foreign affairs
Erotic Travel Tales

foreign affairs
Erotic Travel Tales

Edited by Mitzi Szereto

Published in the United States by Cleis Press Inc.,
P.O. Box 14684, San Francisco, California 94114.
Printed in the United States.
Cover design: Scott Idleman
Text design: Frank Wiedemann
Cleis logo art: Juana Alicia
First Edition.
10 9 8 7 6 5 4 3 2 1

A version of "Broken Windows" by Carole Rosenthal appears in *It Doesn't Have to Be
Me* by Carole Rosenthal (Hamilton Stone Editions, 2001); "One Day on 375" originally
appeared at erotica-readers.com, the Erotica Readers and Writers Association website,
March 2003; a portion of "Ukiyo" by Donna George Storey was originally published as
"The New Libertine" on cleansheets.com, August 2003; "Peking Duck" excerpt from
Eat Me by Linda Jaivin. Copyright © 1997 by Linda Jaivin. Reprinted by permission of
Broadway Books, a division of Random House, Inc.; Chatto & Windus, a division of the
Random House Group Ltd; and The Text Publishing Company, Melbourne, Australia.

Library of Congress Cataloging-in-Publication Data

Foreign affairs : erotic travel tales / edited by Mitzi Szereto.
    p. cm.
ISBN 1-57344-192-9 (pbk. : alk. paper)
1. Erotic stories, American. 2. Travelers--Fiction. 3. Travel--Fiction. I. Szereto, Mitzi.
PS648.E7F67 2004
813'.01083538--dc22
                        2004014724

CONTENTS

Introduction

IS IT POSSIBLE TO COMBINE EROTIC WRITING, travelogue, and literature? What's more, can writers retain the integrity of each? As editor of the *Erotic Travel Tales* anthology series, I offer a yes on both counts. We already know that erotic literature has enjoyed a wealth of devotees dating back centuries. Yet what is it about travel literature that makes it so enticing? There are entire bookshops devoted to guidebooks and armchair travel tomes, demonstrating that the reading public's interest in such subject matter is seemingly unquenchable. Add to that interest the sexual buzz of erotic exploration far from home — and you get *Foreign Affairs*.

As you read beyond this introduction, you'll discover that the text on these pages functions as a form of arousal, literary sightseeing and cultural enrichment, taking travel literature to a new level. In other words, with these notes from the road you get a lot more bang for your buck! (Or pound or euro.) The "tourist" reader of erotica can be anyone — from the diehard aficionado with a bookshelf crammed full of Victorian classics, to the adventuring soul who'll hop aboard a plane or train at the drop of a hat, to the armchair traveler who'd rather stay home with the dog, cat, or parakeet. Like the wide world itself, *Foreign Affairs* has something to please everyone.

This collection of stories includes both best-selling novelists and new arrivals to publishing. These writers travel the globe with their prose, taking us along on the kind of daring erotic journeys most of us can only dream of. Grab your suitcase as we flit from

North America to Europe, the Middle East, and the Orient—and many points in between. An itinerant and hungry American searches the world for a five-star lover. A foreign woman becomes an honorary male in the pleasure district of Kyoto. A young couple breaks taboos with their seduction of a Laotian monk. A "ladette" plays the innocent in Tenerife. A pair of lovers spends a languid morning in the Mississippi Delta. A woman's broken relationship takes her to the sultry heat of St. Lucia, where she meets an even sultrier lover. A Westerner attempts to bridge the cultural gap in Dubai. A gay man and his lesbian sidekick pick up an unusual hitchhiker on a road trip through the desert Southwest. A Welsh woman can only find happiness by traveling to exotic islands. A tourist's desire for her absent husband leads to misunderstanding on a Greek island. A gay man returns to Manchester, England, and his poignant memories of an old love. A woman confronts voyeurism and exhibitionism in Rome. An American ends up in a hotbed of sexual jealousy in a quasi-colonialist compound in Baja, Mexico. A violist narrates a memoir of love in Ceausescu's Romania. A sexually frustrated wife discovers that the amenities at a Brittany farmhouse include more than breakfast. An English tourist indulges in a different kind of sightseeing in Jerusalem. A young woman with a fetish for tight stomachs goes on the prowl in the summer heat of teeming Hanoi. An Australian gives her government sentinel the slip to experience adventure in wintry Beijing. A couple stays in a Louisiana plantation B&B haunted by gay literary spirits. A woman finds a bed for the night with a preacher's son in the snowy Colorado Rockies. A gay man relives foreign embraces in the steam of a Brussels bathhouse.

These tales take us around the world—and offer unexplored continents of erotic experiences.

Embark on an all-new itinerary of sensual travel adventures—featuring the sexiest and most sparkling prose to be found streaming from the pens (and the keyboards) of today's hottest writers.

Better hurry, or you'll miss your flight!

Mitzi Szereto
Yorkshire, England
June 2004

vietnamese art

ॐ

CHRISTINE BELLEROSE

"I'M GOING TO SPEND A HELL OF A HORNY SUMMER," I think to myself, perched over the banister of the villa's third-floor balcony. I sip the first coffee of the day, feeling dumb, licking my lips at the sight of cute specimens, T-shirts tucked underneath armpits, showing off their tight stomachs. Hanoi is great! I can never take my eyes off cute boys; well, I've had plenty of eyeballing to do so far in this hot city. I am in heat and it's only partly due to the humid thirty-five degrees Celsius.

I have settled in the oldest capital city of Southeast Asia for a four-month body language research and survey. The new Socialist Republic of Vietnam is bustling with eighty million people, most of them under twenty-five years of age. The decaying streets smell of ancient history and youthful hormones. Busting at the seams, infested with tourists, Hanoi's Old Quarter reigns supreme as the most densely populated neighborhood in the world, even outdoing Calcutta's legendary population density. Locals wearing pajamas (a mark of wealth amongst the poor) spill their live-in digs and bed mats onto the crumbly sidewalks; some, oblivious to the circus, rest for their midday siesta in fortune hammocks hanging from street sign posts and gas pipes coming out of eroded houses. A mist of *bun cha* hovers around. The appellation refers to little pork patties sizzling on a coal BBQ (a noon noodle dish) and is used locally to describe the exhaust fumes coming out of rickety motorbikes. Swarms of bicycles and pedestrians, noisy motorbikes, scooters, taxis, add in a few private cars, are all fighting for an inch of pavement. People everywhere; like ants, marching to and fro in their saturated nest. The city rumbles in my bones; it is the anthem of a developing country.

May's already torrid heat makes it impossible to enjoy a nice walk. I sit in the taxi with a couple of Canadian expatriates. The dusty breeze helps dry the humid air. Our vehicle, too, is part of the pool of gray fumes. The traffic is ruthless and anarchic, albeit intolerably slow. Right and left of our cooking-tin cab, *vrooms* whir by. The driver habitually zigzags around town oblivious to road signs and one-way streets, boldly driving on the wrong side of the lane, with a skill that ticks the meter another thousand Vietnam Dong up. We drive by "Zen" art galleries, convivial European sandwich bars, dingy but delicious *pho* resto-patios, hustlers, buskers, street vendors, beggars, ninety-pound peasants balancing poles set with two wicker baskets on their bony shoulders selling their farmed goods, a heap of tattered conical hats perched on strutting bronze sliver-figures, merchants selling these same brand-new straw hats and the-hang-from-your-driving-mirror souvenir version to groups of overweight tourists, runaway kids in rags chasing after those same tourists with a box of postcards and multilingual-to-Vietnamese phrase books, the aforementioned tourists flapping their doughy arms, frantic to get a moment of peace and a good camera angle, sweating like pigs in their brand-new khaki safari modular shorts and shirts, heavy backpacks strung over their bellies, ready to cross the Gobi Desert with a reserve of hundreds of liters of bottled water. Life outside my rolled-down window looks like a freak circus. Marcy, Ether, and I are heading to Mrs. Nga's silk tailor shop on Hang Gai Street where an *ao dai* (traditional Vietnamese garment) awaits my final approval. Every souvenir bought in a foreign country has a story of its own. This is the story of a sexy Vietnamese escapade.

Zooming in on a cute man: Thang rides his motocross on Li Thai To and Hang Dao, the corner streets of the Smiling Café where I've spent most of my leisure time since my arrival in Hanoi, drinking *café sua* and people-watching from its second-floor terrace. Vocal chaos fills my ears with wads of foreign wool while furious horns compete against screeching birds demanding my attention. Cars are gridlocked in the middle of the roundabout. Swift scooters swoosh by. A grapevine of humans and machines is sprouting through the maze. I think, *This man. I must see him again.* He floats on a curly cloud in front of our taxi. He is mounting his XR650L Honda 644cc like Genghis Khan his warrior horse, charging the plains of Inner Mongolia. The relentless noise of this sleepless city comes to a stop. The traffic ballet freezes.

How Vietnam was born: At the beginning there was a dragon and a lady who mixed their seed together and produced a dozen offspring. When they parted, the lady led her half-dozen children to earth in the land of what is now Vietnam. The dragon took his half dozen children up to the sky. It's as if today the golden dragon paused the world, making a royal descent to earth, homing in on his favorite son. Thang. His buttoned shirt catches the wind, allowing a glimpse of his tight stomach. God, I love a tight stomach. The effect on my pervert brain is what I imagine must be the sensation for a virile penis of the tightness from a virgin sheath. I melt. Thang veers west looking away from me, his long wavy hair taking the corner half a meter after the rest of him, his tight ass perched high on his insect-looking motorbike. His hands hold the handles firmly; I could fit in there. He could be encircling my waist with his open arms. His mouth is stretched in a macho, self-confident and defiant smile. How can he not have seen me? But I know he did; I saw it in that flashing smile. I will meet him again, two days later. The man of my summer 2000.

Let me explain this bit of anatomy: the tight Vietnamese stomach. Because of the heat, in search of a breeze, men roll up their T-shirts just under their pectorals. No fashion style whatsoever, it looks mighty silly. But what a turn-on! These young males are trained in the art of shadow boxing since early childhood. Push-ups, kicks, stretches. Feats of endurance, strength, agility. The North American "six-pack" expression doesn't even begin to describe this glorious vision. It's a stomach all bodybuilders would die for. Beads of sweat like sparkling stars on their copper skin chisel each ripple as if by a sculptor's knife. These teasers walk around, cruise around, and sit around on their hind legs sipping strong Vietnamese tea, bragging like puffed-up peacocks. My brain overrides the macho affront keeping my eyeballs glued to their stomachs. *And their fat lips,* I muse as an afterthought. I want nothing else this summer but to lick the water from their silky-smooth skin, to dig my tongue in and between each muscle, to suck at their shallow navels stretched out by more muscles. Their tummies call for a roll. I dream up a decadent sex game where I would line them all up against a wall, T-shirts pulled over their heads, and lick, lap, suckle, suck, and kiss their taut bellies.

The sun is coming down from its smoggy seat. Bats are chasing mosquitoes. Surveying the national abdominals from the sanctuary of my balcony, now with a gin-and-tonic in hand to fight the blasting heat, I daydream the golden stomach of the flying dragon. Back on earth I treat myself with the sight of hundreds of stomach-baring males strolling in my vision. Perched on my post, I see the perfect puff of their thick upper lips. I think the creator must've pressed their noses a tad too deep in their heads while molding the clay, taking away from their nose bridge and adding the surplus to their lips! Sometimes I am a real genius. I decide to hit the Old Quarter's pubs to share my evolutionary hypothesis. In a slightly inebriated state I hail a *xe om* (moto-taxi). We slice through the traffic toward my first stop.

I come upon Thang at the Jazz Bar. In a flash I recognize his wavy hair, his fat lips, his engaging smile. My brain shuts out the social chitchatting the instant I lay eyes on him. Distress signals leap up and down my spinal cord: "Must-shove-head-underneath-his-buttoned-shirt!" A loose scarf sits on the nape of his sweaty neck. I want to tell him to slip it off. Let the moisture roll down your body. Give it to mama. Give it to me. Give it to baby, she'll lick it all dry and silky. *"Chao anh,"* I say to him using the term for a same-on-same-footing level. He should have said, *"Chao chi"*—I, look older than him. *"Chao em,"* he replies, planting me at the level of a younger sister, or brazenly, as the street language goes: lover. I wonder if the girls next to him, the gorgeous silk-haired maidens brushing their long manes off to the side of one shoulder, are nightgoers or "secretaries," as the locals call their call girls. Usually bronze "flower girls" sell their scented flesh to the lonely white men spending their uneventful weekends in expat waterholes. But Thang is Vietnamese so they wouldn't go for him, I reassure myself. Thus I find the bravery to flirt with him a tad though, to my relief, he beats me to it. "Peanuts?" He passes a bowl of wet seeds to me. "Delicious," he says, smiling at me with his moon-crescent eyes. He's using slang to comment on my cuteness. I hint to him that they are delicious indeed, but that he should try *xoi lac* (sticky rice with peanuts) as they make for a scrumptious nibble. It's my turn to use slang and I've just implied he should try to eat my nipples and breasts. He tells me his doctor agrees, for peanuts abound in vitamin T, a necessary nutrient for a healthy life. (The love vitamin *tinh;* the money vitamin *tien*.)

"Let's go dancing," he suggests. Oh yes. Please. Anything to get closer to that stomach. Let's cram into a sweaty discotheque so I have an excuse to rub against your body!

We haven't passed the door of the Jazz Bar yet, and already half of my organs have slumped down between my thighs. My heart is pounding wildly against my vaginal mucous walls, my lungs are trapped inside of my gummy labia holding their breath, my brain hits rock-bottom clitoris, my saliva dries out from my throat morphing into a tidal wave inside of my tweaked-out cunt. We ride to our next destination on his Genghis Khan motocross. I must sit sidesaddle because of my long wraparound skirt. "Hold on," he says. And do I ever! I could be grabbing the bars running along the seat but instead I curl my arm around his sexy body. My hand rests on his stomach just below his navel. Here's a rhetorical question: how can the millions of other butterflies, expats, and local females in this city not want to take my place on this motocross?! My fingers, looking like a sea star sucking the salt from his belly, slip down his moist flesh; my little finger reaches lower to caress the band of his pants. His conspicuous erection shapes his crotch into a tent at the tip of my fingers, heat pumps like a coal furnace from inside his trousers. My plump white hand, that of a foreigner not yet used to Hanoi's merciless humidity, a swollen hand against his tight slick stomach, must look like a cream pie against his lean body.

We circle Hoan Kiem Lake heading west toward the New Century nightclub. This is the hip hangout favored by government officials' brat kids, cheeky Vietnamese prostitutes, and middle-aged

Caucasian patrons. We are greeted at the door with a courteous smile; we are not asked to pay the entrance cover fee. No doubt this sexy prey of mine once lured a few of the cigarette-girls into dark corners here; I see them cooing and giggling past him. I teeter down the iron steps in my clumsy platform sandals; he follows behind pinching my ass like I'm some vulgar farm girl. I choke a growl of discontent. So I've been too obvious in lurking him. Still it's *my* fleshy ass he's after, and not any other bamboo-stick-figure girl's!

Without further ado, we hit the packed dance floor. I lose no time shoving my plump digits inside his buttoned shirt, feeling the dampness of his skin. He dips his hand in the small of my back. I'm about to let him in on my genius genetic hypothesis when his fat mouth lunges at me, eating my genius pout. He rolls my thin lips between his teeth. My hand goes on a treasure hunt underneath his buttoned shirt. Tactile pleasures; drowsy, erratic, horny, puppy pawings in tune to the epileptic music. Moisture flows out of my body, streaming down my thighs. We waltz a choreography of shame, at each break-tempo grinding his lengthening bird against my pelvis. With so many dancers on the dance floor, I'm squeezed right into him. Tightly pressed as we are against each other's sweaty body, my hand doesn't fit between us anymore; I force him away from me. He understands I'm after his midriff; kindly he unbuttons his shirt from the bottom and rams his sweaty abs to my navel. Instantly my belly spoons his. I let him swallow my lips again, dart his silky tongue between my teeth, flick it, a deliciously thick muscle pressing against my tongue. It sucks, cleans my gums, and stretches the taut skin under my upper lip, sending lubricious shivers from my mouth down to my clitoris. All the while, like I'm searching for a diamond needle in a mound of clay, I roam the ridges of his torso. I moan a sulfurous moan in the deep of his throat, my hands and fingers diligently imitating on his stomach the feats of his tongue inside my mouth.

A group of loudmouthed men, their table set with a bottle of Remy Martin VSOP, loads of imported beer bottles, soda pops for the girls, and a plate of sliced fruits, order waitresses around. Meanwhile their money-hungry girlfriends stretch their necks hawking for a better catch while at the same time entertaining their men, making sure their attentions aren't diverted by other butterflies. There are no witnesses to our mating dance; the other lithe dancers are busy with their own. I float beyond this earthly realm accompanied by naked chubby angels, hanging on to Thang's mouth. His hand slides from the small of my back tracing the curve of my rump, a finger boldly inquiring in the furrow of my ass, bunching a mass of skirt between my legs, poking at my anus through the fabric, trying to reach up between my lower lips, drawing moisture, and darting deeper through the encumbering clothes. Hot salsa dancing to Nirvana's "Nevermind." I let him grope away, while I reach for his cannonball ass, cupping the base of his moons in one hand, and with the other playing among the ripples of his belly. His muscles pack the palm of my hand.

Heat blows; the breeze comes out of the powerful speakers in the shape of washed-out top-forty tunes. I'm going deaf.

I squeeze the side of his tiny waist. Feeling him up. Massaging stiff muscles. Sliding my thumb in, down, and then up the ascent of his pectoral. He is so thin I reach half of him in one hand. But he is not fragile. I'm forced to wrestle against his body otherwise I would be thrown down flat on the floor. Needless to say I'm praying for a near future in which circumstances would allow him to wrestle me to the mat. I grind my teeth in an ultimate effort not to fake a faint.

Thang. His name means victory.

He leans into me. My fingers grow vines up his chest, flowers circling his navel, thorns tugging at the ebony duvet of his flesh, leaves plunging lower inside his waist band, resurfacing as wet roots. He rubs against me. A volcano is about to bubble, I'm tempted to push lower inside his crotch. My hand over his pants, I pull at the shaft of Hades. His kisses stimulate the hell out of me. My little lips barely contain the spit of my inner fire. You get the picture; from here it's straight to hell in a handbasket. His erect penis rolls on my pubic bone. We embrace a disco tactile love. Mouth to mouth, fingers in moisture. I am a dancing vulva brazenly violating the bronze-bellied Buddha.

The Carlsberg-girls flock around us. Thanks for the disruption, little cunts! Thang starts to tease them. The only way to send them away is to order a drink. I order Carlsberg although I'd much rather drink Tiger Thai beer. We both down our beers in a hurry. The bitter liquid parches my dried-out throat, masking the taste of his cigarette saliva on my tongue.

Cha-cha-cha. We could be dancing all night. "I'm blue dabed

idabedadabedidabeda, I am blue" wails from the mega-speakers. Go-go dancers dressed in impossibly tight black vinyl writhe suggestively, caged in *Star-Wars*-sword-of-light beams. Women wearing less clothes than poor people flail their long lustrous black hair like it's an air guitar show while their effeminate male counterparts spread open their knees pumping the empty air, hungry for butts. Welcome to mayhem in Bacchus' hometown! The discotheque reeks of sex vibes. I am sedated. My python lover sinks his venomous fangs in the tendon at the junction of my neck and shoulder. He lets my thumb gingerly run the seam of his pants. Tugging at his shaft, I wrap my soul around it. I stroke from root to head in subtle movements; he pulses in my grip. His tongue licks at the sweat trapped in a pond of salted water at my collarbone, then he showers my ear with feathery kisses. In time with the bass-tempo of cheesy pop tunes, he whips me around, swallows the back of me in his hollow belly; I continue to dance. Emboldened by his hot salsa hip-swirl his cock pushes in the crack of my ass. I go up on tiptoe to let him slide further in between my legs.

We bump into a couple of girls, their boyfriends looking for a fistfight, the girls cooling their roosters, lulling them in an embrace that's a poor reflection of ours. My partner thrusts a stump of warmth at my budding flower. The insides of me cascade out, slimy, to meet his probing scout along the cleft of my thirsty mouth. His arms encircle me, tentacles, moving our bodies to the beat of the cheesy Vietnamese pop music. His lips trace paradise on my skin. My sighs climb the ladder to heaven. After two hours of this erotic body language, he's the first one to take the initiative of breaking our silence. He whispers these words: "I'm going to make something beautiful with you." *He* (meaning "river," a popular girl's name in Vietnam) comes to my estrogen-fogged mind. A beautiful thing from him to me would be *He*. In a flash I remember a legend about a man having to cross a river to meet his lover on the other side and I'm thinking this river is what's coming out of me right now, just swim upstream, honey. "I'm going to make art with you."

Vietnamese life is art. Artists are given the honorary appellation of highest veneration just as doctors, judges, and masters are. Making art is reaching the richest level of refinement in Vietnam's culture — "*savoir vivre*." "I want to paint you." His hushed voice brings me out of my daydream, where art meets beauty meets estrogen-fogged mind meets *He*, and into the land of moisture.

The purple aura of his cock, the fuchsia aura of my cunt are mating in this invisible coitus while we cling to each other in a frenzied dance. *He* fights for her life. The floor empties, the lights are switched on, it's time to go. Everywhere along the exit path and on the steps of the discotheque, across from it, and in the parking lot too, not-so-coy-anymore lovers are cooing, grappling, full of clumsy lust, grazed kisses. I walk giddily in front of him pushed by a wall of hormonal heat toward the exit of the now-drained discotheque. I could be sitting on his dick right now; it feels so real in the shadow pointing toward me. We fetch his motocross. Renew our nocturnal embrace. And I mount sidesaddle. I hold on tight once more to his stomach.

The brisk air feels good on my drenched body. We drive as much to cool off as to try to find a sequel to our lust scenario. We polish the scorching pavement around Hoan Kiem Lake like the rest of the motorized lovers, while I probe his erection. On Li Thai To we pass the rundown post office and head toward the restored opera house. I devour the nape of his neck. Groomed trees, their trunks painted in white, deflect our mount's head beam. On Nguyen Thai Hoc I am afire with desire, franticly wracking my estrogen-filled brain for a lair where my delicious bronze lover and I could embrace for a never-ending night. It's quite late; tourist hotels have all shut down. Besides, how can I politely propose to this man who might be married for all I know, to please please please take pity on my swollen clitoris and ease the erection out of me!

We drive slowly past Van Mieu, the Temple of Literature, oldest university in Vietnam, and kill the engine a foot from the curb. "Do you want to eat?" Is this a loaded question, I wonder? We seat ourselves at a low table on the sidewalk, and hail a sleepy teenager for a double serving of *thit bo pho*. We slurp the noodles, shift on the Toys "R" Us plastic bench. Otherwise the blood pumps hard at my temples and I am thinking this is it. We're eating *pho* noodles which could be his way of telling me he's being an unfaithful husband right now. He'll ask where I live, drive me home, and that'll be the end of it. "*Xin cam on,*" he says, gesturing at the old lady sitting a ways from our table. She hands him the oil lamp so he can light his cigarette. "Tea?" Hum, ya sure. We get up half crouched and limp toward the old lady's tea stand, reseating our butts on another set of Toys "R" Us benches. The old lady asks questions. This is how Thang finds out my name, where I am from, what I do in Hanoi. She asks him and he tells her he is from France and I am his wife. We burst into a laughing fit and he sonorously kisses my cheek. We chug down a few more tiny cups of this bitter green liquid and he announces that it's time to go home. *"Cam on co."*

On Hang Ciao Street we've reached my home. It must be four A.M. He parks his bike in front of an arched doorway. We nestle in the darkness. Once more he crushes his body to mine. He breathes hoarse whispers slobbering my ear: he needs me. What can I tell him? That I want nothing more for the rest of my life than to drink the moisture out of him? "I want to drink you," comes from my yearning mouth. He catches the spoken thought in his open mouth, licks the meaning of it from my own thirsty lips, sucks any further promises from my throat, and swallows avidly. His cock crushes my pelvic bone; he guides my hand inside his pants. I twine my fingers around his shaft, pull at its fleshy boner, bring out more of his delicious fragrant moisture, while he finds his way between the flap of my skirt and beneath my drenched underwear, inserting a playful finger in the soft folds of my hungry pussy, his thumb fighting my clitoris, stroking and drawing more of tonight's thematic moisture. His mouth descends on my body until it meets his fingers inside my loose Indian top, kneading the tip of a breast. His lips follow. He mouths a mound of mammal flesh, crushing the nerves between his plump lips. A scooter whirs by, lovers looking for the salvation of shadow, the headlight flooding the street a pasty yellow flare, yet we are safe, well hidden in our inconspicuous den. I slump myself in the alcove of the doorway, he tickles the tip of my tit with his snake tongue, dribbling saliva on my chest. More of his sap wets my own jerking hand. His member grows long and firm in my grip. His fingers part me open; his left hand lifts my bottom to meet him. I follow in his steps and pull out his obedient cock, greeting his hand busy massaging my vulva. I sit in his hands; he lifts me off the ground and plunges himself inside my belly. Oh, Hanoi! The fuse in my brain shorts out.

I grab on to his shoulders, hang from his neck, let myself be saddled by his pumping vein. We go at it a few clumsy strokes in and out; I bite his shoulder, pushing his head against my breasts, riding his cock, tiptoeing. A bulb lights up behind the wooden plank door. A neighbor is finding his way toward the communal WC. With a grunt of hurry, Thang spills himself inside my flaming sheath. My vaginal muscles crush his penis, drawing more of his boiling sap. I let out a muffled cry, my mouth air-sealed to his sweaty neck, engulfing his ear, eating at its lucky earlobe. He lets me slowly squirm off him. A cocktail of sperm and pussy juice soils his crotch and mine in a frothing slew. The neighbor might have caught on to our nocturnal passion. At any rate I no longer hear his footsteps. It's dark again. As if the light might have been a follow-spot my imagination created illuminating the orgasm, playing tricks on my giddy mind.

"Sleep with me tonight." Gee! I giggle in post-orgasm coyness. What a jolly good idea! I'm trying to think of a polite way to tell him he can't come in my house, I'm torn between lust for him and respect for my roommates who said absolutely no boys in this dorm, no boys at all, just a double-AA powered tool looking like the part of a male. I'm about to give in to the little evil perched on my shoulder, to face the morning rap, but Thang motions me to his insect-engine. So I'm saved. We're going for another *ruoc den*. I manage to ride behind him not sidesaddle this time but my legs espousing his, one of his hands resting as far back as he can reach in my inner thigh, rummaging for my crotch. I ride with my hand resting on the soft cushion of his recoiled cock inside his pants. We drive along the streets of Hanoi, aglow with the scooters carrying lovers riding their lust in the open air. With the lights flooding the night and the lovers dancing their love around the lake we could be at a mid-autumn festival when lovers carry lanterns and walk a ways out of the public eye to talk body language. Here in Hanoi we call this nocturnal ritual *ruoc den*. Beauty and magic are everywhere. In no rush, we cruise around. Besides, I figure Thang needs to build up strength for another fine art painting session. Sounds of 50cc engines cruising by, of nocturnal lovers kissing, suckling, embracing, moaning, coming, fill the night.

On Pho Phan Dinh Phung Street stand proudly the old colonial mansions, competing for grandeur with their Duong Tran Phu Street sister villas. The capital city is asleep. The crickets rest silently until tomorrow's sunny screeching calling session. It is still too early for the old people to stretch their stiff joints in a ballet of *Tai Chi*. Even the guards posted around the Ho Chi Minh Mausoleum slump in their stolen sleep. We ride the Duong Vung Huong Street toward Ho Tai, the Chinese village at the east peninsula. We disembark at the arch of the village because the hill is so steep I would probably fly right over Thang's shoulders and because the narrow street is crammed with piled-up apartments where hardworking people slumber and there's no justification in waking them all up. The less conspicuous we are, the easier it will be to bribe an innkeeper to rent us a room at this hour. I wait by Thang's motorbike while he talks to the sleepy owner of a hotel. He can't take us in, he says, because I am a foreigner. No foreigners are allowed in this part of motel town. Thang doesn't give up; I am glad for it. The man directs us to a nearby hotel where he swears interracial couples are tolerated, provided he gets a hefty commission. Thang pays up. I walk behind him and his motorbike. We ring the bell at the metal gate. A groggy innkeeper rolls up the sheet of metal to allow us in. Thang rides his motocross up the ridge and into the inside lobby of the hotel. I have to show my passport and my visa. Thang catches my hand, says we are married and registers for both of us on the police records. We must take two bedrooms. White and yellow skins are not allowed to sleep in the same room. So we rent two for 100,000 VND. Once upstairs we argue with the innkeeper to leave us alone. There is no need to see what he will have to lie about. We pay him a hefty commission. Thang inserts the key in the lock of my door. I go in. He doesn't. After all this jazz I'm confused that he's going to heed the innkeeper's admonition and sleep in his own room at the far end of the corridor. At least he pockets my key.

I lie down on the bed. It's been quite a night. Rather than making sense of it all I slide a finger between my still humid folds, and lightly stroke my clitoris, pressing deeper in the crack of my pussy, bringing out gulps of come to better play with my clitoris. I caress my body, roll in my sheets, pinch a nipple, feel and massage, recouping the moisture of my flesh, bringing myself close to orgasm again. Just as I am mounting the unicorn I hear a light tap on my door. I lie still on the bed, close my legs, and curl sideways in a fetal position feigning to have dozed off.

Thang strolls in, locks the door behind him. He lies feline beside me. I keep my eyes closed. I feel him I breathe him. I grind my teeth in pain as my interrupted orgasm pleads to be released from the grip of my womb. He carefully caresses my wired body. Insistent yet gentle, his erect self finds my conjuring aperture. I feel the stiff coolness of his cock. He bites and licks at my neck like he is a lion and I the antelope. I nestle further into his belly. A peek at the world sends me back a reflection of our sealed bodies moving in the mirror at the end of our bed. I push my rump toward his pelvis allowing him to grow hotter between my legs. His member fills my cave. It swallows him whole while I start rocking my hips to meet his grinding. Red velvet blankets fall on the floor. My soul is cuddled and penetrated by his song of loving passion. In his story he tells me about honeybees pollinating lush flowers smelling of pepper and faraway love potions, of a graceful crane fishing the sacred waters for the immortal tortoise, of sparkling rivers encircling mountains of worlds, of birds teasing butterflies with colorful songs, of women's eyes like leaves and men's eyes like flamingos, of teenagers catching goldfish in sacred urns, of fertility goddesses allowing one day a year for lovers to get together and patient husbands to raise the love child as their heir. I ride on his wondrous tale. Behind my closed eyelids I see images of rainbows, thunderbolts, and erupting lava feeding fertile pastures. I feel the armored clashes of warriors battling in Angkor Wat, the anxiety of Anubis resurrected by Isis, the intoxicated abdication of shadow puppets mimicking a sacrificial rite. He flows countless times inside me staying hard all night, sliding in and out of glistering velour. I never wake up. I die and I re-birth.

Another searing-hot morning in Hanoi. I finish off my black coffee from the vantage point of my balcony. I go for a walk around my neighborhood, greet merchants and patrons, chat about the weather, comment on their successful business, accept their compliments, skillfully brushing aside their nosy inquiries. Always checking out the tight stomach. A never-fading smile is stamped on my fucked face. I meet up with Thang at an old lady's *pho* stand. My hand greets the sweat on his tummy. He kisses the hump on my belly. I take a seat across the table from him. He orders me a *pho ga* with extra fresh herbs and juicy lime. I am now feeding the art inside my belly.

so cold the Night

๛

CHEYENNE BLUE

STACEY DRIVES INTO THE SUNSET, looking for God, Billy the poet, or a motel for under fifty a night—whichever comes her way first. She lives in Topeka, Kansas; Billy the poet was last heard of heading toward Los Angeles; and God has eluded her in several salvation ministries in the Bible Belt of rural America. Even the cheapest motels here in the white-skinned, rich-bitch ski belt that spreads around Colorado's I-70 are nowhere near as low as fifty a night.

She's heading west out of Denver, the fading car chugging an elderly beat, up toward the Eisenhower Tunnel at the crest of the Rockies. Georgetown is on the left, with an iced-up reservoir and a chain motel. Pinning her hopes that it's far enough away from the ski resorts that the *après ski* is a flop, she turns in. The car splutters and stalls. Nearly eleven thousand feet in altitude and the oxygen is thin, molecules spread like scantily buttered bread.

Seventy-five, says the unsmiling desk clerk, even with

discount, so she leaves again, stealing a breakfast donut on the way out, stale and sugar-crusted, pushed into the corner by the coffee machine.

Up by the tunnel her chest is tight, her breathing rough and quick. She takes her pulse, fumbling the pink sweater back to expose the veiny wrist. The car swerves as she fumbles; one hundred and one, one hundred and two. Too fast, she's unfit, the booze and fried food affecting her arteries already, even at her tender age. The Rocky Mountains crest in an icing sugar wave, ski runs above the tunnel quiet now in the closing of the day.

Stacey descends with relief, swooping past burning-brake rigs, past the runaway truck ramps stacked high with snow, down toward Dillon, down to where she can breathe a little better. She pulls off in Silverthorne. No chance of a cheap motel here, but there's fast food, a church, and it's Sunday night, and if she can't catch up with Billy the poet, then maybe she'll be soul-fed by devotion.

She drops into the Silver Spur bar, a backstreet place, frequented by the snowboarders and workers at the ski resorts, minimum-wagers who cater to the rich. A Bud, a plate of onion rings. The temperature dips to single digits and outside the ice is hoary on the windshield of the Buick, symmetrical patterns of white and light.

The barman—a baggypants boarder by day—tells her of a hostel, but she calls and it's full. A Hallelujah Wagon of Baptists from Memphis down for a week of prayer and powder. Inept green-run skiing, earnest prayer at night, and a hostel bed.

Damn. Damn damndamndamn.

And then, maybe, prayers are answered in a basin-cut Baptist with salvation eyes. Maybe she can find God and a bed in one merger. She flirts, the casual hand on the trembling thigh, curling around, curling up, close to where she knows his turgid cock lies twitching in eager dread. More Budweiser poured foaming into tall glasses. The Baptist springs for a hamburger; thick red blood runs down her chin like menstruation. She wipes it off and licks her fingers. The Baptist stares in trembling fascination.

Stacey kisses him hard, pushing him up against the rough board wall outside the men's bathroom, strokes the inside of his mouth with her tongue, runs a hand around the white-fleshed neck to draw him closer. Scant inches from where they stand, the frigid Colorado night creeps in under the door, where the wood has cracked and there's no seal against the weather.

The Baptist kisses her back, helplessly, his cock aching like toothache in his pants, a sin in the making. His hand rises, hovers like newspapers blown in the wind, and then tentatively strokes her breast. He sees stars. She sees a warm bed for the night and fifty dollars safe in her purse.

Stacey rubs a thigh higher, up the pressed woolen pants, into the wooden cock. "We could go to your room," she suggests, feigning a coyness she doesn't feel. "Do this someplace warm."

He groans. "I share a dorm with five others." Apologetic stuttering and the promise of flesh receding into the cracks in the linoleum.

She thinks briefly about six white virgin bodies all for her enjoyment. But no, she's too tired to teach more than one. But sleep now....

"We could find somewhere now," she purrs, her breath hot on his ear. "And then sleep together in your bed. Just sleep."

He considers, vacillates, an eternity of fire and brimstone warring with this—his first real, first tangible temptation.

She plays her trump card. "Or if you get a motel room for the night we can do it more than once...."

The pictures paint a glowing scenario in his head, but the rigid teaching holds him in a fierce clasp. "I've no money." A weak excuse.

"A credit card?" She runs a hand over the checked cotton shirt, fiddling with the lowest buttons, as if she's about to flick them open and slide her hands over his flesh.

He turns, with a sudden confidence—amazing what two glasses of Bud can do—and presses her up against the wall, grinding his hips into her accommodating pelvis. "We'll find a place now, then you can sleep in my dorm." The rest of them won't tell; they'll be so sick with jealousy, wanking themselves sore all night just wondering what he and she are doing together in his narrow bunk.

Stacey considers; it will have to do. "Come on then."

She draws him by the hand, out into the crystal night. Snow and stars and frozen breath, mosaic of crunched ice and cold so sharp it pierces her to the bone with its knitting needles. Her car has a heater. Taking his hand, she runs with slipping gait to the Buick, fumbles the keys, and draws him inside.

He's on her immediately, panting and eager like a Labrador puppy, his hands fumbling ineptly, but the wooden cock she feels through his pants is respectable. More than. But not here, not in the parking lot. Stacey feels an urge to gild this encounter with romance, some motherly streak that rises within her. It's his first time, it has to be the way he's breathing over her, slobbering like a puppy, and she'll be good to him. Train him right. She pushes him away with one hand, starts the engine, cranks the heater control up high, and pulls out of the parking lot.

Bewildered, he wipes his mouth with his hand. "Where are we going?"

"Someplace private." She squeezes his thigh in reassuring fashion.

The car noses along the icy roads, and the town drops away. Smaller paved road, climbing higher, past a frozen lake, past the pine boughs weighted down with snow, up still smaller roads, dirt roads, and a White River National Forest sign. The road ends at a lake, snow banks all around and snowmobile trails leading off through the trees.

The car is a cocoon of heat against the bitter night. Stacey parks so that she can see the swoop of the mountain above her. With the engine off, the silence is so total she can hear the shift and creak of the ice on the lake, groaning like a fat man after too large a meal.

For a moment all is quiet, poised and waiting, then he's on her, kissing her with wet and urgent mouth, pushing his soft white hands into her sweater. Finds a breast and his breath hitches in his throat. So perfect, so unexpected—for him anyway, the Baptist preacher's boy.

Stacey guides him, softens the clasp of his hands, pulls up the pink acrylic sweater, and shows him how to suckle. He's a quick learner, and the rosy nipple blooms into his mouth. She watches the tawny head against her skin, then her gaze shifts to the outside world. The ice cracks again, and then there's the elongated howl of a lonesome coyote. The stars burn fiercely, bright holes in the black and indigo sky.

The Baptist boy moans something deep in his throat, and she

feels the timbre of the words through her skin. Taking the hint, she pulls at his clothes, parting them enough to feel skin. Emboldened, he moves away from her and strips near naked in the fugged car. She smiles at his socks, at his pliable milky body. A fuzz of chest hair, tissue-soft skin on his hips, awkward knees, and truncheon cock. Long, solid, more permanent than the rest of him. Stripped, he's younger than she first thought, downy body, a youth really, the solidity of manhood not yet developed.

"How old are you?" she asks, shuffling around in the cramped car, preparing to lower her mouth over him.

"Twenty-two." The words end on a squeak as she licks his tip.

"Really?" Skepticism, a gentle ribbing.

He can hardly speak for the wonder of what she's doing, and the glow impels him to tell the truth. "Nineteen, really. But my fake ID says I'm twenty-two."

"You've never done this before, have you?"

He shakes his head. "We're taught to practice abstinence before marriage. The preacher…" She cups his balls, stroking with knowing fingers, smiling at his gasp. "The preacher says it's a sin."

She wonders at his God that obviously doesn't mind his underage drinking and ID fraud, but whose long arm reaches to grasp his virginity and guard it closely. Another rush of emotion; she's older than Baptist Boy, only four years, but there's a lifetime in that short span. She bends again, engulfs him, moving along the shaft with practiced lips.

His hips jerk, he stiffens. "Oh, God…"

She thinks he's going to pray, draws back, presses hard on the point to stop ejaculation.

In the bright wash of moonlight, he's trembling, shaking like dengue. The car is starting to cool off, but there's sweat on his upper lip. Stacey wonders whether to bring him off like that, but she wants to be remembered, later, eons later when he lies with his pale chosen bride, she wants him to be thinking of how it was with her, Stacey.

His face is back against the headrest, raised to the moon. "Please," he says, helplessly. "Please."

She peels her jeans down her legs, awkward in the small space behind the steering wheel, kicks them aside. Her panties are white, small bloodstains on the crotch, dark from much washing. He touches them with tentative fingers, feeling for the cleft beneath.

Pushing his fingers away, she removes the panties, shivers, the temperature's falling, a bloom of ice forming on the inside of the windshield. For a moment, she thinks about straddling him, taking him in, getting this over with so they can find his dorm bed, lie entwined in the narrow space and listen to the sniggers and envy of his friends. But no pleasure for her that way; first time, he'll blow quicker than a frozen faucet and leave her sticky and unfulfilled. Instead she turns, bends one knee, the other up on the dash where the ice gathers and pushes his head between her legs. It's awkward; he can barely move his mouth, his white cleft ass in the air, his chin hitting the cracked vinyl seat. And he doesn't know what to do, tentatively kisses her, touches her with his tongue, retreats in confusion.

She guides him to the right place. "Lick," she instructs, and he licks her like an ice-cream cone, slow deliberate strokes. Not bad, but not good enough. "Faster." With her fingers she spreads herself, lets her wet labia quiver on his mouth. He's a quick learner and he flickers, butterfly trembles, and as she kisses him back, grinding herself into his face, he responds and slurps her enthusiastically so that she comes, the inner clench and fluttering muscles raising her hips off the seat.

He rises, face wet, and she pushes him back, straddles him as she first wanted to do. Warm thick pillar parts her, cleaves its way inside. Long rod, drawn inside, bumps her cervix. His eyes are closed; maybe he's found God. Tenderly she touches his cheek, strokes a thumb under the vulnerable curve of eyelash. His cheeks are cold carved marble.

Rise and fall, stroking up and down. She thinks of Billy the poet, in Utah maybe, headed west for a new life in Los Angeles, herself fluttering along in his wake hundreds of miles behind. Billy's cock plows her in her mind; in the dark and the hard cold, it's Billy's cock that warms her.

She comes again, a gentle vibration, turnover of feeling deep in her belly, and she stills the tidal motion. His head lolls back on the seat, breathing slow, the concave chest barely rising and falling. He's asleep. Stacey moves her hips slightly; his spend slides out of her, mats the hairs together. She didn't even notice when he came. But he's warm. Drowsy now, the cold stealing around them, moving over her skin in deadly embrace. She rests her head on his chest, where the warmth radiates, and lets the images wash over her.

Billy the poet serenades her with his guitar, speaking rhyming words she can't understand, but knows for a rare and beautiful genius. They have an apartment on the beach in Santa Monica, she's wearing Italian leather boots and a silk camisole, and they stroll hand in hand with the beautiful people on the Venice boardwalk.

Billy the poet tells her he loves her, wants to marry her. He's cold underneath her, Billy, his white chest still in the moon-wrapped night. She should get up and pull the drapes, but she's warm here, warm, warm, and she lays her head on Billy the poet's chest and goes to sleep.

It snows in the night, drifts down, settles on the Buick, cocooning it in white. A powder blanket that has the skiers and baggypants boarders rejoicing and rushing out to make first tracks. And the Baptist Boys from Memphis make their awkward snowplows down the bunny runs, and no one notices that one of their congregation is missing, or if they do they don't say anything, for he went off with the girl in pink. Her rusting old Buick has gone too. Maybe they've driven to Los Angeles, run away somewhere where there are palm trees and cheap motels, and the salvation churches stand empty.

The snowplow clears the road to the parking lot at the snowmobile trailhead, and builds the snow banks up on either side. It's a good winter, good snow pack, and the banks rise up, twenty feet on either side. They won't melt until May, thinks the driver. He shivers — so cold the Colorado night — and rushes the job so that he can hurry home to where his wife waits, soup on the table, drapes pulled against the cold.

one Day
on 375

࿐

HELENA SETTIMANA

WE DECIDED TO DRIVE FROM SAN FRANCISCO TO ROSWELL, New Mexico. It was Alonso's idea. She had been standing out on the beach watching the sky. It was something she did a lot: tracking satellites; counting meteors until the fog rolled in and obliterated it all. That night she said she saw strange lights, like nothing she had ever seen before. Strobes strafed the sky. It got her talking about UFOs and visitors from outer space. I thought Alonso simply did too much dope and told her to lay off, but she just clucked at me. I assured her that what she saw was probably a weather balloon.

She called me an idiot and would not be swayed. "The government lies about things, you know."

Within days she said she was going to launch her own "investigation." So, actually, we did not *decide* to drive to New Mexico—she *told* me that was happening, and in three weeks we were on the road, chasing down another one of her grand ideas.

Now, I should tell you something about Alonso. Her real

name is Conchita, but she insists on using her last name for everything. She's about five feet tall and about half as wide, all hard-packed muscular dark-skinned Chicana with a face like an Aztec warrior—tough as one, too. She'd rip your heart out and eat it if you ever crossed her, but she's one hell of a good person to have on your side. She's my best friend and has been since seventh grade. Known her for twenty years—all of it kind of bizarre. The dyke and the queen, that's us—like Frick and Frack. In another life we should have been a couple. My friends say she's all the man I'd ever want—her friends seem to see it, too—only that I'm not her kind of girl. OK—it's kind of weird, but it's our life. I had no idea it could get weirder, but for one day on Highway 375, it did.

Alonso has this old yellow Chevy convertible—the sort you could fill with water and use for a swimming pool. It eats gas like nobody's business, but it's the perfect California car—ancient, but in great shape, and a real treat with the top down. It's a nice one, if impractical to run. Alonso had this idea that we just couldn't zip down the PCH, with all that sea on one side—at least for part of the way. Oh, *no*—we had to take the desert route from the start. Nothing but hills, scrub, and sky and endless ribbons of road; the mountains like rhino herds all around.

I guess it all went swimmingly until, having stopped for a stretch, we were maybe a hundred and fifty miles north of Las Vegas and we had to stop again, for gas. You know how many gas stations there are out there? Place we found had an old rusty Coca-Cola sign tilted at a queer angle. Guy in a pair of faded overalls—a guy with straw-blond hair and a sunburned face—filled the tank. I walked up the porch of the station and inside to pay for the gas, twitching my bum a bit, just for effect.

The old man behind the desk was Indian, and looked like he was a thousand years old. He moved with deliberate, slothlike slowness. Taking my money, moseying to the cash register, ringing in each digit with excruciating care, counting and re-counting the bills I gave him, counting and re-counting the change he made. I drummed my fingers on the countertop.

"You're not from around here are you?" asked the man, wheezing, glottal.

What was your first clue? I fiddled with the lilac chiffon scarf I'd knotted around my neck and draped over my shoulder. *This ain't exactly a serape....* "Nope," I said, "San *Fran*-sisco."

"Ah," said the cashier, nodding as if that explained something. He continued to count.

When I finally broke free and walked out into the searing sun, I saw that Alonso was talking to a really butch guy on a bike. He looked like he had swallowed a medicine ball—his gut was so huge. The blond guy sat down in the shade again, and wiped his brow. The two of them by the bike were laughing, and Alonso had a little paper bag in her hand—one I hadn't seen before. The guy started his bike, which farted and belched down the road and disappeared from sight. A roadrunner dashed out onto the tarmac after him, something lizardlike in its mouth.

"What's in the bag?" I asked.

"Stuff."

I grinned. "What *kind* of stuff?"

She opened the bag—in the bottom were a couple dozen small olive-colored buttons of peyote and a plastic bag of what looked like magic mushrooms. "Woooo," said I, appreciative. I might think she did too much, too often, but hey, I'm not one to judge to excess. I like it once in a while. It looked like it would be a fun trip—metaphorically, at least.

But she made me drive—I wasn't too happy about it because the idea of a party on the way appealed to me, but here we are in the age of *responsibility*. My hair was also bugging me. Normally she was so much less complicated than I—except for her schemes. Her hair was short—it never got in her face, and she didn't muss with makeup. I, on the other hand, was seriously handicapped by hair. I was trying to tie it up in such a way that it wouldn't whip around and flog my eyeballs to shreds. This was complicated by the fact that I was pushing the old car up to about eighty. My scarf tied around my neck stood out like a flag in the wind.

Alonso beat me to the bag. She'd wolfed down a button back at the gas station.

An hour later, she wasn't feeling too well—sort of sweaty and nauseous. She puked over the gunwales of the car onto the road and felt better. It was about two in the afternoon, with a ringed sun blazing high in the sky. Alonso began babbling about pterodons shadowing our car like Stealth bombers. They circled higher and higher in the blue. She spent a lot of time craning her neck, trying to keep an eye on them. Made her worried that maybe they'd swoop down on us, but they seemed to keep their distance. I figured it was no use telling her we were near Area 51. I was wishing that maybe she should keep the flying reptiles to herself when she hollered that the sky had turned the exact shade of her mother's favorite lipstick. I hoped we could find a motel, and fast.

We were maybe thirty miles north of Rachel—all tumbleweed and the occasional broken barbed-wire fence—when I spotted the woman at the side of the road. I blinked. She was wearing a silly-looking shiny silver bodysuit that made me think of those awful fifties sci-fi films. She was terribly pneumatic, with tits that looked like twin howitzers poking out in front of her. She had some kind of a handbag and was holding a book about the size of one of those road atlases—it was shiny and silver, too—that looked like tinfoil from where I sat. What appeared to be a large fishbowl sat on the road beside her. We roared by. Alonso hollered, "STOP!" and I laid down a long strip of smoking rubber.

"Oh, wow," said Alonso, her eyes narrowing to tiny slits as she licked her lips. "*OH, WOW! Let's pick her up!*"

I was worried.

"What about the pterodons?"

"Gone, I think." She looked blissfully stoned and had that dangerous look she gets when seriously horny. She reached for a soda and began swishing it in her mouth. "Back up, backupback-upbackupbackup!"

I threw the Chevy into reverse. Maybe having a sober passenger would be good for me—someone to talk to who made some sense. We backed up the highway until the car idled in front of the hitchhiker.

"Where are you going to?" I asked.

The woman looked at me, dumb as dirt. She had a sixties-style hairdo that flipped above her shoulders, heavy eyeliner, and a puckered Cupid's-bow mouth. She glanced up at the sky.

"Oh, *wow*," said Alonso, again.

"Where to?"

The woman didn't answer.

Oh, great, I thought. *Just what I need. Pink sky, flying lizards, and a dumb refugee from* Lost in Space.

I turned the engine off. No sense in wasting gas.

"Do you speak English?" I yelled, wondering why I bothered. She just stared at me. "*¿Habla Español?*" Nothing. *Nada, niente....*

Alonso got out of the car, still craning her neck and squinting at the sky. I continued, "Are you lost? DO-YOU-WANT-A-RIDE?"

I was losing patience. "Look, get in the car or stay there and fry, it's all the same to me. Alonso, don't go too far. There might be snakes." The thought made me weak.

Alonso had crossed to the other side of the road and was staring at a cactus. "Hey, Gerry," she called, "Doesn't this cactus look like a dick?"

I nearly broke my neck looking back and forth between the two of them. Yes, the cactus looked like a dick. The bigger wonder was standing in front of me. Alonso started to wander further from the roadway.

"Alonso—don't go too far, *dammit*—snakes! If you step on a snake, don't ask me to suck the poison out!"

The mystery woman spoke. My head snapped back to face her. "My name is Gretok."

Take me to your leader, I thought. *Figures.*

"Well, *Gretok*, are you coming or not?"

She studied the tinfoil book in her hands. I sighed and leaned over, opened the door. I motioned for her to get in. She looked at me, so I got out and walked around to her. I picked up the fishbowl, placed it in the back and steered her into the seat.

I looked around for Alonso, who had wandered off about a hundred yards or so. "Wait here," I told Gretok and jogged across the road and into the desert, carefully watching where I was putting my feet. Stepping lightly in my Tevas I still managed to encounter those dreadful little peppercorn-sized burrs that mine the desert ground. My companion stood there holding a one-sided conversation with an armadillo. The animal was curled into a ball. "Let's GO," I said.

"He was just explaining to me something important," she complained as I frog-marched her back to the highway.

Like how to plug your ears and pretend this nightmare is not happening, I said to myself. "I want you to shut up now, or you'll scare our passenger," I told her.

"What passenger?"

"Gretok."

"Who?"

"Oh, forchrissakes, you are hopeless," I said.

"Who's that?" said Alonso when she saw the silver throwback sitting in the backseat.

"Gretok."

"Who?"

"Gretok. She said her name was Gretok," I said through clenched teeth.

"Oh, I like, I like," said Alonso, licking her lips again.

"Get into the fucking car and shut up," I hissed.

"*No problema*," agreed my girl. She got into the back.

"Please forgive my friend," I began. "She's not well." I shot Alonso a killing look.

A dark sedan appeared out of the shimmering heat-mirage on the road. It slowed to pass us, then rolled to a stop and a blackened window slid down. A pair of shaded eyes peered out.

"Are you folks OK?" asked the wearer of the sunglasses.

"Oh, fine, just peachy," I chirruped back. "Just stopped for a pee." I waved gaily at my crotch and glanced nervously at the paper bag.

"There's a rest-station a ways on. You should've stopped there. There's snakes out here."

A second window lowered a bit. Two sets of eyes examined us. I tried to see — it looked like there were three or four people in the car.

"You folks have a nice trip, now, and stay out of trouble," said the glasses. The sedan pulled away.

I looked into the rearview mirror as we pulled off the shoulder to spy Alonso looking moonily up at our fare. She seemed oblivious to anything except her company. Gretok, on the other hand, was furiously studying her book.

I heard Alonso say, "You have great tits, Greta."

I wasn't going to let things get out of hand. "So," I began, taking my inspiration from the gas-station cashier, "You're not from around here, are you?" I was shouting over the wind, my scarf nearly tickling the nose of the stranger.

Gretok was studying her book. She looked up and said, "Ass, gas, or grass, nobody rides for free."

Alonso started to laugh. I burst out, too. This woman was a nutcase for sure. Alonso was staring at those tits.

Gretok looked at the book again. "I can pay," she said.

"You can, can you?"

She consulted the folded tinfoil again. "Me love you lon'-time," she aped.

"Do you know what you are saying?" I asked.

She looked in the book again. "*Voulez-vous…?*" she began.

I sighed. "So what is it, Gretok? Ass, grass, or gas?" I asked.

She looked at her book and then asked, "What is?"

"Um. Well…gas is…gas is the stuff that makes the car run. Fuel." I slapped the dashboard for emphasis. "We just filled 'er, though. Grass, well…" I looked over at Alonso and thought of the pink sky, pterodactyls. Peyote was a helluva step up from grass. "We don't need that stuff. Now, ass is…" and I began to realize that whatever else we had lots of, this was not likely going to be a productive discussion, from my perspective, anyway. "Don't worry about it, Sunshine."

"*Hey,* not so fast." Alonso was running her fingers up and down her own torso, tweaking her nipples while I spoke. "Speak for yourself. The lady asked you." She knelt on the seat and wiggled her bottom at the passenger. Framed it in her hands. "*That* is ass."

Oh, great. Just great.

She turned to Gretok. "Ever made it with a woman, Greta?"

"Alonso," I yelled. "Leave it alone, you tramp! I don't have the stomach for this, you hear?"

I stared furiously at the distant mountains, clouds caught on their peaks like laundry.

"Hey, she asked about ass. She put it on offer." Alonso's eyes rolled as she unbuttoned her shirt.

Next thing I knew she was holding her tits out, saying to our passenger, "Go ahead, suck me dry!"

This was rapidly getting out of control. For one thing, I was getting hard. It was like, well, like aliens had invaded my body. They hijacked my libido. That had to explain it. I'm *queer*, for God's sake. I told you that. OK, so I'm just as vulnerable to being turned-on at the sight of anything humping, really, but this had just never entered my experience. My cock hurt.

We passed a homemade-looking sign welcoming us to UFO territory. We were miles and miles and miles from our destination. Dammit.

Alonso crawled into Gretok's lap and was unzipping that jumpsuit. Gretok had a fine rack, I had to admit. Her tits were bunched in Alonso's little dark fists while she licked them. I could see the spit shining on them. I swatted at my dick. It just freaked me right out. As I unzipped my pants, I told myself I could get some relief and then concentrate on the road, and finding them a motel — the whores. My balls bunched. *Christ*, they were turning me on, and I was helpless against it.

I began to jerk, hoping they wouldn't see me. Just get it done and get on with it. I fixed my eyes on the road, the low scrub, the cactuses.

Something crept into my lap — it came slinking around between the door and the seat and settled into my crotch, right where it was most sensitive. I couldn't see at first because I was trying to keep the Chevy on the road and it was sort of difficult figuring out how she had reached around like that to cop a feel. She sometimes teases me. Then I realized it wasn't Alonso. I spied her in the mirror: she had managed to pop another of those amazing boobs into her mouth and was suckling away like a baby. I tried to locate the bag of goodies. Did I take some shit and then forget about it? Did Alonso put something in my cola? The bag was on the console between the front seats. I got grabbed again, and looked down this time. The car swerved.

What settled in my lap looked like a cross between an elephant's trunk and a ridged vacuum cleaner hose, with two little fingers at the tip. It was fishing around and wrapped itself around my now-impossibly stiff dick. I caught my reflection in the mirror — bug-eyed, open-mouthed lunatic with hair in a messy ponytail, sweating through a pancake foundation.

I glanced at the backseat again. Alonso had her pants down and another of those tentacled arms was writhing up between her legs, but the gawd-awfullest thing was that one of those titties, the one my friend had been sucking on, had turned itself inside out and had lodged over her head the way a snake swallows a mouse. Meanwhile, Ms. Barbarella sat there looking cool as a cucumber. She might as well have been doing a crossword puzzle.

Alonso was making gargling noises, "Mrph, gragelgrmnlsok…" I was going to have to rescue her. That was a problem.

Ever been so freaked out and so horny that you didn't know

whether to shit or go blind? There we were roaring along 375 at about seventy-five miles per hour while this thing simultaneously swallowed my friend and jerked me to the edge. Jerk. Did I say *jerk*? Just before the flash, that damned tentacle-thing opened a little mouth and began swallowing *me* into its entrails. I've never felt anything like that. It was like horse, it was like speed, it was like — nothing I'd ever felt — it was — oh, my God, I can't believe I'm saying this, but it was like *nothing on earth*…. I grabbed the muscular coil and tried to pull it off, but the more I pulled, the harder it sucked and the *sensation*…

Just as I came, speeding down the highway, there was an immense flash of white light and I lost control of the car. I felt it fishtail and slide down the road. I prayed we wouldn't flip. We didn't. When the sky cleared and the car came to a stop, our hitchhiker was gone. Alonso still sat in the back, her tough little mouth open in shock — she looked like a piñata-parody of a blow-up doll. I got out and looked under the car, fearing the worst. Gretok, however, was nowhere to be seen. I wiped my face with a Kleenex.

The dark car appeared again, swimming out of the shimmering light. The window rolled down.

"Having trouble?"

"No…well, yes, but no. My friend was feeling sick. Carsick." The sunglasses turned toward Alonso. I prayed they wouldn't look too closely. There was puke on the door and rear fender, so it seemed a reasonable explanation. Still, her pants were still off and she had this freshly fucked look. I tossed my scarf over her lap, with studied nonchalance.

"Where's your other passenger?" asked the shades.

"Oh, she got out a ways back."

"How far?"

I made it up — "Oh, about ten miles or so." I winced inwardly: that was close to where we'd first met the dark car and its occupants.

"Your friend OK, now?"

"Yessir," said Alonso, smiling. "I'm fine."

"Glad to hear it," said the shades. "Have a safe trip." The car roared off in the direction we had just come from.

" *¡Puta Madre!* What the hell…?"

"Satisfied?" I shrieked. "*Satisfied? You want to go to fucking Roswell?*"

Alonso looked at me, and said, "Satisfied? Yes. Roswell? No. Not this time."

She opened the door and got in the front seat, again. "You OK?" she asked.

"Yeah."

"Then let's go. Turn the car around."

"Sure you don't want to stop in Vegas?"

She started to laugh hysterically. "No—there're enough freaks right here—and I think I've got enough evidence for my 'investigation.'" She seemed quite sober.

Just before the junction with 93 we passed a guy standing on the side of the road, thumb cocked. Tall and cute, with the most precious bubble-butt, he was dressed like the early western film star, Tom Mix, and his chaps showed his derrière to perfection. I slowed. The problem was that he wore what looked like a T-Fal electric wok on his head. It kinda gave me pause.

"Don't you dare stop," said Alonso. "*Don't you dare!*"

I had no problem being obedient. Ten miles along, right about where we met Gretok, we blasted past the black sedan, which was parked by the cactus-dick. One of its occupants stood on the shoulder of the road, yelling into a cell phone. He turned his bug-shaded eyes at us as we sped past, and I could have sworn he had sprouted fly-wings, but I couldn't be sure. I tossed the bag of contraband into the wind as soon as we were out of their sight. Alonso was pissed, but I refused to stop and retrieve it. This place was weird enough without it.

Broken windows

꒦

Carole Rosenthal

I'VE ALWAYS LIKED TO TRAVEL, sampling other people's lives, but when I sampled Eric in graduate school years ago, long before we married other people, I never dreamed that someday we'd be traveling to Mexico together on this whirlwind trip to his wife's hideaway on a Baja beach.

Just friends, of course. I told him so. I'd made a deal with myself before I left New York. I could only leave my husband for a vacation if I didn't sleep with anyone else.

But what was Eric's deal? Typically, he didn't say. Eric was opaque, deliberately concealed in spiffy linens, carefully coordinated olives and pale greens, and he wore funny little woven Italian shoes. But I spent a childhood studying people like him, staring out my apartment window into other people's windows, watching what they were doing, trying to figure out who they were. My parents were never home. My mother illustrated medical books, my father, a professional bohemian, was out all day doing

God knows what. Maybe the neighbors felt sorry for me. They rarely pulled the blinds.

Or maybe they wanted me to spy on them. It made them feel important. Now, driving down the highway past the flesh-colored California hills, I suspected Eric wanted me to spy on him too. He was a dark window.

"How far?"

"Not far."

My vow of summer chastity, like fasting, had aroused me and sharpened my senses. I loved being with Eric, a happy part of my past. And on a more primitive level, although I didn't like admitting it, I was proud of getting Eric away from Meredith this weekend, too. Meredith was Eric's wife, "an international design celebrity" who actually referred to herself that way, a tiny woman with a Hollywood sense of exaggeration and a tinkling well-practiced laugh.

Not that getting Eric away from Meredith was any big thing. Nothing to go giddy over. Eric didn't sleep with Meredith anymore, I'd heard. Or at least Laurie, my friend in L.A. who worked in their design office said that was the general buzz around the water cooler about the tension between them.

It made sense. "I believe it," I told Laurie.

Eric never liked nitty-gritty sex that much. His idea of a sex fantasy was like a Brancusi sculpture, streamlined and spacious, uncluttered; clean. But for some reason Eric's streamlined fantasies excited me. I even appropriated them as my own. I used to slip over the surface of him when we made love, sliding fast. His surface was cool and smooth and light. His hands were subtle and severe and sparkling.

Now Eric lifted his eyes off the road and smiled. His warm, quiet attention on me was like a slash of sunlight through glass. I extended my body toward him and the hair prickled on my arms. He said, "You haven't changed much in thirteen years."

"You haven't changed either." I was flattered, not annoyed, by this lie.

I remembered Eric's reserve as alluring and mysterious when we were young. I hoped he hadn't gotten trapped behind it.

We passed through Customs. On the Mexican side a mosaic of broken beer bottles littered the roadside, glass and plastic dumped down hills topped by tin-roofed shanties. Patches of colorful laundry streamed, and in gullies I spotted abandoned tires, dogs with incised ribs, and children romping through garbage.

Was it really Eric's elusive qualities that attracted me, or his sparkling blankness that I could fill in? A knot of longing wriggled free, and the feeling spread out and loosened my limbs. The car's air-conditioning was on full blast. Outside, Baja shimmered with heat. My nipples puckered hard against my blouse.

Suddenly I felt shy about myself and our journey as I recalled the sweet surge of his cock inside me, years ago, and the voluptuous delicacy of my own long release.

Sunlight shifted over the shapely symmetry of his brow and jaw. He was an intensely good-looking man, almost intimidatingly so, but I recalled how he sobbed when we broke up, scaring me because it was the single time I saw he needed me. His need gave me powers I didn't want back then, but seeing him shattered had been a strange kind of turn-on.

We veered off the highway onto a dusty cliff road nearer the beach.

"This is our little American compound."

Eric parked the car by an oak-slabbed door in a whitewashed wall. The high wall was topped by broken glass, jagged bottle shards set into concrete, decorative and menacing, and surrounded by bougainvilleas that hung deceptively over graceful arches and red-tiled roofs.

He pulled a bank of keys attached to a pine panel from under the car seat. "Oh, hell! I told Meredith to label the keys. I can never remember which key fits what."

He jammed key after key into the lock. Finally he found the key to make the front gate swing open. We passed into a garden with dry fountains and stern square-mouthed statues flanked by cactus with blood-red blooms. Seven or eight houses, each enclosed by its own interior walls and separate gates, were staggered on the beach slope, surrounded by the outside wall that ran along the road and dipped halfway down the cliff to the beach.

At the second gate, Eric cursed Meredith again for forgetting the labels. I thought it certainly was suspicious, even insulting to me, that Meredith hadn't displayed the slightest bit of jealousy that Eric was taking me here for the weekend. Instead, batting her furry false lashes behind Jean Paul Gaultier half-rims, she had apologized for not accompanying us, saying she had to visit some architectural sites — and practically packed us off together. Was Meredith so sure about Eric, that she believed nothing sexual could go on?

"Help me out. Hold this steady while I push."

Eric shoved with his broad, high shoulder, and his fine-boned face turned red. He led me triumphantly down the steps to a house sheathed in glass. It sprawled against high spikes of agave that framed ocean below and the sun setting upon the waves. Gulls drifted on air currents. There were swathes of horseshoe beach and pliant sands.

"Oh, it's beautiful!" I whirled, delighted, pulling back from the view of the sea.

Something stabbed my toe. I looked up and jags of light glinted into my eyes. Broken glass from the top of the wall. Then I lifted my sandal and saw that I had been stepping upon a piece of clear glass that left little white scribbles on the cement. A bead of blood appeared. I bent to examine it.

I saw more glass. "Eric! Look!"

"What? Hold on for a minute. I'll get you a Band-Aid. I've got to unlock the door first."

"No, I mean look, right there next to the door — there's a broken window. Someone's broken in!"

"What are you talking about? Son of a bitch!"

Iron bars on the low slit window by the front door were wrenched out of alignment and a terracotta brick, hurled through the glass, lay amid shards on the kitchen floor.

"Let me see if I can reach the deadbolt."

He rushed through the house. The house was long and narrow with sliding glass walls, terminating in a dark-beamed bedroom on one end and a kitchen with dungeon-like slits on the other.

His breath expelled with a relieved pop. Relief made him happy and excited. "Nobody's hiding. "

He wrapped a Band-Aid around my toe.

There was a knock at the door, and we jumped. The crown of his head struck my jaw because I was leaning toward him. My teeth hit my lip.

A muscular blonde with a Dutch-boy bob and a suspicious face crowded the doorframe. She was about my age, clutching a dingy yellow dog with a very long muzzle.

"Eric, I'm so glad you got here. As soon as I came down from my place this morning to take Ralphie for his walk on the beach I saw the broken window. I drove right over to Oscar down at the *groceria*, and he'll be here to fix the glass within the hour."

"You're great, M.J." Eric hugged the woman with one arm, looking unexpectedly boyish and awkward. The woman was dressed in drip-dry surgical greens. "M.J. is an anesthesiologist from San Diego, a good pal, our compound protector, as you can see."

"You mean I'm the only one lucky enough to have a schedule that lets me get down here during the week."

"Anna is an old college friend of mine, visiting from New York."

"So I heard." She spoke to me sharply. "Your lip is bleeding."

I touched my lip with my tongue.

"Did Meredith tell you I said to be on the lookout? You know who it was who tried to get in, don't you?"

"Of course. Crazy Sarita. The same one who keeps trying to get in all the time." I must have looked puzzled. "There's this crazy Mexican woman," he told me, "who's been trying to break into homes in this compound for the past year, and M.J.'s the only person who ever catches her. Security's the biggest problem here. We have to work to keep the intruders out."

"Not that I can stop her," M.J. sighed. "No matter how many times I catch her. I'm the one who catches her because I'm the one who's here most often—"

"Nothing stops her," Eric interrupted, handing me a napkin to dab my lip. His voice grew light and animated. He liked discussing the thwarted break-ins. "I don't know what she wants. She eats our food and drinks our liquor and even sleeps here if she can get away with it."

"But what about the outside walls?" I pictured a sinewy woman climbing over the glass and scooping her kneecap like a melon.

"Crazy's Sarita's Mexican." M.J. waved her hand. "She knows the terrain."

Eric hummed to himself and unpacked the groceries, opening and closing the refrigerator. Then he checked to make sure Crazy

Sarita hadn't stolen the television, earlier forgotten because it was hidden under the coffee table cube. He joked to M.J., "They say Crazy Sarita's a witch. Maybe she flies over walls." He returned to the kitchen and began rattling mineral water ice cubes for drinks.

"Could be." M.J. laughed softly and jittered her dog up to her face until his long muzzle touched hers. The dog licked her, and M.J. pretended that the dog, Ralphie, was talking to her. "Ralphie says he doesn't like this kind of excitement. Ralphie says whenever we come to Baja to relax we shouldn't have to worry so much about a crazy *Mexicana* breaking in."

"Or a not-so-crazy *Mexicana*," I answered, thinking of the tin-roofed shanties without electricity we'd passed on our way here. "If I lived with no water or anything I'd want to break into gringo luxury for a little while too."

"Not crazy?" M.J. snapped. She dropped Ralphie hard. The dog thumped on the tiles. He yelped and his nails clicked. "Try telling that to poor old Susanna who came to clean my house two weeks ago and found Crazy Sarita in my bathtub leafing through magazines. She scared poor Susanna half to death. How would you like to come home and find someone sleeping in your bed?"

"Like the Three Bears," I murmured.

M.J. scowled contemptuously. It was clear that M.J. disliked me for being here with Eric—which was odd since she'd talked to Meredith and Meredith herself didn't seem to mind. Could Eric be engaged in some strange *ménage à trois*? It occurred to me that everyone I'd ever met named M.J. or B.J. was gay.

"I'll tell you another thing," M.J. said. "If I spot Crazy Sarita again she'd better watch out because I'm going to shoot her. I don't want her hurting somebody."

"You're kidding!" I said.

"I have a shotgun and I know how to use it."

"She's kidding," Eric said.

M.J. whipped her head back and forth, and said, "Nope." Outside, the sand blew in undulant waves across the terrace. M.J. stood in front of the enormous glass windows overlooking the ocean. With the low sun shining through her drip-dries, the outline of breasts and muscular belly was visible. It was a massive convex construction that rippled as she repeated, "No, I'm not kidding. Tell them, Ralphie. I certainly am not."

"Creepy," I whispered, after M.J. left.

Eric shut the kitchen door. He trailed his finger teasingly down my neck. "Nothing to worry about though."

He thought that I was talking about Crazy Sarita.

I said, "I mean M.J."

He straightened up and looked surprised.

After M.J. left, other Americans stopped by, audible first, with much clanking of keys and padlocks and laughter, then pressing their faces against the glass, clutching bottles of beer and Cuervo Gold and bowls of salsa, beckoning us to accompany them.

"Can't we just be alone?"

"That would be rude." Eric urged me up a circular path to M.J.'s, directly overlooking his terrace, where a dozen Americans with comic-strip names like April and Buzz and Jughead and Sundae were lounging in M.J.'s living room on pigskin furniture, eating chicken-stuffed tortillas, and chattering with excitement about how Crazy Sarita had broken in again.

"Remember, Eric, the time she broke the back window and molded a sand dummy onto your bed?"

"And there was the time she scattered cactus on the floor."

"You seem to be her special love, Eric."

Eric laughed. "Well, M.J.'s had run-ins with her too."

Somebody put on music. April and Buzz started dancing groin-to-groin and I pulled Eric to his feet, pressing close, until across the room M.J. made writhing movements with her head and shoulders. It looked to me like she was loosening a muscle cramp from moving furniture, the kind I get when I sporadically work out. Then her yellow dog began barking jealously, and I realized it was a come-hither to Eric. She was a brawny, hulking woman; she didn't work out fitfully for thirty minutes maybe ten times a month to a TV aerobics program like I did. Her muscles looked oiled. Her bullying swagger reminded me of a Harley motorcycle rider—though, like me, she was a little old for that kind of thing. When she flopped in magisterial exhaustion onto the rocker, she patted her knee for Eric to join her. He eased gracefully from me, and perched on her lap. She glared at me and squeezed his shoulder in reproach. He leaned back. His face was a mask, impenetrable—a see-through mask of himself.

"You and M.J.? You're getting it on with M.J.?" I tried not to sound as accusing and incredulous as I felt. We had returned to Meredith's, and Eric had poured the two of us nightcaps before the casual revelation.

"We're just friends now. She wants too much. But M.J.'s not a bad person."

"What do you mean '…now'?"

"I mean M.J. has a bad temper when she doesn't get her way. That's why we're just friends. It's an open-ended category."

"Are we 'just friends' too?"

"Sure, don't you want to be?" He studied me, the corner of his lip turned down. Maybe he hadn't noticed M.J.'s rage when we left together. "Meredith was never jealous of M.J."

I followed him to the bedroom. In a tall mirror above the dresser I saw the scab on my lip. Eric opened the closet. He shook out the bedding, and stared at me hard. I stared back, and he seemed to shudder. I wanted to touch him, or I wanted him to touch me. He shook out more bedding and tossed it out onto the couch in the living room.

"Wait, you're sleeping there?"

"I've spent the night here before when I've had to. It's a comfortable couch."

What was going on? He curled on his side, his arm cradling his head while I waited for him to tell me. Within silent minutes, he was asleep.

If Meredith knew what she was doing when she gave me Eric for the weekend—especially if she wanted me to take his mind off M.J.—she'd forgotten to label the right key.

Eric slept in his own embrace and I opened the door and walked down the steps to the beach. Behind me, through the windows, Eric looked like a beautiful man in a display case. I unlocked the lower gate, and stuffed the clanky keys under a landing.

The surf rolled silver. The tide was going out, and the sand was scalloped. Soon I came to a ledge of low rocks and crept over them; strange spongy rocks, soft with piles of seaweed and trapped shells. The rocks seemed to breathe as I walked on them, letting out an eerie hiss.

"Sneaking off, huh?"

A hand brushed me. The surf's roar had obscured the scrunch of footsteps. I let out a low shriek. Behind me, Eric was rubbing sleep from his eyes.

"Scared you? I woke up and all the lights were on."

"I stuck the keys under the steps by the beach gate," I answered, defensive.

"That's where M.J. always leaves them too. Let's take a walk."

"A walk to where?"

"Come on, Anna. I have something to show you."

He tugged at my arm and yanked me onto the packed sand.

The moon was peaking, full and bright. I shut my eyes. Water laced my ankles. I cracked my eyelids. Waves curled and I imagined fish swimming in backlit breakers.

"Where are we going?"

"It's a surprise."

We came to a sharp curve. Sand disappeared into a steep jut of rocks. Eric helped me to find sure footing on them. I clung to him.

The rocks were slippery and sharp. At the summit I leaned up and kissed him. I unfolded my mouth into his and pressed his bare back and shoulders beneath his shirt. A faint sweet sheen glossed his back. I wriggled my fingers over his buttocks. He pulled me forward and guided me onto a vast expanse of beach with luminous sands on the other side.

"Look!" He clasped my neck hard. His voice was no longer light, but rapt and sensual.

I turned away from the water.

"Look over there, next to the cliff."

A tangle of car chassis and rusting bodies, maybe a dozen or more, lay streamlined in the moonlight like skeletons, naked carcasses gleaming, stripped of hoods and chrome. Above, the road twisted sharply in a sudden turnaround where drivers unfamiliar with the cliff must have crashed through the flimsy barriers and sailed into the air.

"These are car wrecks! You brought me all the way down to Baja, to this beautiful beach, to see these car wrecks?"

"Shhhh! Don't describe it like that." His thumb rubbed me like an eraser. His voice buzzed low near my ear. "These aren't wrecked cars, they're stolen. This is a hot car dumping ground, where local kids push them onto the beach to strip them for parts. I thought you of all people, you with your visual imagination," he whispered, "would appreciate this. The streamlined quality. The way stripped metal just rises up out of sand. Like sculpture," he said.

"Like sculpture?" I felt confused. The entire beach, cliffs against sky, rocks against sand, even I, myself, was frozen and sculptured.

He cupped my breasts and pressed me down. The sand was cool. Wet seaweed clung to my jeans. He rolled on top of me, bunching my shirt, kissing my flesh. He unzipped himself, and his penis sprang forward. He pushed it against my thigh. His length and hardness excited me. I grew languorous and flushed, and I hooked my leg along his back. We fumbled with clasps and buttons, undressing slowly. Then I undulated beneath him, wet as a sea creature, a beckoning anemone, opening, clinging, trying to pull him deep. His scent mingled seaweed and sweat and sweet light cologne.

He stroked me into position, shaping me with his hands, then lifting me onto a small rim of sand like a stage. The sinews of his neck quivered, ridges of muscle hardened across his chest.

His cock was shadowed, pearly in the moonlight. Moonlight sparkled on the drop of liquid poised on its tip. His fingers slid into me, over me, and I heard, far away, the low thrum of ocean, the crash of surf, and the counterpoint of my own breathing. He clasped my shoulder, bunched my hair in his hand, and pressed his penis into my mouth, pushing deep into the softness at the back of my throat. I traced the powerful veins on its underside, and let him feel the tips of my teeth. I tongued his cock's velvety tip, its tiny slit, its complex and mysterious flavor.

He lowered himself over me and thrust deep into my cunt. We rocked slowly, then fast, and I was all movement, gyrating, dancing, expanding over the ocean, into the sky, about to come.

"Eric," I cried.

I felt his tight jerk of attention and I looked over my shoulder and caught the silent scuttle of activity between the cars. Like sand crabs, practically invisible, protectively camouflaged by darting movement and drab clothes, I saw a man, no, some boys—no, no, several boys—it was impossible to tell how many or how old because they were hunched crablike in the shadows, although every now and then one darted forward, picking and plucking inside a car.

"Eric!" I stopped dead and grabbed his shoulder. "There are some other people here. A lot of them. They're watching us."

"Shhh!" He kept on rocking, slowly, stroking his fingers over my eyes, my mouth. "Keep your voice down, don't scare them. It's OK, they don't mind as long as you don't bother them. Act as if we don't know they're here…"

"But they do know. See, they're looking." I braced up on an elbow, twisting around. The moon was bright, like a streetlight. His eyes were bright, like glass.

He pinned me sideways, still rocking, rocking faster inside me, slick and smooth. For a brief moment I tried to push him away, but my body was pulsating.

"Wait a minute, calm down." He rose, silhouetted against the sky, bracing his arms, standing up to offer the boys his gleaming profile, his glorious up-curved erection. "Anna…"

His voice swelled with need. Or greed. He was almost crooning to me, not an explanation but a song. His words didn't matter. "Don't be skittish, don't be a tease. These are nice kids. They're only scavengers, they're not thieves. The good parts of the cars have been taken already."

In the long silence the air shivered. I arched forward and licked down his ribs. He entered me hard. He was pretending to ignore the boys now and yet he was deeply turned-on in a way that made me feel dreamy, unreal, acutely aware of my own physicality, yet unreachable by the boys. His rhythm speeded up. "We can watch them right back if you want to. Do you want me to introduce you? Look, don't be scared."

I imagined myself through their eyes, a spectacle, a part of the stripped pageantry of the beach. My body unfolded suddenly. My womb contracted, pulling him forward.

I wanted to make Eric come. I wanted to make him lose control.

"Do you want me to stop?"

"No." I shut my eyes.

I heard pounding waves, throbbing surf, his voice a hum, and I grew weightless, rising, soaring, almost skimming the moon, swimming toward moonlight, beginning to tremble.

"This is the kind of real life you don't get any hint of inside the compound," he murmured.

I came with a flaunting crash, a series of whimpers, and Eric roared, and rammed, surging forward.

"You knew these boys could see us?" I said afterward, keeping my tone carefully neutral, gathering my clothes. "And that's why you brought me here?" My cunt was still throbbing. I wondered how many times he'd played this scene for boys with M.J. "I think it's horrible the way you lock the Mexicans out. It's their territory, not yours. You just want them to watch."

Eric, already dressed, was again impeccable, almost sparkling. "You wanted to come to Baja to have new experiences and you did. They're just kids, harmless kids. They get a kick out of watching. They live on the beach, they take the basics for granted, it's no big deal. Remember, you came out onto the beach before me tonight—" I jumped up, insides wobbly, my blouse half-on. His words made no sense to me, but many things made no sense to me.

"Anyway, if you want to go now—" Eric pulled crumpled bills out of his pocket, wrapping them around coins to weight them in a practiced maneuver. "Being seen is no crime, no more than seeing is." He tossed the bills onto the sand. The boys fidgeted below, then clamored forward. "But I knew you'd love this, I knew you'd get excited by being watched. To be broken into in front of people, it's a wonderful violation. Boundaries need to be violated once in a while or they trap you inside. I wanted you, you especially, to see what I need. Even Meredith thought you'd like it."

The moon disappeared behind a cloud bank. The boys were beginning to fade too, into the shadows of the stripped cars. For an instant I wanted to run toward them, to know who they were.

Instead, I ran in the opposite direction, toward the house, away from Eric. I lost footing once on the rocks but I reached the beach gate ahead of him. I scrambled for the keys where I had left them under the landing, and when I couldn't find them, I started digging for them in the sand. Had they gotten buried somehow? Frantically, I banged the lock.

"Don't worry about it," Eric panted, catching up. He took off his shoes and dumped out sand. "M.J. probably came back from walking Ralphie and took the keys. She knows my schedule. She probably took the keys just to be safe."

"Safe from what?"

"From Crazy Sarita. Wait here! I'll run down to Jughead and

Sundae's and get up that way. Then I'll let you in."

"No!" I shouted. Sand clasped my ankles. He was already gone. The wind blew hard.

I grabbed at a scrubby tree and started swinging up the cliff toward the enclosing compound wall not far above me, climbing arm over arm, grasping at rocks and plants.

Overhead, the outside lights flashed on.

"What's Ralphie barking for?" M.J.'s voice shouted over the terrace.

I reached the wall. I remembered M.J.'s threats and her shotgun, and realized if she shot me everybody would believe that she'd mistaken me for Crazy Sarita.

But was there a Crazy Sarita? Maybe there was just me and M.J. I suddenly realized that Crazy Sarita must be M.J. Only M.J. claimed to see the Mexican housebreaker. Like me, M.J. was trying to break in, past Eric's high walls. Maybe she would shoot Eric. I imagined Eric shattering with all the splendor of a car wreck.

My feet gave way. I let myself fall. I landed with cactus spines in my hands. The click of insects surrounded me, and the throaty clicking of night lizards. The wind blew. It lifted me.

Then Eric's shadow loomed over me. He was opening the beach gate. He said, "Let's go down to the water. I'll clean your wounds."

My wounds were many and unknowable. His eyes glittered, then reflected me back to myself. Closed windows.

I followed him. His back was luminous. Above, I spotted M.J. in silhouette, prowling the terrace. She raised her gun. Light gleamed. Shards flew.

At the Falls

ॐ

OPAL PALMER ADISA

AS THE PLANE ASCENDED, Evelyn shifted in the seat and her mind drifted, reliving the breakup with Frederick.

They had just sat down to dinner when she blurted out:
"Listen, Frederick, I want something else in my life. I'm calling it quits. We're not working; we're through!"

Frederick held the fork in midair, looked at her, then at the fork of food as if trying to decide whether she or it spoke. Then carefully and slowly he put the fork on the plate, looked at her as if she had lost her mind and said:

"Is what? You going through change of life? If it's married you want, get married, we can do that."

She shook her head no, fearing what might come out of her mouth. She had planned to be more diplomatic. Frederick had looked at her as if assessing her worth. When she didn't say anything, he pushed back from the table, ran his hand through his receding hairline and spoke with painstaking calm.

"You seem not to realize women in their forties are not in demand. I know you are only forty-two, but a man my age can do way better."

Evelyn had been surprised by his unkind remark and felt attacked. How dare he berate her age? she thought. He was fifty years old with a paunch and a baldpate. He was attractive, but not handsome, generous but not indulgent, and apart from his love of the beach and sailing, he had no keen interest in cultural activities. Moreover, she concluded that his lovemaking was routine and not frequent enough to satisfy her desire or need. Maybe she wasn't in demand, she reasoned, but she wasn't prepared to settle either. As if reading her mind, Frederick pulled playfully at her hand, which she yanked away.

"Listen Ev, you been working hard; you need a break and some good loving. Is five years you and I going together. Tell me where you want to go—Miami, New York, London? I can take off in a few weeks and we can go away and have some fun."

"Why we have to go away to have fun?" she pouted.

"You acting like a child. Not even children have fun all the time. Go and sleep it off."

It was his dismissal, coupled with her own frustrated sexual energy, which had been mounting for the last several months, that caused her to move from being direct to rage.

"Listen, Frederick, maybe forty-year-old women are not in demand, but every day I walk these streets, plenty men give me the eyes. I'm a mature woman but I am not old yet. I know what I want and you have not been satisfying my needs, so just clear out my house and let me wallow in my so-called change of life." Then she stalked to the open door, folded her arms tightly at her breasts, and kept her eyes averted, looking only at the gate until he left, ten minutes later, stalling to see if she would capitulate and apologize. She didn't hear from him for two days. On the third day, her mother called her at work, asking if she were mad or reckless to throw out a good man like Frederick; with a thriving contracting business, he was a good catch. Evelyn fumed; she would show him just how reckless she could be. Without even cradling the receiver in its place, she dialed Frederick's number immediately after hanging up from her mother and shouted at him over the phone.

"You didn't go to my mother to ask permission to fuck me, so why go now like some whipped dog. You think I am a child? We're through! Get that in your head. I intend to get what I want and certainly deserve." Then she banged the phone down without giving him a chance to respond. The next day Frederick sent flowers and an apology note. For the next six days he called, until she refused to speak to him.

When the stewardess announced over the intercom, "Fasten seatbelts for landing," Evelyn shook her head as if to shake out all traces of Frederick. She was through pretending to be satisfied with the mundaneness of life.

As the plane hit the tarmac, Evelyn looked out the window and saw a terrain similar to Jamaica, her own island home. The green in the mountain was so crisp it shimmered under the sun and the blue of the sky was washed a clean azure. Evelyn breathed deeply, rubbed her thighs, and pulled down the hem of her skirt as she rose in preparation to disembark. She smiled as she walked down the aisle, thinking, five days alone, no work, no other person, except for the caretaker. She decided she would stop in Castries, the capital, and purchase fruits, bread, juices, and a few other snack items. All she planned to do was sit quietly and try to figure out how she wanted to live the next phase of her life. She had never been to St. Lucia, but Vivian, a St. Lucian and also one of her colleagues and close friends, told her about the cottage on the mountain where she was planning to sequester herself for the next five days. Vivian assured her, "Girl, staying at the cottage is the best place to get over a man and welcome fulfillment back into your life. Besides, the caretaker lives about half a mile down from the cottage and will cook for you, if you want. He'll meet you at the airport."

Evelyn exited into George F. L. Charles Airport, which basically only had a taxi stand and a tourist booth, and felt the suffocating heat. As she walked over to the baggage claim, her eyes gravitated to a lean but muscular smooth cocoa-brown man with dreads to his waist, wearing a knitted red, yellow and green Rasta top, green shorts, and sandals. His muscles rippled and as he turned toward her; she took in his full moist lips, which parted to reveal even white teeth. She was taking him in but pretending as if she weren't, making sure to avoid their eyes connecting. He caught her looking and flashed her a full smile but she turned away as if she didn't see him. Why was she feigning noninterest? she gibed herself. She claimed her bag and stood waiting. Where is that driver? she wondered. When she turned again, the Rasta dread was holding a piece of cardboard on which her name was written crookedly. This can't be the caretaker, Evelyn thought. Her colleague had said he was a middle-aged man.

"I'm Evelyn Bradford," she said, standing her ground, her nose stuck up in the air, her face stiff.

"Miss Bradford?" he asked, nodding his head.

"Yes, that's me," Evelyn replied formally.

"Seen, cool running." The Rasta dread smiled, boldly assessing her from head to toe. "Seen!" he said again, running his tongue over his lips and pulling off his dark glasses to get a better look. "Ispect," he said in Rasta vernacular, which she understood. "One thing about Jamaica, it has pretty-pretty women and the sweetest weed, but it's one crazy place," he concluded.

"People without knowledge are always saying lots of things about Jamaica," Evelyn snapped, feeling her nationalism rearing. "That's my suitcase," she said, indicating her bag.

He reached for it, and without missing a beat rejoined, "I man live in Jamaica for three years. I attended The School of Art off Tom Redcome Drive. Jamaica is all right with me, but too many brethren stuck on angry. Anyway, come. Let we go," he said, stepping aside and directing her. He led her to an old Land Rover that should have belonged to the army. He opened the door and it was clean. Evelyn climbed in, her shift dress hiked up. What possessed me to wear this dress? she admonished herself, pulling at the hem. The Rasta dread put her suitcase in the back, then jumped in and almost immediately the jeep sprang to life. As he pulled into the traffic without looking at her, he remarked:

"That's a nice dress you're wearing, but I hope you brought something else. You're going into the mountains, bush country, nothing and no one around. It's the Garden of Eden you could walk round like Eve before the expulsion."

Goose bumps rose on Evelyn's arms at his suggestive remarks. Who was this man? she wondered, her curiosity piqued. She glanced at his hand as he shifted gears, and sidled closer to the door. There was something elegant about his hands, as if he played an instrument. They didn't seem as if they did much manual labor.

"So how long have you been a caretaker for the cottage?" Evelyn asked, deciding that this was a safe topic.

The Rasta dread burst out laughing and glanced at her.

"I man look like caretaker to you?" His voice was all tease and dare.

For a quick second sweat spread under her arms. Her throat felt parched.

"Take it easy, take it easy. You're safe with me," he said, glancing at her. "My folks take care of the place. Some family problems came up on the other side of the island, so my old man asked me to meet you and see to your needs."

There was something lascivious in the way he said *needs*.

"When will they be back?" she ventured, trying to quiet a mounting agitation.

"Who's to tell? But not to worry. I man will take care of you, cook you some ital food, idle way all your worries. Once you get there and feel that cool breeze and smell the fresh air, whatever you're running away from in Jamaica will disappear in the wind. Mark my word."

"Perhaps we can stop so I can pick up some juice, bread, fruits..."

"Relax yourself. I have everything under control. Just enjoy the ride," he said, and began humming a tune that she didn't recognize.

"Maybe I should check into a hotel."

"Is 'fraid, you 'fraid of I?" he asked. It was only then that Evelyn realized she had spoken her doubt out loud.

"What is your name?" She shifted the attention to him.

"They call I and I Cane Man, but I sweeter than sugarcane," he chuckled. Evelyn thought about all of the sugarcane she chewed on as a child. She hadn't done that in years. She could feel herself relaxing, her body conforming to the seat.

Soon they were off the main road, and turned onto a narrow, partially paved lane that wound up the mountain. The air was instantly cooler, moist, and Evelyn settled back into the jeep and closed her eyes, enjoying the sensation of the wind on her body. Twice she felt as if someone were rubbing her thigh, but both times when she opened her eyes, Cane Man's eyes were straight ahead, both hands on the steering wheel, fingers drumming in rhythm to his humming. After about forty minutes of climbing up the hill, he turned onto a dirt path, and a few miles later turned off the engine.

Evelyn peered around and about a hundred yards from where they parked, she spotted the cottage, nestled by trees and wildflowers. They sat in silence. Evelyn glanced around and inhaled the fragrant air. She felt as if layers of dead skin fell from her body. A bird alighted on the railing of the veranda. Cane Man helped her out of the jeep, and then got her suitcase.

"That's a St. Oriole," Cane Man said, pointing to the bird. They had not spoken since he told her his name, and his voice was a whisper. "Lots of agouti, gecko, and birds round here, especially black finch," he said, his voice the texture of warm, thick liquid. He stepped onto the veranda. A hammock was slung across the width, near the entrance. The cottage was painted three different shades of green. Cane Man pushed open the door, which was unlocked, and stood back for her to enter. Inside was a cool blue-gray, with larger-than-life-sized hibiscus, bird-of-paradise, and red-ginger painted on the wall.

"Your handiwork?" Evelyn asked, indicating the painted flowers.

"My mother's. She's the painter. I'm a jeweler. Fruits," he said, pointing to the bowl of fresh fruits on the table. "There is fresh juice in the fridge and water. Tea, coffee and crackers in the cupboards. That's the bedroom," he said, pointing to the closed door. "I'll leave you to find your way. There is much to discover: trails, if you are adventurous. There is no key, but you're safe. Pull up the door when you go for a walk, and at night there is a bolt at the front door, and one in the bedroom if you feel the need. Rest, and I will bring you dinner around seven o'clock." He smiled full and wide then, unhurriedly stepped through the door and down the three steps, got into the jeep, and reversed out of the path. Instantly, Evelyn felt abandoned. What's gotten into you? she talked to herself, surprised at her feelings. She wanted him to stay, to talk or at least hum his endless tune.

She was alone. Solitude. She walked around the cottage inspecting everything, and nibbling on a guava as she surveyed. The bolt on the bedroom, she noticed, a child could push loose, and although the one at the front door was a little sturdier, even she could pry it open with little effort. But he said she was safe, and her instincts told her she could believe him. She pulled off her dress in the living room, which had no curtains, and walked into the bedroom. "Not sure I'm ready to be Eve yet," she spoke aloud, opening her suitcase and pulling out shorts and a cotton top. Then she went to rest in the hammock.

Mosquitoes buzzing awakened her, but the sun still hung low. Evelyn got up, stretched, then decided to go for a walk and find the source of the water that she had been hearing. She followed the trail closest to the path that ran from the veranda, pausing to examine the foliage. By the time she found the waterfall and river, the sun had jumped behind the mountain. As she approached she heard humming and stopped, glancing around. She crept stealthily, making sure to avoid brambles. About fifty yards from the waterfall, she spied Cane Man and immediately crouched by a tree. He was naked, washing his hair and bathing. She stared long and lustfully at his lean muscular body, perfect in every way, including his penis hanging full between his thighs. Evelyn was transfixed, greedily observing his every move: he lathered his hands and soaped his genitals. A fire-like ache spread in her groin and she sucked in her breath audibly. Momentarily, Cane Man stopped humming and looked around. She crouched down further, hoping the trunk concealed her body. When he began humming again, she slunk away, glancing back. After a few miss-turns, she found her way back to the cottage that was in complete darkness. What had gotten into her?

She was shivering, but not from cold. Evelyn reminded herself that Cane Man was not her type. "He's probably not even thirty. Besides, I'm not here for an affair or sexual fantasy." She felt a tingle and entered the cottage and washed her face and hands. She sat in the semidarkness of the living room with only a light on the veranda. When she heard footsteps and humming her heart pushed against her shirt.

"You decent inside?" a voice inquired as the humming sound got louder.

"Cane Man, is that you?" Evelyn asked, rising and walking toward the door.

"You sound like you expecting someone else," his voice was a tease and laughter.

"Sorry I man late with the dinner. I went to the Falls, not far from here." He paused and stared at her, his eyes roving her body hungrily, boldly, and like at the airport he licked his lips before continuing. "The Falls is magic, the purest water in the entire Caribbean, healing and lustful too like dogs in heat. The best bath you can have. You must try it, I'll wash your back." He laughed and her body shivered with goose bumps again. "What a way this man fresh and confident," Evelyn thought, backing away from him, even though he did not take one step toward her. He placed the pot on the stove and moved deftly about the small kitchen taking out plates, napkin, and even two candles, all of which he set on the table and assembled a perfect table for one.

"Aren't you going to join me?" she asked, not believing her own request. Why was she inviting trouble into her life? Everything about him spelled a furious trouble. He bit his bottom lip and looked at her more brazenly.

"I is a man who like to know if the door is open or close just in case I want to come in. But I'm going to take this for what it is." He pulled out the chair and motioned for her to sit. She did and he gently patted her shoulders and her legs shivered. He smiled. She wondered if he noticed and was laughing at her. He got another setting then served them both ital stew, a spicy vegetable broth with callaloo as the base. There was also roasted sweet potato and sweet yucca and corn.

"Very good," Evelyn said as she chewed on a piece of yucca, which trickled down her chin. She was embarrassed, but he reached across the small table and wiped the corner of her mouth and chin as if it were the most natural thing. Then he took the fork out of her hand and scooped her a spoonful of ital stew and fed it to her. She chewed slowly, and all the while he was staring into her eyes, stripping away her objections about him. She felt as if she were naked before him. He dipped a piece of sweet potato in the stew and offered it to her in the palm of his hand, but first one then another of his fingers were in her mouth and she licked them slowly as if each were a rum-and-raisin ice-cream cone. She could feel the tips of his fingers tracing the outline of her body, stroking under her arms, near her breasts, then gliding down to her waist, just stroking and drinking her in, until the wetness in her spread and the fire flared out, a soft blue-gold, spreading until it consumed her entire body. She didn't know if it was her own feet, sole against skin that were rubbing against each other or his feet were intertwined with hers. He pasted the yuccas on her lips, and she flicked her tongue and licked and licked. She heard a moan and realized that she was clutching the side of the table. She opened her eyes and he was sitting across from her, his eyes closed, a beatific smile on his face.

"That was very satisfying," he said, reaching for her plate that was clean. Was he talking about the food or what he did to her? What did he do to her? Did he touch her? Did he drug her? Was she dreaming? She didn't need to touch herself down there to confirm that she was wet.

"What did you put in the food?" she asked.

"Love. Love sweetens the most meager pot. I see you enjoyed it. There is much more to come." Again he smiled.

"No, no, I am quite full."

"That is how it should be," he laughed, and turned toward the kitchen. "Go and relax on the veranda. I will bring you a slice of banana pudding with some tea."

She felt subdued, satiated. There was something about the tone of his voice that was soothing. She walked out onto the veranda, and looked up at the sky sprinkled and twinkling with stars. It was a dark night otherwise. Evelyn felt as if time had stopped and only she and Cane Man were left alive in this pristine place, nestled in the mountain. Then she felt his body close to hers, even though she hadn't heard him approach. He reached for the bowl over her shoulder, his finger trailing her braids lightly. He was a full head taller than she was. She didn't turn or move away; she took the bowl from him, his fingers wrapping around hers, pressing them lightly before releasing. She tasted the banana-ginger pie, savoring every bite. All the while she ate, he stood behind her, not quite touching, but the heat of his maleness, and his breathing aroused her, bathing her body with desire, a wet longing. When she felt him moving away, her voice held him.

"Tell me about the Falls," Evelyn demanded, her voice a raspy rush as she caressed the empty bowl.

"No matter the drought that might plague the entire island, it never runs dry. They say it is the eternal tears of one of our ancestors, a slave woman whose children were taken from her and sold to another island. The story goes, when that happened she ran away up here and cried so much, her tears flooded the island, including the sugar estate on which she used to work, drowning the overseer and washing away the entire crop. Since then island people come up here to bathe, some leave a little food, get their healing and go on. You know where it is already. Bathe there in the morning. Seen! Check you later." Then he was gone, walking down the steps, ambling onto the path to the left of the house before being swallowed up by the darkness; only his ceaseless humming, evidence of his presence, lingered. She listened until the sound was just a faint memory. She held the bowl close to her chest and caressed it. Just as she turned to go inside the cottage, she felt as if someone kissed her on her back, near her right shoulder. She paused, glanced around then rubbed the spot that felt very warm. She blew out the candles on the table, stripped naked and was asleep as soon as her head hit the pillow.

Evelyn awoke even before the sun had yawned, and sat up on her elbows listening. She felt rested, at peace. Then she rose and stood naked peering out the window at the dawn and suddenly felt an urgent need. She walked over to her suitcase, which was opened but unpacked, and fished out her sarong. She heard the soothing murmur of the water and stepped out into the morning, heeding its call. Lizards and other insects scurried out of her path. She walked for much longer than she remembered walking the evening before, but still the Falls eluded her. Every time she thought she happened upon them, she found herself elsewhere, but the sound of the water was loud in her ears. When the sun was a wide-brimmed yellow hat above her head and her calves ached, Evelyn decided to find her way back to the cottage. At that point she heard the humming, the same endless song. She stood still and listened intently until she could feel the rhythm of his humming in the soles of her feet. She followed his voice and was right there. She had been circling all along.

Cane Man stood naked under the Falls, in almost the exact spot she had spied him the previous night. Without turning he spoke.

"What took you so long? I've been standing right here for eternity."

Evelyn felt lightheaded. "I know you like the view, but come and join me," he said, his voice full with laughter. As he turned toward her, she noticed his erect penis and hesitated—felt nervous. Although she was on the edge of the water, she felt its cold spray. The sun had not yet heated it up. Evelyn looked around to make sure no one else was present. Was this the excitement she had been seeking? "Go to him. You're safe," she heard her inner voice. She turned to Cane Man. He stretched out his hand to her; she undid her sarong, dropped it by her feet and stepped into the water. Cane Man pulled Evelyn to his chest and kissed her with such force that they stumbled and fell laughing, splashing water on each other. They swam and dove, and he held her under the force of the Falls and allowed the water to massage her back. When their fingers and toes were prune-like, they climbed out of the Falls and she stood naked before him, and trembling.

"You're perfect," he said, his eyes feasting on her body.

"This is the Garden of Eden." She heard the wisp of the wind.

"There is no one else here but us," he said, kissing both her hands. He led her to a tree, under which was a piece of foam with a sheet of tie-dyed cloth draped over it and beside it, a bag of fruits.

"The water is healing, but it also makes you hungry." He flopped down and she slumped near him, feeling vulnerable.

"Relax into your body," he said, pulling her close beside him. He took a tangerine from the bag of fruits, pegged it, and offered her half. She wanted to reach for her sarong but instead folded her hands across her breasts. They ate in silence; he peeled then offered her half of three different fruits. Evelyn was certain he had cast a web and lured her, but what reason did she have to complain? Here she was the first official day of her retreat, sitting by the healing Falls with a man she knew nothing about, and whom she suspected was nothing like what she thought. Relax and just enjoy it, she told herself, repeating it inside her head like a mantra.

"Don't drift away," Cane Man said, tracing the shape of her cheekbones with the tips of his fingers. "I'm what you have been seeking. This is your time. I'm here to please you." He smiled mischievously, pulling a condom out of the bag of fruits.

His full lips sucked on her. She closed her eyes, head back and chin up. Hungrily her tongue sought his, and she leaned back into his arms, her back arched, her legs spread. He moved between her like a snake, kissing her mouth, her neck, her breasts, thrusting his pelvis, rotating his hips, clasping her buttocks, penetrating and withdrawing until she wrapped her feet around his waist, held on tightly and pulled him fully into her, their rhythm matched, the fire a dazzling orange-red, rising up and up, until it sparked and flared off and simmered. Their panting was loud and her legs still quivered. When he rolled off her, sweat dripped from their bodies. They lay side by side, their fingers in intimate communication, their breaths finding an easy rhythm. Then as she was about to doze, he stood up.

"Soon come," he said, running off naked into the bushes. She settled down, her head resting on her folded arms, her ears perked to all the sounds, especially the soothing melody of the Falls. She didn't hear him return until she saw his shadow. Squinting, she smiled up at him, standing with a long stalk of cane in his hand. She sat up and he pulled a knife from the pocket of his pants that were near the empty bag of fruits, and peeled the cane, cutting it at the joints and splitting it in four pieces. After she took the first bite, she sat up and kissed him on the mouth.

"I guess they named you correctly. You're as sweet as this cane," she said as juice trickled down her chin.

"Sweeter," Cane Man dared, licking the juice from her chin.

"OK, maybe a little bit sweeter," she said, knowing it to be fact.

"Have you ever been massaged with cane-juice?" he asked.

She shook her head no.

"Lie down," he said, his face concentrated. She lay on her stomach, but he turned her over, saying "I always start with the belly." She watched him bite into a piece of cane, chew, spew the juice on her, then rub it all over her stomach, massaging her abdominal muscles, alternating between his tongue and hands. Then he placed her feet flat and knees bent. He kneeled before her thighs and chewed on another piece of cane, before he buried his head between her parted legs and used his tongue to massage her labia, her vulva, her entire pubic region until her clitoris was hard and her toes curled.

It was almost noon when they returned to the cottage, replete, water-streaked and cane sweet, her sarong slung over her shoulder. On the veranda, he caressed the outline of her body as if she were delicate crystal, kissed her just above her collarbone and walked off, naked, his pants dangling from his fingers, his song seeping into the air. There was a note tacked to the door. She pulled it off before stumbling into the cottage drunk on passionate lovemaking, and falling across the bed. Her snores soon replaced the quiet of the cottage.

"Leaving the door unlocked is an invitation."

She thought she was dreaming, but felt his breath close to her ears. Evelyn opened her eyes slowly and recognized Cane Man sitting on the bed, dressed in dazzling white.

"What? Where?" Evelyn said, dazed. She felt as if she were having an endless dream, the Falls, the cane-juice massage, and even now.

"Time to wake up, sleepyhead. I am no duppy." He turned her on her back and kissed her mouth. "There is a gathering this evening, across the mountain, on the southern side of the island, down by the beach where the sand is dark and volcanic. Drumming, smoke, good fish, and friends. Take the run with me. Here," he said, offering her a pint glass of what looked like milk. "Sour-sop juice with honey and nutmeg." He helped her to sit up and she tasted it. It was delicious, and she drank half of it before going to take a quick shower. When she came out he was draining the glass.

As she got in the jeep that was parked near the cottage door, she noticed his drums in the back.

"You play?" she asked, wanting to know more about him but sensing his reservation, or perhaps it was his illusive nature.

"I man is an artist. I play. I cook. I massage and I well like this lady from Jamaica." He reached over and patted her thigh. They drove for the next two hours in virtual silence. Every now and again, he would point out some landmark to her, then revert to his humming. For a brief moment Evelyn's mind flashed on Vivian and her insisting that she should go and stay at the cottage. Did she know about Cane Man? she wondered, but her mind was too adrift to hold on to any one idea.

"We here," he said, turning off the engine. She looked down at the beach and saw the bonfire. Even from that distance, she could tell there were mostly Rasta dreads. The drums assaulted the air and she inhaled the aroma of weed. Cane Man hoisted the drum from the jeep, rested it on his shoulder, and headed toward the gathering.

Evelyn was surprised to see so many people, most in African

attire, all along the beach, in small clusters, some around fires. Cane Man was hailed and greeted from all sides; someone relieved him of his drum. He reached for her hand and held her fingers tightly, introduced her as his lady. She smiled, nodded, said hello until they were at the circle, where the men sat at their drums and the pipe was being passed around. She counted about ten women, in comparison to about forty men. She knew sessions such as these happened at home, but she had never been to one. She didn't think women were allowed. Cane Man sat with the circle of dreads; he didn't seem like the same man who, earlier that day, had crouched between her parted legs and massaged cane-juice into her entire pubic region with his tongue. She remembered hearing a Rasta back home shouting that "Rasta don't go down." She wondered what they would say or do if they knew Cane Man gladly went down. She smiled to herself and stood off to the side watching him, her groin aching as his hand pounded the belly of the drum. When she got tired of standing, she squatted, then another dread placed a stool near Cane Man's back and signaled to her. She walked over and sat behind him, their backs almost touching, but soon the drums called her feet to dance. Evelyn jumped up and danced and danced even after she was exhausted. Cane Man stopped playing to catch her before she fell.

"I didn't know you could dance like that," he said, steadying her.

"I didn't either," she panted, clutching him.

"Let's eat something," he said, holding up her sweaty body. "Then we will take a swim and make love here in rhythm with the drums." Evelyn stood up, a little wobbly, and scanned the beach. There were about forty people altogether, most of the men shirtless. Four more women had wandered in and she could make out several couples jammed up close. She didn't want to protest, but her upbringing didn't prepare her for sex with an audience.

"There are a lot of people around," she remarked. Cane Man kissed her lightly on the lips, before leading her to where the food was being served by two dreads with turbans and starched faces. While Evelyn got two plates of food, Cane Man ran back to the jeep, returning with blankets and towels.

"I see you came prepared," she said as he jogged back to where she stood.

"Seen," was all he replied as he turned in the direction away from the major gathering. They found a semi-secluded spot where some large rocks formed an enclosure. There he spread the blankets and they ate.

"You seem to know everyone here," she ventured.

"Seen," he replied, eyes glazed. "They are my brethrens."

"Does this event happen often?"

"About twice a year," he said, standing. "Come let's go and wade in the ocean."

"What about jellyfish?" she inquired.

"Come," he insisted, pulling at her hand. "Nothing going to bite you. You're safe with me." She quickly took off her clothes and wrapped herself in the towel. At the shore he pulled it from her and they entered the water. They waded out, then he pulled her to him and hoisted her up. She wrapped her legs around his waist and sucked on his lips.

The moon was a half smile when they emerged from the ocean, their bodies water-drenched. A few dreads milled about. Evelyn hesitated. Cane Man shielded her body with his as they ran-walked to their blankets. The air wafted with weed and the drumming was fast and pulsing. Her fingers traced the outlines of his palms that were warm and through which she felt the pounding of the drums. She kissed and massaged his palms and he caressed her thighs. The flame caught, savoring its own heat. She glanced around.

"There're still so many people," she half pleaded.

"Then I'll have to make sure to please you."

Just then a dread walked nearby with a big spliff in his hand. Evelyn craned her neck.

"What are you worrying about? Relax and enjoy the sea breeze on our bodies."

Cane Man sat up and had her straddle him. He pulled her close and began to hum. The flame rose, an orange-red heat that flared and flared, spreading, consuming, their bodies crashing as he flipped her back, her feet hoisted on his shoulders. She didn't even recognize the ecstatic scream that escaped her throat as their bodies thrashed in rhythm to the drums and the murmur of the waves, and the flame smothered, spent.

For the next four days Evelyn and Cane Man were inseparable. He toured her around the island, including La Soufrière, the active volcano. Daily, he massaged cane-juice into her body near the Falls where they had their morning baths, and cooked her different ital stew. She felt as if she were sleepwalking, and kept thinking any minute she would wake up.

At the break of day of the afternoon she was scheduled to depart, Evelyn met Cane Man at the Falls. He was silent as was often his way, humming an endless tune that she didn't recognize. After they bathed, he massaged her feet, then they lay on the straw mat and the last thing she remembered before she dozed was him kissing her on her right shoulder. When she woke up, he was gone, and all was still except for a black and gold-tipped butterfly fluttering nearby that trailed her back to the cottage.

Evelyn packed, certain that Cane Man would come and take her to the airport. Just as she was done, she heard his jeep pull up and she ran to the door. A man who looked to be in his sixties got out of the jeep.

"Hi," she said hesitantly, glancing to see if Cane Man was walking along the path.

"You must be Mrs. Bradford. I never see you this whole time you were here. I left notes."

Evelyn remembered seeing notes pinned on the door several times after she and Cane Man returned from some adventure, but he always read them.

"Your son took very good care of me."

"My son? Lots of young men call me father. So you leaving today? You want a lift to the airport?"

"Isn't Cane Man coming?" she inquired.

"I really couldn't tell you," the man said, baffled.

Just then Evelyn heard a humming along the path leading to the Falls.

"I'll be right back," she said, dashing to follow the tune.

Although she jogged and called out, "Cane Man," the humming continued at an even pace, but she never caught up with him, even when she arrived at the Falls. He was nowhere to be found. All she saw was a sweet-sop on the foam mat on which he had massaged and made love to her. She walked to the edge of the water and there she saw an empty water bottle. She stooped, held the bottle in the water until it was full, then sealed it closed. She had never for a minute thought that she and Cane Man would last beyond her time in the mountains, but she wanted to say a proper good-bye. She held the bottle of Falls water close to her. The moaning of the Falls penetrated to her heart and she felt suffused. As she turned to leave, she felt Cane Man's lips on her back by her right shoulder. She stood still, savoring the sensation of his mouth on her, then like the wind it was gone. She turned slowly, placed her hand right where he kissed her and smiled as the heat fanned her groin. Yes, he was much sweeter than cane-juice.

twelve days in a week

ॐ

DES ARIEL

TWELVE INTO SEVEN

That was the beginning and the end of you and me: seven days and twelve fucks, which made 1.714285714 fucks a day. But who's calculating? Plus it was the 12th of the 7th month, July, you said. You tried to make this signify, yet the cards aligned stacked in contrary sequence. You got the date wrong. That was all.

12

My return to Manchester brings it back in shockwaves. Now I know why they call it *Mad*chester. I'm walking past the Bridgewater Concert Hall. Twenty years on, and you are there, crossing the road against the traffic. Still the funky street kid. Head now shaved. Earrings. I see you; you look right through me, a vanished ghost from your past, just some gray figure walking toward Albert Square. I plunge back to that first encounter. You stalked me from behind the corner window where a one-armed model in St. Ann's

Square pointed at me. It was outside the Royal Exchange Theatre. Some renovations going on. I was clumsy. The boards clanked on metal pipes under my feet. I was dazed from doing library research on Deansgate. I needed fresh air, a stroll. So there you were. I accidentally brushed rust from the scaffolding on to my hands, and my thumbs looked like wall prints. Some landed near your crotch, a coppery smudge on white, studded denim. I would have cleaned it off gladly on my knees, but you moved fast. I dodged under the tarpaulin to muse on glances shrugged off. Each print on my palms smudging.

You played the tease, the come-and-get-me game.

They say, back home in the Levant, that a man chases a boy — till the boy catches him. I caught many of my uncles that way. And you were of age, though there was a good fifteen years between us. But with the Capricorn placement that was the norm for you: you netted older men like horses to a stable for a feast.

We were perfect strangers (emphasis on *strange*, not *perfect*) since I am the eternal exile, from perhaps Alexandria, or Beirut — I didn't say — I let you guess. Beirut is my hometown, but I had also lived in Alexandria, the place that has long annexed the imagination, locating it on the universal axis of the mind. The actual city is immaterial. It's all in the eyes of fleeting experience, in the angle of intent. As Manchester can be, a collapsible city, intermingling structures, a circle, a square, a triangle, clubs, bars, galleries, people, memories crisscrossing into a mosaic. Your sugar-brown eye seeing only what your heart, looking for a new protector, fancied was there.

I had heard about you before, thanks to a Turkish friend, purveyor of Euro flesh. But — *and you had forgotten this* — this Turk had already introduced us, briefly, on Portland Street. And then again at Affleck's Palace where you sold hand-painted shirts. I was awarded a "Hello," then you barely looked back. The Turk said you were a sweetheart from Martinique who loved the tongues of foreign men basted and spiraled on your flaming cock. But mostly, you were a foreigner to yourself, misplaced in Manchester. My second appearance that day jolted new sensations back to a desensitized domain, your fucked-up life. Your need for a new protector.

I asked you to join me for dinner — *dim sum* barbecued beef, mango ice cream, and a fine Chablis? See — I wasn't all bad. With my Mediterranean good looks, I had you interested, uplifted, till soon you were gagging and curious for more. I recognized the dynamic of thirsting for the "other." Bringing the alien closer through passion. I needed just a few suggestive words to convince you, before you jokingly licked my palms, the remnants of rust now melting orange explosion on your lengthy pink tongue.

You silenced me, hand in my lap. Words can just get in the way. Then what?

Your bedroom? A straight line that amuses me now for all its laughable geometry. Sometimes, to hesitate is fatal. I did laugh as you twisted it, really wanting to talk about something bookish and scholarly. I yawned (my whole life devoted to books!). A mind-fuck (OK, "shag," if you will have it U.K. style) is one route to the bedroom. It works just as well as seduction. "I am no man's trophy," you said. "I want to be appreciated for my mind." So you talked on as I looked out the window at the motion of people dodging each other as they passed. I nodded *yes*, or *no*, or *I don't think so*: Byron's love affairs; Avicenna, or, I corrected, *Ibn Sina* as he is better known to us; Herodotus; and Queen Hatshepsut, you had heard of and studied them all. Then you switched to music, disco fever, and I was lost in admiration. Nina Simone in her *Mississippi Goddamn* phase — you sang it for me — a song you wanted to change to *"Manchester" Goddamn*, or *Cottonopolis* to a Sylvester-style funk beat. You could have been a star, as we all could.

Time bends my memory here. I was spared, I think, the catalogue of further anecdotes that would have made knowing you more complete — rape, (an uncle, of course), a short prison sentence, a series of potato-faced punters, a football club manager that haunted the gents' room at the Thompsons Arms, obsessed with you, and, one true love at school. But then you were good at (inventing your own) history that I discarded along with your clothes on the floor, to ram home my case. And we fucked right there in an ecstasy of discovery. Twice that night I think.

11

Some other excitement was astir the next day too, a storm cloud of news, not limited to our fusion of combusted pheromones. It had all the clamor of a sudden assassination. The early eighties. It hadn't rained for a week, but thunder still rumbled over Didsbury and out to Alderly Edge: race riots exploded right there in Moss Side—yes, street fights, fires, barricades, and attacks on the police. Manchester felt suddenly like it needed its homegrown Martin Luther King, like it was an offshoot of the Deep South. That was long before mills became lofts and hotels, or canals tarted themselves up as quayside entertainments, long before the Gay Village became yuppified, and the *Queer As Folk* craze, though the Rembrandt pub is still wedged there like a toadstool, impervious to change. If you look down into the canal now, the dirt swims in your face ready to reincarnate as mutant fungus, a virulent Mancunian strain.

Wanting to witness the wreckage of streets, we walked across Alexandra Park to Moss Side. We marveled at the boarded-up shops, the splintered windows, the ruptured gates, the upturned Morris Rovers, and the splayed graffiti. I was fearful: I had truly never been in a city where such outbreaks of street violence could happen. *This was England?* It thrilled and appalled in equal measure. I kept close to you, afraid we'd get verbally abused by stray gangs. Gradually, the mayhem frittered out. The fires trailed to nothing. For some, it never did subside, but grew from the inside like a tumor. We put brave faces on, but were sorely rattled. This passion for touching and nuzzling skin to skin became our total universe.

You lived frugally in those rented rooms in an old Victorian mansion in Whalley Range. Right by Alexandra Park. The front gardens were glossy green canopies for prostitutes to cower or do business in. Pop singers lived in adjacent streets. "Whalley 'de' Range," you called it. Money was scarce for ex-students, ex whatever. Any extracurricular cash you made was none of my business, as for me the only charge was electric, the pulse of you touching, no, mauling me, and me you; you trying to gnaw my musky wood-flavored cock that your teeth chewed like licorice, and me collapsed under you, legs splayed. What dominance and verve. I brought dinner and drinks to your place. You rolled a joint. No great feast, but enough to make you grin. Unopened summonses from the local council for nonpayment of rates lay in heaps on the desk. You shoved them on the floor so you could lean back naked on the desktop, me on top of you. How tough the winters must have been with just that two-ring electric fire, a blanket, and a bowl of porridge oats for warmth. I could only imagine, as I come from wealth, from a business family. We have big split-level villas with olive gardens, and an idyllic mountain retreat. But I was adventurous, then. I wanted you. You taught me a new expression, "How to slum it in style." I kept my own more comfortable rooms in Deansgate a private matter.

10

On the third day, I remember sleeping late in your bed (that mere mattress) at your insistence. The curtains doing nothing to stop the light pouring in. An itch (you?) got under my skin, under fingernails, the soft flesh at the back of my knee, and flattened hair on my neck. Your cat, Giordano, had fleas. Then, so did we. It was Giordano you usually slept with, so he was jealous and behaved badly, hiding from me. Perhaps he knew you were just another body to me, lean and nervous. I would pass. A thirsting for sex that couldn't be quenched. How you lusted for it. So unlike the British boys I'd tried who were limp, pale, and inept, with twangy voices. I made up in technical efficiency what I lacked in affection, a trick or two. A genuine affair would only have torn us apart anyway. I was mindful that we needed distance in closeness. Glad that we did not "fall head over heels" — an odd thing to say, as our heads are already over our heels, and thus quite level. But it is not for me to puzzle the English language.

You scribbled me down in your diary, catching, fresh-minted, the things I said: gnomic, paradoxical, but for me, bungled thoughts I just made up on the spot. They were not for discussion, but for instant forgetting. To take them seriously showed lack of irony — for which there is no easy health tonic or cure. You said I was "a sphinx with a blue funk soul." The blue funk bit, you liked; the sphinx part had you foxed. But I was just a guy turned-on till my eyes drank in the view, when the soapy water trailed and splattered down the crack of your shiny brown, hairless, near-perfectly shaped backside, that I would then towel dry for you, just to lick your salience clean and press my tongue deep into your tasty hole to eat and eat and eat. Then to your balls and…there was no end to the feeling we were consuming each other alive.

9

Talking about books flooded a dark stage with light. You were an ex-archaeology student. "Am I just one of your 'digs?'"

I quipped. "You've read too much," you said. "I can't compete." I laughed. "Oh, yes you can. You're starting sooner." But this talk galvanized you back to the library on a mission of rediscovery. To me, you were a book yourself, a slim volume of elegant erotic poems. If I were to take apart your point of axis and smell the binding in the spine, lavished with cocoa butter, hair oil, and finger the slender pages, stroke the hand-painted sleeve to trace my silken thread through your intricate tight labyrinth of pubic hair coils, I would savor the few marks of print where letters scatter like occasional tufts of hair under armpits, or on nipple mounds. My thumbs would pause then, rest on the white spaces. Yes, I was your white space, enveloping you, making you stand out clearer than at any time before, clarifying your sumptuous content. The dog-eared pages would remind me of lovemaking left off, folded back on itself, ready to be refreshed by a longing gaze, a suction kiss the exchange of saliva. The bookmark, a pickup point, to relish rereading, reabsorbing, to backtrack a little, with fresh foreplay, not to rush the climax, not to get so far ahead of ourselves that we are all-semen-spent, but to let the eyes rest leisurely on all the kissed contours, high peaks, blips and serifs, and let the final full stop come, at last, but not before its rightful moment.

8

You asked me, as we lay together, your head back, me fondling your crinkled hair, "Do you have a job?" and I said, "No, not really. Like you, I am a life student. Watching the world is full-time occupation enough for a would-be philosopher and translator." You said, "Work's hard to find. But I don't care for white-man bosses, timetables, and taking orders." "Perhaps, you should be self-employed?" There was a whiff of the gypsy in you that matched the world traveler in me. It would have been good to take off by car somewhere together, the Lake District, Carlisle perhaps, the Scottish Highlands. But it is the inner geography that is hardest to map out. "I suggest you be an artist's model. Come on. Give me Rodin's thinking man please." You threw off your clothes, stood up on a chair in full daylight, vehement in your nudity. You took an imaginary apple in your mouth, then balanced it on your bicep. Your dick had supple weight that made it dangle purposefully. I applauded. Posing came naturally; patience did not. "What now?"

you said, ravenous for more of me. You slithered down, unbuttoned my shirt, and nuzzled me from my nipples to my waist, undoing my belt, opening the underwear, feasting then on my balls, which you said tasted like salted baklava. We made love on the floor, you sitting on top, riding your Arab stallion.

Bodies sufficed the hunger. But then you scavenged your own cupboard for food: a tired old bag of rice, a cup of lentils, soy sauce, traces of peanut butter at the bottom of the jar, and half a block of creamed coconut. You were still naked as you reached, and I feasted on your bare outline, such meaty curves for one so forever starved. You ranted, lights full on. Passersby looked up, and you waved, and wiggled, audacious and carefree. You said, "I once streaked the full length of Alexandra Park on a dare, and it made me so…oh, my God! And I'd do it again. They can all get an eyeful. It gets attention all right." It ended up I had to take you out for dinner in Chinatown, your favorite, and even the fortune cookies warned us — *that which is built on sand subsides from underneath.* "No," I said, "that's wrong. A house built on sand is home to a family of crabs, or in our case, your lover, Giordano's fleas."

7

Day five: the game proceeded. "What is your real name?" you asked and I said, "Let's play chess. I have brought the board." You agreed, and won, two games out of three. Names had escaped us from the first day — in the hurry to make love, it hadn't mattered. Then deliberately. "Come on tell me your name," you persisted. I shrugged. "You've forgotten me once, so you can do it again. What does it matter? Just call me 'foreign.'" You hissed and tutted. But I held ground. My lips were open to suck you off, till juices filled my fatted cheeks, to take this flavor, but not to tell names. This way, I reflected, I'd be safe as buried treasure, an Arab essence lodged somewhere in your synapses, perhaps snap-sprung into life years later as vague reverberations resurface, as you once again brush rust off your crotch under scaffolding, or stand naked on a chair, apple in your arm, or wave at goggle-eyed passersby who see your lithe and tempting genitals on full display. Or, even — and I could not contemplate this ever happening — on your first visit to Alexandria, or Beirut, when you might try to locate me on a slim lead from the Turk. Then I might say "My name is Mohammed. Just ask in the *souk* for me." But that's cruel. The entire *souk* would answer to that name and say, "*ahlaanbiik*. Welcome to you, *Habbeebi darling*. Come right in." So you could, if inspired, make love to a hundred and fifty Mohammeds, while searching for me—why not?

You moved knight to my castle in silence—the best wrapper for all such questions. "It's better we don't know," you said finally, and I nodded. "That's right. You understand, don't you? Why destroy the moment by naming?" We should not name too much if we want to preserve sensation that can't be tied up by words. And in passionate wonderment alone we can intuit the core of ourselves embodied in the other, the familiar in the alien. "Do women," I said, "become different people just because they adopt their husbands' names?" But this reminded me of my own wife, Khadija (why did I just name her?), back at home. I had not mentioned her to you, nor thought it wise to do so. It was important for your concerns to be limited to what was in front of you. I was more tempted to tell you about my son, Ahmed, a fine young man, not five years from your age who might have been your very good friend. "If X and Y give birth to Z. I'll call you 'Z.' " And you then called me, "Constant," since the bitter contradiction pleased you. "Could you ever be constant?" you asked. "I doubt it. No sentiment, no pain," I said, and you grabbed your diary, jabbed me with your pencil. "Such a cynic. Does romance not exist in your world?" Yet, still you wrote it down.

6

Halfway house, and I still did not foresee the end.

We switched the lights out to let the late dusk saunter over us, forming great leafy patterns on the rug, a pale imitation of the Bokhari ones I had at home, but it covered the beveled floorboards. Light gave you greenish eyes that had power to ensnare. With candles this became even more needle-pointed, night-seeing eyes, like Giordano's. I looked at them as through stained-glass windows, but your soul was closed off, evasive—too much hardship, too many battles with clunkheads had locked it tight. Through bamboo blinds there were the rhododendron bushes, and then across the street a neon sign, electric orange and sky blue. Some things that glow tremendously have little warmth. *Latimers, Signmakers*, it said, a detail far more relevant than who you were, since it was not erased long after you'd gone. But I traced my finger over your body aligned to the shaded areas. Then slowly, with my tongue, till I encompassed your entire sea of caramel-brown skin, my very own Sargasso Sea, my mad boy in the attic, and as the light dimmed further, and the candle guttered, wick bending back into wax, I covered more of you, till I'd engorged myself and you were supine, entranced. Clamoring to get me inside you and once there, you gave to me all there was to give, twisting your head to smother me with grateful eager kisses.

Then you jumped up and said, "I've got the *munchies*. Get me some junk food!! It's like instant sex, just add water and stir." And you threw on a coat, practically naked underneath and ran out to the shop on the corner for a tin of soup and a loaf of bread. Passengers on the bus to Manchester town center did not notice that you had no pants on. "Around here, they like that sort of thing. The curb-crawlers thought I was on the game." "But you are, aren't you?" I said, smiling. "To me, being on the game is just a game you understand." And your laugh was wholesome strong, making it echo out of the park through the oak and chestnut trees. (I remember that laugh so clearly. It almost brings back your name...but then...no... it's gone again. No matter, you're Z to me, my A to Z.) "Why didn't you come back sooner?" I asked, alarmed, having seen a police car. "Stop behaving as though this is a B movie," you said. "Think of it more as a silent comedy classic — the gestures are what counts. The big lip movements." And I felt like Buster Keaton, a house falling down around him. My head protruding through calamities.

5

Day-night-night-day. The stereo speakers crackled due to frayed and faulty wiring stuffed under the rug. All the wires needed mending and sockets replacing. The landlord was negligent, never there, you complained. One day, mid-winter, the ceiling had collapsed. It fell exactly on your bed — bang in the middle. Luckily, you were out parading your stuff at Heroes Disco when it happened. You came home to find your sacred space was a pile of frozen concrete rubble. "That could have been my funeral pyre," you moaned. "And could have taken any number of lovers with me to my death." Such a death by crushing would have been fitting, crying out for any tragedy to release and elevate you above the mundane shit of life: from tracking your UB 40 forms, delayed

Housing Benefit payments, summonses, days without food, random abuse, and stand-up quickies in the park, tree bark grazing the backs of your legs. "And when I called the landlord to complain, to get him to fix the roof, guess what happened? I'd prepared a tirade against him. Launched straight into it, screaming and shouting that he had to do something. He said nothing. I expected anger. Then he made noises like a demented person, like he had three tongues in his mouth. He'd had a bloody stroke. His brain had blitzed. Words slurred around like in a lava lamp. There was nothing more to be said, but to wait. So I slept on this sofa with its broken frame, the result of a guy called Ram Rod, who just wouldn't stop when I asked him to. Another story, right?"

Right. I took you in my arms then, pressed you close, to squeeze through the bravado to the vulnerable core, and caught you trembling. Time to make love again. The radio stuttered and fizzed, the hiatus at the late-night show. Absence of noise stalled our rhythm of love, the join-the-dots evaporated in midair, and it was too far to reach to jig it on again. "Melody is dispensable, but rhythm is not," you said. "Oh," I said, reaching over till our arms clasped just out of reach of the plug. "My. You are a good student. You are beginning to sound like me." "No, not *like* you. *Better* than you."

You liked experimental music: John Peel sessions, dissonant forms, jarring to the nerves; Cabaret Voltaire, Shostakovitch, and Sylvester, all eclectic jumble sale, wildly mismatched. Late-night traffic fazed yet another layer into the mix. Then our arms would dandle and dawdle and sag across the coverlet in search of fingers to wrap together, palms to fuse. The radio would come back on of its own accord and lull us back into deep kissing and hip symmetry, bodies collided and meshed, there seemed no end to it, we made love during a half sleep, limbs twisted and wrapped tight till the sweat became ticklish and nasty, yet both secure we had a living mystery right there to touch and greet the morning with.

4

I was gone. And it scared me. I experienced my first dizzy spell, an unknown shadow on the brain, perhaps a little time bomb, set to go off who the hell knows when. You slapped my face and said, "Come back! You are here! I am here!" And eventually I began to see your face full of concern and wonder who it was that looked so distant and strange and why were the lips moving. What did that mean, to move one's lips? Then I knew again, and felt ashamed for being so feeble, but not so far away from home with you there. So much for the horizontal life. To be permanently laid-back is only possible for life's drones. Yet, I stared at the cracks in your living room ceiling and said, "It's like looking at a map of the upper Himalayas." All day you smoked weed scored from a Rasta friend who, you hinted, loved your expert blow jobs, which was all he'd allow you to do, having a wife and kids too. He'd be there on the Front Line, Moss Side, the biggest head of locks, then too heavily policed to risk, so he came to visit. He took one look at me on entering, and froze. He hadn't expected company. You said, "Don't mind him. He's tame." And, neither of us knew which one you meant. But we eyed each other warily. Then you rolled the next big spliff and stuffed it in my mouth to light up, and said, "No. It's not the Himalayas, man. It's an outline of the Polynesian atolls around Easter Island and…I must invest in some paint one day. Perhaps you could help me buy some?"

To stand up with you was to fall down. To lie down was to suffer an overactive mind. Yet to laugh was to laugh seriously. But then I noticed that my lip was bleeding. And I was angry. You had bitten it. My neck was swollen purple from your gorging there. Impossible to hide. Were you practicing some weird ritual skin slicing while I was sleeping? Marking me as yours? "Do you cut my toenails and pubic hair for souvenirs, rude boy?" I shouted. I always checked for missing items when I got back to my rooms to have a real bath and clean up. But the only thing missing was money, snatched stealthily from my pockets. Did you think I didn't notice? I didn't mind. I would have given it, only you, wisely, didn't ask. And I pretended not to notice.

3

Day Ten. I was tired and wanted to go for a breath of fresh air. "No," you said, "not yet," like there was something urgent that had not completed. "I want you to go right inside, and fuck me harder. Please. I can only take it from you. No one else." So I sat down again, a twinge in my loins for you. And we fucked three times that day. And I plunged deeper, more frantic to take us higher, up above the world. You slapped my backside as you pushed me in.

But it soured, and you withdrew to the other room, not looking in my direction. Something snapped. You said nothing in a big way for hours, deep in abstraction that folded over the real like invisible bricks in a wall that hit me on the head. Your need for sensation had boosted your cravings to the point of no return. I got up to go. It felt like time. Demands got louder, more hysterical. Distance reemerged. We drank coffee for longer before returning to bed, this time to sleep. Morning showers taken now separately, the seismic shift. I looked more at the clock, and so did you. I began to think, a chunk of time had passed, and what was the outside world doing. I said, "I have other things to do today, if you don't mind." And you said, "Is this the end?" "Not unless you want it to be." You picked up a magazine and said one of your friends was in it. "Yes, and I have friends of friends who know photographers who would use you." "Big deal," you said. "I'm going." "No. I didn't mean it." So I sat back down, feeling chasms of need inside you engulf me too. Years had taught me to avoid someone's aching neediness, but with you I enjoyed being wanted. Temporarily. Then you got up and struck me in the face. I felt the blow to my eyebrow. I bruised. It wasn't so bad if you were equally needy, I reasoned. I did not retaliate, feeling guilty, but I did start counting. "Not long to go now." And you barred the door.

2

We endured this torture as though it were still a kind of late-phase hyperactive euphoria. Fighting all day, about who said this or that, who did or didn't do what. You left me at the corner with your shopping bags. Then you ran back, hiding tears. Sulking, unable to breathe, convinced that what we had was something it wasn't. I had marginally more grip, that's all. "Why do you drain me so? Are you a vampire? What do you want from me?" "I want to BE you," I said with the sudden fierceness of a suction engine. "I want to steal your essence and lock it in a genie bottle. I'm a soul-snatcher." You gasped and stood back as though avoiding infection. "You're a sick, demented man. Ignorant and cruel. You can't ever be me, even if you swallowed buckets of my sperm a thousand times. You will never know me now." "I know that," I said limply. "But it was worth a try." The relentless in you made you still intent on your goal, full of apologies and promises to behave. Back in your room, you softened and relented. You pulled off your clothes, and buried your contrite head in my groin, to resuscitate my sleeping dick that had hoped to rest, yet had zero resistance to your oral dexterity. I lay back, my arms behind my head, not bored, just disconnected, thinking of Khadija and Ahmed, an ache to see them, and eventually you got me hard again. We came together in chorus, almost like before, a faded dawn reprise. I felt as though in an aquarium, you watching behind glass to see which way I would go. But go I would. I thought, *if I left enough cash in my pocket while in the bathroom, would you now take it? Bait for the baited?* And so you did. It made sense that way: you could pay your debts, get some new clothes, and I could excuse myself for wanting out—a Royal Exchange indeed. So it was understood. Words, once again, would have cluttered the way, like hairy spiders secreting webs off our lips.

Looking at an aquarium, in a pub back on Deansgate, my packed bag at my side, I pondered that the eaten needs the eater just as much. The eater needs his prey; a victim needs a murderer, even courts attack. It's a willing partnership. A choreographed interlude in the overall dance that brings opposites together. In Manchester or anywhere it can catch you. We can't escape bad timing: we are doomed to wait for the soul mate whom we are obliged to despise as he comes too late or too early in life to make a real difference. These bedroom fables have conclusions built in—the climax encompassed from the first "Hello," the Z a hatching egg in the A.

1

I didn't say I was going out, or leaving for good—why attract attention to the obvious? If I had stayed you would have only kicked me out anyway. Giving you the upper hand. You were having a nap, the tasseled pillow twisted between your naked legs, your finger twisted in your hair, when I closed the door, and took my last gasp at beauty. Then the front door that was really a door opening onto the next thing life could hook me with—a taxi through Didsbury to the airport and an MEA flight back to Beirut. Needing to be publicly invisible creates addictions to subterfuge and denial; we Arabs are forced to play that game. It's easier to do what others—family mainly—expect. At that point, it felt like I had never "known" you, only tasted your piquant flavor, extracted a whiff of core stuff. We were perfect strangers again, rested in our lovely, dishonest isolation, a cause for some rejoicing since it doesn't block the flow of options. I took away from Manchester images of you, a Martinique boy bursting out of your dull British-manufactured brick box.

And the twelve fucks into seven — those will remain, I promise. I heard from the Turk, years later, that you had completely strangled me out of your life — and said "I don't know who you're talking about." Your way of killing me off, of editing the screenplay to your advantage? But why then did you have to be so strong in rubbing me out, knowing he would write to me? He said you kept the diary notes intact, and eventually wrote a story called "Manchester Goddamn," which was published somewhere, some obscure journal. But I have ceased to be interested in reading, my eyes are weak and I fear the worst. Calamity may well become your route to salvation. Unseeing eyes may be mine. I do recall though, that as I boarded the plane that time, I heard your laugh echoing down the cabin, telling me to fuck you, now you were ready to give your best. I strapped in for liftoff, and I wanted to wash my hands, but a small smudge of rust appeared on my thumb. I pressed it on the hot lemon-scented cloth the steward gave me. But the mark wouldn't brush off till I had stroked it on my freshly aroused dick under the strap. I held you there, till take off, pang in my dick getting stronger, when I involuntarily orgasmed, embarrassed for my fellow passenger who was too sick to look anyway. And I knew at once that you were smiling at your sudden release, your victory over me. Yet you thanked me too. I closed my eyes and pictured you streaking through that park, clothes in hand, dick flapping then hardening somewhat, a spirit no one could contain — freer than I'd ever be. I look at you now, walking away, now on the far side of Albert Square on Princess Street, maybe going to work, as a DJ maybe, oblivious of me. You might have seen on the periphery an old bald man, dignified, with kindly eyes, whom you but vaguely remember. And I watch you slip out of sight, Manchester having grown more suited to you, where I am once again just passing through, not fitted. The city has caught up at last with you, not you with it. But we cross-fertilized somehow. And I can weigh the benefits. You truly have become that sphinx with a blue funk soul, and I have been varnished with a life-long coat of your island caramel flavor.

74

peking duck

৵৸

Linda Jaivin

WHAT A MAD MAD PLACE. I wonder if I'll ever be back, if I'll ever see Mr. In Your Dreams again, if his snakes made it through the day, if my interpreter will ever recover, if I paid too much for that opera costume, if my films will come out all right, if I'll ever be able to pay off my Visa, if Jake will be waiting at the airport, and if so what I'll say to him. Mengzhong, "In Your Dreams," what a name. Mengzhong, Mengzhong. I'm sure I never pronounced it correctly. But then, he didn't do so well with *Julia*. Never mind.

I'm sure I should have bought that rug. Sure, it'd have cost a fortune to ship, but where are you going to find one like it in Sydney? I wonder if I'll have to declare my tea? Australian customs are so strict. I can't believe I did what I did with Mengzhong. I can't believe it was just this morning. Seems like another universe. God, I'm wired. Hope the neighbors remembered to water my plants. I wonder if there's any interesting mail waiting for me.

Yes, it was my first trip to China. And you? I know I should have closed my eyes. I hope this guy in the next seat isn't going to talk to me the whole way back to Oz. I'll die. I wish they had a special section on planes for "people who are not in the mood to share feelings or exchange experiences or communicate in any other fashion with the person next to them." Unless of course their seat companion happens to be a killer spunk, in which case you could just move straight to the mile-high club lounge. Unfortunately, Mr. 38A is not a killer spunk; in fact, I don't think he'd count as even a mildly threatening spunk. Of course, that's so unfair. You shouldn't judge books by their covers and I suppose I should consider myself lucky that he's waited this long to start talking. It probably helped that I just stuck my nose in *The Wild Girls Club* all the way from Beijing to the stopover in Guangzhou.

Oh really? You do business there? How interesting. Stop it Julia. Don't encourage him. *Yeah, no, actually, I'm a photographer. On a three-week exchange sponsored by the Australia-China Council.* Why are you telling him all this? It's just going to incite more conversation. *Both black and white and color... Yes... For magazines, mostly.* Here we go. Maybe we can just switch on to automatic pilot. Maybe I should pull out *The Wild Girls Club* again. No. I'll never be able to concentrate.

Uh, Julia. Nice to meet you, Mick.

God, aren't the girls going to die when they hear that Mengzhong was a snake-charmer and sword-swallower *and* a contortionist. He had the most amazing stories about sneaking across the border to North Korea and being in jail JESUS that's what you call turbulence! Hate that! It's so scary! *No, I'm right, thanks, Nick. It's only a little turbulence.... Oh, sorry. Mick. I'm so bad with names.*

The interpreter, Mr. Fu, didn't seem highly amused. Still, didn't that woman at the embassy say that in China nothing was as it seemed? I mean, judging from the general picture she painted, Mr. Fu might have been offended politically, or he might just have wanted to be paid off to piss off, or maybe—and I'm no bad judge of body language, especially when it comes to these things—he was just jealous. Wouldn't that have been bizarre!

Tomato juice, no ice, thanks...oh, I said no ice actually, but never mind... Oh really? Minerals exploration and development? That's interesting. Not. Why do I always use the word *interesting* when

I mean exactly the opposite? I shouldn't be unfair. I'm sure it's fascinating, if you're into that kind of thing. It's just that I'm not. That's all. I wonder where he stands on Aboriginal land rights. Oh, God, Julia, don't bring that up. He'll either say the wrong thing and you'll be arguing with him all the way home or he'll turn out to be OK and you'll be so relieved that you'll feel obligated to talk to him. Mengzhong. Mengzhong. It's a bit like the peal of a bell, really. I wonder if I am pronouncing it right?

That rug, I really am beginning to regret not getting it. Damn. Never mind, I'm sure I'll be back someday. Thirty-six kilos of luggage is probably outrageous enough for one trip, especially when I only went with fifteen. Bizarre how they didn't even blink at the overweight luggage at Beijing airport, but then, half the people on this flight seemed to be taking forty or fifty kilos, no worries at all. I don't really want to dwell on the safety implications of that. *Yeah, I had a great time…. Yeah, it's a fascinating country…. Just Beijing and Shanghai…. Sure, the women are beautiful.* Pig. Western men in Asia think they're God's gift. I think he's about to treat me to some tale of conquest. Better nip this one in the bud. *The men are pretty dishy as well, of course.* Ha! That surprised him. *Yes, I do find them attractive, actually.* Look at this guy. He still can't get over it. What a sadster. The second the food comes I'm going to clap on my earphones. *Chicken or beef? Chicken please…oh, you only have beef. Beef then. Thanks.* If they didn't have the chicken, why'd they offer it? Now, on with the headset. Oh dear, what's this channel? Peking opera, I think. Don't think I like this one either. Ah, classical will do. Urgh. Disgusting, even for airline food. Really poxy. Doesn't really matter. I can still taste that Peking duck we had for lunch, or brunch or whatever that was. I'll be back in the land of mesclun salad and real coffee soon.

Can't wait to have a cuppa with the girls and tell them all my stories. I wonder where Mengzhong is now? Is he thinking about me? I can't believe it snowed this morning. Hard to imagine that it'll be summer again when we land in Sydney. The snow was so beautiful. I wonder whether Mr. Fu was spying on us. Is that why he was so stressed out when I caught up with him again back at the car? Wonder how you say, chill out, dude, in Chinese? Oh, I should be fair. He was probably worried that, having safely shepherded me for three whole weeks through the hazards of Beijing traffic, indulged nearly all my mad impulses (except, of course, my idea that we could just kind of talk our way into one of the prisons, which he firmly resisted), and put up with my taste in evening entertainment (Beijing punk rock—what a trip), he was going suddenly to lose me to the clutches of some street performer who would cause me to miss my plane, overstay my visa, possibly even disappear forever and completely derail Sino-Australian relations. He'd be stuck with the responsibility—and the snakes. I can imagine Mr. Fu sitting there in the car, watching the bag with its creepy contents slithering against the sides, certain that they were poisonous and going to get him. I mean, you can't blame the man for being such a gloom merchant when he's had the history he has—deprived of education in the Cultural Revolution, brother persecuted to death, scraping by on a meager government salary when everyone else seems to have gone into business and is saving up for their first Ferrarri.

What IS this meat? I'm sure it's not beef. I think I've had enough of it, whatever it is. *Sorry?* I can't believe he's persisting in speaking to me when I've got my headset on. *No, it's not the best meal I've ever had either, but never mind…. Yes, I like Chinese food…. What? No, I most definitely did not eat dog! Have you eaten dog?* But dog is woman's best friend! Dogs lounge on the sofa and watch videos, dogs play Frisbee and eat ham sandwiches! *Really? You did? How did it make you feel?* If only the hostess would come and clear the tray, I can pretend to go to sleep. *Warm? Oh, that's interesting.* Interesting, hah! Bet it was even more interesting for poor Bluey! Let's put the headset on again before he has a chance to continue. God, Julia, you're terrible. He's probably a perfectly nice man who's just a bit lonely and wants a chat. On the other hand, what am I, a chat machine? Besides, how could a perfectly nice man eat dog!

I hope the neighbors managed to keep the big fern in the entranceway alive. I wonder what the girls have been up to. Wonder if any of them have had any little romances. *No, I won't have any coffee. No, no tea either. Thanks.* Seat back, headset on, eyes closed. I'm going to be so trashed when we arrive, I can tell already. My mind is such a jumble of images and smells and noises. Let's try and focus, why don't we? I know what I want to focus on. I don't want to forget any detail of what happened this morning. It's been such a rush to here from there, packing and checking out. Before I knew it I was saying good-bye to Mr. Fu and Xiao Wang, and I was on the plane—no chance to really savor the events of the morning at all. Let's be disciplined. Start from the beginning.

All right…I wake up very early. I look out my hotel window and see it's been snowing all night. I go for a walk with my camera. *Yes, I'm finished, thanks.* Strangely enough, it doesn't feel that cold. The sparkling white of the snow, untrammeled at that time in the morning, and the soft glow of the dawn makes Beijing seem like a new city, one that's more ancient, pure, and calm. I walk to the Forbidden City and thrill to the sight of the snow piled in uneven drifts on the golden tiles and crenellated red walls of the palace. For nearly two hours I stroll around the palace and Tiananmen Square, taking pictures. When I get back to the hotel, I find a fretful Mr. Fu waiting in the lobby. He tells me there are lots of bad people around in Beijing these days, robbers and thieves and rapists, and that I shouldn't go wandering around like that by myself. I laugh. You would think from the way he was talking that we were in New York! Poor Mr. Fu. He'd see disaster lurking in a well-made bed.

We go to the hotel coffee shop where I warm my hands and cheeks on a cup of coffee and tell him that I want to make another trip to the Old Summer Palace to see it in the snow. He says it's too far away. He says it's too cold. He asks, didn't I have to do some last minute shopping and packing? What about our planned Peking duck lunch in that famous restaurant in the center of town? I insist. I say the plane's at four in the afternoon, we'll be right if we leave right now. I don't care about the duck. And I can forget the shopping. My Visa's expiring anyway, so to speak. (He doesn't get this. Never mind.) Please please please, Mr. Fu. Please please please. Finally he's shaking his head, and saying I'm crazy, but telling me to put on more clothes so I don't catch cold. I'm already as rugged up as I can be, so I just grab some more lenses and batteries and film and we're off. In the hire car driven by the ever-amiable Xiao Wang, we traverse the city. All of its nonstop clamor—the horns, the shouting, the jackhammers and pile drivers—is magically silenced by the blanket of snow.

When we reach Beijing University, tantalizingly close to the Old Palace, Mr. Fu says something to Xiao Wang in Chinese and Xiao Wang pulls up at the side of the road, in front of a restaurant. Mr. Fu tells me we'll have duck first, then we'll go. It's only ten-thirty in the morning, I protest. But I've learned when to give in, and so in we go, all three of us, of course. I really do appreciate the way the Chinese always invite the driver along to meals; from what I can gather, it's one of the few egalitarian customs they've got left these days. Anyway, when the steam fades from Mr. Fu's glasses, he orders our duck.

The restaurant is pretty empty, not surprising given the time. There is an extraordinarily handsome man at the next table. He has the classic single-lidded eyes and strong bone structure of the northern Chinese, and an unusual, somewhat hooked nose, but what's most striking is his beautiful, almost waist-length hair. Like a lot of northerners, he's tall and well built too. He's wearing one of those army greatcoats that you used to see in the photographs from China in the seventies and eighties but which almost no one seems to wear anymore.

But what catches everyone's attention is his leather case on the floor beside his seat. It's moving. Is that an animal in your bag or are you just happy to see me? Mr. Fu and Xiao Wang are as intrigued as I am, though Mr. Fu is clearly nervous. Xiao Wang leans across his seat and asks, "What's in the bag?" The guy answers. Xiao Wang laughs and Mr. Fu shudders. Of course, I don't understand what they are saying. Three weeks in China and I'm not much beyond *ni hao!* – "hello" – and *xiexie* – "thanks." "What is it, Mr. Fu?"

"Snakes," he tells me, shaking his head. "Terrible. Terrible."

Sorry? Oh, you're right. Can you step over me or shall I get up? No worries. Did he touch my leg on purpose? Creepoid. I'll just get up next time. Anyway, back to the restaurant. I'm totally intrigued. Ask him what the snakes are for, Mr. Fu. By now, this guy is checking me out as well, and I wait impatiently for a translation. He tells Mr. Fu that he is a street performer, snake-charmer, sword-swallower, kung fu master, and contortionist. Cool! He doesn't belong to any proper organization, and Mr. Fu tries to explain to me some concept about "rivers and lakes," which I gather refers to people who live outside the system. Mr. Fu clearly doesn't approve.

I'm enthralled. Snake-charmer tells us how he has always wanted to travel, but that he doesn't think he'd ever get a passport, and so, at different times, he's snuck across the border to North Korea or Vietnam. Each time, he was caught and sent back. Each time, the Chinese police interrogated him and let him go.

Apparently, the police think he's a bit of a nut. He doesn't mind. Gives him more freedom to maneuver, he says. North Korea! Of all bizarre places to spend a holiday.

Mr. Fu is nearly hyperventilating as he translates this story. Our Peking duck arrives. I signal to snake-charmer to join us. He hesitates, looking at Mr. Fu. It's obvious that Mr. Fu is not at all happy. Snake-charmer then looks at Xiao Wang, who just picks up a pancake and concentrates on folding it into a little parcel of duck and shallot and plum sauce. Then he looks at me. I've got a big smile on my face and I'm patting the chair next to me. He shrugs, and smiles and, carrying over his bag of snakes, sits down. "I'm Julia," I say. He looks at Mr. Fu for help. Mr. Fu, uncooperative, looks at the duck. I point to my nose — I learned that Chinese people point to their nose when they want to refer to themselves just as we point to our chests — and say, slowly, "Ju-li-a." He smiles, points at his nose and says, "mungjoong." I make Mr. Fu spell it for me: M-E-N-G-Z-H-O-N-G.

I lever up some of the crisp duck skin, meat, plum sauce, and sliced shallot with my chopsticks, drop it onto a pancake, and fold it as best I can, following Xiao Wang's model, but when I raise it to my lips, a fat lubricated piece of shallot pushes up through the corner and tries to escape. Mengzhong looks amused. He signs for me to watch and demonstrates how to create the perfect Chinese blintz, and then hands it to me. Our fingers touch and I feel a spark. I'm sure it's not the same kind of spark that I feel even with the funny, bookish Mr. Fu, thanks to the amazing static electricity of the Beijing winter. Speaking of Mr. Fu, he's gone a bit sullen now. But Xiao Wang chats with Mengzhong and I recognize the word *Yuanmingyuan*, which is Chinese for the Old Summer Palace, so I know he's telling him where we're off to. Impulsively, I point to him and then to us and with a circling motion somehow make it clear that I'm asking him along. He glances at Mr. Fu, and then mimes a bicycle to me. Ah, he's got a bicycle. He says something to Mr. Fu, who tells me, with an air of triumph, that Mengzhong is worried about keeping his snakes warm. He had been thinking about performing in one of the local parks but changed his mind when the snow continued to fall, and was planning to have lunch and go straight home. Xiao Wang says something. Mengzhong says something. Mr. Fu is shaking his head most officiously.

I'm dying to know what's going on. I'm fixated on Mengzhong's hands. They are smooth and totally hairless, with long, fine fingers that throughout the meal, agilely continue to fold and proffer Peking duck crepes to me. We've finished everything by now (Mengzhong's dish of fried tofu and vegetables was delivered to our table and shared around) and Mr. Fu pays for the meal, refusing Mengzhong's vigorous attempt to pay for us all himself. We layer on our jumpers and coats and scarves, and leave the restaurant. The duck is rich, and makes me feel warm inside. Mengzhong is talking to Xiao Wang, who shrugs and says that other phrase I picked up, *meiyou guanxi*, which I gather is sort of like, "no worries, mate."

Mr. Fu does not look thrilled, and I see why when Xiao Wang opens the back door of the car and Mengzhong puts the bag of snakes on the backseat. Mengzhong then collects his bicycle from where it was leaning against the outside of the restaurant, and walks it over. He pats the small shelf over the back wheel that people use to carry everything from groceries to books and parcels, and says something that I gather means, "would you like to dink?" *Oh, sorry, no I'll get up. No worries. You're right.* Now go to sleep and leave me alone.

I nod enthusiastically, ignoring Mr. Fu's censorious look. Mengzhong starts pedaling slowly. Arranging my camera bag on my shoulder, I jump on and throw my arms around his broad back. The bike wobbles a bit on the packed and slippery snow but Mengzhong quickly finds his balance, and we're off. I wave an enthusiastic good-bye to Mr. Fu and Xiao Wang. Mr. Fu tosses off a gesture that seems closer to "piss off then" than "see you soon" but I'll give him the benefit of the cross-cultural doubt. Mr. Fu, Xiao Wang and the snakes, I assume, are going to meet us at the Old Summer Palace. This is so thrilling! It's just started to snow again, and Mengzhong turns his head and grins at me, a very sexy, self-assured smile and I grin back and hug him a bit tighter than I really have to. This part of Beijing is still quite nice and relatively undeveloped, and there are fewer people around as well. I bury my face in his back and breathe in the musty, woolly smell of his greatcoat, which like nearly everything else in Beijing in winter, has a faint aura of garlic. We swerve off the main road and I swivel my head just in time to see the car zoom on ahead, Mr. Fu's panicked face following our progress up a laneway too small for cars to follow us. Mengzhong gestures and says something and I assume he's just explaining he's taking a shortcut. I'm not worried. We're now riding through this really charming rural lane. We pass small peasant homes made of brick, and cheap local eateries with padded blankets hung in the doorways as extra insulation against the cold. When we reach the edge of a large frozen field, he stops the bike. He asks with words I don't understand and hand gestures I do if I'm comfortable back here. Something in my look tells him it's all right to kiss me, and he does, quickly, almost shyly, just brushing my lips with his.

Oh, Jake! But why am I feeling guilty? Jake took pains to make it clear to me before I left that whatever we had between us had been great and all that, but he was making no demands on me to be faithful to him, which, if I know men — and I think, by now, I know men pretty well — meant that he had no intention of being faithful to me. I mean, it was pretty clear that it was over, even if we did sleep together the night before I left. He didn't have to take me to the airport, of course, and that was a really nice gesture, even if I did end up paying for the petrol. And a big breakfast at the airport. I wonder if he'll like the Chinese *punks not dead* T-shirt I got him? We didn't say "it's over." But I can recognize over when I see it. I think. Anyway, even if it's not exactly over, then he's not the sort of guy who's going to be fussed if I had a one-night, no, make that a one-morning stand. Anyway, I don't have to tell him about it. It's probably not a great idea to tell him, even if it is over between us. "Even if" — do I believe it's over or don't I? Goodness, what is this movie? I have to check this in the in-flight magazine, it's just too bizarre. Hmmm. *Joyous National Minorities Celebrate the New Harvest.* Right. Where was I? That's right, not far from the Yuanmingyuan.

We get going again along the path skirting the field. We arrive at one of the entrances to the park, and from there proceed to the famous ruins. It's so hard to imagine this place once housed thirty imperial pleasure palaces. Now it's a sprawling public park with some dramatically collapsed columns and a few other remnants. Last time we were there, Mr. Fu had told me all about its history, how it had been plundered by the British and the French in 1860 and burned to the ground by allied Western forces again forty years later and how the ruins have been preserved as a symbol of China's humiliation at the hands of the imperialists. We spot him first. Mr. Fu is obviously feeling pretty badly done by. He's stamping his feet impatiently in the snow and blowing out anxious little puffs of steam-breath. I assume Xiao Wang's in the heated car with the snakes. I call out and give Mr. Fu a big wave and a smile. He lifts his chin in a curt greeting. He doesn't take his hands out of his pockets. Never mind. I take out my camera and shoot pictures of the ruins, which look even more desolate and dramatic with their lashings of snow. Children are playing at the base of the Old Palace, and their bright red cheeks match their red padded coats and knitted caps. I point the lens playfully at Mengzhong and he signals for me to wait a minute. He takes off his coat and hat and before I know what's happening, he's flying through the air in an extraordinary series of loops and spins and somersaults. He lands on one of the columns, nearly loses his balance on the slippery snow there, spreads his arms and laughs, a big throaty *hahahaha* laugh that sounds straight out of the Peking Opera we saw the other night. Even Mr. Fu is impressed.

I applaud and Mengzhong shakes out his hair. My camera is waiting for him as he makes an equally dramatic descent back to where we are, and I use up nearly an entire roll of film. Mengzhong puts his coat back on, says something to Mr. Fu and the next thing I know, I'm dinking again and we're off and racing down one of the pathways in the park. We're both in high spirits now, and I laugh and hold on tighter as we strike a patch of ice and zigzag madly, nearly taking a tumble. I have no idea where Mr. Fu is, whether he's following, fuming or just planning to meet up with us later.

We arrive at the entrance to a giant maze. The emperors always had the best toys. The gray stone walls of the maze are topped with at least a foot of snow, and it's another popular spot with the kiddies. Mengzhong locks his bike and buys us entry tickets. Before I know what's happening, he dashes into the maze and disappears. I bolt after him. I keep hitting dead ends but finally I collide with him rather suddenly as I round a corner, skidding on ice. He catches me, taking my mittened hands in his. He is a very naughty boy. I see this in his eyes. I'm a naughty girl, too, and I stand on tiptoes to kiss him and this time I slip the tongue in. He's not, shall we say, averse. He says something in Chinese. I look at him blankly, and laugh, and he laughs and shakes his head, and

I say *meng-joong* and he says *jyu-li-ya* and now it's me running off through the labyrinth and him chasing after me. When I find myself in a dead end, I quickly scoop up some of the snow and make it into a snowball, which I pelt him with. I try to make a getaway, but he tackles me and we both fall to the ground. We're just about to kiss again when some schoolchildren in lurid red and pink outfits pour round the corner and, pointing at us, jump up and down and yell something I guess means something like "they're supposed to be out jogging and we caught them snogging." Needless to say, we scramble to our feet and get out of there as fast as we can, giggling like mad.

When we finally reach the end of the maze, we find a gateway that leads to a path up a small hill. We climb up, hand in hand, our feet scrunching through the snow. I look down and I think I see Mr. Fu starting through the maze. But I can't be sure. He's dressed like so many others in padded blue jackets, with caps and glasses. It's started to snow heavily again. We get to the top of the hill and we're panting and our breath is coming out in clouds. We move closer to the little copse of trees at the top of the hill and soon we are embracing and kissing madly, tasting the duck in each other's mouths, trying to grope through eight hundred layers of clothing. It is insane. Although we are among the trees, it is hardly a private spot. The trees are small and bare, and not that densely planted either. We can hear the laughing and whooping and shouting of people enjoying themselves on all sides. Mad mad mad! I barely know the guy and can't communicate with him to save my life and it's freezing cold and snowing and we're in a public park in China, in the middle of the day, for Christ's sake, and Mr. Fu is probably looking for me and I'm supposed to be representing my country, sort of, and here I am with a street performer, a circus acrobat, a snake–charmer, a fire-eater, a sword-swallower with a Beijing opera laugh, and isn't this the most thrilling tryst I've ever had?

He is deftly penetrating my layers with his hand, which, undoing buttons and zippers and pulling fabric this way and that, finally reaches my breasts. The shock of the cold air already has my nipples on full alert, and he pulls and pinches them while we continue our game of tonsil hockey. I sling one arm around his neck, my hand weaving into that lustrous mane of his. With the other, I reach into his coat and stroke his crotch. Even through the layers of trousers and long johns, I feel his cock standing up to say *ni hao!* When I pull my hand away, he picks me up and presses my back against a tree. With both my arms around his neck and my legs around his waist, we dry-hump like teenagers by the back door. I am feeling cold and hot and nervous and bold all at once. He puts me down and digs through others layers now and finds me all juicy and pulsating. His fingers are surprisingly warm. With visions of Mr. Fu and security police and guard dogs and yes, how can you not, even Tiananmen in my head, I pull away from his kiss and look all around. Miraculously, though there is still that babble of Chinese voices from every direction, we are alone.

When I look back, I see that Mengzhong has somehow managed to extricate his dick from his trousers and long johns and *daks*. Amazingly, despite the snow, despite the cold, it is very hard. Impulsively, I kneel down in the snow and swallow the sword of the sword-swallower, charm the snake of the snake-charmer. And he is charmed. I can tell. At one point I'm sure I hear Mr. Fu calling my name and I panic and lift my head and look around but Mengzhong uses his hands to put my head back onto his cock. I'm very nervous, and very turned-on. What would happen if we were caught? This is a communist country after all. Bamboo slivers under the fingernails? Thumbscrews? Deportation for me, labor camp for him? The almost unbearable tension and paranoia are, I'm almost ashamed to admit, only adding to the excitement. He draws me up to my feet and kisses me while loosening my belt and tugging my trousers down on my thighs. I'm trembling so badly my knees are knocking, but I can't tell whether it's with cold, fear, or desire. By now half my brain's between my legs along with his long, hyperactive fingers, and the other, weaker half is envisioning men in uniform, the shocked faces of little Chinese children and a horrified Mr. Fu. I am also thinking about my toes, which despite my boots are so cold they are burning, if that makes any sense.

Mengzhong embraces me more tightly now, tenderly kissing the snowflakes off my eyelashes. How do you say, "Maybe under the circumstances, darling, we should make this a quickie, besides, I'm freezing my tits off and I'm sure that's an icicle hanging off your balls" in Mandarin? I decide to express, in the universal language, the more readily comprehensible message of "Take me right now." But it suddenly occurs to me that we have a bit of a logistics problem. I mean, my pants (and my long johns, and my panties) are down around my knees, but I can't actually take even one pants leg off without removing my laced-up boots and socks. There's no way I'm going to do that given the fact that we might be sprung at any moment. I think I should be prepared to sprint at the first sign of billy clubs, and besides, I can't just lie in the snow or I'll literally freeze my buns off. Mengzhong's obviously thought this through. He murmurs something in Chinese. (I bet you say that to all the foreign girls.) He turns me around and with one hand on my waist, he gently pushes down on my back until I am bent over in the position that is known in yoga (appropriately, in this case anyway) as the dog posture.

I am grasping the base of the trunk of a slim tree for support, and he wraps himself around me like a pancake around duck and slides smoothly inside, a shallot, no, a giant leek, gliding into the plum sauce. He reaches for my tits with one hand, and my clit with the other, and as he fills me up, my mind dances incongruously with images of snakes and policemen and snowflakes and Mr. Fu and crispy duck skin, and steadying myself with one hand on the ground, I reach back with the other to grasp his hard muscled calf. It is definitely the leg of an athlete, an acrobat. I'm absolutely buzzing with the thrill of it all, and he feels so good inside me. But I'm not sure I'm going to be able to come, not before all those people I am convinced are besieging the hill from all sides now reach our little love spot. Yet I'm sure that Mengzhong is holding back until I come. So I decide to fake it.

I don't want to moan or scream or anything that might really bring on the revolutionary masses so I just grip his legs as hard as I can and arch my back as best I can in this damn position, which doesn't really allow for that, and shake my head from side to side and start to unbalance, and grip him even harder. This seems to convince him because he now starts to slam it into me and finally, with a little groan, slumps over my body. We get our clothes back on pretty quickly, and I lend him my brush and he brushes my hair and I brush his. He takes me in his arms again just as a group of schoolchildren come shrieking up the path toward us. We pull apart, but their teacher gives us a lemon-lipped look of disapproval anyway—imagine what sort of look it would've been if they'd come along just fifteen minutes earlier. And I'd mentally compared

Jake to the Guangdong Acrobatic Troupe! Ha! Jake's just a slacker with a reasonably flexible body and even more flexible morals. No, I shouldn't be so hard on him. That's unfair. Oh, Jake, I do miss you!

Anyway, we bike back to the parking lot where Mr. Fu and Xiao Wang are waiting with the snakes, and Mengzhong gives me a very big smile, and reaches out to shake my hand. This, of course, is all we can do under the circumstances, so I clasp it and say *xiexie*, "thank you," and he laughs and says *xiexie* back, and takes his bag of snakes, and opens it up to check on them, and gives a little sign like, I'm a bit worried about them, shrugs, hops on his bicycle and takes off, and Mr. Fu scolds me for talking to strangers yaddayaddayadda, and I put on a contrite expression and pretend to take in what he is saying while concentrating on all the sensations still racing around and through my body. On the way to the airport I ask Mr. Fu whether *Mengzhong* means anything. "In your dreams," he replies. In my dreams indeed. *Breakfast? Uh, yes, thanks. Yeah, no I suppose I did sleep a bit. And you?* Look at me, with my legs crossed and clamped together and creaming myself. You're such a slut, Julia.

Yes, it was really nice to meet you too, Mike... Oh sorry. Mick. Oh, please let my baggage come out nice and early. I wonder if Jake will be there.

(Half an hour later.) *Nothing to declare.... Thank you.*

Will he won't he will he won't he will he won't he? Stop obsessing, you dag! Here we go. Look beautiful. Jake Jake Jake. No Jake? No, definitely no Jake. Never mind. Oh my God, there's Philippa! What a hero. Wonder what moved her to come pick me up? I mean, she doesn't even have a car. *Philippa! Thanks for coming, mate! Yeah, it was great. I'll tell you all about it. But what have you been up to...? Not much? Oh, well. At least your book is coming along. Yeah, I really hope I can go back sometime. I had the most fabulous time.*

odalisque

❦

MITZI SZERETO

SO HOW'S DUBAI? friends ask over the phone. Dubai. How can one possibly describe this mixed-up parcel of sand that's part Arab, part British, part Indian, with some Lebanese, Malaysians, and Iranians thrown in for added spice? Have I left anyone out? I'm sure that I have.

Hot and sandy, I say. I don't say it's a sand beneath which nothing grows…except perhaps, fundamentalism. How long will it be? I wonder. How long will the freedom last in decadent Dubai? In the neighboring emirate of Sharjah a man and woman can't hold hands in public, nor can a woman wear short sleeves. They can get great rugs though. The winds of change blow close, I fear.

I don't tell my callers about the smell of Arabic perfume that has made a permanent home in my nostrils. Oudh, amber, sandalwood, rose. These are the scents that fill my nose, seep into my skin and the skins of everyone around me. Arab perfume is a great equalizer among men and women; there are no His and Hers sections at the perfume counter. Eventually they stop asking about Dubai. Stop ringing to see how I am. Leaving me on my own, a foreigner in a foreign land. Forgotten by the West.

Citizen of the world, that's what I am. What would my American friends think if they saw me now—a woman caught between two cultures? Their only reference points being harems, white slavery, religious fanatics. They know so little about this part of the globe. Only what they see on the news—the extremists, the haters of the West. The *Death to America* coalition. They would not know this beautiful Arab man on the prayer mat, his long limbs bent in supplication as a *muezzin* calls out the afternoon prayer through a loudspeaker hitched to a minaret, his smell of oudh, amber, sandalwood, rose teasing me, making me desire.

They would think I'm not safe here. Yet I am probably safer than on the streets of any American city or town. (Crime is low in the United Arab Emirates; Sharia law makes a powerful deterrent.) They do not hear the lively Arab music coming through the open windows of taxicabs. They do not see burka walking alongside tank top, both of which have breasts bouncing beneath them. They do not taste the salt on the air blowing in from the Gulf. I hear and see and taste all of these things. I love them all.

Especially his prominent nose. We are in the land of prominent noses. Ah…but that is a superficial thing to say. An American thing to say. The cliché springs to mind of big noses and big—no. I won't even go there. Dubai may be a lot of things. A cliché isn't one of them.

We met over the pastry table at Spinney's supermarket in the Mankhool district—the Spinney's with the Filipina hooker who hangs around outside the glass doors day and night, her skintight pants splitting her crotch, her painted face devoid of expression. Perhaps she isn't a hooker at all, but only looks like one. No matter how many times I go to buy my groceries, she's there. Alone. Standing. Waiting, her mobile pinched between her long painted fingernails. Just as the Latino hustler in his tight black T-shirt and jeans is always there on my way home, cruising up and down past the hotels, day and night. Though mostly at night when it's cooler. After all, it can get up to 120 degrees Fahrenheit in the summer, and Gulf winters aren't exactly Zurich either. I've often wondered who his clients are—wealthy Arabs for whom homosexuality might be punishable by death, or lonely sunburned Englishmen working for the big tax-free bucks in Dubai. Probably a bit of both.

They have a pork counter at Spinney's for the foreigners, the heathens, though I've yet to see anyone make a purchase. It's expensive to buy pork in a Muslim country. Not sure I'd want to either. You tend to get away from the taste of pig flesh until it becomes a distant and unmissed memory on the tongue. Booze — well, that's another matter. You can always get booze. Westerners wouldn't come here if they couldn't. Not the Brits, anyway. When I was still the new kid on the block, I asked the waitress at a Chinese restaurant if the dumplings in the wonton soup had pork in them, concerned as I was for the spiritual well-being of my Muslim dinner companions. They're chicken, she said. Of course. What else could it be?

Meanwhile, back at Spinney's: I was in the process of selecting some baklava to have with my meal that evening. This is very important business, I should add — food in general being an important business in the Middle East. I was dying to pop a piece into my mouth right that minute, but it was Ramadan and the sun was still shining. Not that I would have been led away in handcuffs, but the consumption of food or drink during Ramadan is frowned upon. Everything goes on behind closed doors — stuff your face as much as you want, but not in public, please. Unless you're at a hotel, where Islam vanishes the moment you step inside the refrigerated lobby. Even a drink of water on the street is prohibited, though you might see overheated English tourists going about with a plastic bottle of mineral water, their faces running the gamut from lilac to pink to lobster-red. The same English tourists whose ultimate calamity in life is the absence of liquor for the holy month. It's the major topic of conversation — hear an English accent and you can guarantee it'll be complaining about the lack of booze. They'd have happily gone without food and sex for the month, providing they could get a drink. Abstention isn't so hard once you get used to it. You can get used to a lot of things in Dubai.

In my modern air-conditioned apartment in Mankhool it took some getting used to the cold water taps running hot. The water boils beneath the desert sand, and a cold-water wash in the washing machine comes out hot, shrinking all those beefy cotton T-shirts you brought with you from home. The water in the toilet bowl simmers when you sit down to take a pee, the heat from the tank radiating warmth better than the radiators in my old New York apartment. It's hot here. Too hot. The sun's always there, burning into you, judging you like those lamps the cops shine in suspects' faces in those old black-and-white Hollywood movies. Where were you on the night of—? Did you murder—? Movies where women were *dames, tomatas*. God, how I miss those movies! We get plenty on television here, but they're nearly all Bollywood films. Or rather *fil-ums*. Lots of slender women singing in high-pitched voices, lots of slim men with smoldering dark eyes and flashing white teeth. Sometimes I'm not sure what country I'm in. I see as many saris on the streets as *dishdashas*.

He wore a *dishdasha*. My partner in crime at the baklava table, that is. Pristine white against smooth flesh bronzed from generations of Arab blood and unrelenting sunshine. You see a lot of *dishdashas* here, especially in the swanky lobbies and restaurants of the *Bladerunner* city center hotels. Conducting business. Dubai is all business. All money. Slippery with oil. If you don't hold on tight, the *dirham* will slip out from between your fingers.

He must have seen the hunger in my eyes as I perused the staggering variety of pastries laid out on the large table—honeyed and walnutted and pistachioed sacrifices to those who'd spent the day fasting. Yes, there's plenty of temptation here. When he looked at me, he too, had hunger in his eyes, and it wasn't for the trays of sweets. I felt that familiar little tickle of desire between my thighs as my face heated up from his gaze—a heat which shot all the way down to my toes. The eyes beneath his *ghutra* were as black as his neatly trimmed beard and mustache—in fact, as black as the *agal* that held this head covering in place, and they seemed to darken as they studied me, burrowed into me. I'd later learn from resident foreigners that this is called *The Look*. They're a horny bunch round here, my English friend in Abu Dhabi told me. I should have taken that as a warning, though it was surely not meant as such.

He kept a villa at the beach. A villa bought with oil that he lived in all by himself. Massive tiled rooms, ceiling fans, hand-carved furniture, hand-woven silk rugs. The constant hum of the air conditioner in the background. Servants came and went unseen, discreet as a tampon. The place was within walking distance to the Jumeirah Beach Hotel, where we often had dinner. I'm glad it was walking distance, since I hated getting into a car with him. He drove his Range Rover (not a Merc—the police drive Mercs!) through the streets like a madman. Though so did everyone else, cutting in and out of traffic, running up the bumper in front, flinging arms to and fro in exasperation at the sluggish traffic. All this while maintaining a steady stream of Arabic obscenities. There are probably more men in the Middle East whose mothers mated with dogs than anywhere else in the world.

He was distantly related to the Maktoum family, the rulers of Dubai since the early 1800s. Although nearly everyone who's wealthy seems to be related to them in one way or another. He always smelled of sandalwood and rose—of that Arab perfume worn by men and women. He liked to take the little wand from the ornate glass bottle and dab the oil onto me, onto my wrists, behind my ears and knees, the crook of my elbows, in that snug place where inner thigh joins the flesh of my sex. He'd whisper to me that I smelled better than any perfume as his fingers smoothed the amber-colored liquid into my skin, rubbing it in until it was no longer oily. He liked to dab a bit of perfume onto my clitoris, which he'd take a lot of time over, rubbing in circular motions and causing it to heat up from his touch and from the oil itself, not stopping until he had me squealing and shaking with orgasm. I had no protection from his fingers, since I'd taken to removing my pubic hair shortly after our affair began. Not to be the trendy American sporting a Brazilian (which always looks to me like a cunt smoking a cigar), but because of Islamic codes of cleanliness. They make a lot of sense, when you think about it. Besides, he asked me to. How could I refuse? How could I refuse *anything* he asked of me?

In the afternoons after we made love, I'd remain lying in his bed as the call to prayer started up again—a Muslim rave blasting from the loudspeakers at the Jumeirah Mosque, which has a Starbucks across from it. Get in a few prayers, then nip next door for a no-foam double latte. Islam keeps you busy, I'll say that much for it. With wake-up calls at five A.M. you've no need for an alarm clock. He would spread his prayer mat over the cool floor tiles and kneel upon it, still naked and dripping from me, as he began bowing toward Mecca. I suspected his lack of attire might not have been entirely respectful, but who was I to point this out to a good Muslim? I remained still, silent, not even wanting my breath to disrupt him from his link with Allah. Because there are some lines you just don't cross. Not even in Dubai.

When he finished, he'd look up and see me reclining on my side, nude. Like the famous painting, he'd say. *The Odalisque.*

I am his Odalisque.

With lovemaking and praying out of the way, we'd indulge in an afternoon snack. He'd order me to stay in bed while he prepared something in his cavernous kitchen. I didn't argue. I was still glowing from his flesh, his saliva, the heat simmering over the sandy earth beyond the high walls surrounding his villa. He'd return a short while later carrying a hammered gold tray containing plates of grapes, black olives, *labneh,* feta and *hallumi* cheese, and cucumbers, along with some Lebanese sweets. We mustn't forget the sweets! He'd hand-feed me bits of cheese, followed by bits of cucumber, following it up with a spoonful of thick yogurty *labneh* that stung my tongue with its tanginess. Sometimes he tipped the spoon, and a blob landed on my belly. A perfect mountain of creamy desert snow. He bent down to lick it away, his dark head moving lower as his tongue searched out places where the *labneh* could not have possibly gone, the silky black hairs from his beard and mustache tickling the insides of my thighs, which I'd thoughtfully parted for him. He opened me up with his thumbs, taking his dessert where he found it, the sweets he'd brought into bed with us now forgotten.

Do we have a future? I asked.

Inshaallah, he answered. If Allah is willing.

We'd go dancing—the Kasbar or even the Planetarium, where we'd rub up against each other like two cats in heat. Exotic desert cats. Music thundering in our ears, lights flashing, no one watching and everyone watching. Maybe go hear some jazz at Issimo. Sit outside at a *shisha* joint sharing a pipe, arguing good-naturedly about whether we should try strawberry or green apple next time. The smooth smoke slipping down our throats in the warm night air. Just as he had slipped down my throat only moments before, his elixir as sweet as the tobacco.

He took me shopping, buying me the latest clothes the European designers had to offer. He took me to the gold *souk* in Deira, where he had me try on gold headdresses. I was blinded by gold—everywhere I looked it glittered at me, showing off its extravagant beauty. I didn't wear a headscarf, so he had to fit the dangly strands over my hair, which fortunately is straight and rests neatly against my skull. He whispered that he wanted to drape my naked body with strands of gold, place gold rings on my fingers and toes, then burn frankincense and myrrh in homage to me. As he said this, his tongue tickled my earlobe and I shivered, remembering where it had been only that morning. How deeply it had penetrated before he replaced it with his penis, taking me from behind. The Arabic way, he called it. Arabic birth control, more like. Not that I complained. He made it into an art form. I couldn't bend over far enough for him, spread myself wide enough for him. Anything. Just ask. Just take. I am your desert *houri*.

I could tell that the old merchant with his clicking worry beads didn't approve of us, but since the headdress cost about forty grand in American money, he wasn't about to complain. You can't be serious, I'd said, smiling, my mind calculating *dirham* into dollar. I wouldn't be so gauche as to mention cost, but the thought of wearing something this expensive made my bowels knot up. Thieves would chop off your head in the States to steal something like this. Hell, people were killed for only a few dollars back home. And they say the Middle East is dangerous. Maybe the State Department should reevaluate its warnings to Americans traveling abroad and instead issue warnings that they aren't safe at home.

In the end he didn't buy it for me. Maybe it was stupid, but I graciously talked him out of it, squeezing his hand affectionately as the Abra ferried us across Dubai Creek to Bur Dubai. I thought it would make me feel like a kept woman if I accepted a gift like this. Now I realize how shortsighted that was. How stupid. At least I would've been left with something in the end. I could have always tried to sell it back to the man at the gold *souk* or one of the other merchants. Even if I'd only got half its value, it would have been enough. But I had my pride. An Odalisque has her pride.

Of course he played golf. What self-respecting Emirati doesn't? Several times a week he met up with friends for a round or two. He never asked if I wanted to join in. Not that I'd have wanted to, though it might have been nice to be invited, especially since I'd already met most of his golfing buddies. He did take me to the camel races though. He owned several camels and more often than not they won. I'd sit miserably beside him under an oversized umbrella, sweltering in the desert heat as camels loped along the track, their sun-blackened jockeys hitting them with sticks to urge them quicker and quicker toward the finish line. If it happened that his camel was gaining the lead, he'd lean in close to me, his fingers stealing beneath my gauzy skirt, heading toward their own finish line. My thighs would be slippery with perspiration, but I couldn't open them, since we were quite visible sitting alongside the track. I could hear his breath laboring with the excitement of the race and perhaps with the excitement of touching me, his fingers working my clitoris, thrusting inside me, swimming in a pool of my sweat and my own excitement from what he was doing to me. The farther ahead his camel reached, the quicker his fingers moved and I'd climax just as his camel passed the finish line. I could see that his thighs had begun to jerk beneath his *dishdasha,* making me suspect that he, too, had come. Though whether it was from winning the race or from touching me I could never be certain.

For Eid he took me to a beauty salon to get my hands decorated with henna. Beautiful intricate designs that put any ring or bracelet to shame. Graceful floral and vine patterns that performed a sinuous dance all the way down to my fingertips. He got off on the sight of my henna-painted hand pumping him to orgasm. He even made me wear a *shaila.* Nothing else, just this stern black headscarf as my hands—which he'd tied together with the *agal* from his *ghutra*—worked him to a frothy conclusion. My friend in Abu Dhabi had neglected to tell me the Emiratis were a kinky bunch as well.

The henna faded. And so did his desire for me.

He tired of his Western woman. His Odalisque. I suppose it was a matter of practicality. It was time for him to get married. To an Arab woman. To have Arab children. I wasn't the former, I couldn't offer him the latter. There was no argument. Just tears. Mine.

They said they'd cheer me up—take me out for a night on the town. Dubai has a swinging nightlife, if you know where to look. They were just some guys who'd come around to visit sometime, whom we'd meet for dinner, share a *shisha* with. Golfing buddies, camel racing cohorts. His friends. My friends. Or so I thought. *Salaam Ale-Koum* they'd always greet me, and I'd *Walaikum-asalaam* them right back. Young Arab men with *dishdashas* and black beards and mustaches. Going to a nightclub filled with rich Arabs—the

Kasbar, maybe. At least that's where I figured we were going. Instead they took me somewhere I'd never been.

To a house off Sheikh Zayed Road. A villa like the one I'd spent so many days and nights in, simultaneously shivering and sweating with desire and pleasure, my sighs a fusion of English and Arabic as I reached toward my black-eyed love. They seemed surprised when I pushed their hands away, slapped off their offending fingers. I'd slept with their friend — why wouldn't I sleep with them? They didn't know I was an Odalisque. Their dark scowls burned me as they put me in a taxi, threw some *dirham* at the driver, who smirked knowingly, making me feel like the Filipina hooker from Spinney's. He'd driven whores home from a job before. The sun was already high over the tree-barren city, judging me although I'd done nothing to be judged for.

I wanted to tell him about his so-called friends, but I knew he wouldn't be interested. He was gone from me now. I even thought of taking revenge, maybe saying things had happened that hadn't really happened just to show them I wouldn't be disrespected like that. But I'd heard how women were treated, even when they were telling the truth. *Adulterous behavior* they call it.

Here no one's interested in the truth. Not a woman's truth, a Western woman. A former Odalisque. It's all about power and money, where you're from, what you have dangling between your legs. Guess it's not that different from America, when you think about it.

All in a Day's Work

Rachelle Claret

THEY CALL TENERIFE THE ISLAND OF ETERNAL SPRING. I call it the Island of Eternal Sin.

I never meant to go there—had planned to spend the time in Mykonos—but when a flight from Luton turned up I had to take it. I went shopping on the way to the airport and kitted myself out with all the holiday essentials.

Usually I like to turn up in a new place knowing nothing and no one. This enhances the thrill of the unknown and the possibility of getting lost—which is by far the best way to meet people. Everyone loves to take care of people who are lost and "helpless." I do vulnerable well. I'm good at scared, damaged, needy—and occasionally, if I'm in the mood, I like to play innocent. They love that one.

The flight was mundane and unexciting, save for the hostess with perfect breasts who offered more entertainment value than the family-friendly video and the male trolley dollies—they were far too camp for me and she had a smile that made me consider a sensuous diversion. I imagined her stumbling onto me as we rode through a spot of turbulence—her bosom landing dead center on my face.

At Reina Sofía airport, after the initial chaos that follows a four-hour flight with a planeload of drunken holidaymakers, I was feeling playful and so wandered outside, away from the crowd, to smoke a cigarette and scan the waiting taxis. My long blonde hair loose down my back was already receiving appreciative attention. Combined with lip-glossed lips, a low-cut, child-size white vest, and girlie mini, the image was working. Nobody saw me watching him watching me, for my dark glasses hid my gaze. My eye rested on the ninth car down's driver, who stood leaning up against his white Mercedes reading *El País*. He looked about thirty, and had a tall, lanky body that was bronzed and supple. His jeans were tight and his T-shirt a fraction too small, as if shrunk in the wash. My crotch began to burn and I made the cigarette last as the taxis slowly filled up and left. When he was three cars away he got into the driver's seat and prepared for another fare. I got behind the two waiting couples, slid my glasses up to my hair and set my expression to wide-eyed and awestruck. Within seconds he had noticed me and revved his engine. "Where you going?" he asked, in thickly accented English. His smile made his eyes sparkle and I could feel my panties getting wetter.

"Where do you suggest I go?" I replied, smiling ever so sweetly.

"You no have hotel?"

"No. I just booked a flight. I was told there would be plenty of hotels...." I made myself look suddenly worried, the first-holiday-alone type worried, when a man is needed to take care of the situation and be the protector.

"There are lots of hotels in Playa de las Américas. I take you there, yes?"

"Yes, take me there, thank you, you are very kind."

As I climb into the cab, with my bag on the seat beside me, I position myself so that he can see up my skirt, but make it look as if I don't realize this. It is an acquired talent that I have been practicing over the years. I see his eyebrows shoot up in the rearview mirror and open my legs slightly wider as I look with interest out the window. In fact I find the view highly uninteresting but I must appear fascinated and unaware of the exposed silk.

Once we are up on the motorway he speaks, lifting his chin so that he can look into my eyes. "You like have coffee with me first? I tell you a little about island. Very beautiful." I wonder if he is referring to the scenery in the car or outside, and am purposefully hesitant. "Is OK, I no bad man. We have drink on beach. You see."

"Thank you," I say, and grin demurely. He laps it up, and I look forward to stopping so that I can see his arousal.

He chats to me as he drives and I smile and nod charmingly in the right places, appear enthralled by his island despite its barren dryness. We go past the den of hell that is Playa de las Américas—whitewashed concrete and palm trees that houses thousands of Brits every year; spews them out of its cavernous clubs like wounded soldiers; burns their pale bodies pink-raw on the scalding beaches. I have knowledge of the resort that makes me cringe at the thought of driving through it. He tells me his name is Fidel and that he is lonely sometimes. I don't believe him. I tell him little except my name (false) and that I come from a small village in Wales where I still live at home (also false). He accelerates a little when I tell him that. I think he will be a good lover. As we drive down toward the coast—La Gomera on the horizon and the sun blazing—I know he will be just fine.

He parks up outside a small bar on a black-sand, rocky beach that very few people appear to know about. It is empty, save for a group of kids at the far end, and an old couple down near the shore. They are both topless and the woman's breasts sag, her nipples pointing downward. They have the look of Germans and I wince at their disrespect. The village panning out above the beach is untouched by British hands and maintains a traditional, local color. The smell of garlicky grilled fish wafts by and I follow Fidel to a table. I sit on the chair he pulls out for me. I find the demure innocent always brings out the gentleman.

"You want coffee, or maybe wine? We have very good wine here. Make you very happy in sunshine." His arm swoops up toward the cloudless sky and I catch a glimpse of his flat stomach, a streak of dark hair rising up the center. I feel giddy but remain cool on the surface, merely letting out a giggle that makes him presume I am not accustomed to drinking in the early afternoon.

"OK then, I'll try some wine. But just a little." I giggle again and he gestures for the waiter, pulling his chair closer to mine before sitting down. He smells strongly of a not displeasing aftershave and I notice how white his teeth are, how red his lips. I adjust myself on the chair so that my skirt slips up my thigh a little. I sit with my back straight to best present my tits to him. He is a grateful observer and when the waiter arrives he coughs politely. Fidel is a little nervous suddenly, his voice a touch shaky.

"*Un medio de tinto, y aceitunas.*"

"*De acuerdo,*" replies the waiter, with a glance at my legs.

The carafe fills two tumblers and a dish of shiny green olives is placed between us. They make me think of nipples and mine are aching under my vest top. Fidel lifts his glass as if to make a toast. I join him and look into his eyes. "To England," he says, and I don't bother reminding him that I am supposedly from Wales.

"To England," I murmur, and take a thirsty sip. The wine is potent and fruity and very easy to drink. Fidel offers me a Corona Light and I accept. His finger settles fleetingly on my hand when he lights it and I feel the current, the electric vibe that is crackling around us. As I bend my head to take the light I see his erection bulging on his leg and long to stroke it. But I am a good girl and must restrain myself.

We continue in the same vein, i.e., I let Fidel do all the talking — he does so love the sound of his own voice but then so do I — and he tells me about the island he was born on and that he is saving up to leave one day. He tells me he cannot find a wife and that he has a very nice apartment in a place called Adeje. He tells me that the beach we are at is called La Caleta and that he lost his virginity here with a woman who then broke his heart. I am amused by his willingness to pour his heart out to me when I myself have said almost nothing. I am a good listener, when I need to be.

The effect of the wine makes me want to throw Fidel across the table and straddle him but instead I nibble on an olive and watch his lips as I take tiny bites from the bud. He is dying to kiss me but I want to make him suffer too, and maneuver myself so that he can see a tantalizingly teeny patch of white panties. He strains at his denim seams and the wine is replenished with a flick of his fingers and virtually undetectable eyebrow movement.

But we don't manage to finish the second carafe. I pretend to feel faint as he starts to tell me about his last taxi. I want him to focus on driving me, not an old car.

"I think I need to find somewhere to stay. I need a cold bath and a lie-down in the shade. I'm sorry to leave so soon."

"Is no problem. I have solution." As was so easy to predict, Fidel offers to take me to his place and is throwing money on the table as he helps me out of the chair. Not that I am incapable, but his hand is cool in mine and he places the other around my waist, to support me. "Juss for to get well. You must get out of sun and now is *siesta*, nobody want to show apartments."

"Is that why you have time to spend with me now?"

"Yes, of course this why I with you on beach. Is time for to eat and sleep...."

"Oh. You must sleep; I don't want to be a nuisance."

He looks straight into my eyes and says, "You no nuisance, Kim. You very nice girl." I drop my head in mock embarrassment and let Fidel carry my bag as he leads me back to the cab. "You sit in front, next to me. If you no well, I can help you better."

"Thank you," I say, and notice how he looks at my crotch as he helps me into the passenger seat. I can smell myself and hope he doesn't live far; I want him badly.

"Tomorrow I help you find apartment," he says as he starts the engine. I feign shock; look worried. "You very safe with me. I no hurt you." Hurt me. Hurt me.

"If you are sure, that's very sweet of you."

"I sure. You very welcome my house." His hand is on my thigh, just sitting there, wide and cool and burning into me. "You are very nice girl."

He lives about ten minutes away from La Caleta in a fifth-floor apartment with a large, sunny balcony. He makes me lie down on the sun lounger there, which is covered with a thin, plastic mattress, and brings me ice water. "Can I sit with you?" he asks.

"Yes, yes, of course." He is so polite I feel a little mean. I want him to sit on me, not beside me—I want his cock to fill my throat. I go for the flattering, friendly chat now, keen to get moving on this one. I have waited long enough and my nipples need to meet his perfect teeth and be sunk into, hard enough to cause pain.

"You are very handsome, Fidel. You shouldn't have a problem finding a wife, I don't understand…"

"You think?"

"Yes, I do."

"And why you no have husband?"

"Because I am a little shy, you know?"

"But shy is good."

"Yes, but you see I don't have a lot of confidence. I mean, if I see a boy and I like him, I don't know what to say to him to make him notice me."

"You, you don't have say nothing. You juss beautiful." I laugh, not gutsy but high-pitched, girlie. And then he leans over to kiss me and I act as if I am shocked. I pull away, tongue peeking out of my mouth, eyes wide with anticipation. "Is OK," he murmurs, taking my chin in his hand. His other hand reaches behind and lands on my neck and a thrill rushes through me. I ease myself into him and he kisses like an angel, his tongue exploring my mouth as if it were a vagina. His hands wander down, slowly: one toward my chest and the other toward my lower back, as I lift myself to accommodate him. I push my tits into his hand as his fingers run expertly over my vest. I know the nipples are hard as diamonds and my quick breaths signal for him to go further, to strip me naked. His hand disappears under the vest and he lifts it off me. I let him, moaning a little about not being sure until he silences me with deeper kisses. He pulls each breast from its cup but keeps my bra on so that they protrude cramped and pushed together, the nipples straight out in front and aching, red. His fingers find a first nipple and squeeze it so succulently I cry out. He is turning me on so much I struggle to stay in role. I want to scream, the sensations are so painfully erotic.

"Your breast is like the heaven," he mutters, and lowers his head to take it in his mouth. He has been down this road many times before and his tongue does delicious things to me. I feel it would be an acceptable time to try and return the caresses—I lift a trembling hand onto his back and start to stroke him as if he were a stranger's pet, my movements awkward and inexperienced. He reaches behind as I knew he would and takes my hand around to his stomach. My heart skips a beat as I touch his taut skin, so close to his hard-on. "I like it if you touch me here, I show you." I bet you do, I think, but let him guide my veteran fingers to his swollen member. He shows me how he likes to be touched: slow, long strokes but strong ones through the straining denim. I gradually open my legs wider as his free hand makes its way down my stomach and under my skirt. My knickers are stuck to my pussy but as I am an innocent I might not realize this. He will know what it means though and will act accordingly. I want him to taste me, to drink me and hurt me.

I have to get his cock out; I have to touch its blood-filled flesh. I undo his belt and his buttons and my hand is shaking. Although I'm not sure I'm still in role, I really want this guy and I want to see him up close. He rubs the silk and I imagine his tongue there, lapping me up, pinning me down. I squirm and gyrate and accidentally on purpose the silk goes to one side and I am exposed. He lifts his head from my breast to look at me. I want to put him in my mouth but remember I am a good girl.

"Wait!" he says, and I lie there waiting while Fidel runs back inside, his penis jutting comically over his open jeans. He comes back with his erection and two snifters of something clear and yellowy. "Apple *licor*," he says. "Knock back—like this—" he shows me how it is done and I sit up and knock mine back in the same way, making sure I dribble a droplet onto my chin. He bends to kiss me before I can put down my glass and as he fills my mouth with his tongue I rid him of his jeans—they slide easily from his bare feet and I break from the kiss to lift his T-shirt off—he has to be naked.

He sees me as young and hardly handled—yet he brings out the harlot in me and I feel like pulling out one of my toys, bought in haste yet with care for the holiday. But sex toys and Little Miss Wide Eyes don't mix. I accept the length and weight of him without flinching, loving the way he fills me. He works like a pro, hard but tender, I cannot fault his technique. If I really were a virgin I would be eternally grateful to him. As we gather momentum, in perfect time, he pushes harder, pole-vaulting me to the lounger. I take him whole, in and out of me, aching more with each thrust; I love the way this man fucks. When I orgasm, naked except for my bra that oozes flesh, I kick the air and bang my head on the plastic mattress. When he does he collapses onto me and I can taste the salty skin of his neck.

He crawls over to the table and knocks his cigarettes off with a flick of the wrist. He lights two together and we smoke in silence, backs against the lounger, legs sprawled on the floor, stroking skin and nipple and neck and thigh, and I can almost hear us purring.

"I should go," I say, after a second cigarette and another knockback. It is Schnapps, not liqueur, and the hit is sharp.

"But no! You stay here, in my house. I take care of you."

"I don't think so, Fidel. It's not right, and I don't expect anything from you…." I get up and retrieve my skirt and vest from the floor. I leave my panties for him, draped over a cactus, and dress quickly, the smell of him all over me. He gets up and tries to stop me.

"No, you stay here."

"I can't Fidel, I'm sorry. It's just not possible." He doesn't force me; he is a good man, but he wills me to stay with his dark Spanish eyes. I am used to the look and do not succumb.

"Can I see you again?"

"I'm sure we'll meet again. It's a small island, isn't it?"

"Not that small, and you are too beautiful to be alone. I take care of you."

"I take care of myself. I always have."

"You take it very good for shy girl."

"Thank you."

"No thank me. You lie to me."

"Excuse me?" He has me sussed.

"You no innocent."

"Did I say I was?"

"No, but you say you shy, you live in little village…"

"And your point is?"

"I no understand Kim, why you no stay with me?"

"Please take me to Las Américas, Fidel, it's getting late now. And let me pay my fare."

He grumbles and dresses reluctantly. I kiss him wet-mouthed on his neck to make him see I am not angry, that I just cannot stay. In the lift down I squeeze his balls, rub my hand roughly up his erection under the jeans. I am still very wet.

I ask him to drop me in the busiest part of the dreadful Las Américas, where boys too young to drink, let alone pull, are lining the streets and nursing cans of lager. It's like some modern army, where lager is a weapon to ward off boredom. The noise is deafening, with music blaring from a variety of clubs and kids dressed as tarts staggering by, screaming at each other; it's like a school disco gone bad. I put a twenty-euro note in his hand and kiss him long on the lips. He looks around to check that he has not been seen; I never did believe his lonesome sob story. He won't accept the fare and shoves the note back into my hand.

"Thank you, Fidel. Thank you for showing me some of the island. I had a very good time!"

"I can show you more good time. Please. Take this." He scribbles his number on the back of a flyer from his dashboard. "You must call me."

"Thanks, I will, I'm sure."

He is a nice guy and I won't forget him but before nightfall I have to sample some local cuisine and sip on a glass of sangria. I do not stay alone for long. Soon I'm chatting to a second-generation expat called Charlie who is only too eager to give me a lift to the airport. "What a shame that you're leaving," he sighs. I have to agree with him at that point; his prick is making a tent in his shorts and I can smell the sex on my body as if it were still liquid.

"It depends what you're looking for though, doesn't it?" I do a cocky madam type: assertive nymphomaniac.

"Meaning?"

"Meaning that when the jug's finished we should make a move. Drink up."

We drink fast and reduce the *tapas* to a pile of sardine bones and distorted lemon wedges.

I don't object too forcefully when Charlie insists on paying. He leaves a generous tip. And he has a very nice car. Convertible MG, danger red; I like it a lot.

"I don't have to queue," I tell him, as we step into the revolving door at the airport. "Why don't you go grab us a beer or something? To take away." Charlie grins and lets his hand brush my nipple as he unwraps his arm from around my shoulder. I feel myself nearing another holiday high. He will be like putty in my hands, a mere colt. I will enjoy him.

I meet him on the way back from the bar and guide him to the car park. His hand is shamelessly climbing up my arse, his tongue slippery in my ear. "We have fifteen minutes," I say, trying not to laugh at my whorish behavior. "I hope you can deliver."

"Oh, I can, Missy. Here." He hands me a beer; I pull the ring and let the ice-cold lager drop to my stomach, the heat of the sun still warm on my face as I look up at the blue, blue sky. There's going to be a great sunset tonight, I think, as I push Charlie up against a shaded wall behind a fleet of hire cars and pull my boobs out for the second time that day, tight, still confined by whalebone, fighting for attention. There is no one around and it seems secluded enough.

Charlie's cock strains under his Billabongs and his mouth pulls me with urgent kisses. I lean into his hard-on and imagine it inside me, next to Fidel's. I imagine getting fucked by them both together, two holiday romances in one.

Charlie doesn't waste time kissing and moves downward quickly. He holds both nipples between his teeth. "Bite me," I bark, in that *I'm-in-charge* kind of way, but not loudly, I don't want any interruptions. He bites me hard but not too sharply—I have misjudged him and am glad of it; he is older than his years. "Now fuck me," I whisper into his ear as his hands lift my skirt.

"Oh, don't worry girl, I intend to."

Suddenly his hands are on my shoulders, turning me around to face the wall. "I'm going to fuck you like you deserve, you whore." Fuck, I like it when they talk dirty. It makes me drip. I lift myself high for him, wait breathless for that first contact. I reach around to feel him in my hand but he snatches my hands and pushes them above my head, pins them there with one of his own. "Now keep quiet you bitch, or we'll get caught." He plays the role well and I am under his command. I like a bit of role switching and am desperate for him to abuse me. He holds me stretched out long against a cold, dirty wall and sinks his length into me slow, which I adore. I can take it fast as well, of course. I am open to anything, as I'm sure is appreciated.

He makes me come first, superbly; it mirrors the planes taking off, my engines roaring, and when he is also spent he pulls himself out and turns me around; pushes me to my knees, keeping my hands raised above my head. "Now clean me up, you piece of shit." I am loath to obey him, would have preferred some punishment, but there is barely time for this: a mouthful of limp, wet cock. I lick him clean and *feel* him hardening again in my mouth. I know I am pushing it, I need to get inside the terminal, but I can't leave him hanging with a dick the size of a small cucumber. He is young enough to come quicker than he would like and tastes very good: a well-bred, wholesome taste that has to be better than any airplane food.

He leans with one hand against the wall and looks down at me. He grins. I grin back.

Charlie zooms past hooting his horn as I approach the revolving doors for the last time. I feel I'm being watched as I cross the concourse, not by the travelers who gawp at my messed-up appearance but by a solitary guy sitting farther down at the bar. It is Fidel, and by the time he has run up to the gate to find me I have slipped through the door marked *Privado*. I head straight for the staff washrooms and am lucky that they are empty. Within ten minutes I'm scrubbed up and neat as a pin in my British Airways uniform, ready for flight BA450 to Luton.

The wigs I wear are made especially for me by a guy I know on Savile Row. They have never let me down and I always carry one in my holiday bag. I fold this one neatly and place it in tissue paper, under my toys and my lingerie. I pin the BA pillbox hat to my choppy auburn crop and march out, head held high, to face the punters at desk 17, queuing for their return flight home. Another successful day at work, I feel.

BILOXI

~

GWEN MASTERS

I WAS A TENDER TWENTY-FOUR YEARS when my husband told me that he was in love with someone else. Within a week he had moved out of our home and our bed and into hers. Of course I had married too young. Isn't that what we all say when a first marriage falls apart? I had been young and spontaneous and blinded by the belief that love could conquer all, even my husband's fetish for other women. For weeks the pain of his leaving reduced me to lying in our matrimonial bed, unable to do anything but sleep and occasionally stumble my way to the bathroom, where I paused at the medicine cabinet to contemplate the pills that resided within. Some strength I had never known I possessed always moved me past that image of the bastard I had called my husband sobbing at my graveside. It would serve him right, he would deserve it, which is exactly why I didn't do it. I had already given him far too much of all that he didn't deserve. And I would not cry.

I lay in the darkness those long days and watched as the little red light on the little annoying answering machine began to blink faster and faster. Only when the tape was full did I listen to them, one pestering beep at a time, each one helped along with a deep and dark sip of Gentleman Jack, the only man in my life that it made sense to keep around anymore. Through my answering machine I learned that my mother felt I should do anything I could to work it out and uphold the family name. That was par for her course, though it still hurt my feelings and wounded my pride even further. I learned that my best friend had also slept with my husband and she could have told me long ago that this was coming, but of course she kept that to herself, that selfish friend of mine. I learned that the mortgage was past due apparently because the one who called himself my man had once again wasted all granddaddy's hard-earned money on booze and cigars and, of course, women.

My trusty little answering machine also informed me that because I had missed work for a week without calling, I was now fired and I could expect my severance check, including vacation pay and stock-sharing, in the mail. The good old postal service was apparently still running while my world was falling apart, and I made my way out to the mailbox in my sweat suit, an audacity that would likely have brought on a heart attack for my traditional grandmother. After all, it was she who had taught me that a lady never left home without her nails painted, her hair done, and a fake smile plastered on her face to hide the pain within.

I rifled through the mail and discarded all but one item. I ripped the envelope open and dropped the pieces on the ground. In my hand was a check for twenty-five thousand dollars. My own money. Mine. My bare feet turned, seemingly of their own accord, and stopped in front of the garage door.

That was how I wound up on the River Road, chasing my heart down the two-lane at ninety miles an hour. I had no idea where I was going and I found I didn't particularly care, as long as my humming tires were carrying me somewhere more humid and more southern than Kentucky. I didn't want to be in the same state as that man I had married. I left the house unlocked and unclean, the answering machine blinking again, the dishes festering in the sink, the dust convening atop the glass tables. I left all his money in the bank. I took my dresses and only the things I couldn't bear to part with. I left a note for my lawyer saying that the adulterous husband of mine could have everything. Except the car. That was my vehicle into a new life, in more ways than one.

I had twenty-five thousand dollars in my glove compartment and a full tank of gas. It was enough for a small apartment and the necessities to hold me over until I found a job. It was enough for a new start. The ragtop was open and the wind lifted my chestnut hair to cool me as the humidity pressed down. My eyes watered with the sting of freedom. I drove into the approaching twilight with no plans, no destination other than where I already was, the beautiful South. I had crossed the Mississippi line long ago and now I was heading into blues country, nothing but cotton fields stretching their long rows out to my left, the swirling Mississippi River on my right. I slowed my speed as the darkness loomed.

Somewhere between Tupelo and Greenville, I decided on Biloxi. That is where I would begin my new life, on the banks of the Mississippi. I focused my attention on the lights of a distant dam and drove steadily, studying how the lights changed like tiny stars as I came nearer the expanse of steel and concrete. Suddenly the roadway widened and there it was, one of man's foolish attempts to tame the river that had flowed here centuries before man had even known she existed. It was a good place to take a break from the road.

I pulled off onto the dam overlook, gravel crunching under my tires. A few scattered cars were pulled up to the curb, looking precariously close to toppling off the high platform and into the hungry river. I stretched and walked with slow steps around the white Mustang, knowing that surely my husband had heard the message on his machine and had already come back to the home I would never again reside in. I wondered briefly what he must think. Then I decided I didn't care.

The sun began to flirt with the edge of the horizon, turning from yellow to burnt orange. Streams of wispy purple clouds adorned the sky and the first star of the night made its twinkling presence known. I closed my eyes and breathed deeply the heavy scent of the river. I focused on the brush of the moist air across my skin, the way it lifted my hair from my neck and cooled me before moving on to christen the cotton fields and country roads. The swish of the river against the shore was hypnotic, and I swayed with the rhythm of the gently breaking waves.

Another sound drifted to me, this one out of place on the riverfront but seemingly fitting all the same. The mellow notes wafted on the breeze, a natural accompaniment to the setting sun, and I didn't open my eyes to find where they were coming from. I just stood against the railing and let the bluesy sound glide through my thoughts, coloring them in the deepest purples and maroons of the darkening sky. The tears came then, slow as the river and silent, a step into the threshold of healing and forgiveness. My hands were easy on the railing as the tears fell, my body relaxing by degrees to the soft sound of a guitar behind me and the river rolling by under me, the distant call of a heron and the faint call of lead-liners from somewhere downriver. I did not sob or scream, rant or rave against the injustices that had sent me running for solace. There was simply the river, rolling on as she had for centuries before and would for centuries after, all the sounds that were hers, the wind in my face, and the sweet soul of a guitar.

When I opened my eyes the sun had set and the river was dark and ominous. My tears had fallen one by one into the waters below and were on their way to the ocean, mingling with all the other tears I was certain had been shed into the understanding currents of the Mississippi. Behind me the notes were clear and clean, mellow and gentle. I turned and looked across the short expanse of the gridded walkway.

The guitar was dark, almost as dark as the night around it. It was the color of tobacco fields and muddy waters, the essence of the shoreline. His hands moved over the instrument with a reverence that is reserved for holy places, and I had the sudden thought that perhaps this place was sacred, this river that had given birth to the Delta. He played slowly and with a sure hand, his fingers pressing on the strings with the lightest touch, the sounds without a sharp edge or undercurrent of desperation. The notes told of nothing but peace and contentment.

My eyes held the guitar for some time, until the tempo changed and pulled me out of my wandering thoughts. I let my eyes trail up the musician's long body to his face. His eyes were closed, and even in the darkness I could tell that his skin carried the deep tan that only years of hard work under the sweltering Delta sun could create. His hair was dark, as dark as the night that had come so swiftly, and it was rakishly long, curled at the ends, bringing to mind a little boy's soft and unruly hair. Yet his strong, shadowed jaw and skilled hands said immediately that this was no boy that stood before me. He stood against the railing with a stance that spoke of tranquility, a man who was certain of himself and unwavering, yet something about him spoke of a restlessness that was almost puzzling in its power. I couldn't stop staring at him.

In time his eyes opened and I could tell in the dim red warning lights that they were dark, as dark as the dirt that covered the levees and fed the cotton fields. He looked at me and through me with a curious ease that was frightening in its accuracy; I had the sudden belief that he could see everything I was thinking, that everything that had happened to me was knowledge he already owned, this dark stranger with his guitar that spoke everything I felt without any effort. I found the thought a comforting one.

"Thank you," I said, my voice pitching low to blend seamlessly with the music from his voluptuously curved guitar. He nodded, the curled strands of his hair brushing just above his eyes as he dropped his head and cradled the guitar closer. I was almost sorry I had spoken, that I had intruded into the silence that only the notes of the guitar and surrounding nature had a right to trespass upon. I let out the breath I hadn't realized I was holding when he spoke.

"I thought you needed to hear her." His voice was low and reminded me of a sultry summer night in the South, and in some corner of my mind I saw the image of an ice cube melting, tinkling as it shifted with other frozen blocks in a tall glass of iced tea. His drawl was pronounced and yet somehow short, the unique sound of someone born and raised in the Delta. The depth of his tone said that he was older than I had first thought, and I looked more closely at his face. He looked right back at me with a gaze that didn't waver, confident yet with a challenge that seemed born into him, one that he couldn't quite hold back.

I found myself staring at him, my usual shyness gone without a whisper. "Who are you?" I finally asked, my voice sounding strange and foreign in a land I was suddenly gladder I had ventured into.

He chuckled, the sound rolling easily from deep within his chest, the sound of a man who had seen more than his share of laughter. He cocked his head and a strand of hair fell over his forehead. I fought the sudden and inane urge to touch it, then berated myself and tried to remember what had brought me to stand on this dam and cry while he played in the first place. My mind came up blank.

"Does it matter?" he asked, and I was startled, almost forgetting what I had asked him. I contemplated his question for a long moment as he stood with one hand caressing the fret board of his guitar, the other hand resting lightly on the solid and strong curve of her — it seemed she was female somehow. I studied the instrument, as if to impress it into my memory.

"No," I finally admitted, knowing that I would remember him whether I knew his name or not. I felt like I knew him already yet I was certain we had never met.

He chuckled again, this time sounding even more relaxed, and he smiled at me for the first time. His eyes flickered with a lighter brown and perhaps a shade of green as the smile touched them, starting within his eyes before traveling down to his lips. "In that case," he drawled, "my name is Daniel. Daniel Burgess."

Daniel Burgess. The name resounded in my head. I watched as he reached into his pocket, moving deliberately as if he were trying not to frighten away a skittish animal. Out of the deep pocket of his jeans that fit just right, he pulled out a small empty bottle with no cap. He pressed the bottle to the fret board and I realized it was an old-fashioned slide, like one I had once seen an old black man on a street corner in Memphis use to draw strange sounds from his old battered guitar. Daniel Burgess strummed a chord and moved the slide quickly, but not feverishly, and the sound that fell from the strings was as sweet as the iced tea I envisioned in my mind. Almost as the sound died away he did it again, this time drawing the slide forward and back, the sounds tumbling over themselves in such a way that I felt as though he were pouring himself and all his history out through them.

I suddenly realized that I was standing on a dam over the Mississippi River, mesmerized by a sound I had rarely heard and a man who was a perfect stranger; that I had just cried my own river of tears over a man who had cheated and left me with an uncertain future; and that I had been driving for almost an entire day with little direction. Yet it seemed now that my route had taken me right where I should be, standing here perfectly comfortable in the dark with a stranger who could make all my worries and cares go away with a few strings and an old bottle slide.

I don't know how long I watched his hands move on that guitar. The bottle flashed blue and occasionally a pale yellow in the light of the rising moon. The air had grown colder and now my dress swayed around my legs with a carefree ease, not weighted down by the humidity that was the trademark of the South. He finally stopped playing, the notes drifting away into memory, and we both stood in the darkness in silence, looking at each other.

When he spoke it was a whisper. "I saw your tags. Kentucky. You've come a long way. I reckon you have good reason to run so far and so hard." His manner said he wasn't going to ask, and my respect for him solidified at the realization. I felt myself smile.

"I'm Clarice Tanner," I told him, reverting back to my maiden name without thought.

"Welcome to the Delta, Clarice." I watched him move as he unsnapped the guitar strap that held the instrument to his body, kneeling in the same motion to place her reverently in a satin-lined case. The snick and click of the latches seemed inordinately loud out here above the gentle roar of the river. He moved with the same ease with which he had played, standing to his full height and lifting the case in one hand. He took two steps toward the walkway entrance and stopped, turning to look at me over his shoulder, his hair shining here and there with thin strands of silver, almost matching the pristine white of his rumpled button-down shirt. I suddenly felt achingly lonely. I didn't want him to leave.

"Wait," I whispered. Daniel looked at me with an expression of curiosity. A long moment of thought passed. "I'm crazy," I said aloud.

Daniel laughed. The sound rose to the top of the sycamore and birch that surrounded us, mingled with the roar of the river, and sent a chill through me. "Crazy? Why?"

"Because I'm going to ask you to come to Biloxi with me."

My heart pounded with trepidation as he looked at me. His jaw dropped for a second, then he shook his head and looked down at the walkway. I started to speak, to withdraw the ridiculous invitation, when his voice came low and certain into the darkness. "Biloxi isn't far from here. Follow me, Clarice. I'll take you there."

He turned with a gentle ease and hefted his guitar, walked to an old Toyota that had seen much better days, and settled behind the wheel without looking back. Soon I found myself coaxing the engine of my old Mustang to life, pulling out onto the River Road, led through the darkness by a pair of dim taillights and a curiosity I hadn't felt in a very long time.

And that was how I met Daniel Burgess, the man who would become my best friend, my lover, and my confidant. Daniel and I were one of those anomalies. One of those things about which old men shake their heads while chewing on toothpicks and rocking harder in their chairs on the front porch. There were times no one could figure out for the life of them why the restless musician from New Orleans and the high-society gal from Kentucky had chosen to settle in Biloxi and shake things up. Our union was stormy and calm all at once. But when we loved…ah, those were the moments in which we knew exactly why providence had pulled us together that dark night above the Mississippi waters.

One morning not long after we settled in Biloxi, I awoke before Daniel. Quietly slipping from the bed, I padded barefoot through the open French doors. This was my favorite time, when the fog of sleep had not yet lifted, but the promise of a new day was on the horizon.

I took a deep breath weighted with the humid and oppressive air of the South. It was hot enough this early August morning to make Satan himself beg for the slightest breeze. My eyes drifted shut as a bead of sweat made its way between my breasts and was captured by the satin of my black dressing gown. I pressed my hips into the cast-iron railing of my ancient balcony, feeling the early morning dew seep through the fabric to cool my body. The water was cool on my fingertips as I ran them along the ridge in the handcrafted baluster, collecting the drops of moisture on my skin. I brought my hand to my throat and swallowed once, tasting the last vestiges of the sweet tea I had enjoyed just moments before. I let the drops fall, reveling in the coolness that dissipated all too quickly, evaporating away into the still Delta air.

I welcomed the sounds trespassing on my ears, layer after layer, as beautiful Biloxi awoke. The sun was just a promise on the horizon. The damp scent of the great river assaulted my senses, making me aware of the smoke of the hard-working tugs and the lighter aroma of whiskey and stale wine that seemed to creep into everything in this river walk part of town. Below my apartment, the soft strains of a blues club sounded, the trumpet and saxophone and piano drifting up to my waiting ears, then the complement of a deep bass and sweet guitar. I could almost feel the soul of that instrument envelop me and pull me into its own world of melody as I began to sway to the sound.

I listened to the rumble of a wagon on cobblestone streets, followed by the roar of an expensive engine…past and present existing together in this haunted town. A siren rose to the rooftops and echoed back down, the strobe of the lights pressing against my eyelids as the vehicle hurried to remedy trouble somewhere nearby. The bellow of a tugboat from the river announced the means by which these towns lived and died on the shores of the mighty Mississippi. The years of dredging the lands of America down with her waters had formed this, the most fertile of any soil. Gulf birds sang in riotous tones, arguing and echoing one another in their greedy quest for whatever the perpetual barge traffic might pull up from the silt for their enjoyment.

My eyes opened in near-darkness, the only illumination the old-fashioned street lights glowing below me. I looked down at the sound of laughter and watched an elderly gentleman in a bowler hat walk along the narrow sidewalk, a battered guitar case in hand. He paused as if aware of being watched. "Morning, old-timer," I said, my low voice twining with the music from the club below. My words were loud enough. He lifted his eyes to mine and the weathered years of a musician's life creased his face as he smiled at me, doffing his hat in the old fashion of a true southern gentleman. "Young lady," he acknowledged in a quiet voice that carried a surprising tone of respect. I nodded in response, my answering smile seemingly all the thanks he needed. He hefted his guitar again and continued on his way, this time whistling a bluesy tune.

I sighed along with the sound of a release valve on the locks of the dam, the steel and concrete that channeled the river. The sky was tainted with the palest of blues and purples. I watched the elderly gentleman until he disappeared into the shadows of the Mississippi morning, then turned back to look through the French doors at the man I had left lying on the white sheets of my four-poster bed.

Daniel was on his back, one hand draped across his stomach, which rose and fell evenly as he slept. His other hand was above his head, his fingers twined haphazardly with his long brown hair. I reached up and touched my own chestnut curls, felt how the strands fell across my shoulders, the ends dampened by the humidity that surrounded everything about this town and seeped into this room. He was wearing only pajama shorts, and I studied yet another time the strong curves of his shoulders, the strength of his legs, the inviting curve of his neck, and the tiny diamond earring that glinted in the dim light of the nearby candles. I made my way over to them and trailed my finger through the streams of wax that had been left from an entire night of those flames burning low. I caught the warm wax on my fingertip and watched as it hardened in the air. I peeled it off and dropped it back into the flame with a small sizzle and sputter.

Daniel and I had loved all night long. The smell of his sweet cigars still hung in the air, mingling with the scent of my expensive perfume. The remnants of smooth bourbon colored the bottoms of two heavy crystal glasses. I picked up the bottle and poured a stream of the liquor into the waiting tumblers, then dipped my hand into the chilled ice bucket that rested there beside them on the cherry nightstand. The ice cubes floated lazily in the amber liquid. I ran my hands down the satin of my gown, touching my body through it, recalling his hands running over me time and again as we made love to the sounds of the blues that drifted through our open doors all night long. I moved to the old high back chair in the corner of the room, trailing my fingers over the strings of his voluptuous guitar. Life with a musician was rife with uncertainty tempered by certain passion.

I moved to the bed. Daniel was so handsome to me, with his shadowed jaw and hair just the right length to be less than respectable. He was a big man, certainly twice my size, which made me feel all the more powerful when he threw his head back and let me have my way with him in the throes of passion. I let my mind wander over the snapshots I carried of him while he was out chasing his dreams on the road...Daniel sitting with me on a levee, tossing crackers to the white and gray gulls that circled almost menacingly above. Daniel dressing carefully for yet another show, in some small club in some small southern town where he would be remembered as that tall, dark guitar player who played as if his guitar were an extension of his very body. Daniel laughing with me as we let ice cubes melt on our bodies in the unbearable summer heat and later made love in the puddle of melted water on the slate kitchen floor.

I knelt on the bed beside him. Daniel shifted slightly but did not awaken. I settled my lips on his collarbone and moved above him, and then down, settling between his long legs as my mouth caressed every inch of his chest and belly. I kissed each finger of the hand that rested there on his belly button, then moved it so I could have all of his skin to taste. I slid his shorts down his legs and off, revealing his body to my gaze. Daniel moaned, beginning to wake up, as I slid my hands up the insides of his thighs and found the manhood that had pleasured me so many times the night before.

My hands gently cupped his balls and he moaned louder, his eyes opening to look down at me as I gave his semierect cock one long lick with the flat of my tongue. I felt his organ swell under me in response to my touch. I licked downward, in no hurry at all, leaving a cooling trail down his beautiful body. Daniel did not move, allowing me to get him ready, to please him in my own unique ways. I knew that his dark eyes were open and watching as I touched him, then circled my hand around his hardness. I stroked upward before allowing my mouth to join my fingers. I looked at him as I moved my hand in one smooth slow downward stroke. Daniel moaned his approval.

I began to suck him, letting my mouth tighten around him and slide up and down his thick head. I licked him at the end of each stroke, just the way he liked it. Daniel moved and I stopped using my mouth on him to watch as he reached over to the nightstand and picked up the bourbon I had poured. His knowing smile was a delight. He took a long sip before I reached up with one hand to take it from him. I took a sip of my own while my other hand worked, unhurriedly sliding up and down his shaft.

Daniel picked up one of his expensive cigars and with one smooth motion, struck a match on the headboard of my bed. My eyes trailed from the tiny black streak on the cherry wood to the glowing embers of the cigar. He puffed leisurely to start it. I offered him another sip of bourbon. A single drop of sweat left a trail down the tanned skin of his shoulder. At that moment there was nothing in this world sexier than a man leaning back against a headboard with fine liquor in one hand, a fine cigar in the other, and a willing woman in that bed with him. I smiled seductively and waited until he brought the cigar to his lips and just as he took a deep pull of the sweet tobacco, I slid my mouth down the length of his cock. I was rewarded with a low groan that poured out of his throat along with the smoke.

I slid my lips up and down, pulling him in and out of me. I pushed hard with my tongue, pressing him against my upper teeth, and pulled him slowly out, the combination of softness and near-pain making him groan louder than before. He laughed low in his chest. "You are an incredible woman," he murmured, his voice sincere and full of endearment. I heard the thump of the tumbler settling down on a surface, then I felt his long fingers in my hair, twining through it and tightening to just short of pain as he urged me on. I took him deep, then deeper still, until I fought the urge to gag and settled him in my throat. I swallowed once, hard, and the sound of his cry of pleasure rose in the air. He moved then, bucking his hips gently into me, asking silently for more. I took a breath and let his swollen head find my throat again, then swallowed quickly, my mouth a pulsing sheath of pleasure around him.

I listened to the sound of his cigar in his mouth, the deep pull, and the exhalation of sweet smoke. Every time he took a draw, so did I. I sucked his cock like a fine cigar, savoring it, milking the most from it with every pull of my lips and tongue. Daniel arched into me, hard, as I bit gently down on the base of his cock. The pain and pleasure was driving him to that edge we loved. My fingers massaged his balls with more pressure, my other hand sliding down to find that spot just below them that I liked so well. I touched him there and his body tensed, then relaxed as I drove him into my throat again. I swallowed, and then pulled upward with my teeth. Daniel let out another cry. "I'm close," he said in his baritone, and my response was to lick his cock once, then drive him in again. I pulled gently on his balls, knowing I could make him orgasm when I wanted it. And I wanted it now. I sucked him deep and pulled upward with my teeth one last time.

"Oh, God, now," he moaned, and I felt the sweet cream of his body flooding my mouth. I swallowed the scent of his cigar a complement to his bittersweet taste. I sat up in the bed, my hand still caressing him, and let him reach out and tip the glass of bourbon into my mouth. The strong liquor mingled with his taste in a delightful way that I was sure I would never forget.

He was smiling at me. "Darlin', you know just how to please me," he praised with his southern drawl, and I smiled back at him as he tipped the glass again, this time letting a small trail of the liquor splash against my skin. I let my head fall back as the bourbon cooled my heated flesh, sliding between my breasts. Daniel sat up in the bed and let his tongue follow it. His hands found my waist and he held me as his tongue and lips explored, enjoying bourbon and sweat and the skin that seemed made for him alone. I slid my hands through his hair and pulled him closer as he slid the straps of my gown down over my shoulders, exposing my curves for his gaze. The heavy air pressed against me, cooled only by his tongue as he drank the liquid from my skin.

I stretched against him, feeling light and vulnerable in his broad hands. He pushed me back onto the bed and his tongue trailed between my breasts, pulling the gown down as he went. I soon felt the fabric slip against my thighs, then my knees, then it was gone. I opened my legs to him, knowing what he wanted, and I gasped aloud at the shock of the cool bourbon pouring down one hip and over my pussy, coating my hard clit. His tongue followed the path of the liquor, taking the drops up on his tongue. His strong hands pressed into my hips to hold me still so that he could savor at his leisure. He sucked my clit into his mouth with one slow motion and I groaned, my hands clasping at the rumpled sheets on either side of my body. "You taste so much better than bourbon," he whispered to me, sliding one finger inside my wetness. He knew just what I liked, and as his finger slid in and out he sucked my clit with the rhythm. I didn't have to tell him I was close. He knew my body well. I clenched the sheets and his name fell from my lips as the orgasm washed over me.

The bellow of the tugboat mingled with the sound of my voice as I orgasmed on his hand, my body pulsing around him while his tongue flicked my clit, just the way he knew I liked it. I arched, rivers of pleasure flowing through my body. His hands caressed my calves, then found my knees and pulled me up and open for him. His cock slid through my wetness to find that opening he desired. He wasted no time. I cried out as he rammed straight into me, taking what was his with one long, hard thrust. The sweat that ran down his body dripped onto me, heated against my already heated skin. He braced his hands on either side of my head and I ran my fingers up his arms, feeling the muscles flex as he moved in and out, fucking me like a man should fuck a woman...hard and deep with powerful strokes, possessing and loving all at once. I twined my legs around his hips, feeling them slip on the fine sheen of sweat that accompanied our lovemaking.

Daniel thrust deeper, searching out my body, wanting every inch I had to offer. I lifted my hips and felt him press against my womb. I moaned mindlessly at the mixture of pleasure and pain, wanting only more of it. Daniel obliged, his thick cock deliciously stretching me as he lifted my legs to his shoulders and slipped deep into my cunt. I bucked underneath him. My eyes trailed down Daniel's chest to where our bodies joined and I saw my own wetness covering him. Then he pushed forward, slowly impaling me again. And again.

I ran my hands down his chest and touched his cock as he slid out, stroking him each time. He groaned his approval, urging me on, then pulling almost all the way out so I could jack his cock hard with my hand. Our breaths came faster. He watched my fingers move on him and I felt him throb just inside my pussy. "I want you to come for me," he said, his hands finding my nipples and pressing them into my body, then releasing and pulling on them. I touched his face with one hand and he drew one of my fingers inside his mouth, sucking on it as he began thrusting again, riding me with smooth strokes.

I felt my orgasm begin to build inside the fire my body had become. Daniel sensed it, for he began to push harder, driving me up the bed, my body pulling at the sheets under me and wrinkling them more with every jerk against the mattress. Daniel braced himself and rammed deep. "Now," he ordered, giving me all of him with long strokes and no hesitation. My tight sheath burned with the feeling of his body violating mine so thoroughly. I arched one last time, seeking all of him to fill me, and I screamed into the Mississippi heat as I came hard around him. My body sucked on his cock until he came too, spilling his essence inside my softness. Daniel's cry echoed my own. He plunged again and again until he was spent, sure that all his seed was as deep inside my body as it possibly could be.

After long moments he withdrew from me. Together we collapsed onto the bed, letting our breathing calm. Rivers of sweat rolled down my ribs and thighs as I sat up and reached for the glass of bourbon, taking a drink before turning to him and holding the glass while he drank from it. With a sly smile, he reached for the cigar. I beat him to it, taking a pull of the tobacco. I leaned forward to kiss him and release the sweet smoke into his mouth. He laughed low in his throat as he inhaled what I gave him, then pried the cigar from my fingers with an indulgent smile.

I fell back to the bed and stretched on the sheets, feeling the heat press down on me like a solid blanket. My eyes closed as I listened to the sound of him enjoying his cigar, feeling his fingers trace circles on my back. I fell asleep to the sounds of the town waking up below us, cranking up into full swing. I awoke all too soon to the sound of latches closing on his guitar case.

Daniel had showered and shaved, and was dressed in his favorite blue cotton shirt and navy slacks. I watched as he put his watch on his arm, then ran his hands through his damp hair one last time. It fell over his forehead in just the right way to make his eyes look even darker than they really were. He picked up the guitar case and smiled over at me, seeing my eyes on him. I smiled back. He was a musician, after all, and the road was calling yet again.

"When will you be coming back?" I asked him, knowing he would be back.

"I have a show in Tupelo, then in Cairo. I'll be back in a few days." His eyes watched me as I smiled at him. "I drew a cool bath for you," he offered with boyish charm, making me laugh in appreciation.

Daniel stepped toward me and the smell of his cologne added to all the other wonderful scents in the room. He leaned down to give me a lingering kiss. "I'll be back," he assured me one last time, and smiled before he and his lovely guitar stepped out of my door, the latch clicking softly behind him.

Mer Boy

⤳

GERARD WOZEK

I CAN PRETEND THAT IT'S SAFE HERE. Tiny sponges and violet coral are artfully arranged at the bottom of the three-hundred-gallon fish tank that sits in the enclosed lobby of this nameless sauna in Brussels. Youthful men in thin terry-cloth towels pose, almost motionless, like perfectly arranged mannequins. They sip their fruit-infused beers at the spa bar. They gently throw their heads back, close their eyes, and wait for droplets of perspiration to form on their perfectly arched brows. They seem to hardly breathe as the angelfish in the aquarium wriggle through the underwater ferns.

I watch the dozing dream boys. I ponder their perfectly gelled hair and pumped biceps, their semierect bulges beneath their moist toweling, then turn back to the gurgling fish tank. I stare at the way the delicate guppies and mollies glide along the edge of their glass prison, the grace of their translucent fins as they dart and disappear into a replica Chinese pagoda. I lose myself in the swaying of plastic seaweed, the turreted castle with the extended drawbridge over yellow and red rubble, the porcelain sea witch with her arms extended as if casting a spell.

A Moroccan fellow in a white cotton robe glares at the miniature sunken ship wedged into a tiny sand furrow, as the strange, exotic fish move along the sharp edges of their home, turning the corners quickly, then again and again. He taps on the glass of the giant fishbowl and a baby barracuda scampers away. "We're all just like them, aren't we?" And I begin to look closer at the beautiful sad creatures: mute, walleyed, aimless and ultimately, trapped.

Most come to the bathhouse to forget, to lose the memory of what came before, and to sink into foreign embraces. Perhaps it's because Brussels is centrally located in Western Europe, but at this particular sauna, a patron can encounter a smorgasbord of men from different countries. Tonight, a wealthy epicurean from Budapest has made advances on a professional cyclist from Krakow. A Tunisian banker and a Portuguese sailor have been fixated on each other's tan lines for the last half hour. And Hans, a tattoo artist from Hamburg, is carving an anchor onto a British dignitary's shoulder blade. No language skills are necessary here, only skin-to-skin, eye-to-eye, mouth-to-mouth interfacing.

I don't come here looking for that. I like the way the wet steam encloses me, sealing me into its scorching furnace, my skin and lungs merging with the dewy fog. It takes me back to the first time. The dank smell of male crotch that pervades the common areas is mixed with the sour stench of mildew, but still, I smell him. The red bulbs in the light sockets, and the funny way the carpet resembles trampled seaweed, all serve to revive the past. Our past. His and mine in this basement bathhouse in Belgium.

Faceless men whisper in the dark corners of dim orgy rooms, their chests still wet, towels seeping, filthy with oily red rust, the Marquis de Sade chains chafing their bulging shoulders. I am remembering what it is like to have his teeth bite down on my earlobe. What it's like to feel the hairs of his massive chest on my shoulder. The weight of his hand on my neck, pushing me to his nipple ring. The slow gyrations of his torso as he presses himself into me, my body supple and open to his deepest impulse.

Someone moves his damp bulge across my wrist, touches the

trail of sweat laced along my navel hairs, and gently kisses the back of my head. This stranger puts his nose on the nape of my neck and inhales deeply, then takes my hand and presses it into the small of my back. "You like this?"

Several of the dream boys are glancing over their shoulders at us. He is softly licking the top of my back. He is trying to loosen my towel and rub my buttocks with his engorged cock. I can sense the thickness, the oozing head urgent against my now exposed backside. His breath comes out fast and he is thrusting his wet tongue into my ear. He is trying to find the pulse that will unite us. He is looking for a way into me; for a way that I might submit. One of the dream boys opens a condom wrapper with his teeth and begins to move closer.

If I keep my eyes closed I can pretend that the man behind me is really Wilhelm. I can pretend they are his hands that smelled of fish brine and krill, and they are resting softly on my collarbone. I can pretend they are Wilhelm's eyes that were the color of the morning mist that rises off the fishing piers in Holland. I can try to reinvent the tumult of curls in his hair, those perfect black eyelashes, the impossible swagger. If I keep my eyes shut tightly, I can imagine it is my missing companion's distended manhood with its blind urgency. His amorous caress, his soft brown whiskers rubbing my neck.

But I can't. I take a deep breath and step forward. The dream boy who is trying to hand me the rubber rolls his eyes and sighs deeply with exasperation. As I begin to refasten my towel, my predator has moved on to someone else, so I move on as well.

I stare back at the poseurs lined up across mirrored walls here; bore into their bugged-out eyes and languid, nearly drug-induced gestures. The smell of stale poppers and the odor of something that reminds me of dying alewives filters through the air, and I notice the other dreamers, belly-up in the churning pools. Limbs move to the pounding beat, Sylvester's disco from the late seventies I think, and I wander toward the scallop-shaped whirlpool.

I meander along the edge of the basin and step in, and my hand wanders into warm crevices, little cesspools. My fingers dig inside of the clogged jet sprays filled with mucus and condom jelly; the cisterns of these ancient, turgid baths are completely rotted through. But I go on splashing, my head slipping underneath the surface of the water, my coated arms flailing. I go on with my gulping and gasping for air, but no one seems to worry that I might be drowning. I pull myself out of the Jacuzzi and oxygen rushes back into me.

I am revived, but I wonder if the force of anything in this *hammam* could remold me into something wholly new; whether I might emerge from here like some see-through jellyfish, or fighting stingray. But there is nothing that can match the force that was rendered upon me by the Dutchman I met here last June.

I go into the steam room and place my towel over my shoulders. I let my head sink into my chest. I try and piece together the first time we met: the American tourist and the stealthy fisherman from Holland. Our conversation in broken English, "You don't have to speak right now. You're shivering. Let me warm you."

I had stopped in Brussels on my way to Amsterdam to drink the café au lait and eat the impeccable croissants they serve at the Rocco Forte Hotel. I like to wander around the old section of the city, window-shop around the Grand Place with its cobblestone terraces and Flemish architecture. I like to visit the *Manneken Pis*, the famous peeing boy in the corner of the square, and watch the tourists try and cup their hands into his steady stream, or throw begonia petals into the puddle below him.

It was around two in the afternoon. I was exhausted from my climb to the top of Belfort Tower to look down on the labyrinthine streets below, when I was struck with a craving for some of Wittamer's creamy chocolate pralines. But looking for the Place du Grande-Sablon, I somehow got lost.

It was at the edge of an unnamed street that I was taken with a small-etched sign that read *Hammam*. I entered the building, rather nondescript save for the carved female heads holding up the granite windowsills that reminded me of two sea maids carved into a ship's prow. I walked down a spindly staircase and was greeted by the young attendant. I had only come in for a shower, not knowing this sauna in the basement of an apartment house was infamous for brief male-to-male encounters.

I needed to soak. I needed to steam. I needed respite from the urban crush of Barcelona where I had spent the last week nursing a sprained ankle from falling back off a raised perch at an overlook of Gaudi's castle. Having overexerted my sore tendon with touring the central district of Brussels, I felt justified in taking a hot bath.

With my clothes stowed in a locker and nothing but a fraying towel around my waist, I entered the infrared wet sauna. The curls of steam rising from the floor were soothing, so I sat on the wooden bench and closed my eyes.

"It's still swollen." He touched my foot so tenderly it seemed to stop my pulse.

"There was a bird's nest resting on the edge of a waterspout." My breath seemed to be coming out, but haltingly. "I was trying to rescue it actually. To keep it from falling out."

"There were still eggs in it?" He seemed to whisper but it filled the entire room. The only air to breathe was coming from his mouth.

"I wanted to save them. Give them a chance, you know." I felt myself turn red. Was it the temperature of the sauna? "That's when I stumbled back and fell."

"A noble wound." His hand that had been delicately smoothing the ball of my ankle had moved to massage my calf, and now, the back of my knee. "You ever kiss a Dutch fisherman?"

"Never." I felt my heart begin to beat harder.

"Can you imagine what it might be like to be sailing on the ocean in the Netherlands during a storm?" He moved closer to me, his arm replacing the towel around my shoulders. There was something in the way he pronounced the word *Netherlands*, like *Nedderlans*, but it was more like the strains of some mysterious symphony.

"So you like to fish on the open sea?"

"I do." He smiled as though he were in a reverie. His leg was now resting on mine and each tiny hair on my thigh was pulsing from the electricity generated from this place of contact.

"And you don't mind being on the water for so long?"

"When the waves get choppy, the only thing that can keep you stable is this." He was suddenly breathing his story inside of me. His full lips had parted to reveal a tongue that was now deep inside my mouth, coveting my own tongue, saliva covering my chin and neck.

He wiped the excess moisture from the lather of our French kisses onto my chest, then down to my hard cock, making it slick and even stiffer. Then, he balled his towel up behind my head and I fell back onto the cedar slats of the bench. He stood up, straddling his legs over either side of me, his inflamed prick just inches from my mouth.

"You like my fishing pole?" He laughed slyly.

I began to lick him furiously, but before I could caress his scrotum with my lips, he pulled back. "Closer." His whisper was guttural, pressing for a kind of redemption. "Bring me closer, deeper."

There was only the veil of thick steam enshrouding us. I could no longer feel the bench beneath me. Only his broad shoulders above me. Only his sweat pouring into my eyes. Only his mouth breathing life into me. His rhythm pounding me, the bulbous point of his rudder, navigating through me, exposing me, until the waves and foam and froth were all I could own.

Inside me, he told me his life. He told me how he wanted to be a mapmaker. How he worked in the Maritime and later became a professional fisherman. He told me how to string a net. What time of year is best for salmon and walleye. What kind of cheese to use for bait. How to reel in a sturgeon. How to angle against the strongest wind currents.

"You want to be my captain?" I asked him as we gathered our towels from the bench.

"Your captain?" He looked curiously at me then over my shoulder again through the dense haze. "Captain of butterflies?" He seemed somewhat bemused.

I wiped the sweat from my face as I tried to make out his stuttered speech. He continued, "Captain of undertows? Captain of sunken voyages? Captain of black clouds? Captain of untamed grief, of sorrows?"

We soaped each other in the shower afterward and he told me about the vast fishing piers in Holland. How we might sit, the two of us, and watch the waves abrade the moss-covered jetty. How the color of the tulips fades to magnificent amber in late June. How I need to come visit him soon.

He promised to write me at the school in France where I was teaching. We promised to meet in the province of Friesland, in a little seaport town called Harlingen. He said he had friends there and that there was a lighthouse hotel that overlooked the ocean and the islands. He said we'd make love there. He said we would be the radiance in the tower that would guide the sailors home.

"Before I go, I give you a memento." He searched the pocket of his trousers for his keys, then took off the key chain and handed it to me. "You see the picture? It's a famous one, by the Dutch painter Velde."

A replica of the painting *An English Ship in a Gale* had been transferred onto a porcelainlike surface, about the size of a half-dollar. I rubbed my fingers over the black waves that seemed to swallow the helpless vessel.

"We'll stay in touch, won't we Wilhelm?"

If I linger here in this little room with its rising steam, its wooden slats and the bracing smell of eucalyptus and sweat, I can still feel him. How I would move my fingers over his tattoo that spelled *lampe,* the Dutch word for *trouble.* How he liked when I held his craggy face so gingerly in my hands. How I was struck with awe when he showed me the stitched wound left from a boating accident. "The motor almost took my arm." And how I kissed the thin line of scar tissue there until he smiled with relief. How I tried to harness his passionate thrusting, the pulse that moved through his arched back, his mouth that seemed to know each crevice of my body.

On a spongy floor mat I am waiting for the ocean scent of him, the memory that will reel me back into our dreamscape again, and in the long meantime, I touch myself, and wait for my fisherman. But he doesn't enter. The phone number he gave me never rang through. My emails thwarted. This bathhouse, still desolate.

I write poems on the back of matchbooks in my anticipation of him, building him, stoking his mythical iconography: lone ranger, renegade, brutal sea captain, champion of the foggy wharves. I imagine his arrival, wisps of smoke becoming his sturdy flesh, then those calm eyes with anchors in them, that wilted, benign smile yearning to break into pursed lips, and a searching tongue.

The dream boys are watching an old Steve McQueen movie dubbed into some language I don't recognize. McQueen is sporting a buzz cut and fiddling with submarine dials. The men here gape at the movie god on screen and he gives back nautical commands that make the dream boys wipe their palms and lick their lips. But not even this Hollywood idol can lure me in.

I have become kin to all the familiar initiations here. I know every pirate tattoo, the flesh piercings, and the slashed tongues; all the wounds and markings that will distinguish the warriors from the voyeurs here. I watch the naked wrestlers, watch for the times it seems like surrender, when they're rolling around on the hard floor mats, two mouths clamped over each other, trying to inhale the breath that might bring a complete rescue.

But it's always the same routine. A chorus of moans and an uncomfortable parting. A sheepish shaking of the heads after the failed alchemy. They barely look at each other in the shower room when it's over. And I begin to wonder if anyone can ever meet the one to surrender to in a Belgium bathhouse.

Sometimes I linger just outside the building, counseling myself not to go in, not to endure the waiting. I walk around the Place, staring at the fading facades of the Baroque Guildhouses, reading my favorite placards over and over, *Merchand of Gold, Samaritan, Golden Sloop*. I sometimes drink a heady Trappist beer at Café La Becasse and stare at the tourists darting from one basilica to the next. Or I talk out loud to the comic book characters painted onto the brick walls of buildings, and think how my life has become as cartoonish as theirs.

Sometimes, I take the Metro to the suburb of Laken, just outside of city central, and head up to the Royal Residences, just to wander through the exotic Chinese Pavilion and the Japanese Tower. I feel at home with these oddities, bizarre anomalies built by King Leopold the Second. Here, I can pretend I'm not in Belgium anymore; I'm in Yokohama, or Shanghai, thousands of miles away from ever reaching my missing captain, my Wilhelm.

They're putting flecks of fish food into the aquarium. The tetras and swordtails arrive first and leave only scraps for the tiny gold guppies. For nine months I've returned and sat in this room, eating my half-melted pralines from the *chocolaterie* and staring at the dream boys and the glowing tropical fish, but no sign of him.

A biker club from Berlin walks in and all the dream boys lose their stolid composure. One of the more surly looking gentlemen approaches three motionless youths gaping in their soggy towels and gestures for the trio to remove his leather chaps. Wordlessly, they oblige, and in less than five minutes, the lobby has become a free-for-all.

I am the creature who lives at the bottom of the sea. The mer boy hiding in the conch shell whose fins can't propel him to the surface. I possess a two-chambered heart that cannot take in the right oxygen. I want to breathe above the breakwaters because I am starving to death in the chilly depths. Engulfed, weighed down by the wanting of him, hypnotized by the graceful movements of dazzling seahorses, paralyzed somehow. I am sifting through sand, looking for lost treasures I know must be buried under this silt floor, piecing through the hopeless wreckage of a ghost ship.

The sex critic

ॐ

DIANE LeBow

ONCE UPON A TIME, in my younger days, I became a sex critic. Like a food critic, I've sampled dishes around the world. If food is one route into a culture, certainly *l'amour* is another. In fact, a full serving or two is a fine way to burn off some calories. Of course, I always insisted upon the highest standards regarding health, freshness, and sanitary conditions. Ruminations upon my *inamoratos* reflect on quality of service, location, presentation, cost, noise level, and so on. Then there are the five star lovers.

Oral/Aural Peccadilloes

Cross-cultural communication can sometimes be bizarre and amusing. As in many fine restaurants, when waiters or menus translate phrases into English, sometimes the expressions gain unintended meanings in the process: for example, "Cock in Wine," or "French Creeps."

Playing Catch in Egypt

This was certainly the case with Hassan, the Egyptian judge. I met him in the gardens of the Cataract Hotel in Aswan, where Agatha Christie's *Murder on the Nile* was set. After two weeks on a scuba dive boat in the Red Sea followed by a jolting bus trip from Sharm el Sheikh to Cairo and a flight to Aswan, I was ready for some coddling. He invited me to join him for tea, which was served elegantly with silver service and delicate biscuits, the Nile flowing smoothly beside our lounge chairs. After some days together of sightseeing outings to ruins, ancient burial sites carved into the mountains' rocky cliffs, mysterious smoking dens in town, and sailing on the Nile in a felucca, we became lovers.

This was not so simple, as there were guards on each floor of the large and elegant hotel whose job was to allow only those with rooms on that floor to exit the elevator. In addition, Hassan was a well-respected judge and had his reputation to protect. Somehow he slipped past a guard, perhaps offered him a *baksheesh*. His soft full lips, which for once didn't hold his ever-present pipe, caressed me as my hands explored his tanned smooth body. Hassan was a widower and from lack of use his appendage swung more flexibly than a belly dancer's gyrations. Very excited by the exoticism of the situation—my first foray into the Egyptian judicial system— my thighs clamped around his own and with the help of his fingers and the Nile streaming by just outside the window, I had a beautiful release.

Suddenly Hassan shouted, "I am going to throw." I leapt backward out of the bed, thinking he was nauseated or else feeling angry and was about to toss the lovely porcelain knickknacks against the wall or, worse yet, at me. How could I have known that the verb "to throw" was a literal translation of "ejaculate" in colloquial Egyptian Arabic?

Quiet, Please, Allah Is Listening!

We met in a hotel dining room in Nabeul, Tunisia, at a seaside resort. I was on holiday from teaching college in wintry Paris where sun becomes an atavistic memory. The creative *maître d'hôtel* seated me opposite, probably, the only solitary man in the dining room. My usual taste: dark curly hair, amber sympathetic eyes. He spoke French well but with a Tunisian accent. His English was another story. He used wonderful direct translations from Tunisian like: "I have the nose." That is he was getting a cold and congested sinuses. We fell in love and explored the ruins of Tunis, I thinking about how Dido set her bed on fire and climbed into it when Aeneas sailed away from her at this spot. Abdallah was an economist with the Tunisian government, divorced and lonely. "It's difficult for me to meet women, especially educated ones," he told me. "I am totally responsible for my ex-wife's financial needs until she remarries so I haven't much to offer a woman."

Although not quite like Dido, we did set Abdallah's bed ablaze. Skilled at rear entry like many men of Mediterranean cultures, after some exploratory stimulation with his fingers, before I expected it, he gently but deliciously slipped his strong and solid dick into my alternative entrance. Just as I began to vocalize my approval, Abdallah presented me with a completely new experience. Moaning, screaming, panting: all this, my Tunisian lover forbade me. "Shh, you make no sound until you *jouis,* come, and then you say only 'OK,' only that. It is forbidden to make any sound during sex because Allah will hear." It was only later that I wondered what prevented Allah from seeing.

Back Home in California: The Environmentalist
Even in one's native tongue, sometimes verbal signals obfuscate. When I was newly divorced, I joined the Sierra Club. "Want to have dinner one night?" queried the president of my local chapter. He seemed the perfect choice to begin my new dating career. However, his white plastic belt and shoes might have alerted me about possible kinkiness. He seemed so wholesome and normal. As he began to ejaculate, simultaneously he started intense gagging like he was about to vomit all over me. Since he was on top, I couldn't get out of range but turned my head and closed my mouth and eyes, afraid of what was about to come cascading down like waterfalls on our hikes in healthier moments. Fortunately he did not vomit. Afterward, I asked him about it. He replied nonchalantly: "Oh, that's just part of my primal therapy. Usually when we begin my session, I hide behind the couch in my therapist's office. When I start gagging, my therapist knows I am ready to be coaxed out. It's part of our game."

Sailing with the Producer

Sometimes lovemaking is an aural banquet. Such was the case with Dick the Orgy Producer. Dick invited me to join him for a dinner cruise aboard his yacht in San Francisco Bay. He studied sex like a postdoctoral candidate. He had vast photo album collections arranged by theme: breasts, group scenes, and various other parts of male and female anatomy.

Dick's imagination and words peopled our sea-cradled bed. He continually produced new ideas for the many combinations and permutations spilling out of his imagination into the cabin of his boat. "All of us here, we're like an erector set," he shouted. Dick was always patient and encouraging with our performers: "Jennifer, turn over and let me… Antoine, yes, yes, that's excellent." Two straight-laced looking nurses stripped and revealed their orgy outfits to us: tiny chains that connected the nipples across their breasts and similar ones looped from one nether lip to the other.

The cast of characters that joined us in bed during our frolics on his yacht was inexhaustible. Being in bed with Dick took on the aura of a scene from a Woody Allen film. What revels! And I've never been good at remembering names. There was Sam the Ram, Michelle the petite Parisian raven-haired dominatrix in her leather bustier and crotch-high stockings, Ramon the Argentinean gaucho, and Anita who loved to drape her milk-chocolate breasts over your face. Also participating was Monty the Tantra man, who with one finger could milk a woman's G-spot. Dick gave me stage directions: "You and Michelle, press your pussies together. Let your double dildoes do their job."

It was always surprising to open my eyes during one of our bacchanals and realize that, out there in the middle of San Francisco Bay, aside from the waves lapping at the sides of the yacht, Dick and I were the only ones present.

No Touching, Please, I'm from New England!

He used direct lawyer-speak: "Here's what I want. You sit over there, on that side of the room, and see if you can get me off by talking dirty to me. No touching. Stay away!" An attorney general from a New England state, we met at a Club Med on the west coast of Mexico. I was new to traveling alone in those days and thought a Club Med experience would be a gentle introduction to single wanderlust. When I booked my reservation, I didn't know that, at that time, Club Med was a swinging scene and attracted cartloads of American males out to score. In my innocence, I went there ready to swim and make friends at the advertised family-style dining tables.

Allen walked by at the far end of the beach where some of us went to sunbathe topless. His curly red hair stood up all over his head in an appealing manner from the salt water. Later, on the way in to dinner, he said "Hi" and asked if we could eat together. The next day we spent some beach and hiking time together. When we climbed up or down rocky spots, he insisted on holding my hand in an oddly authoritarian manner. "Just be a girl," he'd command. Since I was by far the more experienced hiker and he was slipping and sliding all over the place, it seemed that he was the one who needed some assistance.

When we got together in his room, it was another story. As I tried to hold his hand or hug him, he jumped back. He sat against the wall about fifteen feet away from me and challenged me to receive his words until I climaxed, with only my own digital dexterity for encouragement. "Now your turn to do me," he announced. "No, no, stay over there." He and his penis all alone in the corner, he pumped away.

I wonder what his Bostonian constituents back home would think.

Location, Location, Location!

Long the mantra in real estate, location is also a factor in the restaurant business. When you think about it, environs are of course a factor in lovemaking. You never know where your next love might lie.

Working Out in Paris

Jogging in the chic sixteenth *arrondissement* where I was living at the time, I was startled out of my jogger's meditation. A handsome forty-something Frenchman, wearing perfectly cut T-shirt and shorts over his well-toned and tanned body said, "May I jog beside you?" He had the self-assurance and directness of the *gauche caviar*, those wealthy French who retain socialist sentiments but live like royalty.

"I especially admire *votre décolleté*," he said, "the way they jounce as you run. Would you step into my garden with me and stand across the rose beds, lift your blouse and caress your breasts while I stimulate myself to climax?" Always curious about people's eccentricities, especially Parisian millionaires', I followed him on a path through the well-manicured rosebushes and hydrangeas outside his villa. It was early spring and I enjoyed the fragrance of his budding bushes as I tickled my own nipples. With classic French flair, he guided himself to a tidy climax with the same aplomb as a gifted cellist sliding his bow across his instrument.

Later he queried: "Have you ever been to the Bois de Boulogne—the special area where *les filles* are? We will drive through and watch them perform all sorts of acts. They are dressed in outrageous provocative clothing. It's all very interesting, very exciting. Would you like to do that?" I thought about cruising through the Bois in his red Lamborghini, which was parked in the curve of the tree-lined driveway, and scribbled down my phone number in his little book.

Cruising at Sea

On one unmercifully long cruise with my mother, we traveled for three weeks from the Caribbean through the Panama Canal and up to San Francisco. At meals, a man who sat at the next table from us and I eyed each other, spoke, then danced, and finally tried to find a private place. He was sharing his cabin with his young son and I mine with my mother. After midnight, wandering around the ship, we discovered an odd room off the gambling casino that strangely enough had a phone booth in it. The room appeared to be deserted so we started to hug and kiss, and finally I ended up on the little seat in the phone booth, as there was no other chair or place to recline in the room. He lifted the skirt of my evening gown, smiled approvingly and said: "Ah, dessert." As he licked and sucked as though I was a strawberry mousse tart, the door from the main casino opened.

We doubled up with laughter when a member of the crew started to enter the room, saw us, and grew wide-eyed. "We're entering the first lock. Did you want to come up on deck?" he asked.

Hay Bales: The Perfect Elevation

His lean cowboy thighs wrapped around a high-stepping, half out of control, five-gaited filly caught my eye. "I haven't seen that fine a gaited horse since I left the East Coast," I remarked to the young horseman trotting on the side of the road past my house. Such was the start of one of the most passionate love affairs of my life.

"Someone is coming down the aisle, just around the corner. We must hurry." When two hay bales are piled atop each other and when a five-foot, three-inch-tall woman lies facedown across the top of the bales, only her toes graze the stable floor. So when a wiry Levi-legged lover comes up behind her, he can easily slip himself inside her. The angle, the amount of pressure assisted by gravity, make it oh so perfect. Add to this the exhilaration of possible discovery by clients entering the stable where Rob and I were the trainers and you might say this was a recipe for a horse-country climax.

The Ninety Feet Under Club

My head inside a cave, fins floating upward behind me, I was concentrating on my underwater photography, when suddenly I realized those pleasant caresses were not the sea's undulations. Of course, an experienced scuba diver knows not to make any sudden moves so it took awhile before I pulled myself back out of the cave, sea life and soft gorgonian corals undulating all around me—along with my scuba boat escort, just off the coast of Cozumel. Under my bikini, which he had pulled aside, I felt warm and sticky, in contrast to the refreshing Caribbean water. I raised my eyebrows and we stared at each other through our masks, but there's no way to say, "What the hell were you doing?" at ninety feet under.

In a Tomb at Giza

The most embarrassing aspect of this episode is that I forgot to visit the sphinx. We drove out to Giza, Ahmad—my archaeological guide—and me. We had already spent several days together in rainy, muddy, December Cairo. After galloping Arabian horses around the Pyramids at sunset, we stopped to investigate some tombs that lay at the outskirts of the larger pyramid area. Inside the tomb, the air was still and warmer. He touched my shoulder and pulled me toward him. The idea of embracing inside a stranger's tomb, someone whose last climax finished a few thousand years ago, intrigued me. But it was rocky and dusty there. There was nowhere to even sit. "No problem," said Ahmad. He ran outside and after a few moments returned waving the saddle blanket from one of our horses that was tethered near the entrance. "Here we are." Ahmad carefully settled the blanket out on the widest area of the floor in the center.

Ahmad lowered his trousers and I pulled up my long skirt. My traveling skirt is especially useful in countries where squatting on sandy expanses without even a cactus to hide behind isn't uncommon. Rather than letting something out, on this trip, I took in a delicious firm young cock as it made its way around my hiked-up skirt and plunged into my juicy folds. As this five-thousand-year-old cavity let us enter its depths, my body opened up to this — perhaps — descendent of an early-Dynasty pharaoh, or maybe a layer of pyramid stones.

The only fresco left on the walls was a faded fishing scene, barely visible in the dusty light wafting through the open doorway. I thought about who was buried here and where they did their fishing as Ahmad and I threw our lines into each other.

Extraordinary Service:

The Cornwallian Chef's Special Sandwich

Returning my greeting, the chef opened his lips in a grin, allowing a large fish eye to protrude from the space where his teeth should have been. On a scuba diving boat off the Sinai Peninsula in the Red Sea, the ship's chef offered amusing and special services.

One evening under a starry Red Sea sky, he and I ended up in the rubber lifeboat up on the top deck. "Have you ever been in a sandwich? Shall I call Ted over?" offered my gracious host, eager to expand my menu. Since it's always my fantasy to have as many apertures as possible filled at once, I agreed. At the far end of the same deck, another diver lay either sleeping or enjoying the gorgeous night. He was a young Canadian, reserved, polite, but willing to participate in our bizarre diving activities. Like three buoys, we all cried out our succulent satisfaction, as the tan sands of the Sinai rose and fell in the moonlight just over the edge of our rubber dinghy.

Five-Star Lovers:

A Caymanian Prince Charming

I was scuba diving on Cayman Brac. Ed strummed his guitar and sang as I stepped off the plane onto the dirt runway. He owned a popular local restaurant, called Big Ed's, for reasons that became obvious as our acquaintance grew. The two hotels were full so I had a room in a private home, empty except for me.

"Oh, so sweet, it's so sweet," he chanted like a mantra as he slipped his thick, large, burnished licorice stick into me. I was both startled and pleased as I felt the breadth of his instrument part my lips and push fully, so very fully, deep inside me. Before I realized what was happening, I was swimming in a timeless flow of one perfect release after another. It is rare to have an instrument of such size and duration, attached to a man who knows how to make his rhythm, speed, and depth suit your every whim. Never since have I soared so outside of time and space as that night with Big Ed.

"I would like you to spend New Year's Eve with me at the party." In those days, this island was like a village where everyone knew everyone and celebrated events together at The Party at whoever's house was hosting it each time. At the lonely local hotel bar on the beach I sat waiting for Big Ed. When I told the woman bartender, she said, "What? He invited me too! Let's just go. I'll close the bar."

At the party, Big Ed was gyrating Soca, or Soul Calypso, with six women. He was, for obvious reasons, very popular with the women of the island.

Several years later I received news from the island. Ed had married, caught his wife in bed with another man, tried to shoot the other man, and was sent over to Jamaica to prison. I sigh to think of his gorgeous cock languishing in captivity. Perhaps he's been paroled by now. Time for another dive trip?

Prices Not Listed

A special meal, each course unique, offering a deeper comprehension of new worlds; music playing, candles, perhaps the sea just outside the window, your every desire anticipated and satisfied: do you worry about the final bill? I never did. *Bon appétit!*

sightseeing in the Holy Land

꒳

TABITHA FLYTE

ON THE THIRD FROM LAST DAY, Bob decided to stop talking to me. He said I was driving him mad, eyeing up boys like some kind of hussy.

"I'm not," I protested. "They're just kids!"

They were eighteen, nineteen, twenty years old, I suppose. Tall, broad boys in tight green or gray military shirts stretched over worked-out chests. Sun-roasted skin, sensual lips, and chiseled jaws. 'Course I was looking.

Bob never looked. Bob looked at his guidebook. It was Bob's life dream to go to the Holy Land, but we had our money stolen in Netanyah, Bob had stomach problems in Haifa, and Jerusalem was dirty. At first, he didn't even know we were in Israel, and when he cottoned on, I think he was kind of annoyed. "Israel?" he kept saying, "If I had known these holy places were in a dangerous place like Israel I wouldn't have come." Two weeks with Bob were proving arduous—and I had just vowed to spend the rest of my life with him.

The arguments started on the beach in Eilat. We lay frying on golden waves of sand under fringed sun umbrellas. Bob was snoring but I didn't even shut my eyes because I had never seen bodies like the ones there in my life. I was only interested for anthropological reasons of course. Bob thought I was getting at him. I wasn't; I thought we could share our awe and wonder; call it another thing on our "sights to see" list.

On the way up from Eilat, we saw a woman hitching at the side of the road. Bob, loving his neighbor and all that, didn't want to stop but I said "Come on, what's the problem? A girl on her own?" so he slowed down and must have decided it was safe. The girl threw a large rucksack in but then a man came running out from the bushes. "Thanks, thanks," they insisted; so we really had no choice, and all the while Bob was shaking his head at me, *see what you've done now*?

I was glad we had picked them up because we were on the kind of tour where you don't get to meet the locals. We had been shuttled around from sight to restaurant to anonymous hotel room and it was only in the last few days that we had dared strike out a bit. And now, we had two locals in our hire-car. I called that progress. The guy's name was Effi. He had olive skin, and his T-shirt was really small but I think it must have been deliberate because it made his arms look huge, like arms in those before and after adverts for weightlifting equipment (his were the "after," naturally). I couldn't stop staring at him. This was a better sight than the sun rising over freezing Mt. Sinai. This was better than getting salt in my eyes at the Dead Sea. I thought maybe he was looking at me then told myself not to be so silly. I didn't catch the girl's name and she didn't speak much English but she was gorgeous. Her breasts were like fat grapefruits squashed in a blue T-shirt and she was wearing cut-down shorts only she had cut them really, really high up her cheeks.

Bob didn't look.

Effi was a talker like me. He said that sometimes they found people lost or desperate in the desert — and they were the lucky ones. He talked about the sharks in the Red Sea and how they prey on menstruating women. Bob flushed. He hated words like

144

menstruating. Or perhaps it was the word *women* he disagreed with. "Danger is everywhere," Effi continued, oblivious. I didn't know if he was joking or not. He had mirrored sunglasses and when I gazed at him, I saw myself peering straight back. My hair was greased wet, and I had turned pink. Bob blew his nose; he hated the heat.

Effi played in a band. Bob smirked at me when he told us, like men in bands was some running joke with us. Effi shoved a tape at me and I put it on. The car was invaded by rock music. It wasn't great, lots of guitars and shouting, but it wasn't as awful as Bob evidently thought it was. Sand drizzled against the windows and it was so hot my bottom was sticky on the plastic seat.

The next time I looked behind me I saw that Effi had his hand right up the girl's shorts. She was pretending to look out the window, acting as though that tree over there was *so* interesting. It was right up there though, she wriggled and he put his arm around her and she sucked the fingers of the hand that wasn't. Then the cassette stopped and the silence in that car, apart from the failing air conditioner, was deafening.

"See that cactus," Effi finally said, pointing out the window. "It's said we Israelis are like cactus. Spiky on the outside…"

Bob smirked at me. *Sounds like you,* his look said.

"And soft on the inside."

"So, are you — like a cactus?" I said.

"I'm soft on the inside, yeah," he said proudly. Bob groaned even before Effi managed his punch line. "And hard on the outside, very hard."

Bob mouthed, *What an idiot.*

We were almost out of the desert when I saw the girl's jumper was over Effi's lap, and her hand was working up and down, up and down. Hard, very hard. He didn't even pretend to look out the window. He looked straight at me with his sleepy, down-turned eyes.

"Turn over."

"What?"

"The tape. Turn it over, please."

Reaching town, it was a relief to see wet greenery after that interminable landscape of sand. I felt elated like I had come out of a tunnel, or had just emerged from seeing a movie in the day and realized that it was still light. We ate falafel at a stand in the street crowded with trees, cabs, and people standing reading newspapers or chatting in groups and it sounded like they were arguing but Effi said they weren't. Until now, Bob and I had been eating neutral-colored international food at bland international hotels so this was a treat. I knew Bob wasn't happy though; this place wasn't in his guidebook so he wasn't sure if it existed or not. I could smell onions on Effi's breath but I still liked it when he stood next to me. The girl rested her elbows at the counter and appeared to go to sleep.

"She's tired," he said, "she don't sleep enough."

She muttered something in Hebrew and he laughed, his white teeth gleaming.

"What did she say?"

"She said, I don't *let* her sleep...."

I was just about to ask why he didn't let her, when I noticed his smile.

"Oh," I said. I wanted to change the subject. "How do you do this?" I was making a mess with my food.

"You open the pita bread carefully, you don't want to spoil it." He held a bread out to me, "then stuff it, it's good right? Squirt some of that, yeah, that stuff there, oh yes, cover it all, and then pop it in your mouth, mmm, tastes good."

"What was so funny?" Bob asked later. "What were you laughing about with Effi?" Bob said *Effi* like it was a swearword.

"No reason," I said.

They knew a cheap hostel where we could stay. It was over a vegetable shop and the drains outside were full of old leaves. There was only one room vacant but because it was getting too late to find anywhere else, we agreed to share it. We lugged our bags up three flights of stairs with peeling banisters. When Effi took my suitcase as well as his rucksack, I knew Bob's scowl was becoming permanent. We reached a room with oppressively low ceilings, a dirty stone floor, and two double beds. Both were covered with the kind of quilt your Grandmother would make. There was nothing else there except for a huge cockroach that scuttled across the floor to my toes. I screamed. Bob said scornfully, "It's no big deal." I couldn't tell what annoyed Bob more: the cockroach or my reaction. I realized he was trying to outdo Effi on the brave man front. But Effi wasn't playing. "The mouse follows the cockroach and the snake follows the mouse. And the snake," he said ominously, "is a very big deal."

Effi had food caught between his teeth, but it didn't detract from his looks. I don't know why but that and the onions somehow made him more real.

"Can I have a word?" Bob hissed at me. Effi winked, and said, "Sure, you honeymooners need some time alone," and he and the girl went out on the balcony. With the door open, the sounds of car horns and police sirens filled up the room.

Bob was angry with me as if it were my fault they only had the one room. He didn't want to get to know Effi and the girl. He said, "I didn't know they would be like this."

"They?"

"The Israelites, the Palestinians, or whoever they are. I thought it would be like on those films, Moses, Adam, and Eve. I thought people here would be more gentle, more religious."

"Jesus, Bob," I said, and he looked at me as if he didn't know me and then he started twitching his nose. He looked ridiculous.

"Now they are getting stoned out there!"

"I know." I was mildly impressed that he recognized the smell.

"Tell them that they have to leave."

"I can't do that," I said. "It's only one night—eight hours at the most. What can happen in that time?"

I sat with them on the balcony while Bob folded, packed and repacked his clothes, and checked his guidebooks. If you leaned over the iron railings and pushed your neck to the side and looked over ninety degrees, you could just catch a glimpse of the golden dome of a mosque in the distance. The scent of incense almost but not quite concealed the stench of cabbage from downstairs. The sun was setting. Purple streaks filled the sky, which makes it sound like an angry sky but it wasn't; it was tender and I would have liked Bob to sit with me out there, but he wouldn't. Two days to go, I thought. Two days and the rest of my life.

Effi went and got a watermelon from the shop downstairs. He sawed through its big red head and distributed the slices among us. My hands grew sticky. "You gotta suck the juice out of life," he said. I was sure he was looking at my tits. Through the doors, I could see Bob was still arranging his socks; I don't know what Bob was sucking out of life but it wasn't juice.

I noticed the chain around Effi's neck, the six points of the Star of David, and if I had known him better I would have touched it. I had a sudden image of that chain swinging in my face, his body sliding over me, his eyes shutting me out. Then the girl sat on Effi's lap. She smiled like a woman in a tourist board photograph. They started pawing each other and I felt lonely so I went indoors.

Bob was already in bed. I got in and gave him a kiss. The room vibrated with the sound of the call to prayer. "For heaven's sake," he said, and put in the earplugs we got on the plane. He was wearing the free socks too. "We're getting up at the crack of dawn. I can't cope with this!" For all his worrying, he still managed to fall asleep within seconds.

The other noise started after midnight. At first I thought it was animals. It sounded like a cat licking milk. Then I realized what it was. I tried not to think of anything, but the noise blotted everything out. And then the noise turned to groaning and whining and I could see the outlines of Effi and the girl in bed. She was under him and her legs were bent around him. He was pushing on her. I could see the movement of his buttocks rocking up and down. And they were groaning like I had never heard before, big fat groans, and I could hear him speaking to her, speaking disgusting things, *fuck, suck,* and *give it to me.*

It made me feel sick.

Of course, Bob slept through it all, oblivious.

After their noise had stopped and even the sound of the traffic had died down, I slipped out on the balcony. I didn't know the time but I knew it was late. The stars were brighter here and I thought of the star that led the Wise Men to Jesus all those years ago—that was what Bob would think if he saw it—and you could believe it because this was definitely the kind of place things happen. This was a place you could lose yourself. I went through the ashtray and found a cigarette end. I used to smoke before Bob. I sat on a plastic chair, which made ugly mosaics on my thighs, and lit up. I looked out on those old stone buildings, the narrow paved streets. In the daytime there would be a market, Effi said, where we could buy plates, sarongs—the things we tourists like.

If only something would happen.

I thought about everything we'd seen. I remembered the mud bath we took at the side of the Dead Sea but my mind was playing tricks on me. I imagined sliding on the mud, rolling in it, and then more people coming in. And I wouldn't know them, but they would be big men, like Effi and there would be women too, in those bikinis with the strings at the side, and they would ask me if I wanted a massage and I would say no, but they would make me, they would hold me down and their fingers would squelch and slime everywhere.

And I told myself, *Don't be so stupid, think about something else, anything else,* so I remembered the Dead Sea. OK, I was floating on the Dead Sea, reading a novel as you do, happy as Larry, then I pictured someone approaching. He would look like Effi, and before I could say anything he would part my legs, and start licking me there in the water, and of course, in real life, it would be too salty, but as I sat there, squirming on my chair, I thought, *Hmmmm, that would really be very nice.*

Even the Mea Sherim didn't escape my treatment. We had to cover our legs and shoulders to visit the religious quarter and the tour guide taking us around had warned that the male students must avert their eyes from all women. Now, I imagined that one of them, a horny teenager perhaps, couldn't help looking at my blouse. He saw my nipples poking through the fine cotton and he couldn't hold back any longer. I had him taking me into his schoolroom, having me there on his desk amid all his books, and when his fellow students came to chastise him, they would be so overwhelmed at the sight, they would pull off their capes and hats and take turns having me on the table, nailing me down, coming together in an Almighty Frenzy.

I'm going mad, I thought.

I must have been out on the balcony for about ten minutes when the door opened and Effi stood there in white vest, gold chain, black shorts, and fucking gorgeous body. I looked away.

"What you doing?" he asked.

"Nothing."

He asked for a cigarette. I said I only had this. We shared it. It seemed intimate and then I felt guilty and knew I should go back indoors but there was this lovely breeze now, and it was so warm, the air smelled so tempting.

"He's a bit boring," he said, nodding back at the room where Bob was flat out.

"Yeah," I said. I wasn't going to start making excuses for him. Bob *was* boring. I knew that. But he was comfortable and faithful. He didn't drink. He didn't beat me. You can't see the appeal?

Effi stood close to me. He was sweating slightly; a nice line of water ran down his forearm.

"Is she asleep?" I asked.

He smiled as though proud of his hard work. "They're both asleep. And we're both WIDE awake."

"Yeah."

I liked the way he said that. WIDE awake.

"You enjoying the trip?"

"I don't think it's what Bob expected." I fanned myself with my hands, *pheewww,* blowing bits of water off my upper lip.

"It's what you expected?" he asked, gazing into my eyes.

"It's different."

He stood closer. The heat of his thigh mingled with mine.

"You can't see much in three weeks. You should stay longer."

"Yes, well, Bob has his job."

"I don't think Bob likes me."

"He does," I lied.

"I don't care, I'm used to being disliked."

"What do you care about?"

"I want to have a good time—it's my right to have a good time."

I didn't know what he was talking about. I put it down to the age difference. He was much younger than me.

"You're looking for something, you're searching, right?" he said. He had the sort of stare you can't break away from.

"Sort of."

"Looking for satisfaction. The things you don't have at home."

"That's not true. But well, Bob is religious man. I think he was expecting to have a spiritual experience."

"Spiritual yeah?"

His breath was on mine. His cheek stubble was almost scraping me. He had strong hands. He was the same height as I was, but he was muscular, hard but lean. I thought again of the pale bookish students of the Mea Sherim. It was hard to believe they were of the same world let alone the same country.

"All that trust in God stuff is OK," he said, "but you have to have men of action." He paused. "Don't tell me Bob does it for you…in the bedroom?" His silver necklace shone.

"He does it for me," I said weakly.

"Yeah?" He was closer. "You get excited when you're with him?" His face was so near to mine that he was almost blurry.

"Move again, and I'll call him."

"Yeah," he said. His fingers were on my wrist. "Call Bob."

"I will," I whispered, knowing that I wouldn't. "I most definitely will."

"And what will you tell him?" He imitated me in this high-pitched silly voice: "Bob honey, I wanted to fuck this Israeli guy so bad."

"No," I said. I was backed right against the railings now. I felt like crying, but I didn't want him to go away, and I knew if I cried, he would. I kept my eyes fixed on a star, the star.

"Calm down," he said, and I thought about straddling him, bouncing on his cock, and watching his face as he came. "I'm not going to touch you."

I thought, *You're not?* and disappointment made my heart beat faster.

"That's my girlfriend in there. You think I'm going to screw around?"

That was exactly what I had thought. I felt ashamed and at the same time, I liked him even more for it. So he wasn't just after anything he could get.

"Hell no, I'm just sightseeing," he said, and smirked at me. I think I understood. "Tell me more about Bob."

"What do you want to know?"

"How often do you…fuck?"

The word gave me goose bumps. I was shocked. No one spoke to me like that. For the last few years, I had just been Bob Hague's girlfriend. Now I was his wife. "Once, maybe twice a week."

"It's not often."

"Often enough," I said, which was true. I gazed out over the balcony and noticed the dark shape of mountains beyond that I hadn't seen before. I thought it was funny how you could miss something so obvious.

"Does he ever lick you?"

"Occasionally." He had once.

"Tie you up?"

"No."

"Does he ever put his finger up your arse?"

"I'll tell you this," I said defensively, "one, he never ever has tried to fuck my friends; two, he doesn't go to lap-dancing clubs; three, he doesn't write dirty emails...."

"Yeah," he said. "You're right. That's the way to live."

I started to feel bad. "I'm going to bed," I said, but he grabbed my wrist. He had a small plaited band on his—a friendship bracelet, I think they're called.

"I can't sleep. I don't sleep. Really. I get bad dreams. It's much better to stay up all night. Really."

"Really?" I was laughing, but he wasn't.

"Come on, stay here with me. Take off your dressing gown."

"No...I can't...not with Bob just there."

"Bob's flat out with his earplugs in. It's just you and me." As an afterthought he added, "and the stars and the sky."

"He might wake up."

"So what if he does?" To tell the truth I wasn't completely against the idea. I mean, I *was* on holiday, and it hadn't been much of a holiday so far.

"Undo your dressing gown," he said again.

"I..."

"Come on," he said more gently, "I just want to look at you." I was breathless. "You're so pretty. You've got such a great body. I want to have a look at you."

"What about her?" I mumbled helplessly.

"She's sleeping too. Hey, I know you are looking for an adventure that you can't get at home. If you want I'll untie it for you."

"No, I...I will," I said preciously. I tugged at the dressing gown; it parted, revealing my legs, my white thighs. I looked up at him helplessly.

"Go on. Show me more," he said sweetly. "You're so attractive. I like your look."

I was wearing knickers and a vest and they were plain

white, not the sort of thing a guy like him would like, surely? I felt vulnerable, my hair stood out in the wrong way and I could feel my damp knickers were glued to me. Still, I spread the dressing gown so that he could see my tummy.

"Beautiful," he said. He didn't touch me. He just looked. I shrugged the gown off my shoulders and stood there in my underwear. If Bob came out now, I could just say I was hot. It was true.

"Now put your fingers down your knickers," he said.

"I won't."

"Do it," he said. He leaned against the balcony as though he was certain I would. "Come on. You've got to take care of yourself. That's the important thing to remember."

"I can't," but even as I said it, I moved my finger to the top of the knicker band. I remembered tracing the map of Israel with my fingers before we left. I remember thinking: it's so small, so tiny, yet everyone makes such a fuss about it. To touch myself properly, I had to spread my legs wider. He gazed at me longingly, and I could feel everything rush together yet at the same time move in slow motion. I parted my thighs for greater access, and each time I shifted he nodded, "That's it, get in there, get your fingers nice and wet. Take care of yourself."

I was thinking, *I will* not *show you how much I love it.*

"Show me what you won't show Bob."

So I did. He said he wanted to see my fingers right inside my cunt, so I showed him. I held myself open and I rubbed my clit, I masturbated myself, and I stopped feeling silly. I held on to his arm and after all these years, I felt I was letting go. I felt safe. I was going to come.

"I can't," I said and stopped. "I can't do this."

"Yes, you can, look at how well you've done so far."

"Please touch me," I whispered.

He shook his head. "I can't. You have to take care of yourself... but if you don't mind I'm busting out of here." I watched as he pulled down his shorts and his hard cock was fantastic and I would have done anything to touch it, but I knew that I couldn't. It required effort to keep my mouth from dropping open. I rubbed myself more. I was putting on a show—the best show in town and this one definitely wasn't in the guidebooks. We wouldn't touch each other.

We were only sightseeing. He stroked himself. His fingers were nimble around the head. He got into an expert rhythm down the purple shaft. *Land of Milk and Honey,* I thought; his milk, my honey.

"I don't want you to think about Bob or even me. I want you to think of hard cock and wet pussy, and how you are showing your cunt to a man you don't know."

"Yes," I breathed. And I knew he wouldn't believe how wet I was. Maybe it was a mirage but I knew I wouldn't last long. I was so desperate for it, I don't think even if Bob had come out then that I would have been able to stop.

I could hear him moaning softly, "This is good. You look hot. Tell me how you like it."

"Oh, yes," I moaned. "I love it. Feels so good." I felt like I was in one of those videos that Bob campaigned against. I was wet but I still managed to get some friction going. My fingers were scrabbling away in my wet cunt, all for me, all for him, his eyes on me. I thought I was dying, and I wanted the whole world to see me playing with myself, doing it for myself, feeling myself, in front of the best-looking man in the world and coming, yes, honey, coming, like everyone should and then the milk arched out from his cock over my thighs.

Afterward, we slid open the doors, stealing into the room like thieves and even when I tripped over a sandal, they didn't wake up. At 5:30 A.M. there was the deep, compulsive cry to prayer and Bob cuddled up to me, "Wakey, wakey." I hadn't slept at all. I had just dwelled on the mattress thinking of everything I had seen. "We've got a busy day ahead." The room still smelled of tired vegetables, but it was mixed with the smell of fresh bread too.

I could hear the others waking. I knew Effi would have a hard-on.

"I'm going to get ready." Bob kissed me on the forehead. He was refreshed. "Staying here wasn't too bad after all. Perhaps it's good to get off the beaten track now and then. You see more that way." I went out on the balcony ready to see the town wake up. The taxis and the busses had started up again, and there were people setting out their market stalls. Effi came out a few seconds later: black shorts, white vest, gold chain. We shared the end of a cigarette in the bright Middle Eastern light.

through the Looking glass

❦

GREVEL LINDOP

IT WAS THE LAST THING SHE WANTED TO SEE. She was so taken aback that she flinched on the threshold, almost causing the man who had insisted on carrying her case up to bump into her. For a moment she thought of complaining, but found she could not remember the Italian for "mirror." Instead the words *miroir* and *Spiegel* circled confusingly, and by the time she had banished them in favor of *specchio*, he was flitting about the room, showing her the minibar, the dimmer for the lights, and the switch for the air-conditioning.

Once she was alone she looked at it again, sidelong. Bad enough to have spent two days trailing around Next and Monsoon without finding anything remotely suitable. Why did the mirrors in shops always make you look so hideous? By the end of that first day's shopping she was telling herself it was no wonder David had dumped her. Though if a man asks you to marry him, then spends six months secretly dating someone else, there has to be more in the equation than an inadequacy of looks. On the second day she had bought herself several pairs of tights and settled for a black dress, short but not too short, for evenings. But the idea of this frumpish, twentysomething woman setting out for the *bella figura* world of Rome had almost scared her into canceling the trip. Only a reluctance to see the cost of a nonrefundable flight disappear into the black hole that had swallowed the rest of her life had kept her on course. I'll make myself inconspicuous, she told herself. I'll stay invisible, and perhaps Rome will lift my spirits.

And now here she was in what should have been the refuge of her hotel room on the via Margutta, confronted yet again by her own unwelcome image—weary from the flight, mousy hair lank and unkempt, face reddish and sweaty from the airport taxi—reflected in a huge mirror that occupied far too much of the wall behind the bed.

She turned away from it to look down into the slanting street, which blazed, yellowish-white and dusty, already thronged again after the midday lull. She wrestled with the catches and discovered how to open the window while partly closing the wooden shutter to shade the room. Then she tried to immerse herself in the childlike sense of nesting that goes with occupying a new hotel room: filling drawers, positioning hangers in the closet. But the mirror was always there at the edge of vision like another, colder window with someone else—her cumbersome self—moving behind it. It was better when she went to take a shower. The bathroom was a cool refuge and its small mirrors were intimate, like miniature portraits. They showed a face that was provisional, that would be cleansed and freshened in a moment.

The shower did its magic so well that when she wandered back to the other room, hugging herself dry in a huge, shaggy towel, it was a shock to see the pink, white-wrapped stranger turn to greet her as she approached the bed. She looked even more unkempt now, but, she thought, distinctly better. She let the towel drop and scrutinized her image. Breasts firm and still quite high. Tummy—well, easy enough to hold in, only needed toning really. Certainly not fat. She swiveled a little and peered over her shoulder, rising on tiptoe as if wearing heels. Ass—well, not huge. Cellulite? Maybe a little. Presentable. Would anyone take pleasure in looking at this body again? Could she, honestly? She didn't know.

But she knew she didn't want to see her every move matched by this full-scale reflection. The mirror was bigger than the bed, for God's sake. Who on earth would want something like that in their room?

And as soon as she asked the question she knew the answer. God, how naïve she was. A mirror that big at the head of the bed? It was for people who wanted to watch themselves. Honeymoon couples — or would honeymooners be jaded enough for that? Surely not. Middle-aged *second*-honeymooners, more likely. Or men who brought prostitutes here. She felt slightly sick. Was this a hotel where those things happened? She had asked the travel agent not to book her into a tourist hotel, to find a modest place where Italians themselves might stay. It looked sober enough — the little marble entrance hall, the old brassy lift in its rattling cage — but perhaps local people knew it for other things.

She had heard of mirrors on the ceiling — she glanced up at the unbroken white plaster — but behind the bedstead? Well, maybe. The head of the bed was white wrought-iron, a thin swirl that hardly obstructed the mirror. For an instant she imagined herself on the bed, straddling a man, thrusting down over his hardness, watching her movements in the glass. How could she want to do such a thing? Or crouching while he entered her from behind, meeting his eyes in that glass (she tried not to see David's eyes, and clenched her teeth). She felt hot and ridiculous. She clutched the towel around her and padded back to the bathroom to finish drying. Certainly she need not put up with it. She would rehearse the phrases, for her Italian was minimal, and ask to be given a different room, a room without a large mirror. *Senza uno grande specchio.* She plugged in the hairdryer decisively. OK. Nothing simpler. And better do it at once, or they might wonder why she hadn't made the decision immediately. It was, after all, a slightly odd request. Why would a woman *not* want a big mirror? Would they think she didn't like to see herself? She didn't, of course, but that wasn't the kind of thing you could so much as hint at, still less to a young male desk clerk, least of all in Rome. And she could hardly come out and say "Look, from the size of the mirror I can see whores come here, I can see this is a brothel."

She shook her hair out. With the shutters closed the mirror had taken on a slight amber tinge, and from where she stood by the window alcove, the images in it seemed to have a faint doubling, as if there were two layers of glass. She could no longer see herself but the glass reflected oblique strips of light thrown on the far wall from the louvered gaps in the shutter. Something made her murmur the word *brothel* to herself; and then, rolling the *r* extravagantly, *borrrdel-lo*. Was this a bordello? There was some subtle agitation at the back of her mind. She gazed at the mirror, at its dim and slightly distorted angular image of the room, its odd creamy sheen, and then her stomach gave a lurch, and she recognized what she had really known the moment she walked in. *A two-way mirror.*

That was what they had in bordellos. Of course it couldn't be on the ceiling. People watched each other. Some people *wanted* to be watched. Without moving, she gazed at the mirror—its curious honey-colored surface, its slightly multiplied reflections, the tiny speckles of inscrutable darkness here and there beneath its glaze—feeling as if it might turn her to stone. What sights had it seen? And—naked, she grabbed convulsively for the towel—who might be watching right now? She felt the hair prickling on the back of her neck, and goose bumps raising themselves over her breasts and spreading to her shoulders, followed by a scalding blush. Just a few minutes earlier she had paraded there, lifting and squeezing her breasts, turning her bare ass to the mirror. Thank God she hadn't touched herself anywhere really…special. Had she moved her hips around at that moment when she had thought of having sex on that bed? Surely not. Oh, God. As the blush fell away she grew cold. She felt lumpy, graceless, defenseless. Drawing the towel tight, she almost ran into the bathroom.

The one thing she wanted now was to get out of that room. Out of the hotel would have been better still, but how could she manage that? They would have to be paid, she had a firm booking. She felt tears pricking her eyelids. No, there must be rooms here that didn't have these mirrors. Maybe hers was the only one that did. Oh, God. A worse thought struck her. Suppose hers *was* the only one, did they reserve it for young women so that some pervert, some voyeur next door could watch them undress? But there was a double bed, they had warned her that the hotel had few single rooms and she hadn't minded. Did they sometimes put young couples there and hire the next room to someone who wanted to watch them?

Planning her campaign as if about to come under enemy fire, she considered exactly what she would need to fetch from the bedroom. Underwear, dress, shoes, makeup. Her purse. Italian phrasebook. She didn't want to spend a moment longer than necessary in that room. She took the bath towel and bound it around herself until she was swathed like an Egyptian mummy. To use her hands she had to wrap it under her arms, so she put another towel like a shawl over her shoulders. If some pervert were watching now, he wouldn't see a thing. Stiff with fake unconcern, she marched into the bedroom and grabbed what she needed. She couldn't resist stealing a glance at herself in the broad surface of the mirror, glowing now as the late afternoon sunlight melted toward evening. Was there a hint of light from behind it, some insidious gleam leaking from the next room? She almost hoped someone was watching. How disappointed he would be, how bored. He wouldn't get so much as a glimpse of her body.

Nonetheless as she dressed and made up in the bathroom she couldn't suppress a tinge of mischief. She applied the deeper red lipstick and rejoiced in her highlights. In the rich, slanting light that found its way through the frosted glass of the bathroom window her hair looked more a dark gold than the "mouse" she self-mockingly called it. She pouted at herself, widened her eyes challengingly, contemptuously. *Can't catch me,* she thought. Let him have a glimpse of her face, at least, and let him eat his heart out over what he was missing.

Her interview with the desk clerk was easier than she'd expected, and less productive. Yes, he understood, the room was noisy, it was right over the street, there were motorbikes and Vespas, yes. She did not need the large mirror, in fact she particularly did not *want* a room with a large mirror. (She was surprised to find her most unanswerable schoolteacher glare coming to her aid: he would know damn well what she meant when she mentioned the mirror, of course, and would understand that she had guessed.) And indeed he did seem a little flustered, a little confused, as if caught out. But she could not possibly be moved, he told her, before Monday, when the weekend guests would leave. Then they would have a perfect room for her, across the corridor. She argued, but he was adamant, his politeness became more and more perfect, he began to tidy the desk, he excused himself and spoke on the telephone, his eyes wandered away. She accepted provisional defeat. She would hold out until Monday.

Taking the lift down and wandering out through the vast double-doors into the warm, echoing street, she began to feel better. She had asserted herself. And what a story for her friends. My stay in a Roman bordello. It had a sleazy charm. They would laugh, and sympathize, and secretly they would envy her.

She strolled down the Via Vittoria and into the Corso. The shops were wonderful: the beautiful leather goods, the designer dress shops with their electrifying, minimalist window displays. Why were English shops so awful, half warehouse and half jumble sale? But would she dare enter these sheer, classic, art-gallery-like shops, even if she had the money? She ran her eyes lovingly over the gorgeous displays of shoes, the sparse dazzle of perfect jewelry in Bulgari and Tiffany.

As she made her way down toward the Victor Emmanuel Monument, the evening crowds seemed friendly rather than threatening. People walked the streets for pleasure, not just to get somewhere. They strolled, they spoke eloquently, they laughed a lot. She envied the effortless grace of the women, the way they clicked lightly along in their heels, negotiating with innate poise the awful pavements, a patchwork of cobbles and blobby tar, never putting a foot wrong. She admired the young men circling and swerving on their Vespas, pillion-riding girlfriends clinging to their waists.

Reaching the district of the pavement cafés, she wandered into the Piazza Navona, the long square walled with Renaissance palaces, each end decorated with a huge Baroque fountain and its crowd of lazily arguing people. She chose a restaurant. Dining alone didn't bother her: a teacher of French with half a dozen school trips behind her, she had learned to value solitary meals as a time for relaxation and people-watching. Lamps were lit. Further along the square a guitarist, a violinist, and a plump tenor began their sentimental repertoire. Rome, after all, was an adventure in itself. As for men, who needed them? Though she enjoyed it when the waiter arrived and began to pamper her outrageously, with just a hint of wistful flirtation.

After eating (the wine had been good too) she strolled over to look at the fountains. She was fascinated by Bernini's fountain representing the four great rivers; the titanic marble figures sprawled joyously, pouring their bountiful currents into the stone basin. She paged through her guidebook to identify the figures: fatherly, bearded Ganges; muscular young Danube; the River Plate, pudgy and elf-like (did Bernini imagine Native Americans looked like that?). But it was the Nile that enchanted her most, that beautiful, enigmatic figure (was it male or female?), hiding its face with a veil. The face was certainly there—you knew that from the position of the head and hands—but the sculptor had contrived it so that no matter where she stood, how she craned her neck, there was always something between her and the statue's face: one of the other figures, a corner of the great rock in the fountain's center, the Nile's own knee, veil, or hand. The guidebook said it was because people believed the source of the Nile could never be found, that it was eternally hidden. Her heart turned over as she read the words. What a pity men had insisted on tracing the Nile, she thought. Why couldn't people leave anything alone, why couldn't they just enjoy the mystery, the endless possibilities? She challenged the statue again, trying to find new perspectives that would let her glimpse the face. But no matter how she moved and craned, twisted and turned, that other face remained hidden from her, and she was glad. Let it stay a secret, she thought, let it keep its privacy.

A breeze sprang up and she felt spray from the fountain first dusting and then soaking a tract of her skirt. Goose bumps rose on her skin and she shivered. It was time to go back.

Rome, she found, was a city where you could walk alone at night without feeling afraid. She enjoyed the stroll and felt less reluctant to return to the hotel. No one was on the desk. To reach the lift you had to go up a small flight of stairs. She heard Italian voices, a man's and a girl's. Hanging back, she peered around the corner from the reception area to see them, the girl clinging to the man's arm, laughing helplessly, swinging one bare foot and clutching a shoe with a broken heel. The lift clashed and rattled its way down and the couple got in, the girl's giggles echoing as the cage closed and the lift began to rise. A call girl and her customer? she wondered. Or just a lively couple up for a few days in Rome, tipsy on wine and the excitement of the city?

Back in her own corridor, she took her shoes off and trod lightly. There was just one room beyond hers. She found a light switch and put the corridor into darkness for a moment. There was no light under the door, and surely no one would sit in darkness all evening waiting for her to come in. She let herself in as quietly as possible and without switching on the light pondered the huge mirror again in the soft glow from the street. How much could be seen from the other side? She put her face up close to its edge to estimate which parts of the room it commanded. Impossible to be sure. Perhaps the best guide would be which parts of her own room it reflected. She gazed into it, trying to imagine the room beyond. Was it luxurious, a fantasy of decadence, all gilded ebony statues and silk cushions? Was it a grubby, office-like space, a projection room in reverse, with the cold eye of a camcorder trained on the unforgiving glass? Surely not. It would be a bedroom like hers, with just that one extra facility.

But even as she tried to picture it she distinguished footsteps approaching rapidly along the passage, followed by the gentle click and crunch of a key in the lock next door. She jumped back from the glass as if caught in some shameful childhood act, as if she herself were the voyeur. She heard the light go on in the next room. Was it imagination, or did her room grow marginally lighter? Again, the mirror had that mild amber glow. Was it just the street lamps?

She had crushed herself against the wall beside the head of the bed so she would be invisible to anyone peering through. Now she felt stupid. She would not creep about and go to bed in darkness as if intimidated. Yet how could she switch her light on without making it known that she had been hiding? Irrationally, she felt herself blushing. In the end, feeling silly, she crept out of her room, key in hand, sweating lest someone came along the corridor, and noisily let herself in again, switching the light on at once, making believe that she had only just returned. God, was this kind of playacting going to rule her life until Monday? She couldn't bear it. Bracing herself to move around the room she turned the light down in favor of the lamp by the bed.

She collected her night things and marched into the bathroom to get ready for bed. Would it be possible to drape a sheet or towel over the mirror and so mask it off? Wrapping herself in the deliciously soft hotel bathrobe she padded back, stone-faced, to the bedroom. The mirror had a surround of flat gilded wood so broad that it was impossible to tell whether the glass was set into, or merely laid on, the wall. Nothing would hang on that frame, it was too flat. She would need thumbtacks to keep a sheet in place, and might be accused of causing damage. She would have to live with it. She took a pile of magazines, fetched a bottle of mineral water from the fridge and went to bed. At least, she told herself, no one could see more than the back of her head as she sat there. If they were watching now, fine, let them go fuck themselves.

She put the light out soon—darkness was her refuge—but found it impossible to sleep. Rationally she knew no one could be watching now, yet her body refused to relax. Gently she ran her fingers, feather-light, over her belly to calm herself. The sensation was soothing. It seemed to take her out of her thoughts. She moved her hand down a little further, wondering whether to masturbate. No one could see, no one could know. She stroked her inner thighs, moving her fingertips inward to her labia, caressing herself subtly. She thought of the young men she had seen that evening on the Corso: the toned bodies in the immaculate designer T-shirts, the mischievous smiles, the touch of chivalry in the way a young man moved a hand back to reassure the miniskirted girl riding pillion on his Vespa.

She imagined catching his eye, attracting his interest so that he swerved gracefully, pulling the Vespa over alongside her, his dark-haired girlfriend petulant that he was paying attention to *her*. She ran her fingers up his bare arm and he leaned over to kiss her but as he did so she dodged him flirtatiously and took the soft hand of the girl on the backseat. He would just have to watch first, she would show him something that would drive him crazy. She pulled the girl down on top of her, slipping her hands deftly up the tiny skirt and running a finger along the line of the thong. Knowing just what was wanted, the Italian girl knelt, bowed her head and began gently to tongue her, tracing teasing concentric circles around her clitoris. The boyfriend was appalled, astonished, excited. He protested, but his girlfriend wouldn't be stopped, she slid her tongue deep inside, then returned to a relentless teasing, sliding a finger in gently, concentrating on treating her to an exquisite orgasm.

But now it was time for the boyfriend. Over the dark girl's head she met his eyes and they had a secret understanding, he had his cock ready and at the critical moment she pushed the Italian girl aside, grabbed her boyfriend and guided his hardness right inside her, still massaging her clit and making him fuck her deeply, expertly, while the other girl watched, helpless, in a torment of mingled excitement and jealousy.

She came, shuddering and arching her back, so caught up in her orgasm that she allowed a little moan to escape her before it occurred to her that whoever was in the next room had probably heard her. But so what if he *had*? The idea fired a tiny spark of power within her. In this darkness, she could be her own person, perform the most intimate act, and he could never know for certain what she did. She imagined a man with his face pressed against the glass, peering through into the darkness above her, desperate to know what exactly she had done. Serve him right, she thought. Let him be driven crazy with unsatisfied curiosity, unquenched desire, his voyeuristic hopes unfulfilled. Maybe she'd torment him every night in different ways, letting him guess that she was undressing, masturbating, making love with some boy she picked up on the street or even—yes—some woman, but always in darkness and with tiny muffled sounds so that he could never, never be certain. In fact, she thought jubilantly, *break his fucking heart.*

She let the fantasy fade. But the after-bliss of her self-pleasuring still soothed her and as she let go of her thoughts she was already floating, nameless and invisible, into the boundless mirror of sleep.

When she awoke it was daylight and still early. She felt a renewed energy: all she had to do was stay out of her room. Easy, there was the whole of Rome to explore. She waited to go to breakfast until after she had heard the door of the next room open and shut, so was thoroughly nonplussed when she stepped out of her door straight into the path of a tall man just leaving the room next to her own. He stood back and bowed slightly but beyond registering dark eyes and what seemed an enigmatic smile she was too paralyzed by shock to take in his appearance, or respond in any way. She had no alternative but to walk along the corridor in front of him, feeling his eyes boring into her back and seething inwardly at the thought that this man was quite possibly spying on her, had perhaps been booked into the hotel specifically on the understanding that a young woman would be in the next room for his visual pleasure. Well, she just hoped he felt thoroughly cheated.

He sat alone at breakfast, which was self-service, and when

she crossed the room to fetch coffee she heard him speaking to one of the other guests in an accented Italian that suggested he might be French. She stayed as far from him as possible.

She spent the day exploring, seeking out a few sights that aroused her curiosity but otherwise ignoring the guidebook. By late afternoon she was footsore and made her way, reluctantly, toward the hotel. At the foot of the Spanish Steps she threaded her way through the gabbling crowds of tourists to the sanctuary of Babington's English Tea Rooms. There she sank gratefully into the cushions to take comfort in exquisite chocolate cake and Earl Grey tea. Browsing in the guidebook she luxuriated in the thought of the literary tourists who had sat there before her: Henry James, Katherine Mansfield, E. M. Forster. In the house opposite, she read, Keats had died in 1821. It was now a museum, maybe she'd visit tomorrow. Keats was a bit of a voyeur himself, she reflected. Didn't the hero of *The Eve of St. Agnes* hide in a closet to watch his girlfriend undressing? They'd studied it at school and she'd found it silly but exciting. She'd imagined herself sometimes as the heroine, letting that dress slip slowly half off — a line came back to her now, "Her rich attire creeps rustling to her knees." That wasn't the way a girl undressed on a freezing night. Keats' heroine must have known her lover was watching, she was just playing with him, teasing him. Turning his voyeurism into her power.

Was that how it worked? If you knew someone was watching, did that hand you the power? Her fantasy of last night came back to her. *I can drive him mad,* she told herself with a little flush of excitement. *I can't get back at the bastard who dumped me but I can tear this guy to pieces with unsatisfied desire.*

It was evening and she'd been out again for a meal and a little too much sparkling white wine before she had a chance to put her resolve into practice. With the wine it made her feel almost too high, so that as she got into the lift she found herself giggling with nervousness, and had to hold her breath while she checked for light under the door of the next room. This time she left the corridor in darkness. The light in the room next to hers was on and — wouldn't you know it — as she put her key a little shakily into the lock of her own room the light next door clicked off. He knew she had come in. He was waiting.

She flooded her room with light. *Damn you,* she thought, *I'm going to make you wait.* A kind of inspiration seized her and, unable to hold back, she strolled toward the huge mirror, kicked her shoes off, knelt on the bed and checked her makeup, narrowing her eyes and pouting her lips an inch or two from the glass to apply a new coat of lipstick, pressing her lips voluptuously together. She could clearly see a minute black speckling at the back of the mirror: a sign of imperfect silvering, the microscopic gaps that let light through so that someone, in darkness, could watch from the far side.

She found that she was enjoying this moment of theater. The actress's role gave her protection. She was untouchable and in charge. She had deliberately put on a low-cut top, and now, casually and with concentration, she leaned forward to adjust her bra, giving the watcher a long moment to gaze down into her cleavage, between the generous curves of her breasts. She could guess how alluring she must look to him. No matter what she might or might not see in herself, she could read her body now as if it were someone else's and knew she had beauty enough to rip any man apart.

Moving away from the mirror she slipped off her top and dropped it on the bed. Turning this way and that she pretended to admire her breasts and then, almost trembling with the excitement of it and yet desperate not to let the trembling show, again with her back to the mirror, she unfastened her skirt. Her lace panties were nothing special but she sensed that for the watcher they promised everything. He would be praying that she would take them off. Perhaps he was already stroking himself, building his climax for the magical instant when she would turn to the mirror utterly naked. And she would not give him that satisfaction. Her nipples were erect and she felt moist between her thighs as she tremblingly unfastened her bra, slipping the straps from her shoulders so that it stayed loosely perched on the fullness of her breasts, ready to slide off at any second. *Shall I put the light out now,* she wondered, *or shall I flash him a nipple to let him see what he's missing?* Supporting the bra with one forearm she faced the mirror and, with an air of consummate casualness, let one cup fall away. Elated by the beauty of what she found herself revealing to another, she stepped quickly to one side and turned out the light. *Show's over,* she whispered to the mirror. *Sleep well, you poor bastard.*

He was there again at breakfast. She felt him looking at her.

When, later, he left the hotel, she followed him through the streets. She wanted to know what kind of man he was, who could do this to a total stranger. He was dark and quick-eyed and wore an Armani suit — he looked to be in his thirties — and went to a gallery full of marble tables and small sculpture. He spent a long time in the back while she browsed in and out of dress shops opposite — everything seemed to be open although it was Sunday — keeping an eye on the door. When he left she went after him again. Where was he going? Would he visit a brothel, or was the one she was staying in sufficient? Did he have a wife, a mistress, a girlfriend? When he had lunch at a restaurant near the Borghese Palace, outside under a trellis of vines, she found a table in a far corner, and was embarrassed when, having paid his bill, he nodded to her on his way out.

By the time she'd settled her own bill he'd vanished, so she followed the other part of her plan and walked down to the Corso where she nerved herself to go into a shop called Intimissimi, whose windows displayed an achingly beautiful range of lingerie. One assistant spoke charming English and took delight in helping her to choose the most minimal and stylish white bra and G-string. She pressed her face into the filmy fabric and felt ready to fall in love with herself. This was it, she told herself, now she'd rip his heart out with desire. He'd never forget her. She'd haunt his dreams.

She drank coffee in the bar opposite the hotel until she saw him return, late in the afternoon. She gave it five minutes by her watch and then followed him in; she didn't know why, maybe it was that now she was playing cat and mouse with him, closing in for the kill. It was almost as if he were her property. He had arranged to spy on her, to take advantage of her, and she'd turned the tables.

She made sure he was in his room (she could hear water running, the creak of boards as he moved about inside) before entering her own, taking her clothes to the bathroom to dress for the evening. The fabulous Intimissimi lingerie caressed her body, she applied her makeup with artistry. Ready at last, she twirled in front of the big mirror to let him see what would never be his. She felt his eyes on her, his longing like a magnet tugging through the glass and she lay back a little on the air, resisting the tug, knowing that she had control. It was like learning to fly.

When he went out for dinner she followed, invisible. She

felt she could anticipate his every move, know which street he would turn into, which shop window he would pause to glance at. Her steps matched his so closely that she felt the need to take extra care on the uneven pavements: if she stumbled, he too might miss his step. He made his way to a modest restaurant and she followed him in after an interval, passing his table without a sign and taking care to sit in a back room, just beyond the *ortolano* buffet spread with its wonderful array of vegetable dishes, fish, cold meats. There she would not be trapped between him and the door. Now he was the one trapped. And so she kept him when at last he walked, by way of the Piazza del Popolo, back to the hotel. Instinct told her he would be waiting, that the mirror would be at its most permeable that evening. She wished she had thought of setting candles in her room.

Leaving the lift on the second floor she found he had taken the stairs. He appeared at the top, a smile playing about his lips, his dark eyes suddenly warm as they met hers. His look was conspiratorial. He knew all right. Yet how could he *do* this to her? she asked herself. How could he time it like this, match his return so neatly to hers, turn with such amused politeness to stroll up the corridor—she refused to walk ahead of him—and let himself into his room with a polite "*Bonsoir, mademoiselle*" to relax by his mirror to await the show, as if she were some stripper, some porn actress, some call girl hired to give an exhibition?

God, she'd show him. She let herself in and flicked on the lights: soft, but bright enough so the bastard could see through that mirror, see what he'd never be allowed to touch. She pirouetted, slipping her hands under her silk jacket to caress the outline of her breasts. Then she slid it off. She lay back on the bed, bending one leg, letting the skirt slide back to show the top of her lacy holdup stocking. She was wearing her highest heels and she knew how long her legs would look, how any man would thirst to run his fingers over them and palpate the creamy softness of her thighs. She knew how desperate he would be to see more, that he must already be stroking his cock, praying for the next revelation.

Well, she thought, *let him. By the time I've finished with him he'll be out of control, he won't need his hand, he'll come prematurely, the pervert bastard.* She stood up, facing away from the mirror, and glanced back teasingly over her shoulder. She moved a small green velvet-covered chair to the center of the room. Languorously and with increasing delight, she began to strip. As she discarded her clothes she made love to her body, teased and caressed and worshipped herself as never before, cupping her breasts in the lacy white bra then, once she had removed it with tormenting slowness, squeezing and bouncing them, circling each aureole with a fingertip, teasing each nipple until it stood up stiffly, forcing him to see how she could love and seduce and pleasure herself. She stroked her thighs, slipping her hand into the tiny frill of the thong, delicately parting the moist, sensitive lips and momentarily running a finger, feather-light, over her clitoris—it felt enlarged and sensitive as never before—imagining how he would beg to be allowed to touch her and how she would always refuse him. Then turning from the mirror she began to slide the thong down, letting him see the lovely curves of her ass which she knew would drive him crazy, though not as crazy as what she would show him when she turned to loll back into the velvet chair, bend one beautiful knee—she felt a melting deep in her belly as she saw herself in the mirror, haloed with raging and indecent beauty—and parted her labia to show the naked crystal of the mirror the glistening shell-pink of her inner lips and the taut bud of her clitoris.

Now for the *coup de grâce*. She felt her whole body go into meltdown as she opened herself to the stranger's gaze and her own, slid a finger between her thighs and began to pleasure herself, wriggling and moaning to torture him and to express the overwhelming pleasure which unfurled like a burning flower through her body. She held back as long as she could, tormenting herself and him, and at last, shaking and panting in the contractions which flooded through her, she came and came, knowing that he too had lost control and was unmanned, his hardness turned to irretrievable liquid, while she gasped "You bastard, you bastard, you fucking bastard" over and over again.

A while later she put the light out. "Don't tell me you'll ever find another woman like me," she told him. "Don't tell me you'll ever forget me. Don't tell me you'll ever even be able to *sleep* again for thinking about me, you bastard, you bastard." And as she lay in bed spent and waiting for sleep it seemed only natural that silent tears should be running down her cheeks and soaking the pillow.

It was a surprise in the morning when the desk clerk spoke to her. At first, seeing the Frenchman passing through the reception area — he looked more melancholy than usual, tired and preoccupied, and no wonder after the mind-blowing show she'd given him last night — she hardly took in what the clerk was saying. He repeated it. The Signora could now leave her room. If she would have her things ready by ten, he told her, she could change to another. Guests had left, the new room would be ready for her.

She felt panic. She didn't want to go. The room with its mirror was the place of her power. How else, she wondered, would she communicate with her victim? How else devise further punishment for him? But then she realized that her move, her disappearance from his magic window, would be his final torment, the act that would burn her into his memory forever. He might never see her again.

So she moved. The new room was on the other side of the corridor, away from the street. An ordinary mirror hung on the wall by a chain as well-behaved mirrors should. There were no telltale dark specks in its depths, no amber tinge, no double image. It was a tame mirror. She looked at it with a certain contempt. *You don't know what you're missing,* she told it with a little grimace.

Handing in her key at reception a few minutes later she was surprised to find the Frenchman once again at her elbow. He bowed, and the ironic, conspiratorial smile blossomed slowly on his face. *"Mademoiselle,"* he greeted her. He offered his hand. *"On m'a dit que vous allez partir ce matin, est-ce vrai?"*

For a moment she was paralyzed. She felt herself blushing. How dare he? Was he going to apologize, or what? *"Non, non,"* she tried to explain. *"On s'est trompé, il ne s'agit que d'un changement de chambres."* He must have overheard the earlier conversation at the desk and thought she was leaving rather than changing rooms.

The stranger seemed to brighten up. His eyes widened. *"En ce cas..."* In that case he would be delighted if she would be kind enough to join him for lunch, especially as he believed that they preferred the same type of restaurant? He raised his eyebrows and the teasing smile returned.

She couldn't believe it. He was actually asking her out, after all that had happened. For a long moment she stared at him, trying to come to terms with it. She knew that he'd been spying on her. And he knew she knew. And she knew he knew she knew...and so on, like a pair of mirrors reflecting each other to infinity. And yet, and yet: if neither mentioned it, if no one admitted to knowing it, it would all stay in the land of secret things, things that happened that had never really happened, hidden like the source of the Nile. No, she must confront him, she would go out with him, she would take the chance to tell him what she thought of men like that. Stiffly, she accepted. She went to her new room to arrange her things, steady her nerves, decide what to wear.

This time the restaurant was tiny, hidden above a shop in the Via Vittoria. She wanted to know what he would eat, and ordered the same. He ordered a sweet musky wine she'd never tasted before. He seemed gently protective, subtly amused at everything she said. Was he laughing at her or with her? They talked about Rome, which he knew well. He was from Lyon, he ran the family business in partnership with his brother. He came to Rome every few months to buy Italian reproduction furniture to sell in France. He had gentle, expressive hands with long fingers. He wore no wedding ring. She didn't ask if he was married.

She tried to keep herself aloof, to avoid laughing at his jokes, though his warmth and the conspiratorial twinkle in his eye made it hard. After the pudding—an exquisite concoction of ice cream, chocolate, orange zest, liqueur—she tried to challenge him. So he came to Rome often, did he? And always to the same hotel? Yes, he told her, nearly always: not just to the same hotel but to the same room.

She was astonished at his blatancy. How many women had he watched through that mirror, she wondered. "*Et pourquoi choisissez vous toujours la même chambre?*" she challenged. "*Ah!*' he raised his hands a little. "*C'est pas toutes les chambres qui ont un tel panorama!*" Not every room has a view like that, all right, she thought. His complacency astounded her. "And what," she asked him in her best and iciest French, but in a voice that trembled, "what gives you the right to watch me as you have done?"

To her amazement he laughed. "*Mademoiselle,*" he replied, "I believe it is you who have on occasion followed me, *non?*"

She felt furious. As if her observation of him were on the same level with his invasion of her privacy, as if it cancelled everything out. "And the mirror?" she asked, "That huge and horrible mirror? In *my* room? In the hotel?"

"*Le miroir?*" Startled, he seemed not to know where to look. "*Le miroir? Ah!*" He lifted his hands in an ironic shrug, then glanced around at the other tables, the glint of conspiratorial humor sparkling again in his eyes. "*Oui, c'est une vulgarité; si j'ose dire, une vulgarité*" (and he whispered) "*un peu Italienne.*"

So a two-way mirror was a typical piece of Italian vulgarity, and that was that. He took no responsibility. She struggled for words but found none. Impossible to hate him, he hardly seemed to know what he'd done, what he'd inflicted on her. She gave it up. He paid the bill and they strolled back, and it all happened just as she had known it would. So that when, back at the hotel, he invited her into his room, she faced a choice that, she realized in a dazed way, she had always known would come. She could slap his face, turn away and leave him to his own demons. Or she could cross the threshold, step into the Looking Glass room, take the unknown that would come.

And, as she had known she would, she chose the latter. He unlocked the door (the sound of that lock so strangely familiar to her) and she entered the room like a sleepwalker, sure that she walked into a trap but unable to hold back, needing at all costs just to *know*. Hearing him close the door behind her she stared numbly ahead, her heart pounding. This room was almost a duplicate of the other, its window toward the street shuttered, but at her left were small French doors to a balcony looking out on the Borghese Gardens. She could hardly pull her eyes away from the view they offered, dreading the bleak, cavernous hollow of her previous room that would loom through the unsilvered side of the mirror. Her stomach clutched as she thought of what she would have to say to him.

He spoke but she couldn't take it in and with a clenched effort turned toward the bed. And there it was, the great surface of glass. Through it she saw an empty bed, the shadowy depth of a room; and at the far end, pastel-bright French doors. Disoriented, for a frozen irrational second she lost all sense of which way she was facing, which room she was even standing in. Of course, she told herself, the light from outside must be too bright now for the other room to be clearly seen. It *must* be so. He spoke again, questioningly, but she was kicking off her shoes and kneeling on the bed. She pressed her palms flat against the glass and gazed into it. Only her own eyes met her, staring back. Here and there was a dark speckle of imperfect silvering, the mellow, blemished complexion of an old looking glass. There was no two-way mirror. Had she ever thought there would be?

She felt at once huge relief and dreadful disappointment, an impulse to laugh and cry simultaneously. Then she felt his hand gently caress the hair at the nape of her neck. She stiffened but again looked into her own eyes. The thought came to her, *You're through the looking glass now. You can do whatever you like.* With a sudden impulse she turned and pulled him down on top of her, feeling his lips and then the tip of his tongue against hers as she parted her lips and opened to his kiss. Tenderly his hand stroked and kneaded her breast — she craved for more pressure and luxuriated, pressing herself against him, as he gave it. He reached down to trace feather-light patterns on her inner thighs. She shivered with pleasure, stroking the back of his head as his mouth burrowed exquisitely into her neck.

Then, leaning up on one elbow, she turned the tables, kneeling astride him, helping him to undress her, struggling out of her top, leaning forward so he could unfasten her bra, then swaying her breasts temptingly over his face, arching her neck and clutching his shoulders as he sucked her nipples. She dragged her skirt and panties off, kicking them out of the way, keeping her stockings on, crouching over him and opening her thighs as his hands explored, tantalizingly stroked the fine fuzz of hair, teased the lips of her cunt. Already she could feel herself growing slippery and open. His finger began to circle around her clitoris, then slipped just inside her and began a tender massage at the most sensitive spot while his thumb kept up a rhythm on her clit.

Loving her naked vulnerability but determined not to lose control yet, she began unbuttoning his shirt, kissing his chest as she worked her way downward, gently removing his hand and pressing it down for a moment on the duvet as if he were her prisoner. Soon he was naked and from the tension in his body she could tell what he wanted. She wriggled down the bed and took his cock in both hands. It was firm, fully erect, charged with tension. Trailing her fingertips up and down the shaft, she watched him shiver and heard him gasp at her touch; then, leaning forward, she ran her tongue lightly around the rim, almost laughing at the sense of power it gave her to see him so helpless, drawing back to watch the drop of moisture that appeared like dew at the tip, then taking the head into her mouth, twirling her tongue around it, sucking hard and then letting her teeth to glide over the rim so that he gasped again, arching his neck as if he couldn't stand any more.

But she knew there'd be plenty more. She looked into his eyes. "Oh, my darling," she told him, "how I'm going to *fuck* you," reveling in the hardness of the English word. She sat astride him again, stroking the tip of his cock against her clit, slipping him a little way into her soaking cunt and then out again, using him as a toy, letting him thrust with his hips but controlling him to bring herself each time closer to orgasm yet not quite allowing herself to reach it. When she was biting her lip and shaking with the tension she at last permitted herself to mount him fully, sliding his cock deep inside her, swaying her hips to and fro, riding him to gather his firm thrusts at exactly the right spot, leaning forward to press her clit hard—and still harder—against him. And she stared into the mirror to watch herself, shameless and victorious, until she could take the unbearable rhythm no longer and had to close her eyes, shuddering and gasping as her orgasm welled up again and again, melting, flooding and uncontrollable.

Later he fetched champagne from the fridge, leaving the bottle and two glasses on the table while he went into the bathroom. Deliciously lazy, she lolled in bed, watching herself in the tall mirrored door of the wardrobe opposite. Reflecting the glass behind the bed, it multiplied her image to infinity. She scrutinized her reflection. So many selves, she thought. So many moments, so many possibilities. Her other bodies—her other selves—stretched away, further and further, more and more mysterious, into the shadowy depths. At the center of it all, gazing back at her, was her own present face. It hid all the faces of those other selves. She challenged the glass, trying to find new perspectives that would let her glimpse her other faces. But no matter how she moved and craned, twisted and turned, those other faces remained hidden from her, and she was glad.

whitewood

༄

A. F. WADDELL

"AL, ARE YOU PACKED YET? Be sure to take something light and cool."

"Almost finished!"

"And make sure to color-coordinate! Oh, here. Just let me do it for you. Ecru, oatmeal, cream, tan. These go together. See?"

"Yes," he sighed. "But I'm not wearing pink."

"Your walking shorts are salmon, not pink."

"Whatever. Wow. A long weekend! It's going be great to get out of Baton Rouge for a few days."

Alan and Bethany Bateman had recently moved from Oklahoma. They were originally from Northern California, and had experienced culture shock as they moved from region to region across the United States. Alan's career in industrial consultancy had brought them to Baton Rouge, Louisiana. Bethany was a nutritionist. She could work in almost any city.

As they drove south on Highway 1, the odor of the Mississippi drifted from the east, across the two-lane blacktop.

Alan crinkled his nose. "Wow, the river smells really rank today. Imagine...PCBs, pesticides, volatile organic compounds, oils, heavy metals, and dioxins. Nasty!"

"Al, that's frightening."

"As it should be. In parts of Iberville parish, drinking water can be the color of tea and smell like rotten eggs."

"You need aromatherapy. 'Honeysuckle,' isn't that a lovely word? I like it as a verb too!"

"A verb? Use it in a sentence."

" 'She honeysuckled. He honeysuckled. They honeysuckled.' "

Her hand drifted down and rested on his thigh. "Hey, I'm driving here!" he laughed. "But don't stop."

She smiled and rubbed his thigh before slowly moving her hand over his cotton-covered cock, its lines and curves teasing his shorts, pink straining against pink. She unfastened his pants and pulled down his cotton briefs. Her head moved over his lap. Eye to eye with his monster, she licked and kissed its tip, taking it into her mouth, sucking it, moving her mouth up and down its shaft. Blow Job Protocol applied: lips together, teeth apart. Tongue on the sensitive underside. Lay out a tongue cushion. Slack the throat.

"Beth! Let me pull over. Let me find a place!" He made a right turn onto a narrow secondary road, went a distance, and pulled over. Dappled sunlight played through the trees and into the car. Through his Ray-Bans he noticed that Beth's copper hair looked especially good today as her head moved in his lap. He sat up straight, affecting a casual air, prepared to wave to motorists if necessary.

She took him deeper into her mouth and upper throat. His rhythm, intensity, and moans told her he was coming; tension and expectancy preceded the jetting of his semen. Warm and heavy, it splurged the back of her throat. She had a system: quick, swallow, there will be more. His come had a unique taste; he had a unique taste. Aesthetes considered ejaculate to be an acquired taste, allegedly deriving from the producer's diet. Cannibals allegedly said it: vegetarians tasted best. The taste of semen was described with difficulty. To her it was salty, slightly pungent though pleasant, an exotic food of sorts; a thick rich comfort food. Its ingestion seemed to affect her chemistry, its cocktail giving her a hormonal dose. Penises should perhaps have food labels: *ascorbic acid, blood-group antigens, calcium, chlorine, cholesterol, choline, citric acid, creatine, deoxyribonucleic acid, fructose, glutathione, hyaluronidase, inositol, lactic acid, magnesium, nitrogen, phosphorus, potassium, purine, pyrimidine, pyruvic acid, sodium, sorbitol, spermidine, spermine, urea, uric acid, vitamin B12, and zinc. Low fat. Low calorie.*

His left arm angled through the car window, Alan moaned and grimaced in orgasm as he waved to a friendly fellow in a passing pickup.

Highway 1 centered patches of oak, cypress, grasses, and marsh. There was the occasional roadside store. 7-Elevens and Quick Stops were unlikely to be found on this stretch of road. The convenience store had married the Mom and Pop, breeding a unique child. Shelves were well stocked with basic toiletries and food items, but individual ownership and regional idiosyncrasies lent their quirks. Pickled pig's feet, pickled eggs, and hot sausages floated in an opaque liquid in large, homey, three-gallon glass jars. In separate containers, fishing bait was available: night crawlers, crickets, and minnows. Ammunition was a complement to the brisk sale of liquor, wine, and beer.

Cheery folk art often decorated the front exterior. Hubcap collections, junked car art, and Mason jar curiosities upon aged wooden shelving competed with parking space. Weird local legend was often documented by plaques and tattered art-covered flyers posted on the storefront. There was a propensity for the sighting of reptilian/humanoid creatures, their horrific forms being reminiscent of American horror/science fiction films of the 1950s and 1960s.

"Hon, I have to go to the bathroom."

"OK. Keep an eye out for a place to stop."

Bethany fumbled in her shoulder bag. It was large, of black leather, and had no compartments. It seemed a black hole of sorts. It was perhaps even a portal to other dimensions. Who knew? For the time being she did inventory primarily by sense of touch. Paperbacks. Notebook. Pens. Disposable camera. Makeup. Kleenex. Toilet tissue. Hairbrush and comb. Billfold...

"HERE! Here's a place!" Alan yelled as he hit the brakes and prepared to turn. They were jarred, thrown forward. His sudden braking never failed to irritate her.

The Family Pantry was open for business.

She got out of the car and entered the store. To the right was a long cluttered wooden counter; behind it was tall built-in shelving that held liquors and cigarettes. A woman stood behind the counter.

"Excuse me, where is your restroom?"

"It's at the back. Wait. You'll need a key. Here you go."

"Thank you." The key was attached to a motor oil spout.

She prayed for a clean restroom, but well knew the horrors of the road. No toilet paper. No hand soap. Filth. Germs. Overflowing wastebaskets. Broken door locks. For protection she would perhaps need to swathe herself in toilet tissue or wear a level four Hazardous Materials Suit. She strode from the store and made a right turn, then another, wandering to the rear of the property. Distracted, mentally removed from her environment, she tripped, dropping her shoulder bag and dumping the contents onto the asphalt. Her stuff went flying and rolling. She knelt and began to gather her things.

"Missy, I do believe that you possess contraband. Yes, ma'am."

She first saw his shoes. Black and shiny, they were draped by gray pant cuffs. Her eyes traveled up his leaning form. A holstered firearm decorated his hip. A tight gray uniform shirt sported a badge: Officer Lowell Howell. He surveyed her, slightly smiling, his mirrored aviator shades glinting in the sun.

"Excuse me? What do you mean, officer?" She looked up at him.

"I mean, you're in violation of Louisiana state law. Sex toys are illegal here. Ignorance of the law is no excuse, Missy."

Bethany wilted. She glanced at her belongings on the pavement. Paperbacks. Personal notebooks. Makeup bag. Grocery receipts. The vibrator! It rolled and collected dirt. Eight inches long and one and a quarter inches in diameter, it was a white plastic ribbed model with a smooth tip. "The Retro" they called it at the Babe Toy website where she ordered it.

"Officer, it's for my neck. I swear!"

Officer Howell smiled and discreetly glanced to his right, then left. "Well, gal, I do believe there is a solution."

"Yes? What?"

"I'll let you go this time. But I'll have to confiscate the...uh... device. Hand it over, please. Slowly..."

She smiled at the thought of activating it. She almost laughed at the bizarre thought of chasing him with it.

Back at the car she opened the passenger door and got in, slamming her bag onto the floorboard.

"What took you so long?"

"Nothing!"

"What's the matter with you? Is it time for your period?"

"No, it's not time for my period. You always ask that. 'Is it time for your PEeeeRIOD?'" she mocked. "Good grief."

"Oh. OK. Sorry, hon! Ready to hit the road? We're almost there." He smiled.

"Please. Let's go!"

Located west of 1 on Big Wet Road, Whitewood beckoned from the end of its wide drive. Ancient red oaks lined it. They drove the canopied lane. Whitewood's tall colonnade accented verandas and balconies. Dark-green louvered shutters spotted off-white walls. Black wrought-iron accents curled against white and green. Guest cottages lined the rear of the grounds.

Marigolds, magnolias, camellias, hydrangeas, and roses surrounded Whitewood, creating a wall of fragrance. Humidity and aroma seemed an oppressive, invisible weight as the couple walked from the parking area to the entrance.

"Kaaaaaa... KaaaaaAAAA KAAAAAAaaaa..."

"Oh, Al...allergies again, hon? You sound like Jack Lemmon in *The Odd Couple*."

"Kaaaaa kaaa kaa..."

"Getting clear?"

"Kaaa kaa...yes. A little better, thanks."

After check-in, they paused outside their door and read the plaque: *The Southern Gothic—Whitewood boasts a proud guest history of literati and artists, among them Mr. Tennessee Williams, Miss Carson McCullers, Miss Harper Lee, and Mr. Truman Capote. Please enjoy your stay in the special ambiance of our Southern Gothic cottage.*

"Isn't this fascinating? Imagine such greatness...having been in these very rooms!"

"Beth, it's probably just a gimmick to help fill up the place."

"Oh, Al...even if that's so, isn't it fun to believe, to imagine?"

He smiled and pushed open the door. "After you."

The accommodation sported Queen Anne furniture, eclectic

estate sale finds, and Capistrano ceiling fans. French doors opened to gardens and oaks. An adjacent sitting room provided a small book selection, and a rattan ensemble of settee, table, and chairs. Large low windows were artistically, randomly draped in lengths of transparent white cotton.

Bethany unpacked soaps and cosmetics in the bathroom. She peeled off her damp tank top, tube skirt, and panties and threw them to the floor. The humidity was murder. She knew that she'd shower, step out, get dressed, and five minutes later feel sticky again. She stepped into the shower and tested the plumbing. The water pressure was decent. Water cascaded through her hair and over her face, neck, and body. She worked her hands with liquid coconut soap. She soaped her face, neck, and shoulders, working her way over her breasts. Her hands slid, fingers teasing her nipples. Her hands slipped under her breasts' slope where their softness met her ribcage.

Lather. Repeat. Again she soaped her hands, her right hand moving down her belly, over her bush, to her cunt. She cupped herself and lathered and rinsed, before slightly parting herself, her slit, her concavity, her nooks and crannies, folds and hollows.

He stood naked in the doorway and watched her through semitransparent fabric. Steam and scent hissed at him. He stroked himself, gripping his cock, imagining it slippery with soap and water and cunt. His testicles tightened against him; he imagined his cock a steel rod with wings, pulling upward skin and muscle and blood.

Beth's hand rhythmically moved between her legs. Her eyes were slits; her lips parted, jaw slackened. With her left hand she supported herself as she leaned into the anterior shower wall. Alan pulled back the shower curtain and stepped inside, positioning himself behind her. He reached around and held her breasts, as he pushed his cock against her buttocks. She shivered. He slid his hands and arms lower in support. "Lean forward. Relax." She leaned, and pulled apart her buttocks, and tilted her cunt opening upward. His cock slid the gauntlet of her ass cheeks, up to down. Her tiny brown eye winked, as he moved to pink. The head of his cock teased her, before she enveloped him. Snatched. Snatch. Funny words.

"Aaaahhhh!" she let out. The position afforded an exquisite contact and depth, the angle of cock from the rear pounding clit on the downside.

"AAAAHHHH!" His cock slammed into a place seemingly just behind her belly button. She arched her ass and pushed herself against him. He held her hips, pulling and releasing her, pulling and releasing, as his cock passed through wet gripping muscle and bounced from a deep wall. Her cunt convulsed around him, hot and wet and deep. He drew in a breath and gritted his teeth and splashed her flesh walls with his thick warm come.

In the darkened sitting room figures could be seen seated at a rattan table. From behind, tiny patches of light projected through angled shutters, filtering through plumes of cigarette smoke. A dark intense man in a white linen suit, brown wingtips, and white Panama hat chain-smoked Pall Malls, downed Wild Turkey, and animatedly talked to a man seated opposite him.

"Just listen to them go at it, would you? Their paroxysms of passion make me positively dyspeptic. It's always the same, people from the other side inhabiting our special places and invading our space. And entities capitalizing on our names. The Southern Gothic. Indeed! How long have we been here now? I wouldn't have predicted qualities of the afterlife. It takes a period of adjustment."

"I suppose. I was here for weeks before I figured it out. I have difficulty keeping track of time. Senses seem to blend. What's the word?...synesthesia!"

"Crossing over can be a delicious submission, an enervation, a stroll down St. Peter in the rain. But I sometimes yearn for the other side."

"Oh, Tenn, relax now." He smiled. "Tell me a story from the old days."

"Well, all right, Tru...be quiet and listen now!

"Once, Anna Magnani and I were in Rome, having drinks with friends at Caffe Sul Quadrato. We sat outside...

"From a distance I spied a pathetic creature, a wisp of a girl, sunken face, arms like twigs...

"She walked past our table, her rose perfume wafting...

" 'Anna!' I whispered. 'Look! Anorexia Nervosa!'

" 'Oh, Tenn!' Anna said. 'You know EVERYONE!'"

The small blond listener collapsed in laughter. "Oh, Tenn! Now let me tell you about a Johnny Carson appearance."

"Maybe later, Tru. Maybe later."

That night at White! Bethany and Alan shared a booth and perused menus. The simple yet sophisticated restaurant decor displayed shades of white: bright white, off-white, soft white, milk-white, and cream. Louvered shutters and Mission-style slatted booths lined the rectangular main dining room; tables dotted the center. Everything was done in white.

Alan skimmed his menu. Creamed Chicken. Creamed Mashed Potatoes. Creamed Cod. Steamed Cauliflower. Pureed Turnips. Lima Beans. Herb Bread. Cream Sauce.

"This food seems awfully bland."

"I randomly chose this restaurant. But since we're here and we're seated, let's order. Then we can go back to our room and get some sleep. It's been a long day."

They ordered the creamed chicken, mashed potatoes, steamed cauliflower, and herb bread. It turned out to be a very satisfying meal, a study in comfort food. Their systems were unexcited by peppers and spicy sauces; bathed in bland protein and creamy carbohydrate. They nodded and drooped at the table. It was almost like doing drugs. It was said that locals were often arrested for DUI: driving under the influence of carbohydrates.

"Please stay awake, Beth. Help me find Whitewood. Don't let me nod off at the wheel."

"OK, hon. Steady now…" The drive was fortunately a short one.

They were beat. Back in their room, they undressed. The Queen Anne four-poster was dressed in white cotton. The AC wall unit cranked away. The ceiling fans spun, their slow rotation reminiscent of implied cinematic evil. At least the air was moving.

Bethany walked into the sitting room and perused the bookshelves. Skimming *A Streetcar Named Desire* brought back memories of the film. She'd seen three versions of it; they were each unique. Releases from 1951, 1984, and 1995 starred Brando and Leigh, Ann-Margret and Treat Williams, and Jessica Lange and Alec Baldwin. She wondered what a politically correct version might be like, and smiled.

In the darkened bedroom they slept, dreamily mumbling and moaning. Bethany lay on her side, spoon style, her breasts and belly softly pushed against Alan's back. Her left arm draped his middle.

His erection moved up and out.

"Look at that, Tru. What a waste of a fine specimen. Heterosexuals! I don't understand them. I truly enjoy women as friends and business associates, they can be such darlings, but the thought of sharing romance and physical intimacy with them... hmm..."

"We share meaningful relationships with women. We simply have no need to fuck them."

"Tru, must you use that word? It's not very gentlemanly."

"Oh, come off it. You know you get a thrill when I say it."

The two men then quietly and closely sat, watching the woman and man sleep.

Breakfast the next day at Breakfast!, a franchise on restaurant row, presented little or no food-ordering challenge for Alan and Bethany. Eggs. Toast. Grits. Cereal. Sausage. Bacon. Pancakes. Fruit.

"Al, what exactly is a grit?"

He smiled. "Beth, it's simply a finely ground corn product. You should know that."

The coffee list was refreshingly simple. Unlike trendy coffee bars, it didn't have dozens of choices; it boasted only regular and decaf. Even if the beans were arabica, the brew could still be a fine cup a' joe, they'd discovered in their travels.

Over scrambled eggs, toast, and coffee, they discussed the day's itinerary of shopping, eating, and museums.

Stoked, the man sat in a bathrobe and pounded away at his Remington. It was often work. It was occasionally magic. Whether by effort or organic flow or both, when the words came he felt potent. Omnipotent!

"Tru, I've composed a new poem! Tell me what you think... Listen!

"fingertips ache!
tumid lips part
warm tongues meet!
liquidity...
flesh through air
flesh against flesh

flesh into flesh!…
pink thrust glissades
between wet rouged walls…
force across boundaries
skin tingle!
nerve throb!
cell rage!
brain craze!…
liquid heat thump
warm ooze pump
bleed seep weep
into
under
skin & flesh…
through skin & air & skin,
…vibrations!
…of words & touch
…cries & tears
…mark
…time & space!
…mind & flesh!"

"Tenn, this doesn't sound like your style. What are you doing, channeling Walt Whitman and Allen Ginsberg?"
"Truuuu. Don't you like it?"
"Yes! I like it, I really like it!"

In the evening Alan and Bethany returned to the Southern Gothic and settled in. Alan eyed the bottle of lotion that Beth had just bought. He smiled as he thought of the variety of products on the market, and Beth's delight in them. He picked up the bottle and read: Rainbow Farm's Organic Honeysuckle Elixir Moisturizer & Esculent. The flower essence herein is produced without pesticides, herbicides, or machinery. Planted and harvested by moonlight by naked vegetarian virgin Goddesses, it offers the highest available quality to our Elixir. May be used as a general or personal lubricant and is edible. May also be used as a hair conditioner.

She lay on her back on the bed wearing a camisole and panties. The ceiling fan whirred. The wall unit had given up the ghost. The humidity was a bitch. It sapped her strength and mentally fogged her. In its moisture it was perhaps akin to drowning: allegedly not so bad if one stopped struggling. She gave in to it.

She lifted her arms as he slipped her camisole over her head and laid it aside. He slipped her panties down and off. She turned and lay on her stomach as he undressed.

He dispensed the lotion and rubbed it into his hands. Skin universe, top to bottom, back to front, hard to soft, moist flesh press. Lips to lips, warm wet tongue tangles, mouth on neck, mouth on breast. Hand between parted thighs, fingers stroke, stroke...

He marveled at pussies. Pussies were beautiful in a strange sort of way, reminiscent of deep mouthy sea creatures and small slippery consumptive creatures from science fiction films. In some ways there seemed to be more variation in pussies than pricks. A pussy could be a delicate cleft or an askew slash, or several sizes and shapes in between. Its lips might be a mere slit, tiny and tight, gathered inward; larger and slightly splayed with scalloped edges; larger still, with distended stretched lips. It could vary in shade from pink to brown to purple to black.

Pussies had a melting candy/ice cream quality. An artful finger or tongue or prick could set free their flow. He drizzled lotion onto hungry lips. Tasting and testing, he felt smothered yet driven. Drugged. As he tongued her his taste buds processed sweet/sour/salty. *Pyridine, squalene, urea, acetic acid, lactic acid, propionic, isovaleric, isobutyric, propanoic, and butanoic acids, oviductal fluids, cervical mucus, sebum, perspiration, alcohols, glycols, ketones, and aldehydes.*

Bethany's heels dug into the mattress; she rocked her hips and propelled herself toward the headboard. She held his head and pulled Alan's hair. She pulled him up and seized his cock. Cocks could be interesting in a general kind of way: multicolored, hued from white to pink to yellow to tan to ebony and in between; multisized, from diminutive to jumbo to colossal; multi-textured, from soft to firm to hard; multi-shaped, from straight to curvy to bent. They seemed one-eyed teary spurting monsters, looking for caves to rave and rage and bang in, before going back out into the open world of exploration.

His cock deeply entered her, was now hers. *My cock. MY cock.* She claimed it: between spasmodic wet walls that wafted honeysuckle; between splayed flailing legs as she dug her nails into his back; in her cries as she spoke a primitive language that begged.

Alan and Bethany soon slept, under the gaze of curious wizened eyes. Through the night, minds, forms, and voices thought moved and talked softly across time and space.

"Al, are you packed yet? And be sure to dress comfortably for the trip home."

"Help me pick out something to wear."

"Here you are. Ecru polo shirt, beige walking shorts, white cotton socks, and Birkenstocks."

"OK, then."

The couple dressed, finished packing, gave the room a last glance, and were gone.

"Tru, tell me a story."

"Of course, I'd love to tell you a story. A short one. All right?"

"Yeeeessss...a short one." Tenn nodded, bright-eyed though heavy-lidded, a smile on his face.

"I told this one on the Carson show. The 1970s were a blur. I was writing my last books, traveling, doing the talk show circuit. I took pills for my nerves. I drank a little. I was occasionally booked for Carson appearances. I tended to make TV executives nervous, did you know that, Tenn? So there I was, sitting between Johnny and Ed, telling my little story...

"So I was at this party. A very rude drunken gentleman began to bother me. He demanded that I give him my autograph...

"We could find no paper. He suddenly unzips his pants and whips it out! 'Autograph THIS!' he exclaims, dick in hand. Pulling out my pen and considering the available writing space, I told him, 'Well, I'm not sure if I can autograph it, but perhaps I can initial it!'

"Johnny almost lost it. GOD, I was good!

"Tenn...Tenn...are you awake?"

A dark man nodded in his chair, as a small blond man closely sat and deeply sighed.

A man and woman drove north on a two-lane blacktop.

"Hon, I have to go to the bathroom."

"OK. Keep an eye out for a place to stop."

More Moments
of sheer joy

꜅

JAI CLARE

ISLANDS ARE LIKE MOMENTS; sheer moments of joy in water.
Tiny perfections lasting a finite time; situated in a particular space
and occupying the ecstasy side of the brain. The more moments you
have the more you want. Just like islands. One is rarely enough.

I wonder if you can get addicted to them.

The boat, approaching the island — an iridescent mass of shellac,
green and blue in the ocean — clunks to a stop. Waves sting at my
hands. Another island waits for me. The boat rocks; the boatman
steadies himself. A breeze lifts from the water and runs through my
hair with a lover's touch. I look at the boatman. He is so tanned, so
healthy-looking.

I can smell the island. Smell its limits; sense its end and sheer joy
of completion. An island, no matter its actual shape, is like a circle.
It completes and surrenders itself. It is perfection composed of

granite, earth, and sand. I set foot on an island and am infused with joy like a religious ecstasy.

I am waiting for the moment to begin. The boat swerves; the man, silent, weather-mocked, his pointed ears like they'd been wind-bitten, tries hard to keep it still. Children, like small mannequins, brightly colored and shoeless, just like in the Sunday supplements, race to the pier; sounds of thumps on wooden slatting, bright smiles, laughter, tiny hands. Around them annoying insects flit over small, distended puddles in sand. The air is exotic, warm, consuming.

I am not alone.

Back on the main ferry I saw a man. Just an ordinary man, hair the color of sodden matchsticks, face delicately shaped like fragile wax moldings, legs thin and elegant like a tango dancer, bending over, tying up his shoelaces, and then he knocked his head on the railing and smiled sheepishly at me, looking quite silly. His smile made me ache. I decided then it was time I had an affair. I didn't ache for him in particular: more a general ache for fresh faces, fresh skin, and moments in my body to match the exquisite islands. I remembered my husband then, for a moment.

You leave me parched. I lay spread out before you, your semen dribbling down my thigh. Everything about me is vulnerable and more honest than any moment in my life. If you would but look. Look at me, I want to scream, look at me. Can't you see now is when I want you? Now! Don't leave me like this. You think I am done just because you are? My head bent toward your toes, my back bending away from your head, you lying flat beneath me, my hips uplifted, my body expectant. This is me. I have moved for you. I have tried every trick I know and still you finish. Oh so satisfied. Read me, just read me. Read the words of my body, read the contours, the shapes I am making. I make these shapes for you. For me. For us both. I stretch out my arms before me — it triangulates me — and lift my hips slightly away from you, my cunt contracting as if grasping for air or flesh; my body would beg if it could say the words. I shape the word...I want to feel you so much, feel you against me and inside me. I wait, pressing down on my hands. I wait. You've not seen, you've not guessed I need more touch than what you've given me. You think that's it. I wait still. You lift up your leg, you smile, I move away, you kiss me. You are happy and wordless. You leave me parched.

The first step onto the island is always the most important. Someone takes a picture of me and I smile. A practiced smile. I shake hands with important people. People with large hands. I say how happy I am to be here in this tropical paradise. They tell me what I will see: waterfalls, lakes, rivers, interiors of excellent schools, hotels for exotic carefree tourists. I move up dark-tiled stairs and into a white and yellow hotel room, an anonymous shower and coolness on my body. Water drenches me. Yellow tile patterns on the wall, making the image of a fat box.

The first island was cold, and off Norway: Bolga — far north, a small island, freezing water everywhere, with views of other islands: Storvika, Åmnøya, Meløy. My intent is to avoid the major islands, as I said in my press release. Just minor islands; islands off islands. They asked me how long it would take. I said a year. They asked how my husband felt about me being absent so long. I said it was for charity. He understood. He agreed with what I was doing. He could join me on any island. It didn't need to be a lonely sojourn. He was welcome anytime.

Now I am glad I am alone. I have been doing this for five months, three weeks, and five days, and possibly forty minutes. This is island number fourteen or is it fifteen? Norway and then Bornholm, Elba, Sicily — including smaller islands off; islands caught in a day sweep around the coast, like fish in a net — Malta, then Greece, which was a dream. I wandered around the Cyclades like Odysseus.

Yet I yearn to see Zanzibar: a place strangely exotic, unknown; to walk the Stone Town with the scent of cinnamon in my hair, sleep with the aroma of cumin on my pillow, enclosed in the drifting aroma of cloves on the night air: somewhere completely unreal. Impossible, yes.

Sponsors give me money for mentioning their products everywhere I go, for the publicity I get for them and for each island I visit. Sometimes islands give me gifts and money, though I usually leave them with armfuls of sponsors' products. On Karos, in the

Cyclades, I was given a donkey, which I had to leave behind. Good publicity usually breeds more money. The time the ferry sank off the coast of Turkey, and I had to pull in unexpectedly into southern Cyprus, brought me in more money than I could ever dream of. I pledged I would raise a million, when I've reached that figure I can go home. How many more islands before then?

On Madeira I caught chickenpox after my lucky Buddha fell into the water. It was small, shiny red and much touched, for reassurance, and now it's in the harbor water, run over by fishing boats and pleasure cruisers. On Madeira a Frenchman in a dark suit smelling slightly of petrol and coffee walked over to me and we talked. He walked me into an alleyway. I was scared. I smiled at him. He reached his hand toward my neck, resting it behind me on the wall, pinning me from escape. He was pretty in a grown-up sort of way. Pretty and charming with gray hair. I could have just let him finger me, at least. I wish I had. I wasn't ready then.

The islands seem to be getting smaller. I've been to medium islands and then large ones—avoiding the really big country islands, the continent islands, such as Australia, Japan—and now back to intimate islands. How many islands are there in the world? Has anyone ever counted? And Asia is like one big splotch surrounded by hundreds of lesser dots. Now I'm on the smallest of the British Virgin Islands, fearing that when I get to Polynesia I may slip off the edge of an island and vanish into the ocean. I could spend my life doing this and never go back. This place is truly paradise. Oh, such horseshit clichés. But just look at it. I don't want to leave. There is only one other thing I would need to keep me here. What is my life in England to compare to here?

A yacht moves into focus, pulling in for the night. A big yacht. Four sails in a beautifully symmetrical pattern, like dancers. The yacht glides in, like Arthur's boat floating to Avalon. Just two people on the beach. Can a place be more unreal? My footsteps on the wooden-slatted balcony confirm its physicality. How is it that some people get to live in such a place? Endless bougainvillea around the door, clean white floors, a balcony view overlooking deep green hills and the ocean. The endless ocean. Down below is the beach:

fine, wide, empty. This is a tiny island. I could go snorkeling, scuba diving. I've never had sex underwater! I don't need to ever leave. I think I am going to cry or die or blow up fat like Big Daddy. Become an eccentric Welsh woman gone mad under the sun, drinking mint juleps by the ferry-load. Here I could have a lover who fucks me in daylight, on the beach, under trees, spreading my body over a rock, water at my feet, sun burning me, his body over me, in me. We'd meet casually on hot street corners and run to a sheltered spot, brushing overreaching bougainvillea from our faces. I'd feel alive and wanted. I'd feel alive.

Here I am. Alone, doing almost exactly what I want to do at this moment. All the books say you should do what liberates you. They say listen to your inner voice. They tell me what I want. They tell me I have to look after number one: *"and number one is you! Yeah!"* What happens when bolstering your self-esteem hurts others?

I send you a postcard from here, portraying big fluffy clouds, blue sky, azure waters — the whole caboodle of clichés. I send you a postcard from every island I go to. They are pictures of the world I now inhabit. Of course you have the photos people take and the sponsors keep you informed and you see me in the press — once placed just inside the front page, now hiding further and further in the back pages; no doubt you'll expect to see me on the tiny gossip pages soon enough! Do you expect me to fail? I think you do. I send you love and kisses and describe what I see. Indeed I do love you. Sometimes I even miss you.

Once I had a lover who knew how to treat me. Many lovers, even, before I met my husband. Lovers who knew their way joyfully around a woman's body; lovers who excelled at teasing and taunting and licking my clit; lovers who lingered and lovers who knew when to be aggressive, when my body needed force and when I needed delicate beautiful tentative strokes inside me; who knew when to turn me around, how to touch me inside to make me squeal and leap from the bed in amazement, touching the ceiling with the thrill of it all; lovers who would caress me with words and music and wine, as well as the power of who they were. Lovers who were certain of themselves. I miss that. It's been a long time.

I remember Zeb, who would spend hours with me, whole

afternoons, in a sun-drenched room, central heating way up, wandering the Victorian flat naked, drinking wine, talking, dancing energetically to Cuban music on the stereo. His speciality was to make sure I'd come at least three times before he did. He had seduced me when I was nineteen. His body shone. He was fit, young, and toned. I loved running my hands over his body, having him caressing my thighs, stroking me, looking at me, telling me I could do anything I wanted. Filling me with confidence from his sure touch. He would kiss my thighs, kiss my labia, kiss every part of me, loving the taste of my juices in his mouth. I loved those sun-soaked hot winter afternoons.

I take a trip on a sleek yacht, polished, chromed, and efficient like an ideal robot. I tie back my unruly hair—a mass of maddening brown curls—and thrust my bikini-clad body into the sun. We land on an uninhabited rocky island where my host and I stride about the barren place like conquerors. He's tall with an Irish voice, blue eyes, and wrinkles from too much sun; too much sailing around the world, and he is a master of harbors and islands and weather conditions. He cooks exquisite cleanly sharp meals on a tiny hob and I marvel at the tiny space he inhabits physically and the infinite space he roams mentally. I think it would be good for him to touch me. I look at his thin bony freckled hand. Those fingers that untie knots so deftly. I smile at him.

The sand is hot. The speckled rocks are hot, covered with vibrant insects. The air is full of them and the sound of birds. I watch the small boat bobbing, tucking my legs under me, admiring the depth of tan I am acquiring.

Island number sixteen. I hope someone has taken a picture. I shout to the guy left on the yacht, over the small chasm of water, "Hey, get the camera! Take a picture of me! I need proof!"

Without proof I cannot get the money. All those corporate sponsors and their tax-deductible donations, garnering free publicity and great PR. Look, they care about African Orphans, Disappearing Cheetahs, Cystic Fibrosis. The charity I'm doing this for right now protects gorillas and orangutans.

Where do you start choosing who is the most deserving? I began with my distaste for the trouble humanity embroils itself in—even though it may not be each individual's absolute fault—and my love for an old toy orangutan I had when I was eight called Herbert, and picked an animal charity. You have to start somewhere.

We are alone on the island; exploring red-sand cliffs, red the color of the evening sun, exploring the edge of the water, the tidemarks, the rock pools, the inner oasis, the greenness of the ground past the soft sand. I laugh uncontrollably when, standing under the cliff, he asks to sleep with me. He doesn't touch. He doesn't reach down to me, my back rubbing against the hard rock, to touch my cheek, or pull down a fragile bikini string, or unravel my hair from its loose tie, but instead he looks at me as if I am immobile, and says, "Rachael, let's lie down under this rock and make love." Without touch it is simple to refuse. When actually I want the authority of touch on me, skin on skin. There is nothing like it. Not even islands can compete. He brushes against me in the yacht. I lean against him so one breast presses against his arm. But he does nothing. He uses his voice when I want his skin. I wish I could say yes. Zeb would be able to seduce me easily.

I have a strong fantasy life. Sometimes I take refuge in there for hours at a time, especially at night, or alone in my bed in the morning. I am like a teenager imagining her first kiss. I don't caress my arm, but if it wasn't so silly maybe I would. Sometimes what I imagine frightens me but it's only thoughts and dreams.

People on the island ask about my life at home in England. I have a strange English accent, they say. I laugh and say that's because I'm Welsh and grew up outside Hay-on-Wye, a town of bookshops where literary men come once a year to pontificate. We've had presidents, ex-presidents, famous novelists bothered by controversy like wasps on a summer's afternoon. Now I live in Canterbury, a town of sacrifices and martyrs. The town is a martyr to tourists. See how it subjugates itself. Henry II would adore it.

They ask about children. They are sweet, these islanders. Some incomers are runaways from America. The hotel owners are obviously gay. Their cooking is superb: shrimp so fresh, so tender and crisp, I swear I saw it out in a small rock pool just hours earlier.

I say I have one child, Elissa, with her speech impediment and fascination for insects. She is six—the same age as my marriage. Doesn't she miss you? Oh, yes, I imagine. Don't you miss her? Indeed, more than you can know, but I have to do this. Sometimes I wonder how I could have left her. But she is safe with my husband. It is only for a year.

My mind is like a black box whose hinged lid you have no way of lifting. It used to embarrass me. The dreams I could see. Daylight with you makes me bashful. There, I am no one a friend would recognize. I am no one daylight would greet with familiar smiles. Now I can truly let my inhibitions fall away like coverings. I can dream openly of what I want, now I am away from you. I can imagine a lover who explores my body, who takes time and care, who has fingers that probe and delve and search and liquefy. A man to whom I could shout aloud "Fuck me" without it sounding silly, whom I could invite into my ass without fear or trepidation of reaction. A man who could pull my nipples and bite me and tease my clit with his strong teeth. A man whose hands would firmly, delicately grab my throat as I was about to come. A man who could wrap me in soaking sheets and pull me to him. I dream of such freedom. I don't know when it changed or was it you that changed? All I want to do is marry the world of imagination with daylight. Is that so wrong? And I will do so but without you.

"Rachael! Rachael! Rachael!" Children and parents are shouting and waving. The boat pulls away. They have covered me with cerise and white flowers. Big white petals with cerise spots like dribbled blood. Flowers fall on the quayside as if this is a wedding departure. This is all too much: I am only a small businesswoman with a flair for spotting talent, for spotting an idea and going for it. I am no goddess, I want to shout to them. All I did is come to your island, bring reporters and cameras and leave again. I didn't even fuck! My flair is flawed.

Airports and dry hotel rooms. I am an expert at quayside tasteless coffee and at keeping my sweet tooth amused with fat Snickers bars and popcorn in a packet, while waiting. I come ashore on America, like a seasonal tornado. I miss my moments. I miss my islands already.

There is something about the limitations of islands. Pure

pleasure, whereas the mainland seems infinite and thus the pleasure diffused. Some islands are long and thin, some curl around and touch their other sides. Some are two but called one. Some are dots literally and one big wave would swallow them. Some are mountainous. Some are windblown and empty.

We all need more moments of sheer joy. What is the point of it all without it? The bathroom here has flaking yellow wallpaper. I can see homes of spiders and cobwebs around the windows. I sit on the toilet and think of tomorrow: of Martha's Vineyard, Nantucket. Sometimes I just decide to call in on an island on the spur of the moment. I see a name on a map and I want to go there. Islands in Chesapeake Bay look interesting…or the islands down the coast from Savannah. Are there any countries that don't have islands at all?

I stare at maps to give me answers. I love just figuring out how an island once fitted, slotted in like a jigsaw to the mainland. I do that at night when everyone has gone to bed and my feet ache and the lights are low and I pool light over my map and my malt whisky and I lie naked on the bed, if I'm somewhere hot. It's hot tonight. Mainland America. I miss Europe; its smallness and odd customs, like driving on the right side of the road, like saying the word *curtains,* and posting something instead of mailing. People here are rather too friendly. Not a surly voice in the lobby. Even the press ask me nice questions. Rachael Driscoll comes to America, like some otherworld circus clown.

How big this place is—I have a map open now. Even the mainland is composed of islands: Manhattan, Staten Island, Long Island. Florida isn't real. Is it? It sticks out the bottom like a monkey's tail. Night falls. The hotel is quiet. It's hot. Unbearably hot. The air-conditioning makes too much noise. I shall never sleep. I have with me, on the side cabinet, as I do wherever I go, my wedding photo in a small metal frame, a plastic purple beaker covered with white daisies that Elissa gave me for water. The bed is yellow. Cowardice.

I do not know much about the man who is helping me now, only that his name is Daniel and he interests me. Everything thrills me, even this clean harbor here on the west coast of America; I raced through islands like a baby suckles milk, and now we are preparing for the islands off Los Angeles, and then Guadeloupe and then Polynesia. I am resigned, almost, to never seeing Zanzibar, which feels like the end of the world.

I say to Daniel, "It's got to be the end of the world, how many other islands have two Zs in them? Do you even know where it is?" He hums and ahs and guesses. "Wrong coast of Africa," I say.

It's September; we are short of a million by just £100,000.

You seem very far away from me now. I don't even know if you exist, even though you sent me a letter and here it is on my bed waiting for me unopened. I guess you'll tell me the summer is over in England, before it even began. I guess you're going to tell me Elissa wants new trainers, or braces, or wants to stay up all night to watch MTV. You'll be saying in these fragments of news that I should come home. You'll never tell me so openly. But that's what you think. You'll say the garden misses my touch and should you paint the kitchen in yellow? And your mother has to go into hospital and your father wants to buy a new car even though he's nearly eighty. Your boss is driving you mad. I can guess all these things. I can't even begin to tell you what I am thinking, that I do not miss your touch. I want touch. But not yours and yet there is an inexplicable bond between us still, it is as if you planted a spirit within me that watches and holds me tight, constricting all movement but thought. Am I haunted? I am not looking for love, I say. Rest assured. I don't want fissure. I just want to be reached where you cannot reach me. I am a selfish woman. Is it your spirit in me that stops me being truly uninhibited? I am moral; it is tearing me apart.

More moments. Never to see Zanzibar. It is too far away, and my time is nearly up. I fret at it. I look it up on the Internet. I stare at its shape on the map. I point it out to Daniel beside me. I have discovered that he is from Boston originally, his accent is kind of quaint and tortured, and sometimes I cannot understand him. He has trouble with my Welsh vowels and so I tone them down just for him. He cannot understand my fascination with Zanzibar. I say its name over and over again: Zanzibar. It speaks of myth, dreams, spices, fragrance, and Arabs. It speaks of something unattainable. We touch accidentally over the map of Africa. I can smell him, sense him, imagine him touching me. I lean toward him. I wonder if he's a caring empathetic lover, and how his mouth will feel on my mouth. He rests his hand on mine as I point out the coastline of Zanzibar on the map. "I have to go there!" I shout, looking at pictures then appearing on my laptop screen. Coconuts, cloves, little islets, the House of Wonders, Aldabra turtles, 560 carved doors.

"Sublimation is a dangerous thing," he says to me with so much understanding I feel like shouting. I look at him. He touches my shoulder. He pulls on my hair. My cunt wants him so badly I almost am not me.

"You sound like a self-help book."

I decide on Mexico instead of Guadeloupe. Mexican islands; there must be others. Daniel accompanies me smelling of cinnamon and ginseng shampoo. I am in a boat traveling down the length of Baja California, stopping off at islands with beautiful Spanish names. Cameras capture me climbing onto the island of Margarita, smiling. My last island. Daniel tells me, enthusiastically, how the name of California came about, from some Spanish guy's book.

It's not Zanzibar. The world doesn't come to an end. They take their last photos; I am a success. They leave me alone with one New Englander who is holding my hand delicately, and a dozen Mexicans in light clothing watching me. It feels so alien. We have the million pounds for the furry creatures. I have to return home. Rachael Driscoll returns home in triumph.

The wind gets up. Plankton float past. Mosaic water glints and washes. We head back to the boat, stand on the water's edge. I make sure the spirit of my husband is left in the land, on Margarita with the children and the trees. After all, I am so far from home. This place is so unreal, surely the rules don't apply here? Surely now I can take a moment from my marriage, from my promises, and have just one moment for me? Daniel's hand holds on to mine even harder. He turns and begins to unbutton my shirt. The sun hits my breasts. I glance up into the sky looking at the sun, feeling heat, seeing seagulls flying, hearing sounds of wind in exotic trees. Heat on my breasts as he runs his hands over them, cups them. Everyone is gone. There is just us on the water's edge, as his head bends down. I can see his dark hair. I touch his hair as his lips wrap around a nipple and firmly begin to pull softly between the very white edges of his teeth.

He lifts up and smiles and removes my sarong, my shirt, and my underwear. I stand naked, water on my feet. He looks at me and smiles again and puts one finger between my legs. I spread. For a few minutes I close my eyes as he fingers me. Abruptly he stops, takes my hand and leads me back across the wooden slatting into the boat. No sounds on the boat. No one here at all. Just seagulls in the sky, and heat.

Lost in the moment, eyes closed breathing hard, lost in the moment the island purple mosaics flashing tunnels inside outside going through hands gripping feel your breath. The blue sea the sheer blue sea, islands that kiss like crabs, the swaying boat deck, the sound of gulls. Wet wood beneath my feet. He touched my breast his lips, his hands, his pinching fingers his fingers inside me naked now his mouth and tongue between my legs, he holds my back, holding me with the palm of his hand, stopping me from swaying from falling – I can feel his concern for my body with every touch. This exultation of touch is what I needed. The caress of his cock, the feel of it. He pushes me to the floor with the force of his body. He says nothing but I can feel his breath on me. The mad touch he's inside me now. I'm on the deck, legs spread out no shame no embarrassment he's looking down at me he holds his cock – I love that, a man proudly holding out his cock – pushing now inside of me, riding me like this is all he has thought about since we met. I can feel and feel it and it's beautiful, I can't believe I can't believe is there anything more than this? Best feeling air kissing skin clouds as voyeurs stranded spirits catching up with me.

I am on the sofa. There's the key in the door. He is home. I open my eyes, close my legs, jump up to meet him, and smile, scattering mementoes: cloves and maps.

VOWS

ॐ

LISABET SARAI

I SAW HIM FIRST.

Our boat had just rounded the tip of the peninsula that divides the Nam Khan from the Mekong. The driver cut the noisy motor and let us drift with the current through the golden haze of late afternoon. Peace. Birdsong and the mother river lapping against our hull were the only sounds. The highland breeze danced cool and sweet in my nostrils. I took a deep breath and let my tension ripple out and away like the river before us.

Lush jungle vegetation climbed up the right bank, into the hills. The left bank, on the city side (but who would have imagined that we were in a city, the ancient capital of a potent empire?) was carpeted with the same tangled greenery, but less steep. All at once the slanting sun struck a gleam of gold ahead. As we drew closer, I saw a temple pier jutting into the water, a carved and gilded pavilion with traditional eaves sweeping toward the ground.

A Buddha image nestled in an alcove near the peak of the roof.

The man stood on the platform below, as motionless as a statue himself, and yet there was a kind of movement in his stillness. He was one with the river and the forest, breathing in slow unison with them as he gazed at us.

Orange robes draped his lithe, slender body. The honey-colored skin of his naked shoulder glowed in the waning sun. His shaven head highlighted a broad forehead, fine cheekbones, and full lips. He looked young, no more than eighteen. Then our eyes locked and I saw wisdom in his, grace, perhaps humor, but definitely not innocence.

His beauty made me ache. Tears congealed into a knot in my throat. Then Danielle noticed him.

"I'd like to fuck him," she commented softly. I whipped around, embarrassed and concerned that the driver had heard, but he had his palms together, offering the ritual *nop* gesture of respect as we passed the pavilion.

"Dani! Really! You should be ashamed of yourself! I'm sure you know that it's strictly forbidden for a Buddhist monk to touch a woman."

"So? Vows were made to be broken. Besides," she said slyly, sneaking a hand into my lap, "you can't pretend that you don't want him as well."

I hadn't realized that I was half hard. I had thought that my appreciation of him was wholly aesthetic. Under Dani's skillful fingers, I swelled to a full erection in seconds. Grinning, she grasped the tab of my zipper and started to pull.

"Stop it!" I whispered urgently, grabbing for her invading hand. "Have a little respect!"

"Oh, but baby, I do respect you," she cooed. "I just want to make sure that you get what you want. Sometimes you're too shy to go after it yourself."

She'll never let me live it down. The fact that I'm attracted to men as well as women, but even more, the uncomfortable truth that I might never have realized it if she hadn't bullied me into my first homosexual encounter. Not that I regret it. I'll never forget that incandescent night with the audacious young punk she bought for me in Amsterdam.

There have been others since. Only when we're traveling, though. Travel brings out a strange recklessness in my wife, a hunger for extremes that I don't see when we are in New York. At home, Danielle is energetic and competent, affectionate and attentive, seemingly content with our life. It feels as though we are connected, in bed and out of it. When we're on the road though (and our mutual love of travel was part of what brought us together), she becomes somehow sharper, prickly, and less accessible. She seeks out risks. She sometimes reveals a catlike streak of cheerful cruelty.

In Vientiane, for instance, she had insisted on tracking down rumors of still-flourishing opium dens somewhere in the city. Reluctantly, I had accompanied her, concerned for her safety. I had romantic images of dim chambers fragrant with incense, brocade-upholstered couches of carved ebony, an ancient crone with bound feet preparing and offering the pipes with a toothless grin. Instead, we found ourselves in a thatched hut on the riverbank a few kilometers west of the city center, in the care of a strapping Lao youth with lurid tattoos on his chest and a Led Zeppelin T-shirt.

Watching Danielle's immobile form lying on the woven mat, her eyes wide and empty, I wondered for the hundredth time what drives her to such places. The sickly sweet odor of the drug tickled my nostrils. The proprietor tried once again to interest me in a pipe. I shook my head, but I couldn't help wondering whether the narcotic would have dulled my loneliness.

Dani was still stroking my penis surreptitiously as the boat pulled up to the public dock. "Why don't we go back to the hotel? We can—talk—about our new friend." She paid the boatman, and handed me my straw hat, which I used to hide my raging erection as we strolled the few blocks back to our guesthouse. I barely had time to close the door and slip out of my sandals before Dani was down on her knees in front of me, undoing my fly.

Here in the privacy of our room, I didn't object. I was painfully hard; it seemed as though the taut skin sheathing my organ would burst at the slightest touch. Danielle squeezed; I could scarcely bear it. She gazed up at me, mischief in her hazel eyes. "Pretend that it's him, sucking you," she murmured, and then she swallowed me whole.

Her mouth was a steaming tropical jungle, her muscular tongue a snake twining around me. I closed my eyes and allowed myself to sink into pure sensation.

After five years with me, she knew how I liked it: languorous strokes from base to tip alternating with energetic sucking that must have left her jaw sore, but which brought me to the edge again and again. I filled my mind with images of her: the ginger thatch of her pubis matching the fringe on her head; the slick folds hidden among those curls; her palm-sized breasts with their extravagant nipples; her lively, intelligent, sometimes mocking face. I imagined that she was stroking herself as she worked on me. That might well be true. I remembered her wild, almost inhuman expression when she came.

But as she brought me inexorably closer to orgasm, these images slipped away, though I tried to hold them. Instead, I saw a pair of ripe lips curved in a half-smile, brown eyes sparkling with gentle challenge, smooth curves of golden flesh that cried out to be kissed. I imagined bare feet, muscular buttocks, a slim cock rearing like a rod of ivory, hairless and pure. She was broadcasting these images to me, I knew it, but that didn't help me to resist. I moaned, guiltily and overwhelmingly aroused. I saw a cloud of saffron-hued fabric drifting down, covering twined limbs, white and honey-colored, and I spilled myself into Danielle's greedy mouth.

We were sitting on the hotel veranda around eleven the next morning, taking a late breakfast of *café au lait* and croissants, when we saw him again. He had draped the end of his robe across his chest and raised a parasol against the sun, but neither Dani nor I had any doubt that this was the same monk. The grace that I had sensed in his immobility was fully realized in his fluid walk. Each step was sure, balanced, controlled and yet free. I was reminded of the classical dancers we had seen in Thailand, whose bodies morph from one pose to another without seeming to move.

We were hidden in the cool shade of the porch. The starched white linen of our tablecloth might have drawn his eyes, but he did not turn in our direction. I noticed a circular item tucked under his arm.

I pointed it out to Dani. "His begging bowl. The monks leave their temples at dawn to collect food from the people. They only eat what is donated to them. Meanwhile, the people gain merit from their offerings to the *Sangha*. They hope that the accumulated merit will help liberate them from the cycles of rebirth."

Dani laughed. "You've done your research, haven't you?" She leaned closer to me, placing her hand on my thigh under the table. Her skin was feverishly hot. "How would you like to get up at dawn tomorrow and make some merit?" Her fingers inched upward, toying with the edge of my shorts.

"Danielle, you are truly incorrigible!" I said. Still, I understood what she had in mind. I burned with shame, but I knew that I wouldn't be able to resist her.

We spent the afternoon in the Dala Market, marveling at the intricate, vivid textiles and the tribal silver jewelry. The evening we spent in bed, Danielle teasing me until I was agonizingly close to climax, but never allowing me to finish. "Save it," she whispered to me as she squatted over my face and gave my eager tongue access to her sex. I hardly minded. Watching her orgasm was nearly as arousing as coming myself.

The next morning, in the wan six o'clock light, we waited uncertainly on the guesthouse steps. Dawn was misty, cool, and silent. Even the birds were abed. The stucco buildings across Thanon Photisalat were shuttered. The dirt surface of the road was damp with dew.

I shivered in my cotton shirt and pants, more from nervousness than cold. I could hear my own heartbeat. With both hands, I clutched the circular tray of artfully carved fresh fruit that we had bought in the market. We had to be crazy, didn't we? I glanced over at Danielle. She was absolutely motionless, save for her breathing. Her lips were parted and her eyes sparked with fierce excitement. I thought of a tiger, crouched and ready to pounce on its prey, and shivered again.

Fifteen, twenty minutes passed in this peculiar state. At last a sound reached me, the soft crunch of leather soles on gravel. I looked down the street to my right and saw a splash of orange coming toward us. Even at a distance of fifty meters, I recognized him by his grace.

Vague panic surged through me. At the same time, my cock stirred in my pants. What were we supposed to do? How could we avoid offending him? Despite the ache in my groin, I wanted more than anything to please him, to honor him and his vows.

Danielle whispered to me urgently, "It's him!" I nodded, finding nothing to reply. I could tell that for her, it was his supposed inviolability that was the turn-on. His purity and grace did not arouse her; rather, it was the prospect of sullying that purity. At some level, I found this horrible, and yet, I know that her perversity is part of what draws me to my Danielle.

I remained frozen, rooted to the spot as one is in dreams. I felt helpless, unable to escape whatever fate was approaching on sandal-shod feet. All at once there was motion across the way. A slatted wooden gate swung open silently, and a barefoot woman in a sarong stepped into the lane. The monk stopped in front of her. She sank to her knees and placed a blue ceramic bowl on the ground at his feet. Then she bowed her head, palms pressed together, fingers grazing her forehead, as the monk bent to pick up the bowl.

He murmured something to her, and she raised her eyes, a hint of a smile on her lips. For a brief, poignant moment, his hand hovered over her brow in an obvious gesture of blessing, before he turned and continued his progress toward us.

His eyes were straight ahead, though surely he knew we were there. He had almost passed us when, desperately, I stepped forward, crouched down, and placed the fruit on the dirt surface of the road. "Honored one," I croaked, barely able to get the words out. "Please accept this humble offering."

He turned to me, his smile like the dawning sun. "Thank you," he said softly, with only a trace of an accent. "It is rare that a guest considers the needs of our poor monks. May your reward be fitting to your generosity."

"Sir." It was Danielle's silkiest voice. I realized that she was at my side, on one knee in front the monk. "We are pleased to serve a holy one like you." She was laying it on so thick, I felt slightly disgusted. The monk, however, gave her a look of gentle welcome.

Encouraged, she continued. "We are surprised, though, that you speak English, and so well."

"When I was still a *samnera*, a novice, an American man came to our temple, seeking the *Dhamma*. He taught me many things." There was a faraway look in our monk's eyes. I wondered what he was remembering. "It was from him, from Sam, that I learned to speak your language. That was many years ago, though, not long after the war. These days, I do not get much opportunity to practice."

Could he mean the Vietnam War? I was astonished. Surely this youthful-looking man could not be in his forties?

He seemed to read my thoughts. "Living in the light of

Dhamma keeps one young," he said simply. "I have spent most of my life trying to walk the true path."

He picked up our offering and slipped it into his alms bowl. I held my breath at the grace with which he endowed this ordinary act. "My name is Souvannaphone. I live at Wat Xieng Thong, near the river. Let me invite you to come visit us. I would be very pleased to show you the temple, and to talk to you further."

"We would be honored," murmured Danielle. "Would this afternoon be convenient? We are leaving Luang Prabang tomorrow."

"This afternoon would be ideal. I will look forward to seeing you then."

Souvannaphone raised his hand in benediction over our heads. I closed my eyes, flooded by diverse emotions. I could identify shame, relief, joy, and lust. I was painfully aware of my cock, throbbing inside my drawstring pants.

I don't know what was going through Dani's mind. When I dared to look again, the monk was already fifty meters further down Thanon Photisalat, receiving alms from an elderly woman who looked too frail to walk. Dani was watching his progress, her eyes glittering.

"This afternoon..." she purred. "I suspect that it's going to be a long morning."

"I'm not going anywhere this afternoon." I was determined to follow my higher instincts for once. I was not going to let Dani drag me down.

"Oh, really? Should I go by myself, then?"

"Do what you want, but I'm not going to participate. This is a good man, a holy man. I don't want to watch you ruin him by subverting his vows."

"Ruin? How dramatic! We're only talking about sex, baby. Between consenting adults! It's hardly a crime."

"For Souvannaphone it might be. What do you know of his beliefs, his commitments? He has been a monk for twenty years, maybe more. You might destroy the very foundations of his life."

She smiled to herself. "Well, if he hasn't been laid in twenty years, he's probably the horniest guy I'm ever likely to meet...."

I turned my back on her in disgust.

"Where are you going?"

"Back to bed. It's ridiculously early."

"Wait, I'll come with you." She caught up with me and grabbed my hand, accompanying me into the cool inner depths of the slumbering hotel. I knew that she had something other than sleep in mind. "Even if we don't visit him," she murmured in my ear, "there's no harm in fantasizing."

I tried to pretend that I wasn't interested. I wanted to punish her for her selfish lust. Yet I couldn't deny the aching hardness in my groin, or the exquisite sensitivity of my skin.

Dani was gentler than usual, seeming more open, more submissive. I hoped that I had convinced her to drop the notion of seducing the charismatic Souvannaphone. Yet as I poured my release into her welcoming cunt, I couldn't shut out an image of the beautiful monk, unabashedly naked, an ambiguous smile on his ripe lips. I prayed earnestly that it was a sight I would never see in the real world.

We slept for a while, the breeze from the ceiling fan drying the sweat on our bodies. Mid-morning brightness filtering through the gaps of the curtains finally woke us. I was ravenously hungry. We found an airy stall in the next lane and ordered big bowls of *foe*. Dani seemed very gay, slurping up her noodles while making arch comments about passersby. I hoped against hope that she had given up on our assignation with Souvannaphone. Certainly we didn't speak of it.

We changed some money, hauling the huge bundle of *kip* back to our hotel in a plastic bag, and then went out shopping for gifts: a carved teak figurine for my editor, richly embroidered tablecloth for my mother, hammered silver bangles for Dani's best friend. We wandered through the bustling midday streets, examining the wares of the hawkers and dodging bicycles.

As it got later, my body hummed with anticipation, vibrating with the muted roar of some engine hidden in my gut. My cock remained semi-hard, even though Dani had drained me dry earlier. I tried to ignore all that and concentrate on the lively and exotic scenes around me.

Finally, around 2 P.M., Dani turned to me. "Don't you think we should go back to the hotel and get ready for our visit?" she asked sweetly.

"I told you, I don't want to go." I wished fervently that I had an excuse that would save me from her scorn. "Anyway, I have a headache," I ventured, and sure enough even as I voiced this thought, the throbbing of my pulse in my temples turned to pain.

"Poor baby," she crooned. "Let's go and get you some aspirin." She led the way back to the guesthouse. I followed, in both physical and mental misery.

I lay on the bed with a cool cloth over my eyes, breathing deeply, trying not to think. Dani was in the shower. I felt rather than heard her approach me. She closed a damp hand around my half-erect penis and began to stroke me slowly.

"It wouldn't be polite to ignore his invitation, Michael," she said. "Anyway, if he's as righteous as you seem to think, I'm sure that even with our best efforts, we won't be able to seduce him."

"I don't want to try," I replied irritably. But my cock told another story. With a sigh, I got up and went to stand in the shower, wishing that the cool water could cleanse me of my impure desire.

When I emerged from the bathroom, I donned a loose shirt of unbleached linen, and a fresh pair of drawstring trousers. That was all.

Dani grinned but said nothing. She put on a deceptively modest ankle-length dress she had bought in Thailand, a gorgeous batik in greens and golds that made her hair flame. I say "deceptively modest" because of the long row of buttons up the front. No underwear for her, either.

I was embarrassed by our lascivious scheming, yet I couldn't deny that I was excited. Never had I felt so conflicted. Resentment surged in me as I looked at Dani, so devious and so delectable. Why didn't I have more spine, to stand up to her when she got like this? Why was I perennially unable to refuse her?

We strolled northeast toward the far end of the peninsula, where Wat Xieng Thong was situated. The jewel of Luang Prabang, according to our guidebook. We had visited several of the other famous temples in the city; I had been saving this one for last.

Dani took my hand as we made our way through the quiet streets, in the lengthening shadow of Phu Si hill. "Relax," she said. "Don't worry. I'll handle things. Just leave everything to me."

That was exactly what I was worried about.

The vegetation thickened around us as we left the city center behind. We passed rough wooden houses on stilts, chickens scrabbling in the shade underneath, laundry swaying in the gentle breeze. Occasionally, we heard the muted babble of a television or radio, but we saw no one. It felt as though the whole of the city-village was dozing in the afternoon. I took a deep breath, and then another, trying to release the awful tension that gripped me, but it was no use. I was consumed by desire and dread.

Finally we reached the arched gateway to Wat Xieng Thong. Souvannaphone's home. Gilded *nagas*, the serpent-dragons that sheltered the Buddha while he meditated, guarded the entry, their scales a riot of multicolored mirrors. As we stepped over the sill and into the sacred compound, I felt something shift inside me. The choice was made, the effects would follow. Let karma do its worst.

At first, the place seemed deserted. Directly in front of us was the magnificent *sim*, or ordination chapel, with its five-layered, flame-tipped roof swept into dramatic earthward curves. Smaller but equally ornate buildings were scattered around it. Blue tile and gold leaf were everywhere.

An enormous, fantastically twisted tree shaded the entire courtyard. At the same moment (I could tell from the way her hand tightened in mine), Dani and I noticed the figure seated, full lotus, on the turf at the foot of its main trunk.

It was, of course, Souvannaphone. His eyes were closed; his chest was bare. The golden, hairless flesh fascinated me. His nipples, more bronze than gold, drew my eyes and made my balls contract and ache.

It was his expression, though, that once again brought up my tears. It gave me a glimpse of total peace. Bliss. Perfect stillness and unearthly beauty. My craving to know his exquisite body faded and transformed into exquisite longing to know what he knew, to experience this state of completion.

And Dani? Had she abandoned her perverse plans for this man, this saint (for so he seemed to me at that moment)? I ventured a glance in her direction and saw that she too was transfixed by the vision of him. Her cheeks were flushed and her breathing was ragged. Her eyes were fever-bright. Her mind was closed to me.

A huge sigh shuddered through my chest. At that sound, or perhaps just from the sense of our presence, Souvannaphone opened his eyes. He smiled at us, a smile at once simple and wise.

"My friends!" he exclaimed, untangling his limbs and rising

fluidly to meet us. "I am delighted that you came. I had begun to wonder if you were simply being polite this morning."

His English was truly amazingly good. It disarmed me. As he approached, I wondered about protocol. Should I bow or try a *nop*? Should I offer to shake hands? He seemed so informal, and in some sense, so Westernized.

He overrode all my concerns by grasping my hand in both of his. His skin was silk against mine, cool and luxurious. "But you never told me your names!"

"This is Danielle," I replied, amazed at how steady my voice was, given my inner trembling. "And I'm Michael."

The monk inclined his head in a little bow to Dani, but of course he made no move to touch her. A nasty twinge of vengeful satisfaction swept through me as I noted his reticence. This was followed almost immediately by guilt. We were husband and wife, after all. We were supposed to desire each other's happiness. And to share.

"Welcome to Wat Xieng Thong, Danielle and Michael. Normally, the temple is a good deal busier, but at this time of day, most of the monks are in their rooms, meditating. That is just as well, though, as we won't disturb anyone. Come with me, and I'll give you a bit of a tour."

He glided off toward the *sim* on bare feet. We followed, dazed by his grace, overwhelmed by his enthusiasm.

The temple was, as promised by the travel writer, full of wonders. The solid gold Buddha images ranged in the cloister gleamed benevolently, but not so brightly as Souvannaphone's smile. The Tree of Life mosaic in the main sanctuary, fashioned of mirrors and precious stones, by all rights should have astounded me. But I was already stupefied by the incredible beauty of our human guide.

Finally, he showed us a scattered collection of stucco-walled, palm-thatched huts, shaded by a canopy of gnarled tree limbs and flowering vines. "These are the monks' quarters," he said. He led us to the furthest building and pulled aside the saffron and red cloth covering the door. "This is my room. Please, come in and be comfortable."

Making our way past him, we found ourselves in a simple cell, with whitewashed walls and a cement floor. There were no windows, but fresh air and light entered through louvered vents under the eaves. The overall effect was a cool, delicious dimness.

A rough bamboo platform covered with a mat of woven reeds, a chair, and a three-legged table: these were the room's only furnishings. In the corner, near the roof, I noticed a teak shelf holding a bronze figure of the Buddha. Unlike most of such shrines I had seen in Laos, this one did not include flowers, incense, or other offerings. Souvannaphone noted my interest. He shrugged, a Western gesture made peculiarly charming by his smooth, bare shoulders. "The Lord Buddha does not need food or drink or even prayer. All He asks is pure simplicity and honesty when we look within ourselves."

I winced inwardly, thinking of Dani's and my impure motives.

"Sit down, please. I will go and get some refreshment." Before we could protest, he was gone, leaving the door-cloth swaying in the breeze of his passage.

Dani and I sat down next to each other on what must have been the monk's bed. I looked at her, silently pleading for release from this sordid enterprise. She gazed back at me, almost defiant.

I shut my eyes and breathed deeply, willing my racing heart to slow. We must have been close to the river; I could smell the sharp, rusty scent I had noticed during our boat ride, along with a hint of fishiness. The temple compound was so silent, I could hardly believe that it housed the three-dozen souls that Souvannaphone claimed. A low humming hovered just above the threshold of my hearing. Chanting, perhaps.

My body hummed, too, taut and ready. Despite my shame, I was unquestionably, unrelentingly hard. As I shifted position on the stiff bamboo, my trousers grazed the head of my penis. I gritted my teeth, swallowing my moan of pleasure, but Dani saw, and smiled knowingly. She took my hand and gave it a squeeze that reverberated in my groin.

"Relax, baby," she whispered. "Everything is under control."

The door-cloth swayed, and Souvannaphone entered, carrying a teak tray that he set upon the table. It held three glasses of water, and a plate of coconut-milk sweets like those we had seen in the market.

"Please," said our host, seating himself on the chair opposite us. "Help yourselves."

"After you, honored Souvannaphone," said Dani, that mock humility back in her voice.

"Buddhist monks are not allowed to eat after midday," I told her, annoyed by what seemed to me to be her willful ignorance and insensitivity.

Souvannaphone laughed, a liquid sound that bubbled like champagne. "True, Michael, but the living obligations of hospitality override the dusty strictures of traditional discipline." He picked up a *khanom* and bit into it delicately. His pink tongue flicked out to lick a bit of the coconut from his ripe lips. My cock surged at the sight of this simple and sensual gesture.

Dani took one of the little sweets and ate it in a single bite. "Delicious," she said. "Thank you."

"My pleasure," replied our host, and indeed he seemed to be enjoying himself. "After all, the Lord Buddha preached against extreme asceticism. He taught that ruthless self-denial was as empty a path as mindless self-indulgence. That is the essence of the Middle Way."

The room fell uncomfortably silent. My cheeks burned with shame. I feared that the beautiful man before us could read my lascivious thoughts. Clearly, he was modern and enlightened, rather than a rigid creature of tradition, but I felt certain that he would not sanction my immediate and overwhelming urge to strip the saffron robes away from his hips and devour his nakedness.

I could hear Dani's breathing, fast and shallow. I did not dare look at her. The monk gazed at us calmly, kindly, apparently not the least disturbed by our lack of conversation.

Finally he spoke again.

"The Lord Buddha told us that desire is the cause of suffering. If one can release the desire, one can know peace."

I couldn't stand it anymore. "Excuse me," I blurted out, stumbling to my feet. I pushed my way past our host, my body brushing against his robes, and ran out the door in a kind of panic.

The stillness of the afternoon rose around me, thick as mist. The chanting was barely audible, rising and falling like the hum of a distant beehive.

I didn't know where I was going. I just needed to get away from Souvannaphone's luminous, compassionate gaze, and Dani's lustful one. My feet found a path through the tangled jungle; a glint of sun on water told me I was approaching the river. Sure enough, in a moment I found myself at the peak-roofed pier where I had first caught sight of the monk.

I leaned against the railing, panting from my crazy flight. The waters of the Mekong slid serenely past, seeming to mock my inner turmoil. I remembered with a pang of mixed fear and jealousy that I had left Dani alone with the monk. Well, she was not my responsibility. I could only control myself and my own desires. I had acted rightly, removing myself from a situation so fraught with moral danger.

Yet now that I had escaped, I desperately wanted to be back in the welcome dimness of that hut. There was something that I needed, that I ached for, something far more significant than physical satisfaction. I closed my eyes against the brightness of the sun on the river, refracted through my tears.

There was a stirring in the vegetation behind me. I kept my eyes shut, holding my breath, wanting, not wanting, waiting for whatever would come next.

"Michael." It was him. I turned to face his beauty.

"Are you unwell?"

I wanted to embrace him, to kneel before him. I blushed deeply. "Uh—no, I just suddenly felt the need for some air."

"I understand," he said with a half-smile, and I believed him. "Where is Dani—my wife?"

"She is still in my room. Waiting for you. Come, Michael." He took my hand and led me back along the shady trail. His skin was cool against my feverish flesh. I caught a hint of sandalwood in the air that moved around him.

Dani was half-reclining on the bamboo bed but sat up hastily as we entered. I could see that her dress was unbuttoned to the waist. Her pale skin shone through the gap.

The monk seemed not to notice. He handed me a glass of water and I drank it down, more thirsty than I had ever been. Souvannaphone looked from me to my wife and back.

"I was speaking of the desire and the nature of suffering. When you surrender all attachments and let the world wash over you like water, your suffering will fade to nothingness.

"Sometimes, however, it is not possible to simply will desire away. The more you try to let go of the desire, the more attached you become. Sometimes, you must satisfy the desire. Then, when you are sated, the desire evaporates like the morning dew, and you are free."

Souvannaphone stood up with the conscious grace that marked all his movement. With a simple gesture, he untucked the fabric wrapped around his waist and let it fall to the ground. Through sudden tears, I had a confused impression of tawny skin, rounded limbs, a center of darkness, and a spear of ivory gleaming like the moon.

"Surrender, Michael," he murmured, and I let go, finally, of my resistance, kneeling at his bare feet to worship him.

He was smooth and hard as polished river stone. I bathed him with my tongue, reverent, grateful, sucking him deep into my throat, but always gently, always with respect. In response, he reared and bucked in my mouth, slamming his slim but relentless cock against my palette, asking me for the roughness that seethed inside me, but which I hadn't dared to release.

I gave him what he wanted. What I wanted. I sucked him, gnawed him, devoured him as I had dreamed. On and on, for hours, for eternity, his cock ramming me again and again, till my jaws ached, till I was dizzy and delirious with lust.

My own penis was a rod of granite, threatening constantly to spill over. In this endless sucking, I would sometimes feel a tremor run through him, and think, triumphant and joyful, yes, now he will bless me with his flood, and I will be saved. He did not come, though. I had the sense that he was totally in control of his reactions, even as his erection grew constantly fuller and stronger.

Finally, I raised my eyes to his, gasping, saliva dripping down my face. "Please," I begged him, holding his slicked hardness between my palms in an attitude of prayer. "I can't bear it, Souvannaphone. Please, please fuck me."

"No!" Dani growled from the bed behind me. "No, that's not fair! It was my idea! Fuck—me, damn it, fuck me now!"

With deep guilt, I realized that I had totally forgotten her. She was sprawled on the bed, her dress hanging open, her knees pulled up, one hand pinching her nipple, the other probing frantically in her cunt.

Her usually creamy skin was mottled with arousal. Her hair was plastered in auburn ringlets on her sweat-beaded forehead.

The curls around her sex were equally soaked. Now that I was paying attention, I noted that the small room was thick with her musk. When I looked at her, the anger in her eyes flickered out, leaving only desperate need. My lust for the holy man melted away, replaced by ravaging desire for her.

"Please," she whispered. "Souvannaphone. Someone. Fuck me."

In one stride, the monk was by her side. His hands hovered in the air over her bare flesh. I held my breath, suppressed my jealousy. She deserved him as much as I did. She needed him, too. Possibly more than I. I waited for the moment when he would caress her, knowing he would not be able to resist her wanton beauty.

That moment did not arrive, though. His hands shaped in the air the ritual gesture of benediction that we had seen that morning. His rigid cock waved, only inches from her mouth. Then he stepped away.

His eyes, ageless and pure, met mine. "Make love to your wife, Michael." I needed no second invitation. In an instant, I threw off my clothes and joined her on the bed.

I slipped into her like I was going home. Her lushness, her heat, her complex and familiar scent, welcomed me. There was no struggle, no challenge, no games, only a silent and sublime connection as we rose together toward ecstasy. I could feel her need, and I answered it, simply and completely, in a way that was new but somehow not surprising.

We forgot about Souvannaphone. We forgot about the world. There was Danielle and Michael, Michael and Danielle, and then finally, only One, nameless.

When we came back to ourselves, the hut was full of shadows. There was no sign of our host. "I'll bet he was watching the whole time," whispered Dani, tickling my ear with her tongue. "I'll bet that he really got his rocks off." I was about to chide her for profaning such a holy moment. Then she kissed me deeply, and I understood that she was not in the least bit serious.

We did not see him again. As we made our way through the quiet dusk, holding hands, the *wat* seemed deserted, a glittering relic abandoned by some long-disappeared empire. I could sense his spirit though, hovering, flowing through me as a new peace.

We flew out, headed back to Vientiane, the next morning. The propeller-driven, Soviet-era plane smelled of mold, and rattled ominously when the mountain updrafts seized it. It had gotten us to Luang Prabang safely, though. We just had to trust that it would survive the return trip.

The hills were emerald, stitched with the silver of cascading streams. We took off to the north, then circled the city once before climbing into the clouds. The twin rivers cradling the ancient capital of Lang Xang gleamed with reflected sunlight. Then I caught a brighter glint, obviously the spire gracing the roof of some temple. The image of Souvannaphone at the river's edge flashed again in my mind. Beauty simultaneously sacred and earthly. Wisdom of both the soul and the body.

Dani squeezed my hand. I turned to smile at my gorgeous, perverse, and blessed wife.

Three Days
on Santorini

꒦

SAGE VIVANT

SHE TURNED TO MIKE as they shuffled their way up Lufthansa's crowded jetway. Carry-ons were slung over both their shoulders.

"Doesn't Greece have an airline?"

He chuckled derisively. "Yeah, they have an airline. But you wouldn't want to fly it across the world. Trust me."

"Why not? Is it bad?"

The dark, swarthy man in front of them glanced back, smiling and nodding knowingly.

"See? Everybody knows! Olympic went bad after Onassis sold it, and it never got better," Mike went on authoritatively. The man voiced his agreement and they almost immediately lapsed into a loud Greek exchange.

She got so hot whenever he spoke Greek. Not knowing what he was saying should have disconcerted her, but instead, it intrigued and excited her. She imagined he said things that couldn't be expressed in English; concepts so profound that only an ancient language could capture their nuances.

The men stopped talking and she leaned toward Mike, her heart racing with curiosity.

"So, what did you talk about?"

"I asked him if he knew the basketball standings in Greece."

Sometimes it was just better for her to fantasize about the content of his Greek conversations.

"Well, it's still fun to listen to you. Maybe I'll learn some Greek while we're there!" she said, lifting her face to his for a kiss.

"Silly woman. Hoosiers can't learn Greek!"

She turned her body to jettison a carry-on toward him.

They settled into their seats for the relatively short flight from Frankfurt to Athens. He took her hand.

"I wish you could join me in Thessaloniki. It's so beautiful, you would lose your mind."

She smiled and squeezed his big hand. "I just can't picture myself at a reunion of Greek basketball players," she replied.

"It will be better for you to come another time. When you can spend time, meet my family and we can all be together. Now is not good."

It pained him to exclude her, she knew. But she assured him this wouldn't be the last of their trips to Greece.

"When you meet me in Santorini," she said, speaking close enough to his ear so her hot breath would be felt, "we won't much care about what happened in Thessaloniki." She flicked his ear with her tongue.

He sighed and let his seatback support his head. "Ah, Santorini!" He placed a hand on her thigh and squeezed. Even through her jeans, she felt the wild warmth of him. With the raw sexual power he exuded every moment of every day, he was the most potent aphrodisiac she'd ever known.

"See you in three days," she said into his big chest when they got to Athens. They confirmed they had each other's contact information and headed for their gates.

She quickly discovered how Olympic had earned its reputation as the aging plane rattled its way south toward Santorini. The setting sun painted brilliant streaks of orange and purple, distracting Ingrid from the plane's inadequacies. She could hardly wait to see the island Mike couldn't stop talking about.

There was still enough light in the sky to see the enormous caldera of Santorini. As tiny reflections of sunlight sparked the tips of tiny Mediterranean waves, the water glistened with seductive allure.

A simple unimposing façade greeted her at the front of her hotel in Oia, where the pace was slower and the volume lower. The expanse of sea behind it and the glittering lights of Thira to her left foretold of the view that awaited from her room.

She did not sleep in her modest room's small but clean bed. Unable to tear herself away from the singular beauty of her patio's vista, she reclined in a low-slung, canvas chair facing the sea and spent the night there, mesmerized and longing for Mike.

This kind of beauty, pure and perfect as it was, evoked urges of an inexplicably carnal nature. The cool night breeze licked at her skin and she closed her eyes, surrendering to it, unraveling under its relentless calm. She must have slept because, periodically, she woke. But she was awakened by dreams so vivid, they pushed into reality. Mike's lips on her neck, making their way down to her breasts. His generous tongue lapping at her happy, erect nipples. She felt his touch, his very presence, whenever she drifted to sleep. And it consistently woke her.

A rooster jarred her even before any suggestion of daybreak threatened the horizon. In all other circumstances, the harsh call would have annoyed her, but here in Oia, it melded into the agrarian landscape.

Despite the travel and the erratic night's sleep, Ingrid vibrated with the energy of the mysterious island. At 8:00 A.M., she roamed the labyrinth of whitewashed stairs that lined the island's edges. Few *kahfehneos* were open at such an early hour—life on Santorini did not stir until at least 10:00 A.M. She explored what seemed like every nook and cranny, fascinated by the ancient freshness that permeated every breath of life.

When the sun was high overhead and a thin film of perspiration lay on her, she realized she was hungry. More tourists roamed the town now. She had no wish to eat where they did—she was actually beginning to feel Greek!

She found a restaurant displaying the sign of an octopus and the name of the establishment in Greek. A couple of tables were occupied and only animated Greek conversations were audible.

She walked in.

For the next three days, she took all her meals at the octopus restaurant. The three brothers (Giorgos, Lambros, and Stavros) who owned the place attended to her like she was a child under their tutelage. They introduced her to *marides, fassolia gigantes,* and, of course, octopus in its many culinary iterations.

Stavros spoke English the best of the brothers and soon she found herself telling him about Mike and his imminent visit. By the second night, each of the brothers had treated her to either a glass of local wine or ouzo. (The ouzo made her head spin, so she stuck with wine thereafter.)

Stavros showed her how to make a call with a phone card at the pay phone next to the restaurant. She punched in the numbers that would ring Mike in Thessaloniki.

"*Neh!*" A gruff male voice nearly shouted in greeting.

"May I speak to Mike, *parakalo*?"

"Eh?"

She corrected herself. "Michalis!"

"*Ohi!*" The voice said something else she didn't understand and then left the phone. She assumed Mike was now being paged to come to the phone.

"*Neh.*"

"Mike? It's me!"

More unintelligible Greek ensued. She heard the man say "Michalis" several times and she came to intuit that the wrong Mike had been summoned.

"Michalis from America!" She shouted, desperately hoping there wasn't more than one of those, too.

The man said a bit more, waited for her response, then hung up when she was silent. Tears of frustration welled in her eyes and she replaced the receiver with hopeless finality. She missed him so much and suddenly hated this unfamiliar country and its complicated language.

Even a simple phone call was fraught with confusion and difficulty in this quirky place. She knew Mike wouldn't have given her an incorrect phone number—her inability to reach him by phone was purely a language problem. She considered asking Stavros to make the call and ask for Mike, but she was embarrassed by what she feared he might view as her ineptitude. Did she want to risk Stavros telling his brothers that Americans couldn't even manage a basic telephone call?

When she returned to her hotel that evening, she checked with the mild-mannered owner to see if there were any messages for her (the rooms were not equipped with telephones). The woman's English was worse than Ingrid's Greek and she just kept nodding pleasantly at the phone when Ingrid pointed to it, smiling as if to give her guest permission to use it. If Mike had called, he would've been able to communicate with the woman, explaining who Ingrid was and leaving a message. But could the woman then deliver the message to her? Ingrid decided, dejectedly, that she could not and returned to her room.

On day two, Ingrid attempted to rent a motorbike. But when the vendor saw her lack of coordination and her complete discomfiture with the braking and acceleration mechanisms, he urged her to spend her money on a bicycle instead. She was disappointed—the motorbikes were so sexy, so European!

But it had also been some time since she'd been on a bike. As she swung her leg over the back of the first one, she misjudged the position of the wire basket behind the seat and flung the inside of her thigh right into it. Infuriated, she couldn't help but notice the vendor's attempt to stifle his laughter. As gracefully as she could, she slid demurely across the front of the bike and landed unceremoniously on the seat. Her thigh stung from the earlier impact but she refused to let the vendor know her pain.

She rode to Akrotiri that day and spent hours reviewing the remains of the island's most ancient civilization. Hot and sweaty from her ride, she again felt consumed by the urge to touch Mike, to feel him touch her. What was it about this island, anyway? Was it because lovers were everywhere, kissing, fondling, and hugging? Was it some mysterious mood that rose from the caldera and insinuated its libidinous nature in the unsuspecting populace? Or was it just that her man was capable of arousing her even in his absence?

Despite the penetrating sun and her growing exhaustion, as she pedaled back to Oia, the heavy heat between her legs was more than a distraction; it rapidly became an urgent need. She pedaled quickly but kept an eye open for private, remote areas where she could steal a few quick minutes.

What was she doing? What if she found some hidden spot, used it to gratify herself and then got caught by Greek police? How could she ever explain such an indiscretion to her family, or even to Mike? Especially to Mike...

Her legs pumped the pedals furiously; she was less than a mile from Stromboli, her hotel. The bike wasn't due back until six. She swerved into the hotel's small parking area and leapt off, forgetting about the wire basket and once again whacking her thigh.

But pain that close to her sex helped alleviate the incredible knot of lust that sat so solidly there. She leaned the bike against the building and sprinted into her room, passing the innkeeper on her way.

As her hands grabbed at her breasts, they became his hands, squeezing and kneading her. She tore off her jeans and shoved a hand into her panties. Furtively, she ran her fingers along her now-slick labia before pushing a desperate hand into her vagina. She stood in the middle of the room, seething with desire, one hand massaging a breast, the other sliding in and out of her wetness.

Her hand was his cock, plunging into her, feeding her what she needed. Her juices coated her hand now and her speed increased. In seconds, tremors wracked her body and her eyes rolled backward. Her fingers did not stop their probing and rubbing, even as she surrendered to her body's release. But when her knees gave out and she lurched to find support, her hand ceased moving and gently cupped her hairy triangle, holding it like an egg that couldn't be jarred for fear of breakage.

She moved to the bed and lay down, where she slept for several hours, until it was close to 10:00 P.M. Dinnertime in Greece. She showered, dressed, and walked in new serenity to the octopus restaurant, where Lambros made her try the greens he'd prepared with a lemon-garlic sauce.

She tried to phone Mike again from the pay phone, but this time there was no answer. He'd arrive tomorrow. She had to be patient.

The next day, after returning the bike and incurring a late charge, she meandered about the spiraling, uneven steps overlooking the sea, just as she'd done the previous morning. She didn't know when Mike would return exactly—he'd alluded to an early afternoon departure but she didn't have his itinerary. She decided to have a Greek coffee shortly before noon and then head for the airport.

The bus retraced the route it followed when it delivered her to Oia days before. She stared out the window at the glistening Mediterranean but the bus passing in the opposite direction briefly obstructed her view.

A flash of Mike's face jolted her. He was on that bus, headed for Oia! Had he seen her, too? She sprang from her seat and scrambled toward the driver, whom she convinced to let her out immediately. Her panic transcended her inadequate mastery of Greek in this case.

She burst from the motor coach and began running in the direction of the other bus. As she rounded the sharp bend, nearly a precipice over the crystal clear sea, she saw him getting off the bus with his suitcase. When he saw her, he dropped his luggage and ran toward her.

Under the strong midday sun, they laughed and collapsed in a needy, ecstatic embrace. His body, strong and hard, emanated some new aura she'd not known before. He seemed like part of this rich landscape, like a caldera in his own right. Hugely powerful but at one with his surroundings. The sun and the water flowed through him.

His kiss fed her as she knew it would, and his hands in her hair, his palms running down the length of her back; these were her reasons for living.

Because of his suitcase, the two waited in the hot sun for the next bus, rather than walk toward Oia. He related his basketball reunion to her with almost childlike animation.

"Well, *you* must have been having a good time," he added. "I tried to call you both nights but they said you were out."

"Damn it! I tried to find out if you'd called but nobody told me anything! Why wouldn't they tell me you called?"

"I didn't leave a message."

She looked at him quizzically. "Why not?"

"You obviously weren't waiting for my call, so I didn't want to disturb your fun."

"Mike! What's the matter with you? I've missed you desperately!" She decided that now, however, was not the time to describe yesterday's consequences of missing him. "I tried to phone you, too!"

"Tried?"

"Well, the first time, I think the wrong Michalis answered."

He grinned. "Yes. There were four of us by that name! And none of them speak English but me."

"Yeah, so that was a bust. Then, the next night, there was no answer at all!"

"We had a game last night."

She refused to let this foolishness be an obstacle between them. Leaning into him, she pressed her breasts against his chest.

"But we're together now," she purred, kissing his parted lips. She felt him relax a bit as the bus pulled up.

He said he was hungry so they went directly to her octopus restaurant, suitcase and all. Stavros greeted her warmly.

"This must be Mike!" he said, extending his hand for Mike to shake. The two men exchanged pleasantries in Greek, then Stavros seated them at the table with the best view of the water.

"You know this man?" Mike said when the man was a safe distance away.

"Isn't he nice? He and his brothers own the restaurant. They taught me so much about Greek food! In fact, let me order—you'll be impressed!"

"You know the brothers, too?"

"Miss Ingrid! *Kalimèra sas!*" Lambros and Giorgos called from the bar.

"Well, I don't really *know* them," she said cautiously, suddenly understanding where Mike was headed with his questions.

"They seem to know *you!*"

"Mike, you're being ridiculous. They've been kind to me, that's all. I told them all about you. Stavros even knew your name when you came in! Stop imagining things."

"American women are easy targets for Greek men. They would see someone like you and not give up!" His jaw was clenched and he pretended to read the menu. She reached for his hand.

"It's sweet that you're jealous, but trust me when I say you've got nothing to worry about," she assured him, making him meet her gaze.

He ordered for them both (he would not let her do so) and ate in awkward silence. Fresh breezes swirled with seductive undercurrents through the open-air restaurant. The tension between them triggered something primal and the moistness between her legs returned. When he'd finished eating, she spoke quietly.

"I want to show you something special. It's not far. You can leave your suitcase here."

She led him down the main street, which now flowed with a never-ending stream of tourists. Just before the tourist office, she tugged at him to follow her down one of the myriad staircases that snaked around the small, whitewashed houses. In her hours of exploration, she'd come to know the paths of the endless stairs throughout Oia. The couple descended what seemed like several flights. Finally, they arrived at a cave tucked between two buildings. It was small, maybe seven feet wide and shaded, yet it afforded a panoramic view of the glittering Mediterranean. They stared at the clear, calm beauty, speechless with appreciation. She stood behind him and slipped her arms around him.

"I've been dying to take you here. I found it on my first day," she whispered. Her hand moved to his crotch, where a prominent bulge grew. She rubbed it with a slow, circular motion. His neck was hot near her mouth.

Completely forgetting about their luncheon conversation, he turned and pressed her up against the cool stone wall behind her. He encased her breasts in his wide palms. He squeezed them, eyeing them as if they had answered some silent prayer.

"I've been wanting these," he whispered hoarsely. He quickly peeled her knit top over her head and snapped the hooks of her bra apart. Her full breasts fell out of their restraints with their own unique urgency.

His mouth was on them immediately, sucking, licking and kissing her hard, pink nipples. She struggled to get his shirt off so she could feel his skin against her. He helped her but never stopped sucking her breasts.

Then, he unbuttoned and pulled down her pants. As she stepped out of them, he took off his own. She watched his cock pop out and swing to attention, bobbing with the effort. She immediately grabbed it.

There was a small stone step two feet high, incongruous and seemingly useless, in their cave. But he sat her down on it, knelt before her and spread her legs. The cool breeze felt wonderful as it rushed over her steamy center. The scent of her arousal rose up between them. He held her legs open at her thighs and started to move his face toward her succulence.

"What's this?" he asked, touching the black and blue patch on the inside of her thigh.

She rolled her eyes in self-deprecation. "I had a run-in with a bike," she explained.

"These look like finger marks. Look! It's exactly where I would touch you!"

And damn if he wasn't right.

"You've been with one of those men at the restaurant, haven't you?" he demanded, still holding her thighs open.

"No! Mike! Come on, now!" She wanted his face between her legs so badly now. "I told you. I fell off a bike!"

"A bike with fingers."

She was burning up. The heat, her anger, the passion between them…

"What do I have to do to convince you I've been faithful?" She put her hand between her legs and dragged a finger slowly between her creamy lips, letting him see her pink, slippery folds open and close under her roving finger.

"Yesterday, I had to please myself because I was so hungry for you," she continued in a low voice. "No man could substitute for you." She ran the fingers of her other hand through his hair. As she watched his face relax, watched his eyes follow the massaging fingers between her legs, she subtly drew his head toward her until she felt his nose at her clit.

He lapped at her juice, flicking his tongue with absolutely perfect precision over and over her swollen clit until she called out, pulling at his hair. Once the waves had passed through her body, she became aware of her own mouth's need to consume her lover.

Her knees were too weak to support her, she knew. She looked down at Mike, whose face was shiny with her juices.

"Stand up," she urged.

When he did, he was harder than ever. It hovered before her, tempting her.

She dove at it, hungrily sucking, sliding her lips up and down his shaft while she swirled her tongue around his cock knob. She held his tight balls in one hand with the tips of her fingers wedged between his asscheeks.

An intake of breath alerted her to his impending orgasm, so she pulled him out of her mouth. He yelped softly, with an endearing helplessness.

Her strength returned and she got to her feet. She turned her back to him and held on to the strange little stair for support. Her ass was exposed to him. She wiggled it a little. Looking over her shoulder, she grinned.

"Fuck me, Michalis," she purred.

His thickness was inside her instantly, plowing into her, pulling nearly all the way out, then ramming back in again. Every thrust sent ripples of pleasure through her and she pushed her ass into him with the same rhythm.

They came quickly and together. The gorgeous sea, the heavenly blue sky, that incorrigible breeze—all of it became a sensuous, blurry backdrop to their wild, passionate melding.

When they returned to the octopus restaurant to get Mike's suitcase, the Greek brothers could not refrain from smiling at the couple's dirty, disheveled appearance.

"I think you have learned to enjoy Santorini, eh, Miss Ingrid?" Stavros teased her quietly, believing himself to be out of Mike's earshot.

She blushed and walked out, holding on to Mike's arm.

"What did he say to you?" Mike demanded as they walked.

She rolled her eyes and did not answer. She hoped by making light of the exchange to get him to drop his fixation on it.

"Why won't you tell me?" he insisted.

She sighed and relented. "He pretty much congratulated me on having sex," she laughed, a little uncertainly.

Mike stopped walking. "How did he know you had sex?" His eyes blazed.

"Well, let's face it, we both look a little less than fresh."

"I don't understand. Has he ever seen you after sex? How does he know what you look like after you make love?"

She stared at him, speechless. She waited until the silence magnified his paranoia enough for him to see it. When his epiphany finally hit him, a broad smile spread across his face.

"I'm behaving badly, aren't I?"

"You're cute when you're jealous, but yes, you're behaving

badly."

"It's just that I've missed you," he said, slipping his arms around her waist. "I imagined every man was after you while I was away."

"Well, they were. I just didn't sleep with any of them," she giggled. They embraced and she smiled as he squeezed her affectionately.

"Let's go rent bikes," he suggested.

"Now?" She had hoped a different physical activity would be next on their agenda; something requiring fewer clothes and more contact. Then she realized what lurked behind his request.

"You want to verify that a bike bruised my thigh, don't you?" Her hands were on her hips but she kept a teasing smile on her face.

"What can I say?" He shrugged, grinning. "I can't imagine any Greek man could keep his hands off you!"

ukiyo

ॐ

DONNA GEORGE STOREY

IT BEGINS RESPECTABLY ENOUGH.

My longtime colleague and friend, Yutaka Yamaguchi, invites me to dinner at one of Kyoto's oldest restaurants. We're celebrating. He's published his second Tanizaki volume, I just got tenure. Along the way I lost a husband, too. Work kept me so frantic this past year it took a month to notice he'd moved out.

My goal this summer, I tell Yutaka, is to rediscover pleasure. Not in books or dreams—I've had plenty of that—but in something I can savor, something I can hold in my hand. The real thing.

For the moment I've found it. We have a table on the terrace to catch the river breeze. The evening sky stretches over us, a bolt of violet silk fading to silver. Young waiters murmur excuses as they bring course after course: slices of sea bream and fluffy, snow-white conger sailing on a miniature boat of ice, eggplant and broiled river eel, wisps of ivory-colored noodles in chilled soy broth.

Yutaka pours more cold sake into my cup, a small work of

art in itself with frothy air bubbles suspended like jewels in the depths of the thick glass. "What other pleasures shall we rediscover tonight? We're in the right part of town for it."

"I don't know. How about one of those image clubs where I can play company president and screw my 'secretary' on the desk? Or maybe a soapland. How much would it cost to have two or three naked women soap me up with their bodies?" The sake is clearly taking effect.

He laughs.

"Gion is for men," I remind him. "Rich men."

"Perhaps, but foreign women are the 'third sex.' Legend has it you possess magic powers."

It's true enough my status as honorary male has come in handy in my profession, but I never considered matters of the flesh. I feel a surge of warmth between my thighs as if a cock is dangling there, thick and florid. The sensation is oddly exciting.

"No magic I know can turn me into a gentleman profligate. Not even for one night."

Yutaka smiles.

We drift through the canyons of the pleasure district. Signs for bars and clubs twine up dark glass buildings like neon ivy. Two college boys hold up a friend, his body sagging like martyred Saint Sebastian, his chin glistening with vomit. A gray-haired man and a young woman in an office lady's uniform hurry down a side street toward a blinking lavender sign for a rent-by-the-hour hotel.

Suddenly the sky shrinks and blushes. I'm inside a tiny room. Everything is red, the ceiling, the floor, the banquettes, the leather-upholstered bar. Only the mirrors on the walls lend a silvery glint to the infinite reflections of red. A man in shirtsleeves with a loosened tie sits at a table near the entrance, his face ruddy with drink. Two young women, one thin and feline, the other with a round, luminous face, lounge on either side of him.

It's a hostess bar, the classic choice for the evening's "second party" — if I were a man.

A handsome middle-aged woman in a kimono walks out from behind the bar to greet us. Yutaka introduces me as his colleague from a prominent American university. Her eyes flicker with new respect. In an instant I've changed from foreign girlfriend into a member of that inscrutable subspecies — the third sex.

Bowing, she gestures to an empty table. A tuxedoed waiter brings out a tray with ice, mineral water, and a bottle of Chivas wearing a silver necklace on its glass shoulders printed with the name *Yamaguchi*.

The moon-faced woman slinks over from the other table and introduces herself as Kazumi. Her modest silk dress only accentuates her curves. I've glimpsed my share of female flesh in the public baths here, but never anything so lush. In spite of myself, I imagine her kneeling before one of those low faucets, her heavy breasts dangling like cones of white wisteria tinted dark rose at the tips.

I blink and swallow hard.

As Kazumi busies herself mixing us whisky-and-waters, she chides Yutaka for not visiting her in so many months. Who else can recommend good books to her? Then she turns her sloe eyes to me, the honorable American professor. How young I look for a lady of such marvelous accomplishment; how perfectly my summer dress becomes my fair complexion. Her low, husky voice makes my skin tingle as if I'm being stroked with a piece of velvet. It's a long time since I've been courted. I admire her skill, but I don't believe a word she says. Even though I'm not the one paying.

My eyes wander to the next table where the slender, catlike hostess is doing something strange. She is touching herself — first her ears, then her eyes, nostrils, mouth — and counting. "Eight," she says, tracing a small, coy circle where her dress creases in her lap. She pauses, eyes narrowed, as if struggling against the urge to pleasure herself then and there, but she shifts her weight to one haunch and trails her finger around to the cleft of her ass. "Nine." I hear the word *ana*: hole, orifice.

If I were that man, I think, I'd touch her now.

But he only stares, his face flushing scarlet.

Back out on the street, we float through the summer night. The sky is black satin, embroidered with points of silver thread. Eleven-thirty and it's still warm, so warm it's hard to tell where the night air ends and my body begins.

"That hostess was lying through her teeth," I tease Yutaka. "Only a man would be fool enough to believe it."

"Carolyn, you're resisting."

"Maybe a pink salon would do the trick? Some throbbing music, a quick hand job from a stranger in the dark?" To my surprise, I'm half-serious. I've always wondered about those places, with the flashing photo galleries of women in tawdry lingerie and the permed gangster barkers calling out to men's crudest, most desperate desires.

"It's a bit early for such extreme measures." Yutaka claps me on the shoulder. "I think we need another drink. A little liquid courage?"

He leads me down a narrow side street. Glass and neon turn to weathered lattice doors illuminated by plump red lanterns. The oily, bittersweet fragrance of *yakitori* hangs in the air. As we move deeper into the maze of alleyways, even the walls vanish. In a haze of cigarette smoke, we pass gaming parlors, noodle stands, and tiny pharmacies hawking condoms and vitality drinks for every blood type. The stylish young women of Gion proper have suddenly grown older, their bodies thickened by childbirth, their smiles flashing gold. The men, grizzled and bent over mahjong tables, might have been frozen in place for fifty years. A final turn and Yutaka ducks under a blue curtain into a tiny bar, no different from its neighbors.

"*Irasshaimase!*" The aproned proprietress glances up from the low wooden bar. Her harried expression melts into genuine pleasure. "*Yamaguchi sensei. Ohisashiburi desu ne!*"

Her smile enfolds me, pulls me in. Any friend of Yutaka's is a friend of hers.

All six seats at the bar are occupied by middle-aged salarymen, some grinning, others soulful depending on the number of drinks they've consumed, but there's space in a *tatami* alcove tucked beside the bar. The mama-san sets a plate of cold soybean pods between us and returns with two tall glasses of *chuhai*, a cocktail of sweet potato liquor that goes down as easy as lemonade.

I catch myself studying my friend across the table: lean, high cheekbones; fine, leather-grained lines around his eyes; elegant fingers, the color of old parchment. Catholic girl that I am, it's no stretch to make him into a confessor after a *chuhai* or two.

"Everyone thinks it's easy being an academic. You teach a few classes a week, have the summers off. What a joke. I haven't had a break from work since I started grad school. Jason never got it."

Yutaka murmurs that his wife, too, can be less than understanding at times. We're talking in English, the natural language of complaint.

Of course it only got worse when Jason's dot-com company went belly-up. I was at the computer all day and most of the night, racing to finish the revisions on my book so I could have my contract in hand for the tenure committee. At first I scheduled regular breaks in the evening to be with him, but if I tried to get romantic, he'd snarl something about being tired. Then, when I was back at work, he'd creep into the study and start massaging my shoulders. I'd shrug his hands away—I had no time for games—and he'd go off to mope. But one day last fall he didn't go away. He only pressed down harder, kneading my muscles with brisk, defiant strokes. I was surprised how good it felt. After a minute or two, I closed my eyes and relaxed into it. Soon I felt a hand moving down my chest, undoing the top buttons of my shirt.

I asked him what he was doing. As if I didn't know.

Hush, he murmured into my neck. He pulled my shirt down over my shoulders and yanked up my camisole. The cool air licked my nipples.

Open your eyes, he said. Watch me play with your tits.

I winced, but did as I was told, gazing down at his big tanned hands squeezing my flesh. They looked foreign—a stranger's hands—but, oddly enough, I liked that. My chest was already speckled with flowery pink blotches of arousal.

Does the Japanese scholar like to have her nipples pinched?

I bit back a moan.

I think you do. Look at the way you're rocking your hips. Is it possible Madame Professor might have other things on her mind right now than work?

I glanced at the computer. The lines of text trembled and blurred.

Let me help you out of these pants, Professor.

I tilted my ass up to make it easier for him. Leaving my jeans and panties dangling around one ankle, he slid his hands between my knees and spread my legs wide, then wider still until they hung over the sides of the chair. He started to strum my clit—that much he could still do just right—and I bucked against his hand, whimpering as my tender asshole rubbed against the scratchy fabric of the chair seat.

Jason clicked his tongue. My, my, what would the tenure committee think if they saw you now, squirming around in your own juices?

Fuck me.

I'm sorry, I didn't hear you, Professor. Let's have a nice loud voice so the students napping in the back row can hear.

Fuck me, you bastard. Forget the kids in the back row, my shouting probably woke the neighbors two blocks away.

Jason reached down and fumbled with his zipper. His cock sprang out, an angry red baton. He lifted me to my feet and positioned me against the horizontal filing cabinet. We often used to do it standing up in the early days, me on tiptoe, Jason crouching a bit to get it in. I loved the sensation of his cock moving in and out, pressing up against my clit. I felt like I was flying. This time was different, though. Rougher. The denim of his jeans chafed against my tender pubes and each thrust knocked my asscheeks against the cabinet drawer. We weren't making love. He was punishing me, spanking me with a chilly, rattling metal hand, but I wasn't a helpless little girl, I was fighting back, grinding into him, soaring up higher, a witch on her broomstick. I came before he did, shrieking sweet victory.

It was the last time he touched me.

Will I ever have sex again?

"You're a very attractive woman, Carolyn."

I jump guiltily, but Yutaka's face holds nothing but mild concern. I must have been drifting off, mumbling to myself in drunken reverie. *Ukiyo*, the floating world, that's what they call it in Japan. Dreams and sex and sorrow all mixed up together. If I did say it all out loud, Yutaka is friend enough to forget in the morning.

I lean toward him. "You see, Yu-kun, it's not working. I'm still a woman. Even if I just want a little comfort, the warmth of another body beside me, I have to find the right guy who loves and respects me and fits in at the department's wine and cheese parties. I have to follow the goddamn rules."

"There are no rules here," Yutaka whispers back. His eyes twinkle.

I know a dare when I hear one. There it is again, that strange, tugging warmth between my legs. I go to smooth my skirt, but stop, suddenly afraid of what I will find.

A cell phone call and a taxi ride later, we're sitting on cushions in a well-appointed *zashiki*. Yutaka sips cold sake. I nurse a glass of barley tea. The place doesn't look like a brothel. We could be guests in any traditional inn with tasteful pretensions, except for the fact my heart is pounding in my throat.

The *shoji* door opens with a whisper. A young woman kneels on the glossy straw matting and bows low, first to me, then Yutaka.

She is lovely.

"This young lady will perform a traditional dance for us," Yutaka explains. "Her name is Ohisa." I bite back a smile. Ohisa is the name of a character in a Tanizaki novel, an old man's doll-like mistress, who, even in 1928, was a relic of the past. We've both published articles on her, mine a feminist reading of her submissive behavior as theater, masking a deeper rebellion. In private, on lazy afternoons, I'm less politically correct. I sometimes pretend I'm spying on her and the old man as he forces her to act out arcane sexual practices from erotic prints; beneath her dainty protests, I know she enjoys it.

And now she sits before us in the flesh.

The wizened grandma in the corner strikes up a geisha love song on her *samisen*. Ohisa rises to her feet. By some trick of the hand, her red sash slithers to the *tatami*, a gaudy, sleepy snake. Her summer kimono follows, pooling at her feet in ripples of midnight blue cotton and morning glories. What's left: Ohisa in a robe of nearly transparent silk that hugs her slender hips, her small round breasts. The nipples, a pale tender pink, poke through the thin cloth.

This is no ordinary dance.

My face grows hot, my hands throb and twitch in my lap. Has it finally happened? Am I seeing with a man's eyes?

I reach into my bag and pull out my sketchpad, full of amateur renderings of a fox shrine tucked beside a tofu shop, a corner of the iris garden at the Heian Shrine. I draw quickly, the curves of her buttock and shoulder, a faint shading of aureole. The kind of sexy picture a voyeur who thinks he has talent might dash off as a souvenir. But I also see what few men would in the proud tilt of her chin, the precision of her gestures. Ohisa—or whatever her real name is—is an artist.

When the dance is over, Yutaka stands, flashes me a smile and disappears. The *samisen* player leaves, too, but not before she removes the screen in the corner to reveal a futon, the top quilt folded back in invitation. A small brigade of sex toys stands ready by the pillow, all for a lady's pleasure. Images flash into my head, cartoon obscenities. Ohisa trussed up in the dildo harness, her vein-brocaded rubber tool bobbing with each wanton thrust. Or myself, the mad professor, leering over her supine form, a vibrator wand buzzing in each hand.

I catch Ohisa's eye. We both look away. Right now this room is a foreign land to us both.

Flustered, I push the drawing toward her. My offering for her putting up with Yutaka's absurd joke.

Ohisa studies the picture. She looks up at me again. Then she smiles.

It is Ohisa's idea to pose for me. She vamps, makes silly faces. We giggle like girls at a slumber party. I find, to my surprise, I'm having a very good time. Of course for her it might be nothing more than an act, a canny reading of a novice customer's mood. She's a professional woman. Like me.

At last she kneels on the bed with her back to me, her head turned in profile. Connoisseurs claim no vision is more erotic: the contrast of pale, slender neck and rich black hair.

It's my best sketch yet.

"Very nice," she murmurs.

It is now that I allow myself one indulgence. I touch her. Lightly on the shoulder, then again on her cool, smooth hair. I mean to stop here—and give her what I hope is an easy night's work—but for what she does. She sighs. A sound of such melancholy yearning, I feel it in my own body, an ache like hunger, but lower. Suddenly I want to comfort her, give her something, even if it's selfish. I wrap my arms around her and pull her back against me. She doesn't resist.

"May I touch your breasts?" My voice is strange, deeper.

"Please," she whispers. Her chest rises in quick, shallow breaths.

In the cups of my palms, her skin is padded satin. I circle the nipples with my fingertips, feel tiny goose bumps rise. Once, as if by accident, I brush the stiffened tips.

She sighs again. The sound makes my fingers sing like electric wire. I understand it now, how a man can get so hot and bothered just by touching a woman.

My hand skates down the curve of her belly.

"May I..." I want to say "...play with your cunt," but the proper words escape me.

She seems to understand. She parts the robe, drops her legs open.

The hair down there is slightly damp as if she's fresh from a bath.

"How do you make yourself feel good when you're alone?" I'm fumbling for words, absurdly polite. "Teach me. Please."

Obediently she guides my finger to a soft hollow just to the right of her springy little clit. As I strum, I flick her nipple with the pad of my thumb, the way I do when I masturbate. She moans. I drink it all in, the slurpy kiss of finger on pussy, the spice-and-seawater smell of her. Or is it me? Rubbing her in her secret place is enough to make my own cunt drool like an old drunk. My skirt is hiked up to my waist and I'm pushing myself against her ass and she squirms back and we're riding together on a wet spot as wide as the ocean, floating in that place where only sex can take you. No rules. No boundaries. Only pleasure.

Suddenly Ohisa's body goes rigid. "*Iku, iku wa.*" The Japanese don't come, they "go," but I need no translation as she sways in my embrace, mewing and shuddering.

I hold her until her breath is even and soft.

The curbside door of the taxi opens as if by magic. I slide in, lean back, glide through the summer night. The whine of an *enka* ballad drifts from the radio.

Heedless of the white-gloved driver, I bring my fingers to my nose. In novels and floating world prints the journey from pleasure back to ordinary life is the time of contemplation. The lies I'll tell Yutaka. The way I'll remember her cunt, soft as wet rose petals, when I bring myself off later in my bed. A touch of teenage-boy glee — *I made a girl come!* — though I know I didn't touch Ohisa in the way that counts.

I take a long, slow breath. A woman's pleasure. The perfume those libertines of old ruined fortunes to possess. I have it right here in my hand. The real thing.

Remembering Andrei

⤜

DEBRA HYDE

AT ONE TIME, Romania was a beautiful country. Bucharest was a city of pristine white buildings and colorful public flowerbeds, the Transylvanian Alps were wonders of steep climbs and hairpin turns, and castles, whether intact or in ruins, scowled down over small towns, invoking thoughts of Dracula. Romania was a country of contrasts, where a luxury automobile would draw alongside a horse-drawn wagon, where one field of hay was machine-baled and the next gathered by hand. And I was privileged to have witnessed these stunning disparities firsthand.

But that was before Ceausescu went nuts, before he banned birth control and progressive medical practices. Before Romania's common man, weary of too many mouths to feed and greedy for commodities, sold his excess children for quick cash and television sets. Before shoddy medical practices meant dirty needles and mass exposure to HIV. Before the country's people withered, then rebelled, then withered further.

I remember the Romania of the mid-1970s, a time when Ceausescu emulated Western culture by wooing then-President Nixon. As a result, cultural programs brought American performing arts groups to this Old World country.

I was a musician in one of those many touring groups, a violist in a college orchestra. Neither a virtuoso nor a principal chair, I was capable enough to earn a seat and determined enough to keep it. That summer, my orchestra worked its way through five weeks of touring, performing at every little city we came upon — Timosoara, Cluj, Galati, Drobeta-Turnu Severin, and more. We even played at a castle rumored to have been owned by Dracula where a television crew filmed us as pigeons, upset by the noise and commotion, flew overhead and aimed for the darkest of the men's suits to soil. By the time we reached the Black Sea, we were a ragtag troupe of tired gypsies primed for some R&R.

The Black Sea offered that restive peace. Like an American Great Lake, it was vast and magnificent. Its water lapped gently at its shores, its air breezed warm but never hot, and its people were — to our ignorant surprise — tourists from all over Europe.

There among those tourists, I met a local, Andrei. Although this will read like a bad sexual cliché, I have to tell you that I met him over sausage, at breakfast. I saw the sausage getting dished onto my plate, glanced up, and beheld a lean young man with hair so blonde it was a childlike yellow. As our eyes connected, I saw his were filled with amazement.

I'd seen that look before. In fact, I'd spent most of the trip adjusting to the fact that I amazed Romanians. I'm nothing special, mind you, except one thing: dark, copper-colored hair. Romanians had never seen anything like it and to them I was like some ethereal fairy creature. People stopped in their tracks and watched me. Children would come up behind me, their little hands touching my hair hesitantly, lightly, as if it were gossamer and the slightest touch might break it.

The children I silently adored, even as I pretended to ignore them. Their touch was just as much magic to me as my hair was to them. Now, I had this blond young man staring at me in stunned, unmistakable love-at-first-sight infatuation. As he stood there, platter in hand, he didn't know what to do next except to offer me another sausage. I begged off, but Andrei still spent the rest of the meal tending to me personally. He offered up sausage after sausage, eggs galore, bread, and, by meal's end, I was so stuffed with food and infatuation, I could barely rise from the table.

Later that day, while out walking, I saw him leave work on his bike. I smiled and said hello. He rode by and, as I turned to watch him pedal past, his steering grew just a touch wobbly, just enough for me to find it charming. The next day, he noticed that I ignored the onion soup at lunch but eagerly gobbled up the cream of chicken soup at dinner. Onion soup disappeared from the menu, never to plague me again.

Andrei was wooing me. And I liked it, so much that I decided to woo back. I watched the staff's habits, learned where he parked his bike, when his shift let out, and waited for him. Just what any hot-blooded and sexually aware American girl in pursuit would do.

"What's your name?" I asked him when he saw me by his bicycle. Andrei, I learned after we'd negotiated our way through language barriers. "Janice," I told him. I smiled and looked into his eyes as I said it. I even touched his hand. He was warm to my touch, though his body seemed frozen in place, stunned by my attention.

In time, we learned about each other. He learned I was your average conservatory student. I learned that he longed to perform professionally—classical guitar, it turned out—and he had been intrigued by every touring group that came through the hotel. When he saw me, that intrigue flared into immediate attraction.

We sat on the lawn behind the hotel and taught each other folk songs from our respective countries, my viola the melody to his guitar's harmonies. We cheered when our improvisations worked, laughed when they didn't. And sometimes, when the music and laughter fell away, we were left with that knowing silence, the silence of attraction.

Eventually, he showed me to a place in the rear of a maintenance building, a space forgotten by workers and big enough to spread a blanket on the ground and him over me. I remember two things: how, at first, he caressed my jean jacket, even leaned forward to smell it. I smiled and indulged his innocent curiosity. Back then, behind the iron curtain, denim was almost as rare as red hair but far more sought after. The second thing, though, still arouses me: how we kissed. How we mingled tongues, how we caressed, how hot we grew at each other's touch. But always, we'd stop. Coming up for air and common sense, we'd stop.

Eventually, we tried not to. Eventually, we lurched toward something more than denim and red hair and soft lips and wet kisses.

It's all so strange to write about this now, using words like *eventually* and phrases like *in time* because, in actuality, time was fleeting. We only had nine days' time to come together, share, then part.

I was keenly aware of that fact the day I took Andrei's hand and put it to my breast. Andrei looked at me questioningly. I squeezed his hand, making him grasp my breast. "Please," I said. "I want you to." I wanted him to unbutton my blouse, to see me. I wanted his lips locked around my nipple. I wanted to get wet as he aroused me. I wanted to rub myself against him, letting him know he could explore more.

Andrei wouldn't.

"No," he told me. "I cannot."

"Why?"

The look on his face told me everything: it was fear, a fear that, as it passed, melted into guilt.

We talked about it as best we could. As near as I could tell, Andrei struggled over the conflicting expectations of modern communism and old Christian orthodoxy. Where one embraced equality of the sexes, the other eschewed worldly things and vices, demanding submission to an older doctrine. Andrei lived wedged between two worlds, and now he had come in contact with yet a third one: mine. Mine, which was a place of newly won feminism, sexual freedom, and rock and roll, of birth control pills from Planned Parenthood and plugging in the viola to play Emerson, Lake, and Palmer while flirting with the emerging sentiments of punk rock.

No wonder he was confused. Still, a day later, democracy and communism beat out religion, and Andrei caressed my bared breasts with mounting excitement. His breath was ragged in my ear, his hands urgent. I pulled away from him and unzipped my pants. Anxiety spread across his face as I did and I'm sure he wondered whether seeing my cunt would doom him to hell or make him a good communist.

He survived his first glance but almost died of shock when I showed him where my clit was. "Never forget this spot," I advised him. "Women will adore you." I figured that if I made Andrei feel like a god, maybe he would forget the fear of being mortal.

My approach seemed to work. Or maybe our overwhelming heat persuaded him. Either way, Andrei became adept at pleasuring me, at slipping his fingers into me, at catering to my clit. He learned to thrill at my lively arousal, at my boisterous coming. He learned that in bringing me off, he could set aside old fears, at least for awhile.

Then again, when I coaxed him out of his pants, we found that he had something to teach me. He was uncircumcised, and I didn't have a clue how to handle his foreskin, what to do with it. "American boys are circumcised," I told him. He looked puzzled and bore the same look I'd seen at various checkpoints where the guards would linger over my roommate's passport longer than they did mine. *Jewish. He thinks Jewish when he hears "circumcised."*

I didn't know what to say or how to confront him. How could I? Raised by liberal, civil rights believing parents, I only knew about prejudice intellectually; I'd never had cultural bias laid right at my feet before. I said nothing, challenged nothing. I plunged back into our mutual infatuation, deciding that just as we'd forged our way through our language barriers and cultural differences, now we'd ignore each other's prejudices. I'm not proud to admit that holding Andrei's uncut cock in my hand prompted me to such a selfish course—that lust did that to me—but it did. Memory, however, does not permit me the comfort of denial that lust did. Today I sit uncomfortably with the memory of things left unchallenged.

There, then, lust urged me forward. I learned how to pull back Andrei's foreskin, where best to tease his slender cockhead, how to work Andrei into such a state that he ached for release. I introduced him to the breathtaking magic of a mouth slipping over his length and a tongue toying, wet with possibilities.

"I...I..." he panted, hesitating yet again. I reached up, put his hand on the back of my head, and made him push himself deep into my mouth when he came.

Later, I rested my head in his naked lap and watched his cock in repose, gently limp, satiated, its head tucked away in its foreskin.

The prejudice forgotten, the balance between us had restored itself in afterglow.

The blow job turned Andrei into a proletariat. He abandoned his orthodoxy and embraced modern existence. But time was pressing us into action. "Three days left," I told him. "And I have to perform tomorrow night."

I saw him in the audience that night, clapping in that respectful, orderly unison favored by the Eastern Bloc. I smiled, wondering if he'd find America's way of applauding chaotic and senseless. I know I certainly found the unison clapping disconcerting the first time I heard it.

That night, I met him behind the hotel. We rushed through kissing and petting and I went straight to my knees, hastily freeing his cock and sucking him off for the sheer pleasure of a stolen moment. I can still picture him, back to the wall, still hear him moan as he came, still imagine the feel of his cock as it shot its liquid essence into my mouth.

The next day, while my chaperones and the lobby staff watched Ilie Nastase battle Jimmy Connors in tennis on the hotel's only television set, I smuggled Andrei into my room. There, I found him so thankful for the previous night's spontaneity that he lay me down, pulled off my pants, and reached tongue-first between my legs. Like most men going down on a woman for the first time, he hesitated. But when he saw me arch and buck at his tongue's touch, he forgot whatever anxieties he had. He teased my clit, explored every crevice, and slipped his tongue deep into me. He savored me. And, when I could stand no more, I rode his tongue, his face, him, in furious abandon. He gasped for breath as I moaned and came.

After that, passion plunged us into stolen erotic moments and friendship obliged us to share simple moments. I showed Andrei how Europeans had it all wrong when it came to bumper cars, that they weren't for polite cruising but for smashing into each other. Andrei taught me how to barter with cigarettes for deals from kiosk merchants along the pier. Together we waded into the sea to swim and cavort, to lap kisses from each other as the water lapped around us.

The first time we swam together, Andrei noticed the hair on

my legs. "I stopped shaving in Bucharest," I told him. In Bucharest, imitating American feminine habits was a calling card for prostitutes, and men, when they spotted shaved legs, treated whore and tourist alike with indiscriminate, pushy disrespect.

"You would be safe here," he told me. The cosmopolitan, seaside Romanians knew better than to make assumptions.

The more we swam, the more the sea beckoned us. First, it only whispered as its waves lapped the shoreline, but as time passed, as we swam in it and grew familiar with each other, it became part of our attraction for each other. I would lie in bed at night, thinking of him in the water, swimming up to me, grabbing me from behind and pressing his erection between my legs. I thought of his hands at my breasts, always wet. His kisses were wet too, as if the sea were about to spill from his mouth to mine.

Then I'd recognize a more personal wetness and I'd press my fingers into service to relieve myself from the tormenting image of Andrei in the water.

Finally, our last night together arrived. We suffered, knowing our final good-byes lurked nearby. We tried to ride the Wave Swinger and the carousel with our usual cheer. We tried to walk the pier, looking for trinkets to buy. We shared a dark beer at a small sidewalk cafe. But our poignant sadness permeated our efforts to feign happiness. As the evening wore on, we became desperate to escape that unhappiness. We needed to forget, if only for a time, and to forget, we had to lose ourselves in each other. The Black Sea offered us that.

At twilight, we made our way to the water's edge. We took off our shoes, walked barefoot, and let the water soothe our feet. When the beach gave way to a rocky outcropping, we scrambled over the rough rocks until we found a spot where we could hide, just us and the water.

The water. Calf deep in the sea, I murmured, "Andrei," as I removed my blouse, my bra. "Andrei." My words brought him to my breasts, first with his hands, then his mouth. His touch electrified me. I slipped from the rest of my clothes and pressed my nakedness against him. "Please," I asked one last time.

Andrei groaned and pulled me close. His mouth searched, along my neck, my cheek, finally, my mouth. We kissed in agony. Around us, the water lapped.

"Take off your clothes," I moaned. "Let me feel you against me."

In moments, his naked body pressed against mine. My cunt convulsed in hope and desire. I kissed him urgently, caressed him in desperation. He returned my passion.

Around us, the water lapped.

We reached down for each other, my hand at his cock, his at my cunt, feeling, probing, currying our lust. As we slid into the water, Andrei latched onto my hard nipple and sucked. I spread my legs and urged his cock to nestle there. I guided it to my lips, water all around, my intent unmistakable.

"We only have now, tonight," I whispered. Andrei said nothing, but moved away from my breast, bringing his face ear-level as he pushed into me. The feel of his cock entering me made my breath catch in my throat, the sigh that escaped him blasted against me in ecstasy.

He rested a hand on my breast as he worked himself into me. But it didn't require much effort — I was eager and ready. I flowered for him, accepted him, and beckoned him deeper. Andrei began to fuck me and, as he felt me encompass him, he groaned. I nibbled at his ear and caressed the length of his back, held his asscheeks in my hands as he took me in long, slow strokes. I looked down to watch us fuck, but the darkness had deepened and the shadows only hinted at what we were doing.

My cunt knew what it was experiencing, though, and it gushed over Andrei's cock, then grabbed at him, clutching him greedily. I wanted to feel myself tight around him. I wanted to drive him to frenzy, to come and feel him come, yet I wanted the fucking to last forever. I wanted to never let go.

It didn't, though. We thrashed our way to quick orgasms, me squealing and squirming as he slammed into me, Andrei crying out as he flooded me.

Around us, the water lapped.

We rested there, in the water, long enough for Andrei to grow hard again, to fuck again. This time, he was bold and decisive. He turned me away from him, propped me against a rock and took me from behind. The rocks scraped at my belly as he bit into my neck, as we huffed and groaned wildly with his every stroke. When he finished, Andrei pulled from me and rested against me. I felt his success run from me, down my leg, into the water.

When we finally returned to my hotel, Andrei reached into his pocket and presented me with two necklaces, one a copper cross, the other a string of tiny shells from the sea. He placed them around my neck and kissed me. Tears choked me; I did my best to swallow them.

Likewise, I left a piece of myself with Andrei, a keepsake as American as his necklaces were Romanian. As our kiss ended, I took my denim jacket off and handed it to him. I smiled, weakly, and whispered my good-bye.

Our lives separated then. Andrei returned to his life of classical guitar, communism, and orthodoxy. I returned home—scrapes on my belly and a hickey on my neck—to contemplate dropping out of conservatory for the sake of spiked hair. But that night, before my orchestra returned home, I cried myself to sleep. Two days later, I touched native soil. Two weeks after that, my sorrow faded into sweet memory.

Andrei and I wrote to each other for a while. In time, he succeeded in getting into a Romanian folk troupe that performed for tourists. He even secured classical guitar work and achieved a measure of local fame. Eventually, he married. I finished college, went punk, and traveled the small bar circuit before discovering performance art via an MFA. Sadly, my travel took its toll on our letter writing and soon we lost touch with each other.

But in 1989, when Romania rose up against Ceausescu, the memory of Andrei came back to me. As news footage of Romanians rioting flashed on my television, I remembered the sound of his voice, the touch of his lips, the feel of him inside me. Tears welled up, just like that night we kissed good-bye, but this time I didn't choke them back. I cried. I cried because I feared seeing his body lying on the street of some ravaged city, or that I might see him in the face of a suffering Romanian orphan. I wept because it felt like sacrilege to remember the sex we shared as his country violently convulsed its way toward freedom.

But I couldn't help it. My body had its own memories.

While my feelings were raw with remembrance and worry, I rediscovered and reclaimed those necklaces that Andrei had given me and wore them for a time. I prayed for him and hoped for him, but I never heard from him. To this day, I don't know his fate.

Now, more than a decade after communism's end, Andrei's necklaces sit in a little wooden box, a Romanian folk design burned into its lid. And just as the design is etched onto the box, Andrei is etched in my heart. Just as those necklaces are tucked away inside, he is tucked away in my mind. Andrei endures, ever only a thought away.

continental Breakfast

⤲

HOLLY FARRIS

WHEN MELISSA SET DOWN THE RUINED SUITCASE, she swore she would never travel again. Not for pleasure. She needed a vacation so badly that she and her second husband, Ned, had hitched a ride to Paris on the airline she was preparing to retire from. Immediately upon touching down, they had set out on the 530 kilometer drive west to Riec-sur-Belon in south Finistere, a quiet corner of Brittany. Their destination was a farmhouse cottage surrounded by field and countryside.

"Being a flight attendant," Melissa had said at parties for almost twenty years, "is being a big cat trainer in heels." However glamorous it was on the outside, industry problems and colleague pettiness threatened to shred her middle-aged composure at any moment.

France carried many sensual memories. During the time her first husband was an older bachelor courting her, he had flown tourist class from New York to Paris on a flight when she hadn't been part of the crew, knocked at her city suite on a lovely April afternoon, and then bathed her in champagne he poured into a dented zinc tub. He soaped her breasts, molded her wet hair into ringlets and swirls reminiscent of thirties movie stars. When at last he frothed shampoo in his palms and began on the hair between her legs, placing each of her heels delicately over the tub's rim, virginal Melissa's vulva pounded. Open to his gaze, her coral pudendum was a joy, as precious as a masterpiece in the Louvre. He "found" a platinum engagement ring among the bubbles, and she wore it first on her spiking clitoris.

A superb lover, his treasures were too great to hoard. What she had taken as inspired foreplay, the bath she celebrated, was, in fact, a betrayal. When she found many of her colleagues could boast of similar trysts with him, they divorced when Melissa was barely twenty-five.

"A whole week," Melissa said. She placed Ned's free hand between her breasts, drawing down the peasant blouse's elastic neckline. She was hot enough to feel his wedding band warm nicely. Ever her chaperone, he shot the bolt on their guestroom's door. Their relationship was more tied to economics than sex, more about maintaining gym memberships than erotic gymnastics. Passion was pesky, inconvenient, and tiring to Ned. What marital property they shared — friends, money, status — required upkeep.

Her husband pulled his hand away from her cleavage as if burned, and unbuttoned his wilted shirt collar. Undeterred, Melissa sprung the front hook joining lacy bra cups, spilling herself toward Ned. Pale breasts with nipple discs became jewels displayed on gauze. Framing the still life, her chestnut hair rippled. Though Melissa wore tailored Capri pants and strappy sandals, she felt earthy and loose above her waist. She had pulled the tortoiseshell clasp from her long hair as soon as Ned turned the rental car on the A-10 and drove 39 kilometers to the southwest, fleeing the city. Melissa flew often to Paris, but she had never made this trek ending in stone fences decayed into rubble, concrete benches encircling elms.

"Let's go to sleep," Ned said in the darkness, draping his sweated-through dress shirt on the suitcase carcass. Their troubles had begun at ticketing when the agent misjudged the baggage conveyer belt's mood. Transparent at the end of a thirty-hour day,

Ned's shirt poorly concealed the cracked wheel and ripped fabric, but it curtained their misfortune, for which Melissa was grateful.

He took Melissa, stretched across the still-made bed in the dark, from behind hastily, flattening her buttocks against his pelvis, pumping for all he was worth. Her moist cunt, always the object of Ned's selfish lovemaking, held the least sensation for Melissa. He offered to play between the sheets after he was finished, but his lips were cracked and his unshaven chin chafed spots she had bikini waxed.

Lying to one side of the wet spot they had made, her husband turned peevish. "I couldn't understand a word MaDAME"—he lengthened the second syllable with everyone's parody of French—"what the bitch said when we checked in." Melissa found her comforting, grandmotherly. The older woman's body hid under a starched apron, her wispy hair tucked into a gray bun at the rear of her head. Upon arrival, the proprietress had quoted rates and terms. "*Quel prix!*" she said, which Ned recognized as "What a price!" from their tourist book. Sure that Madame had doubled the cost since they booked, Ned complained about their flight and car. Turning away from his whining, Madame had taken Melissa's hands between hers, murmuring "*bonus,*" a word that sounded the same as in English.

Ned, not having touched a towel or his toothbrush since they left home, turned down the bed's sumptuous linens, flopping on the side Melissa usually took. When she stood at the side of the bed to allow him access, he wiggled across to his accustomed place while the carved bed squealed. Curtains hung from rods spanning finials atop the bed's posts, conjuring the illusion that they inhabited a tree-house encased in fog. From her seat against the headboard, Melissa pounded the pillows, and then lined the top sheet's scalloped hem across her naked breasts. Something besides cotton scratched her hip, and she pulled out tiny foil-wrapped chocolate squares that must have rested on the pillows.

"Pink peppercorns in chocolate?" Ned said, squinting at the English on the label. It was worth his clicking the bedside lamp on to learn what he ingested. He chewed his treat, chasing bits off a side tooth with his tongue. Near as Melissa could tell, Ned fell asleep with the second souvenir melting inside his cheek.

Only a week before, she and he lay in bed at home on one

of her few overnights with him. Travel brochures, bearing French she knew would sound sexy if she tried to pronounce the words to Ned, fanned across the comforter. She'd had a grueling schedule, coast-to-coast flights and too little sleep, but she couldn't settle.

"A canopied bed and 1800s wallpaper," Melissa prattled. "No tours, no ruins, no crowds. How a trip to Brittany should be." She said this as a test. It might not be too late for romance at this hideaway, a working farm doubling as a guesthouse. Ned watched Bill Dance, the professional bass fisherman, catch a few on TV from a lake in Mexico. All of Bill's guides spoke unaccented English, and Bill was in his element. The entire expedition played out as far away as Ned's lumpy toes.

"Wonder how the food will be in France?" Ned said, sounding worried. He never ate fish. "Tiny portions and silly sauces?"

"You won't starve," Melissa said. "After a week, we'll be buffed."

She said this knowing her taut figure in her uniform was businessman eye candy. Her small waist showed the short jacket's cut to advantage, and her middle lay flat beneath the tailored skirt's waistband. The striped silk shirt fell beautifully from her high, small breasts. Unbuttoned a single pearl stop at the neck, Melissa flashed a feminine collarbone rising into an athlete's neck when she bent to serve. Pewter wings she wore pinned to her jacket lent tantalizing authority. She'd heard all the stale jokes: mile-high clubs, party planes, and so forth.

During this special trip interlude, she prayed to herself, Ned would stumble over her physical need, satisfy her pent-up desires as the couple became anonymous time-travelers cavorting in the 1800s. Gauze canopy panels would bind her wrists and ankles, a restraint freeing her to request nastiness from her husband. When it was her turn, she would tickle the same fabric over his nipples, tie his cock and balls into a frontal package. Unaware of Melissa's fantasies (he was a house husband happily retired from his own corporation), Ned switched off the TV and carefully put his glasses inside their case on the bedside table.

"You know the complimentary continental breakfast American hotels serve?" Ned groused. "In Finistere, I bet I'd kill for bacon and eggs."

When Melissa awoke in Brittany, she floated in rich coffee. In fact, the odor was strong enough to seem a mocha vapor hovering in their well-appointed room. Surprised but relieved that Ned continued to snore, Melissa retrieved her short silk robe and new slippers from beneath Ned's shirt on the suitcase. Unlike the night before, she groomed and primped leisurely in the bathroom at the end of their hall. Homemade soaps, lotions, and gels in reed baskets on an *étagère* lured Melissa to sample. She experimented with several blends, dabbing wrists, one knee, both elbows. Hearing scratching of some sort, she opened the window panels outward, knocking against the ladder of a workman.

Hayfields and orchards stretched as far as she could make out in the misty light. Odd structures she knew to be grape trellises were rounded parallels, and hedgerows intersected in brambles. Blocky rectangles around the window bolstered the stone cottage façade, lending an air of architectural stability. There was nothing whimsical about the place at dawn, and weathered shutters were missing louvers and hung crooked.

A painter in white coveralls, brushes dangling from loops at his hips, made her heart race. He scraped horizontal lines under the eaves, then wiped his rasp against a green-flecked leg. As Melissa ducked out of view, the man climbed down the ladder two steps at a time, a motion which wrinkled his coveralls where his legs became his flat rear. He stood on the ground for an instant, and reached down to the soil, evaluating the next place the ladder might stand. When all looked satisfactory, the athletic painter hauled the upright ladder a few inches, and launched himself, springing from the balls of his feet to the second rung. That tiny exertion, the step up, pinched his trousers in a *V* at his crotch that made Melissa salivate.

She was accustomed to model-handsome pilots, but this country man intrigued her. That she observed him undetected added to the wickedness. I should lean out this window to grab his butt, she thought. She envisioned the man naked, descending the ladder beside the window. Leaning out, she could flick her tongue across his fabulous buns, licking the places sweat began trickling. After spanking his schoolboy rear with her hairbrush, she would sternly order him to turn and give her his front, where she would nuzzle his balls and perineum. She could hear him whimper and plead — French she couldn't understand — to be allowed to descend enough to put his penis between breasts she squeezed together while she sucked its purple tip. Such slutty daydreams!

Totally appreciating the talents of a housepainter for the first time in her life, Melissa touched the bathroom mirror's whitewashed frame, satisfied she was radiant enough at forty to snare the workman, had she been so brash as her imaginings. She brushed her hair until it shone, decided against putting it up or even tying it back, and stepped into the narrow hallway.

Madame surprised her by being right outside with a bundle of clean sheets, and Melissa held the door open for the woman to set the linen inside their room on a chair. Ned, fingers spread at his sides and his stubble denting the pillow, didn't move. Melissa was embarrassed to see a stain speckling a path from Ned's face to his chest. If Madame noticed what had become of the chocolate, she didn't say.

"What's the hour?" Melissa said. The hallway admitted some exterior light, and Melissa assumed the guests always slept later than the hosts, but it would be rude for her and Ned to have cocooned their entire first day.

"Early," Madame said to her in perfect English. Melissa heard water run and the bidet flush in the bathroom where she had completed her *toilette*. Mindful of other visitors, she pulled the robe lapels together, retied the sash belt. Madame plaited her fingers through Melissa's like a schoolgirl, right hand in left, and winked. "*Café au lait, mon chère,*" Madame said. "Mocha for Ned. Come to my kitchen as you are."

Their hostess intended to pamper them, the brochure that arrived by mail had said. Melissa and Ned had filled out an extensive survey about their likes and dislikes in advance. European chocolate was at the top of Ned's list of desires; eating it gave Melissa hives.

Madame ran a tight kitchen. White wainscoting set against blue and yellow tiles made the place clean and intimate. Tawny baguettes lay horizontal to one another in rows on the rough-hewn table. Tins of gooseberry, raspberry, and strawberry jam were within arm's reach. Wire baskets of brown *oeufs* stood at the ready, enough to make omelettes for twenty. Country butter, dew-slick round pats as big as fists, sat on marble, which was sprinkled with flour to accept pastry. A slab of bacon for Ned, a fat-streaked rectangle crusted in black pepper, hung from a hook plastered into the tile wall over the wood cookstove. Madame tossed a fine-grained log into the fire, removing and recapping the stove's cast-iron eyes in sequence.

Synchronized to Madame's selecting the last log in the wood box, a bear of a man, wearing a leather apron with canvas sleeves over a white dress shirt, entered the kitchen from the porch. Logs were heaped in arms he held rigid at his waist, a firewood pyramid as high as his nose. He flashed a huge smile at Melissa, who lowered her eyes, even when he tossed all the logs together into the box as if they were matchsticks. Admiring his strength, Melissa was astonished at the man's fluidity. Shucked of his smock, he frothed his arms and hands in lavender-smelling soap at the farm sink, turning up his cuffs. He chose a thin-bladed knife out of the marquetry block on the counter, and set about scoring the skins of red potatoes.

Mopping trickles condensed on its surface, Madame poured milk from a stoneware pitcher into a copper pot for heating. She used a tiny ladle, as silvery and precise as a dental instrument, to capture an extra portion of cream. This last she swirled on top of Melissa's brew once the heavy coffee bowl was filled to the rim.

Thinking this hub would get busy, and wondering if Ned were wandering around the dining room, Melissa excused herself. As she went through the swinging servants' door, She admired the antiques. Many pieces had been primitive workstations: a wooden breadbox, a cast-iron pot for rendering lard. A formal buffet's mirror reflected back her self-indulgent dress. Licking appreciatively at the foamed coffee, she was annoyed at the memory of Ned back home saying he wanted predictable continental breakfasts, the dregs imprisoned in a steam table. This is the Continent, she thought, and I am a sophisticated traveler blessed with a glorious kitchen. God knows Madame can make a breakfast to remember.

Melissa wanted to devour the whole spread, send Ned back to their room gnawing only a bread crust dipped in fresh country milk. *No*, she whispered to herself, *he needs his strength. I am owed sex and romance, the former if not the latter. I'll drag Ned away from convention on this trip, throw him across our duvet before Madame has cleared the dishes.*

Four places were set at the table. Plates were heavy cream-ware, bowls decorated in yellow and blue foliage or fruits. They rested on mats with variable stripes, so rustic they could have been homespun. Two couples are here, thought Melissa. She hoped the other husband would be better company than Ned. And that the other woman thought nothing of dining in her robe.

Melissa became aware of a sideboard mirror she had missed. She leaned in to toy with pewter drawer pulls, to run a finger over some distortions in the glass. The thing gleamed with age and value.

Fiddling at the mirror's back, checking how pegs anchored it in its frame, Melissa spotted a small note, its mauve card stock dented from engraving her fingers traced. It was probably someone's place marker from a long-ago formal dinner. After holding it at a reading distance, then remembering her reading knowledge of French was worse than her speaking ability, Melissa was about to replace the paper behind the mirror when she caught a word she knew: raspberry. Rushing to read it, wondering if the antique had spent time in America, Melissa made out what seemed too many words for the short lines:

> I yearn to paint your pretty toes, covering the mother-of-pearl nails with warm raspberry jam. Stiffened cream will bind the trifle, and I will savor the dessert I have fashioned.
> C.

Melissa sat down heavily on the nearest chair, unaware it creaked under her slight weight. Her hair caught in the shallow at the base of her throat, which slicked with sweat. The tops of her ears burned. She felt her cheeks heat as the lover's note shamed her.

Where was Ned? Melissa, worried that exploring on her own had already gotten her in trouble, craved company. Baking smells hit her as she swung open the door from the dining room to the kitchen, scuttling back to Madame. The older woman stirred and sautéed, pausing to ladle a hazelnut concoction into Melissa's empty coffee bowl this time. Unneeded in the active kitchen, Melissa wandered to study the austere china cabinet, whose placement transitioned the living from dining space.

A brass hand bell drew her eye. The piece bespoke country

origin; it was not unlike what rural American schoolhouses had used to convene or recess class. This Melissa knew from her grandmother, whose stories about teaching as a young woman just out of high school had intrigued their family. Gram was adventurous, Melissa thought, for her time. *So I shall be.*

Set beside gold-edged demitasse cups and saucers, the bell flashed a modest patina, weathered through in spots to gray metal. Turning a filigreed key in the cabinet's heart-shaped lock, Melissa opened the case's glass door and poked at the bell on its polished shelf. Hearing no sound from the clapper, and certain she could investigate so quickly she couldn't be found out, Melissa lifted the mute bell by its walnut handle. She carried the artifact to a window, and peered under its brass skirt to see the interior. Where a wire hook suspending lead shot should be, the usual sound apparatus, ivory paper curled instead. Deep-cut lettering was explicit:

> *I must plow russet moss at the point where your body forks. My earth will mingle with your scent.*
>   *B.*

Melissa reeled away from the window. The bell tumbled to the carpet, and she felt her eyes sting as tears came. How could she invent these fiery communications? Ned hadn't made love to her before last night in months, but she had quit counting. Perhaps she was exhausted from the trip, wrung out from anticipating a breakfast delayed until a late hour. It could be afternoon or evening if she had misread the outdoor light. Was it getting darker, or was the sunlight truly building?

A cottage garden waved in the window glass, a profusion of old-fashioned blossoms. Hollyhocks opened phallus-centered flowers beside flame azaleas, and Melissa calculated how sun-loving and shade-tolerant flowers grew in such harmony. The landscape was impeccable, and she realized maintenance fostered the botanic chaos.

As her eyes scanned the outdoors, a gesture she wanted to take her away from the erotic overload inside, Melissa noticed a sculpture pedestal overgrown with a wild rose, its sugar-cube buds softening the briers. Thinking the stone cold and severe, a rebuff to the physical turmoil she felt, Melissa was sure she could will sex to become secondary. No, the sculpture morphed into a communal cunt. There was the obvious tunnel, but soapstone wings had been polished on their internal aspects, left coarse outside. She was so aroused she would have fucked the artist on the spot.

She saw a man some distance from the private nook. The gardener was shirtless, his silhouette composed of stained pants tucked into high boots. Tan flesh from toiling outdoors ranged beyond his clothes. He shoveled mulch from a pile under a budding peach tree, heaping the handcart until crumbs fell away. She was riveted for a series of his trips, and was able to confirm he tanned naked. As he stooped to grasp the cart's handles on either side of his thighs, the unbelted pants slung low on his hips and abdomen. Melissa, admiring his precision, searched for a white line. The gardener strolled the stone walk, upended the cart effortlessly, and never paused to drink water or mop his bearded face. Once, she imagined he flipped the bandanna from his pants pocket toward the window where she peeked. *Does this man go home tired to a wife at night,* Melissa said to herself, *or does he bed down alone in a room off the stable? Surely I can carry him ice water one morning, memorize his chest up close. In fact, if he is actually the sculptor, his hands hold memories of me already. He will touch me as a lover reacquaints following an absence.*

Aware that her shoulders quaked to maintain her balance, Melissa toed the china cabinet's bell under a radiator to hide it. The swinging door slapped. Madame, bearing an ironstone platter, swooped into the dining room, setting sausages and crisped red potatoes on the table. Melissa smiled weakly. She X'd the air over her coffee cup to signal she'd had enough.

"Here, Melissa," Madame said. She scooted a chair out from beneath the table, patted the seat's tufted cushion, and waved her guest over. Although it was opposite the place at which Melissa had set her lipstick-marked cup, she was glad Madame commanded her to do something. She heard voices, people moving around the kitchen, no doubt collecting their own magical coffee. Melissa arranged her face to welcome strangers, to chide Ned for being a slugabed. Madame, calling to the others in the kitchen, whooshed back through the door. Melissa lifted her heavy plate, checking the factory mark on its back.

She nearly screamed. The pastel card she found glued to the back of the plate was the same insistent blue as the borage flowers she'd seen the gardener pick. In fact, a platter of yellow sliced tomatoes before her was garnished with dozens of the cucumber-smelling blossoms. Melissa took in the card's message as if it were a gulp of spring water:

> I am wild to frost your breasts in tempered bittersweet. Almond or citron to garnish, your whim will guide my hand. Let my tongue solder you.
>   A.

She was having a breakdown. Melissa's vision went out of focus until the mantel blurred. She squirmed in her seat, clamping her knees together, crossing her ankles primly. Her breasts and belly flushed underneath the silk, making her feel exposed. She was about to mash an erect nipple with a palm to hide her arousal when she took a calming breath and sneaked a look around the room. The painter and gardener sat on either side of her.

The men she had spied upon were spectacular. Muscles betrayed that they did physical labor, but the specimens were as unblemished as flight attendants'. Rugged work clothes were shocking in the refined dining room, but her dress was also inappropriate. Their arms windmilled as they gestured and laughed, sinews hard as cable. Uncallused skin was as fair on the painter as bluish skimmed milk. Sienna, the gardener's hue, sprouted saffron-bright body hair. Melissa sized up the shirtless man while the two talked in French. They drank coffee, jabbed fingers in the air to emphasize a point, and tapped perfect nails against the cloth. Wonderful, she thought, to invite the employees to her and Ned's first breakfast in Brittany.

"I am Melissa," she said, extending her right hand. She needed to interrupt, make them reward her attempt at being social. She felt guilty for having checked out their anatomy from the windows, but protocol governed everyone now.

"Ned?" Melissa said when the swinging door opened. Madame carried an impossibly huge platter, and the white-shirted assistant Melissa had seen in the kitchen held a porcelain condiment dish in each hand. Madame removed an apron that had kept its starched pleats throughout her *hôtesse* duties. She settled into an upholstered wing chair near the window, beaming at her guests around the table while the last man to arrive took up utensils to serve from his place. Did Madame relax? No, she sat up stiffer against her chair's sloped back, and addressed the gathering.

"You have met my boys, Melissa? They are Anton, Basil, and Clement."

"No, Madame," she said, coughing politely. "So these handsome helpers about the place are your sons?"

Melissa, distracted as she was, had noticed each gorgeous man's varied features, skin color, and dress—or lack thereof. Trying to remember the rules of marriage, hers or the way it was done in France, she assumed Madame had offspring from three striking paramours. This lady's amorous imagination trumps mine, she thought.

"Your Ned," Madame said to Melissa, not that anyone asked. No empty chair remained. "Ned will not join us today or tomorrow," she said. "I'm afraid, *ma chère*, that I took the *libérte* of tranquilizing him. He so relishes his *chocolat*."

Melissa's mouth fell open; her temples pounded. She twisted her hair into a rope with a sweaty hand, desperate to recover her tranquility, force out her voice in protest. She would control the situation, stack the odds in her favor, as she did with airline passengers every day. Failing that, she would flee, lock her room door, tend to poor Ned.

Madame paced her words. "Your cravings, Melissa, are scattered throughout the house. Literally."

Beginning at her left and continuing around the table, each man produced a card. She saw mauve, ivory, and blue paper pass in her direction. Colors lined on the plate at her right, for Melissa refused to touch anything. "I am Clement," the man who collected the vellum rainbow next to her said gently. "At last it is time."

Without a word, Madame, apron in hand, ducked through the door into her kitchen. Rising to stand, undoing gold links from his wide French cuffs, Clement continued to speak. Melissa waited, mesmerized, for each syllable. "You must be famished," he said. "And I believe you ordered raspberry jam."

Where to begin? The workmen had written of her longing better than she could express it. Liberated, she would ride the gardener among wild roses, clawing his brown back until she was nauseated from the airborne musk and his cream clotted between her legs. The painter would knead his club, posed against a spattered drop cloth while Melissa fellated fruit ice mounded in a paper cone. The cook would thumbprint her in flour on each asscheek, meticulously butter his fists.

Ned awoke in two days' time. Melissa told him she had been unfaithful. "Twice," she said. "With Clement and Basil. Anton is waiting his turn. Can you believe it? Anton works as a housepainter, but his passion is sculpting chocolate."

Ned walked to the train, carrying his toothbrush, and left Paris on the first flight. His ruined suitcase stood in the foyer at Riec-sur-Belon as a shrine to vacations gone bad.

"I'll never travel again," Melissa often said. "Not for pleasure." Indeed, she ran the little guesthouse, she and the boys welcoming visitors, who were for the most part ravenous women. Madame retired to her roses, entering the kitchen on holidays to whisk up special omelettes. The bounty of France never flagged, and Melissa never hungered again.

about the authors

OPAL PALMER ADISA is a literary critic, poet, prose writer, storyteller, and artist. Her published works include *Caribbean Passion, The Tongue Is a Drum* (poetry/jazz CD with Devorah Major), *Leaf-of-Life, It Begins With Tears, Tamarind and Mango Women* (PEN Oakland/Josephine Miles Award winner), *traveling women, Bake-Face and Other Guava Stories,* and *Pina, The Many-Eyed Fruit,* a children's book, as well as *Fierce/Love* (poetry/jazz recording with Devorah Major). Her poetry has appeared in numerous journals in the United States, London, Canada, and Jamaica. She lives in Oakland, California.

DES ARIEL has been writing for many years now. He is from the north of England. He lives a quiet life, traveling sometimes, but in various other guises has done editing, teaching, and book reviewing for *Publishers Weekly.* He has also published fiction and essays in well-known erotica anthologies. As well as the occasional erotica story, he writes essays, bibliographic material and is taking his time on a novel and a story collection. He is currently living in the United Arab Emirates.

CHRISTINE BELLEROSE, aka "cricri," aka "Gui Hua," was born in Montreal, Canada. She has dabbled in an eclectic procession of arts, from poetry, playwriting, classical guitar, stage drama, classical and modern dance, fashion design, fashion styling, to writing. In the midst of it, she has traveled to many countries. In May 2004, Christine exhibited her writing at Imagine Gallery in Beijing, breaking the rule that writers can't show. She is now writing her first novel — *Grasshopper* — and has published many stories online at *Rêve Bébé* and *Plume Rose*. Today she lives in the artists' village of Songzhuang (outside of Beijing), China.

CHEYENNE BLUE combines her two passions in life and writes travel guides and erotica. Her erotica has appeared in *Best Women's Erotica, Playgirl, Mammoth Best New Erotica, Best Lesbian Erotica, Best Lesbian Love Stories*, and on many websites. Her travel guides cover backcountry and rural travel in the southwestern United States and Europe. She divides her time between Colorado and Ireland, and is currently working on a book about the quiet and quirky areas of Ireland. You can see more of her erotica on her website: www.cheyenneblue.com.

JAI CLARE lives in the southwest of England. Her fiction has appeared in *The London Magazine, Agni, The Barcelona Review, Night Train, Zoetrope: All-Story Extra, QWF, Buzzwords, Cadenza*, and *Aesthetica* magazine. She's just finished writing her psychological drama/thriller novel before starting a PhD at the University of Gloucestershire. Website: www.jaiclare.co.uk.

RACHELLE CLARET is trilingual, with a first-class BA, and currently works as a recruitment consultant in Somerset, a part-time research/writer in London, and a professional freelance proofreader. Her interests and, subsequently, her writing focus largely on the food and sex industries — and on the quirks of human behavior and sexual relationships. Although she aspires to writing novels, it is mainly her erotic writing that gets accepted for publication in books, anthologies, and magazines, such as *Diva, For Women, Desire,* and *Grunt & Groan*, a Canadian anthology about sex in the workplace.

HOLLY FARRIS is an Appalachian who has worked as an autopsy assistant, restaurant baker, and beekeeper. She has fifty-plus articles, short stories, and poems published to date, and more of her erotica can be seen in the Venus Book Club's *The Big Book of Hot Women's Erotica 2004*. Holly's literary short fiction is forthcoming from *Home Planet News*. She divides her time between Virginia and Saint Louis.

TABITHA FLYTE lives in a small seaside town forty miles to the east of London. She teaches creative writing and beginner's Japanese to (mostly) enthusiastic adults and recently completed a writing MA. She has written four erotic novels, including *Tongue in Cheek*, *The Hottest Place*, and *Full Steam Ahead*. Her latest, *Coming Round the Mountain*, was released in 2004. Tabitha's work has been included in *Erotic Travel Tales*, *Best Women's Erotica*, *Aqua Erotica*, and *Herotica*.

DEBRA HYDE's wanderlust began at the tender age of ten months when she traveled across the Atlantic from England and then sat on her mother's lap during a cross-country drive to new digs in Nevada. For most of her life since, Connecticut has been her home. Her work has appeared in many anthologies, most recently *Best Lesbian Erotica 2004*, *The Mammoth Book of Best New Erotica*, *Heat Wave*, several Venus Book Club editions, *Erotic Travel Tales,* and *Erotic Travel Tales 2*. Visit her at her weblog, Pursed Lips. And rest assured, she still travels — even just to quell her wanderlust.

LINDA JAIVIN is the author of the international best-seller *Eat Me,* which has been published in over a dozen countries and ten languages and was recently chosen as one of twelve novels for Vintage UK's Summer Reading Promotion 2004 on the theme of sexual love. Her other fiction includes *Rock n Roll Babes from Outer Space; Miles Walker, You're Dead;* and *Dead Sexy* as well as short fiction. She is also a playwright, essayist, and nonfiction author; her most recent book is the China memoir *The Monkey and the Dragon*. She is working on her fifth novel. She lives in Sydney, Australia.

DIANE LEBOW, based in San Francisco, has published stories in *Erotic Travel Tales 2*, Salon.com, *Travelers Tales* anthologies, *B for Savvy Brides*, *Women's Studies Quarterly*, and numerous national newspapers and magazines. Her work will appear in the soon-to-be published collection, *France: A Love Story,* and she has the lead chapter, "Rethinking Matriliny among the Hopi," in *Women in Search of Utopia*. She has spent time with Afghan women, the Hopi, Amazon people, Tuvans, Mongolians, Corsicans, and Parisians, as well as scuba diving with sharks in the Red Sea and training champion Morgan horses. A pioneer of college women's studies programs, she received her PhD from the University of California in the History of Consciousness and was a college professor for many years in Paris, New York City, and California.

GREVEL LINDOP lives in Manchester, England, where he was formerly Professor of Romantic Studies at the Victoria University. He writes regularly on poetry, biography, and theater for the *Times Literary Supplement, PN Review, Stand,* and other magazines. His books include a biography of Thomas De Quincey, a twenty-one-volume edition of De Quincey's complete works, *A Literary Guide to the Lake District,* and five collections of poems, most recently, *Selected Poems.* He is currently working on a volume of erotic poems, provisionally entitled *Playing with Fire,* and on a biography of the poet, novelist, and occultist Charles Williams.

GWEN MASTERS is a twentysomething woman living in the shadow of Nashville's famous Music Row. She enjoys guitars and readily admits to a shameless fetish for musicians. Her work has appeared in *Ruthie's Club, voracitybeat,* various magazines, and in the upcoming *Naughty Stories from A to Z.* Her current novel, *Better Judgment: Confessions of a Mistress* is on shelves now. Gwen currently has several projects in the works, including *Crossroads,* an honest and cutting erotic novel focusing on the bedroom politics of the country music industry.

CAROLE ROSENTHAL's fiction has been published in commercial and literary magazines that range from the experimental (such as *Cream City Review* and *Minnesota Review*), to the mainstream (*Confrontation, Other Voices, Transatlantic Review, Ellery Queen's Mystery Magazine*), to the political (*Mother Jones, MS*). Frequently anthologized (*Powers of Desire, Masterpieces of Modern Mystery, Love Stories by New Women*), her writing has also been dramatized for radio, television, and stage. Rosenthal's new collection is entitled *It Doesn't Have to Be Me,* and she is currently completing a novel called *St. Daddy in Santa Fe.* She is Professor of English and Humanities at the Pratt Institute in New York City.

LISABET SARAI has been writing ever since she learned how to hold a pencil. She is the author of three erotic novels, *Raw Silk, Incognito,* and *Ruby's Rules,* and the co-editor, with S. F. Mayfair, of the groundbreaking anthology *Sacred Exchange*, which explores the spiritual aspects of BDSM relationships. Her stories have appeared in a variety of print collections, including *Erotic Travel Tales 2; Wicked Words 8; Leather, Lace and Lust; Delicate Friction; The Big Book of Hot Women's Erotica;* and *The Mammoth Book of Best New Erotica*. Visit her website, Lisabet Sarai's Fantasy Factory (www.lisabetsarai.com). She lives in Southeast Asia.

HELENA SETTIMANA lives an otherwise uneventful life in Toronto, Canada, where she wears funny hats and teaches pottery to women and men exercising *Ghost* fantasies. Her short fiction, poetry, and essays have appeared on the web at Erotica-Readers.com, ScarletLetters.com, and CleanSheets.com. In print, her work has been featured in *Erotic Travel Tales; Best Women's Erotica 2001, 2002,* and *2004; Penthouse; Best Bondage Erotica; The Mammoth Book of Best New Erotica; Hot and Bothered 4;* and many others. In addition to moonlighting as Features Editor at the Erotica Readers and Writers Association, she is busy assembling her first collection of short fiction, and there is a novel in the works.

DONNA GEORGE STOREY has taught English in Japan and Japanese in the United States. During her two-year stay in Kyoto, she spent many memorable evenings in the pleasure district of old Gion. She now lives a quieter life in northern California with her husband and two sons. Her fiction has appeared in *The Absinthe Literary Review, AGNI,* CleanSheets.com, *The Gettysburg Review*, ScarletLetters.com, and *Taboo: Forbidden Fantasies for Couples*. A story published in *Prairie Schooner* received special mention in *Pushcart Prize Stories 2004*.

SAGE VIVANT is the founder of Custom Erotica Source (www.customeroticasource.com), the online resource for tailor-made erotic fiction. Her work has been published in a wide range of anthologies, from *Best Women's Erotica* to *The Mammoth Book of Best New Erotica* to *Heat Wave*. She is the editor of *Swing!* and co-editor with M. Christian of *Leather, Lace and Lust* and *Binary: The Best of Both Worlds*. She lives in San Francisco.

A. F. WADDELL writes multi-genre fiction, is a film lover, lives in California, and works in the business field. Works include the *Thelma and Louise* parody "Tina and Lucille" in *The Mammoth Book of on the Road*; "Cashmeres Must Die" in *Leather, Lace and Lust*, which will also be published later this year in *The Mammoth Book of Best New Erotica*; and "The Road Killers" in *The Wildest Ones: Hot Biker Tales*. For more, visit the Web presence at www.afwaddell.com.

GERARD WOZEK is the author of *Dervish*, which won the Gival Press 2000 Poetry Book Award. His poems and prose have appeared in various journals and anthologies, including two volumes of *Erotic Travel Tales, Queer Dog, The Road Less Traveled, Best Gay Erotica 1998, Rebel Yell 2, Blithe House Quarterly, The Harrington Fiction Review, Bend Don't Shatter: Poets on the Beginning of Desire,* and *Reclaiming the Heartland*. In 2003, Wozek received a Finalist Grant Award in Poetry from the Illinois Arts Council for selections from an unpublished manuscript entitled *Lost Saints*. He teaches creative writing at Robert Morris College in Chicago.

about the editor

MITZI SZERETO is editor of two previous volumes of *Erotic Travel Tales* as well as author of *Erotic Fairy Tales: A Romp Through the Classics,* and the novella *highway* (Renaissance E Books). Her writing appears in various books and publications including *The Mammoth Book of Best New Erotica, Wicked Words 4, Joyful Desires, Erotic Review, Writers' Forum,* and *Moist.* As M. S. Valentine, she's the author of the erotic novels *The Martinet* (Chimera U.K. and Venus Book Club), *The Captivity of Celia, Elysian Days and Nights, The Governess, The Possession of Celia* (all from Blue Moon and Venus Book Club), and the double-volume *Celia Collection* (Blue Moon) She's the pioneer of the erotic writing workshop in the U.K. and Europe, which she conducts for arts organizations and literary festivals. When not writing or editing, she's a university lecturer in creative writing. She's appeared in the Bravo television documentary series *3001: A Sex Oddity* and frequently on BBC radio. Her work as an anthology editor has earned her the American Society of Authors and Writers' Meritorious Achievement Award. Her next anthology, a collection of speculative erotic fiction featuring famous historical characters, will be out in 2005 from Cleis Press. An itinerant spirit, she has lived in South Florida, upstate New York, Los Angeles, Seattle, and the San Francisco Bay Area. She presently resides in Yorkshire, England.